THE FUTURE OF FLIGHT

LEIK MYRABO AND DEAN ING

A BAEN BOOK

THE FUTURE OF FLIGHT

Copyright © 1985 by Leik Myrabo and Dean Ing

A Baen Book

Baen Enterprises
8-10 W. 36th Street
New York, N.Y. 10018

First printing, February 1985

ISBN: 0-671-55941-9

Cover art by Attila Hejja

Printed in the United States of America

Distributed by
SIMON & SCHUSTER
MASS MERCHANDISE SALES COMPANY
1230 Avenue of the Americas
New York, N.Y. 10020

ABOUT THE AUTHORS

Dr. Leik N. Myrabo took his Ph.D. in Engineering Physics from the University of California at San Diego in 1976. Much of his attention for over a decade has been devoted to innovative propulsion systems using beamed energy. From 1976 to 1983 he was a research consultant to the government and private industry. One of his studies (for Arthur D. Little, Inc. in 1980) concerned how and when beamed-energy propulsion would begin to impact the commercial aircraft market. He was a member of the AIAA (American Institute of Aeronautics and Astronautics) task group on Future Flight Systems, whose charter was "the application of science and technology to foster the development of promising unconventional propulsion systems for aircraft and spacecraft in the year 2000 and beyond."

Dr. Myrabo annually organizes and chairs a special evening session entitled "Space Transport Beyond the Shuttle" at the annual Joint Propulsion Conference of the AIAA/SAE/ASME. Currently, he is a Professor of Mechanical Engineering at Rensselaer Polytechnic Institute in Troy, New York. He teaches courses in thermodynamics, propulsion and space technology, and conducts research on very advanced propulsion concepts.

Dr. Myrabo's personal interests include outdoor activities, jazz music, ballooning, solar architecture, and high-performance vehicles (he built his personal sportscar, and is keenly interested in ARV/ultralight aircraft development).

Dr. Dean Ing was an Air Force interceptor crew chief and an aerospace Senior Research Engineer before taking his Ph. D. in Communication Theory from the University of Oregon in 1974. As an assistant professor in a midwest university he taught media history, psycholinguistics, and media writing. He then became a full-time writer, focusing on the technological future. He is a member of the Citizens Advisory Council on National Space Policy (sponsored by the L5 Society), and of SFWA. With the original author, General Daniel Graham, he reworked the text *High Frontier* into a book of popular format.

Dr. Ing has been a finalist for science fiction's major awards, the Nebula and Hugo. To date, he has written or co-written ten books, and two of his high-tech novels have edged onto s-f bestseller lists. With Dr. Jerry Pournelle, he recently completed *Mutual Assured Survival*, a nonfiction book on future defenses against nuclear missiles.

Some of Ing's personal interests include fly fishing, backpacking, and chasing vintage model aircraft. He has designed and raced lightweight vehicles; his prototype Magnum GT (*Road & Track*, May 1968) is currently licensed for the street. He develops and tests survival and backpacker equipment; he is contributing editor to *Survive* magazine and *Survival Tomorrow*. His easily-constructed shelter air pump and filter designs are detailed in the book *Pulling Through*. Ing lives in Oregon with his wife and two of his four daughters.

LIST OF ABBREVIATIONS

ACA—agile combat aircraft
ALL—airborne laser lab
ARV—aircraft recreational vehicle
CW—continuous wave
ERH—external radiation heating
FEL—free-electron laser
g—Earth-normal gravity; an acceleration of 32.17 fps^2
GALCIT—Guggenheim Aeronautical Laboratory, Cal Tech
GBL—ground-based laser
GW—gigawatt; one billion watts
HEL—high-energy laser
HLLV—heavy-lift launch vehicle
ILS—instrument landing system
IR—infrared
IRH—internal radiation heating
I_{sp}—specific impulse; a measure of fuel efficiency
L5—favored site for orbital colonies near Earth and Moon
linac—linear accelerator
LSC—laser-supported combustion
LSD—laser-supported detonation
Maser—microwave amplification by stimulated emission of radiation
MHD—magnetohydrodynamics
MLS—microwave landing system
MW—molecular weight; (also) megawatt: one million watts
OTV—orbital transfer vehicle
PRF—pulse repetition frequency
R&D—research and development
RP—repetitively pulsed
RPV—remotely piloted vehicle
SPS—solar power satellite
SST—supersonic transport
SSTO—single stage to orbit
T_c—chamber temperature
TW—terawatt; one trillion watts
UV—ultraviolet
VTOL—vertical takeoff and landing

CONTENTS

FOREWORD

You might expect a book on the future by a propulsion physicist to be a triumph of caution over ambition, and one by a science-fiction writer to be a triumph of ambition over caution. What you hold here is a collaboration for the general reader; so, if we are all lucky, it's also a standoff between caution and ambition. That may be inevitable in any map of the future.

Any decent map will have benchmarks by people who have stood on the very edge of known territory and surveyed the unknown. Here you will see references to quite a few: Tsiolkovski, Kantrowitz, and Dyson, to take familiar examples. Some others have not enjoyed as much notice in the media, but they are all explorers of our future. We owe them more than we can ever repay.

What we owe them *for*, in a phrase, is escape from the limits to growth. This is true because the future of flight depends on new sources of energy and ways to harness it. But future flight, in turn, will boost our ability to tap vast energies that we can use to improve the quality of everyday life. This is especially true for inexpensive flight to orbit and beyond—as we will show. There is a word for this kind of mutual assistance between technologies: *synergism*. In the following pages you will see that some of those new technologies are already proven, and that others are barely on our mental horizons today. But don't bet against our standing squarely on that horizon twenty years from now!

In 1959, the laser was a startling new lab curiosity. It transmitted so little energy that some physicists derided the notion, ever, of the high-energy laser (HEL). Twenty years later we were using HELs to weld refractory metals and more recently, lasers have destroyed missiles in flight. The HEL is here and now—but so is antimatter. So far it has only been demonstrated that antimatter can be created and, at great cost, contained for a day or so. Five years ago, antimatter (like the energy beam of thirty years ago) was a tool of only one trade: science fiction. How long before we are using antimatter to boost starships and orbital hospitals? Another twenty years? Never? The answer may depend more on our determination than on physical laws. That, too, is part of the future of flight.

Gerard O'Neill, in his book *2081*, lists five areas of technology he believes will "drive the changes" we see during the next century. These drivers are computers, automation, communications, space colonies, and energy. After you read his predictions, you may feel with us that a sixth driver of change should be listed: propulsion technology. (It is not the same category as energy, any more than computers and automation are the same.) We think so because the full growth of both space colonies *and* energy will come only after very great improvements in propulsion, which will make solar power satellites and space colonies practical. Put it another way: our favorite driver of change is the advanced spacedrive.

And what of everyday travel; will it be hypersonic? We think some of it will. But the authors are both constructors of racing cars and we assure you that, for most daily uses, other vehicles make more sense. That is why we think today's ultralight and "ARV" sport aircraft are a tipoff of big changes in your future. More on that in Chapter 2.

Still, our intent here is to sketch a map of future

flight with a primary focus on the real "gee-whiz" stuff—but in terms as non-technical as we can manage. If you want more of the hard technical data, you might start with our bibliography (which is not complete, but touches many high spots). If you want to design your own spacecraft or family flyer, some of these designs may help. You may even emerge with some rough preliminary details of starships or supersonic dirigibles. Chiefly, however, we hope to offer some insights into new technologies that link your personal future with the future of flight.

—Leik Myrabo and Dean Ing
August, 1984.

Chapter 1:

COMES THE REVOLUTION

We are dedicating this book to the proposition that all futures are *not* created equally.

Of course, all of those futures are educated guesses. Guessers who assume that all long-established trends must continue will, with Thomas Malthus, often show us gloomy futures; evolution with a vengeance. Yet we know that trends are not always continuous.

The extinction of most dinosaurs, about 64,000,000 years ago, was a natural revolution on Earth; a sudden discontinuity in a *very* long-established trend. Evidence is mounting that a sizeable asteroid struck this planet with such violence that the ecological carpet was suddenly jerked from under the feet of the great reptiles. Early mammals benefited from this sudden change and a different future evolved. The human race is a beneficiary.

Occasionally a new idea rekindles the human spirit, reverses trends, and creates real changes in the quality of life. When the change is discontinuous, a sharp break from predictable step-by-step evolution, we have *revolution*. It may be political and violent, or it may be technological and peaceful.

The future we "create" in these pages has an unfair advantage over some others because ours plugs in the revolutionary stuff. We think that is proper because, when people's backs are against the wall, they turn to any revolutionary help that's handy. As it happens, much of our world is nearing disaster in its energy needs—and we are not finding permanent peaceful solutions in conventional ways. Some leaders are beginning to look hard for revolutionary solutions (in several senses!). We're in luck because, among others we will describe, there is one that left the realm of "pure" science fiction around 1960 and it does not require violence or a new government. But it may cause a few governments to evolve in useful ways.

Revolutionary change is relatively rare. It's also less predictable than the weather, which explains why leaders often greet it with gritted teeth. The best they can do is rush to see how the new revolutionary change might affect them because, after the revolution, evolution takes over again, and that's more predictable.

Thanks in part to outrageous claims by advertising flacks, we have just about wrung all the juice from the word *revolutionary*. Every new kitchen gadget, diet fad and teaching aid is a candidate for the tag, despite the fact that almost all of them evolve, step by painstaking step, from previous ideas without much discontinuity. The marvelous airships of Alberto Santos-Dumont are often mislabeled this way.

Santos-Dumont, an eccentric little Brazilian, became the toast of Europe in the 1890's with his dirigible (which means directable, or steerable) balloons. As a boy, he had read the science fiction of Jules Verne to his saturation point, tinkered with engines on his father's coffee plantation, and built toy hot-air balloons of the type pioneered by the Montgolfiers a century earlier. Arriving in Paris in 1891, he found that cigar-shaped balloons had already been tried; hydrogen and other gases were used to inflate some craft, and one Henri Giffard had tried driving balloons with a steam engine. The young Brazilian suspected that existing gasoline engines might be better.

Santos-Dumont saw the high-tech hardware evolving, and put it together with care and courage. By 1899, after gradual improvements, he was putt-putting over Paris rooftops, steering his little dirigibles where he liked. The Zeppelins and blimbs of a later day owed much to the daring and gadgeteering of this tiny aeronaut. His autobiography reveals how he proceeded with detail improvements until, years before the Wright Brothers succeeded at Kittyhawk, Alberto Santos-Dumont could circle the Eiffel Tower. He won worldwide renown, and deserved it; but his work was not revolutionary.

We cite the case of Santos-Dumont to show the steady march of evolutionary design, and to applaud it. But the future of flight involves something more: truly revolutionary discoveries, technologies that are discontinuous from earlier work where Santos-Dumont's was not.

Now we take a case that *is* revolutionary, even though its discovery was predicted in Santos-Dumont's day. The Russian futurist, Konstantin Tsiolkovsky, wrote during the early years of this century that "... energy may even be supplied to a missile, from the Earth, in the form of radiation of one or another wavelength. ... This source of energy is very attractive to contemplate, but we know little of its possibilities." Of course, there's a huge gulf between predicting something, and demonstrating that it works. Tsiolkovsky risked his reputation by predicting revolutionary changes, with only the sketchiest notion how those changes might be achieved. Many scientists of his time dismissed him as a candidate for a strait-jacket.

Then Albert Einstein, in 1917, wrote a paper on stimulating radiation. On the cover of one issue of Gernsback's *Wonder Stories* in 1932, science fiction fans saw a propulsion beam; but no one had any firm ideas how power might be beamed without tremendous losses in the beamspread. (Every time the area of the beam doubles, its intensity must drop by half.) During the 1930's at least one man, the inventor Nikola Tesla, pursued his dream of wireless transmission of power. Tesla proved himself a genius in his early years with Edison but later became secretive and scornful of criticism. We know that Tesla sought to beam power, but we must suspect that he never succeeded.

But by 1954, experimenters managed to amplify microwaves through a scheme they called "Microwave Amplification by Stimulated Emission of Radiation." They soon reduced this jawbreaking phrase to its initial letters: "maser." Then one of the discoverers, Charles Townes, co-wrote a paper suggesting that the scheme should also work for radiation of visible frequencies: an "optical maser." This created a lot of excitement in laboratories, as scientists worked to demonstrate *light* amplification by stimulating emission of radiation. Of course they soon adopted the short term: "laser."

The first laser was fired by Theodore Maiman of Hughes Aircraft, using a ruby crystal and a flash tube to jolt the crystal with a great wallop of energy. Within a few months, Ali Javan of Bell Labs succeeded using gases instead of rubies.

Both approaches drew instant attention. The amplified beam of light did not spread out like a flashlight beam or even a searchlight. A beam of light as thin as a pencil could be sent for long distances without fanning out much, and had obvious uses such as optical alignment and communication devices. The beam transmitted very low power, but it did transmit a tight beam of wireless power that could be collected by a distant lens. The race was on to develop lasers for special uses—especially lasers of higher power. The revolution had begun.

The Soviets claim that in 1962, Askaryan and Moroz were first to draw attention to the fact that a laser, when vaporizing part of a target, can produce thrust. But researchers credit the U. S.'s Arthur Kantrowitz with the first serious suggestion, in 1971, that lasers might furnish enough power to boost vehicles into orbit. Both in print and in an annual AIAA (American Institute of Aeronautics and Astronautics) meeting, Kantrowitz pointed to the fast-rising power levels of lasers. He suggested that launches to space could be made enormously cheaper by this revolutionary use of beamed power. The AERL scientist added that we were letting naive pessimism put false limits on our future. Always the cautious optimist, Kantrowitz said it might be possible to increase the power of lasers by perhaps *six orders of magnitude.*

A multiple of ten is only one order of magnitude; six orders of magnitude increase meant that a laser transmitting, say, ten watts in 1971 might be the forerunner of *million-watt* lasers one day. History is proving him right, perhaps sooner than he thought. Thanks to stepped-up activity in several related fields—some of it provoked by the redoubtable Kantrowitz—we are now developing lasers measured in megawatts of power output. We see no reason why we cannot keep boosting their power to the gigawatt range. Ten billion watts, furnished for a few minutes' duration, could boost a payload half that of NASA's shuttle from launch pad to orbit at the cost of thirty thousand dollars' worth of electricity. In other words, we could put a payload into orbit for a dollar per pound, instead of nearly a thousand dollars per pound!

Maybe this kind of optimism has a domino effect. In any case, a few scientists began to look around for other ways, in addition to lasers, that we might power vehicles of the future. By now they've come up with several schemes that may rival lasers in the future of flight.

Well then: why aren't we rushing to do it? There are several answers, some of them political. The point to remember is that while the remaining hurdles are real, none of them appear to be basic. This future of flight is a future we can all share. On the other hand, by a general failure of vision or determination, Americans may share a flightless future while others soar above us.

Alan Lovelace, Deputy Administrator of NASA, described part of the problem, and the promise, in 1979. Writing in *Astronautics and Aeronautics* he said, in part, "Let me sketch for you two possible world 'options.' One I will call a fully flight-integrated society. In it everything and everyone flies—not just 65% of the U. S. population, but 100% of the world population. . . . Wherever a person finds himself, there will be a landing site, and he can call for this transportation easier than you can call a cab. . . .

"The other possible world I will call a flight-regressive society, a society that has found no affordable solution to the problems of energy, noise, and pollution, a society in which aviation reverts to the status of a technology too expensive to use. . . .

"The major issue is one of national will. . . . The Wright Brothers did not stick with the bicycle, and I do not think we will either."

Lovelace, in so many words, was calling for a renewal of what historian Joseph Corn calls the "winged gospel." From the early Wright flyers to shortly after World War II, the U. S. raised the dream of flight to something beyond a cult; we viewed flight almost as a religion. We lionized Doolittle, Lindbergh, Earheart, and Halliburton. We doted on our aircraft such as the JN-4 "Jenny," the workhorse DC-3, the advanced little Ercoupe, and strange hybrids like Kellett's autogyro. And if we loved aircraft like those in which we might actually hope to fly, we virtually worshipped the B-29 "Superfortress," the twin-tailed P-38 "Lightning," and the Bell X-1, with the shape of a winged artillery shell, that hangs today in the Smithsonian like a giant's toy. Very few people born after 1945 share the gut-level excitement of their elders whenever a restored P-51 streaks overhead, its in-line Allison snarling a challenge that raises hackles on the old-timer's neck, and perhaps a catch in his throat. Oh yes; we knew a winged gospel in the first half of this century. . . .

Then, somewhere between the German V-2 and the Soviet Sputnik, most of us discarded that fervor. Some have never replaced it with anything. Others replaced it with dreams of wealth, or prowess in sports. True, a few parishioners kept the faith with tiny single-seat air racers or model aircraft. Of those, a very few went on to design hang-gliders and then, like Santos-Dumont, evolved new craft which we call ultralights.

Just as Martin Luther once stirred the world with his new wrinkles on an old religion, the ultralights have produced a storm of controversy among followers of the winged gospel. By now it is becoming clear that ultralights will fill an important niche in the future of flight. Perhaps more important, they have inspired another, more advanced type of new aircraft; the aircraft recreational vehicle, or ARV. That is not to say that everybody likes them yet. We will have more to say on ultralights and ARVs in Chapter 2.

But a latter-day gospel of flight is growing now, and Princeton's Gerard O'Neill is one of its prophets. When Tsiolkovsky predicted manmade worldlets in space, growing their own food, his contemporaries considered him a mad Russian. When Robert Heinlein wrote of a huge spacecraft with a complete ecological system in his 1941 story "Universe"—well, everybody knew science fiction people were a little strange.

O'Neill, however, is a professor of physics at a prestigious university. Since 1969, with the vital help of young scientists who share the dream, he has been working out the problems of living in space. Not just taking brief visits from our planet, but living and working there, in habitats that provide all of Earth's benefits without some of its drawbacks. O'Neill and his colleagues have shown that most hurdles on the way to space habitats have already been cleared; our primary lack now is the will to do it, because it will be very expensive at first. And faced with huge deficits here on Earth, many people ask: why do anything that expensive?

Answer: for the same reason Queen Isabella hocked her jewels for Columbus. Spain was repaid ten thousandfold in riches from the new world, and the countries that create new worldlets in our solar system will reap wealth so tremendous as to make all that Spanish gold look like pocket change. We'll give details in Chapter 9. Soviets know those details as well as we do. Does the word "cosmograd" ring a bell? It's a Russian word meaning "space city," and cosmograds are a Soviet goal. Stefan Possony, an often-quoted scholar of the Hoover Institute, tells us that the Soviets are expanding their space capabilities well beyond anything needed to support their current military *or* civilian work. A moon settlement and a huge space station, says Possony, are among the few things that would explain all this furious activity by the USSR; and they have already told us they intend to build such things. James Oberg of NASA, author of *Red Star In Orbit*, tells us that all this Soviet activity may include a manned Mars mission.

Everyone knows that the Soviets have serious economic problems. They would not be outspending us in the effort to build space cities unless they expected huge returns. They proceed as if they had memorized the books of American engineers like Stine and Pournelle, who are telling everyone who will listen that the wealth is out there, and that it's up for grabs.

A growing fraction of Americans is already impatient to get on with it, to spread the latter-day gospel of flight. The L5 Society is an organization of people working toward permanent settlements beyond the Earth, and toward commerce plying between Earth and those settlements. Anyone can join; its monthly *L5 News* repays the dues handsomely, and its articles are written for ease of understanding. Its board chairman is Arthur Kantrowitz and its officials include world-famous scientists, publishers, legislators, and futurist writers. A careful reading of the *L5 News* shows that members are at odds over the support of military space funding. One side of the issue claims that the U. S. should fund only nonmilitary space efforts. The other side replies that space has already been weaponized by the Soviets, and that the U. S. will reap huge peaceful benefits from military space programs—particularly those that are genuinely defensive, not offensive. [For more on this topic, see *Mutual Assured Survival* by Drs. J. E. Pournelle and Dean Ing, Baen Books, Nov 1984.—Ed.]

What does "L5" mean? The mathematician Lagrange noted that, in the case of two celestial bodies positioned as the Earth and its moon are, there are five points nearby where much smaller bodies can be stationed where they will stay in position, perhaps oscillating slightly around that "libration" point. Some of those points (such as the gravitational midpoint between Earth and the moon) are not very stable; we might have to keep nudging a satellite to keep it there. But libration points L4 and L5, in the same path as the moon but 60° ahead and behind it in Earth orbit, are very stable. Even if we snagged an asteroid a hundred miles thick and placed it at the L5 position, it would stay there, influenced by the gravitational pulls of Earth and the moon.

The L5 Society expects commonplace flight to worldlets in such positions; they say that once you escape Earth, in terms of energy you are halfway to anywhere. Mining the asteroids and colonizing Mars will be fairly straightforward tasks then. Cheap nonpolluting power beamed to Earth from orbit will be a cinch because we already know that structural metals and solar cell chemicals can be extracted from moon dirt—which is known formally as "lunar regolith," and informally as "green cheese," by the way.

O'Neill and his colleagues have developed working models of a device called a "mass driver," a sort of electric catapult which could fling materials up from the moon into lunar orbit. The mass driver is much more efficient in vacuum; though it probably will not be used to hurl payloads up from the Earth, it may be just the thing to boost materials up against the moon's gravity.

Prophets of future flight back their claims with convincing figures, though some claims seem a bit far-fetched at first blush. How can we solve earthly pollution from space? By making fossil fuels obsolete, collecting solar power beyond our atmosphere where it is *eight times* more available and beaming it down to us. How can it help solve overpopulation? By creating so many off-Earth colonies and with flight so cheap that within a century, emigration might well stabilize Earth's population. How will we get there? Several ways, beginning with the present chemical fuels while we develop HEL (High Energy Laser) propulsion systems and some others even more advanced. We'll cover these far-out ideas in later chapters.

Carl Sagan, testifying before a U. S. Congressional subcommittee, has said that the engineering aspects of space cities seem perfectly worked out by study groups. He added, "It is practical."

Still, it will be tremendously expensive until we develop those cheap, clean propulsion systems. Some systems will boost huge payloads to orbit, while others will power the family flivver to Athens for dinner and back to Topeka afterward. Much of the revolutionary work has already been done; now we need to evolve them in practice. That will take more funding of advanced designs.

Astronaut Gordon Cooper, never one to mince words, summed up the situation in conversation last year with one of the present authors. "In the field of propulsion systems," he said, "most of the scientific establishment is about fifty years behind a few little groups of geniuses. I think we should reassess the whole funding process."

Chapter 2:

THE CROWDED SKIES

Where civil aviation is concerned, the skies have been crowded for some time. We are now seeing small aircraft that look very different from those of a decade ago, but they still depend on burning fossil fuels and until the end of this century, at least, we are stuck with that kind of power. The revolutionary changes won't come until we can beam power to our aircraft. We'll start with the recent past and present, move quickly on to cover the aviation changes we expect during the next decade or so, then finally discuss the far-out stuff.

Most of us grew up in a time when inefficient aircraft were the rule. There is an old saying among designers: "With enough power, you can fly a barn door." We could afford to fly barn doors then, installing thirstier engines, and we took cheap fossil fuel for granted. On the ground and in the air, the chief sales gimmick was performance: more speed, more power, more altitude. Private and commercial aircraft got (and still get) their fuel from oil just as our cars did. Largely, they reflected the same goofy assumptions about foreign oil; Buicks and Boeings squandered more and more fuel from the 1950's onward.

All of that came to a screeching halt in 1973, when we seemed to be hopelessly hooked on gas guzzlers and our fuel suppliers suddenly hiked their prices by an order of magnitude. Looking back, we are astonished to see how fast Americans got smart when OPEC slugged us in the wallet. Almost overnight, we learned how to face a future where fuel cost would be a controlling item in air travel. We are still facing it—oil experts say that even in the face of the complete collapse of OPEC prices will never drop below $15 per bbl—and until cheap beamed power becomes available fuel cost will control the future of flight as it never has before.

Today, we have a new way of defining "performance," based on fuel consumption. The new Buicks and Boeings are no faster than they were ten years ago, but how they save on fuel! Instead of circling their destinations, wasting fuel while waiting for a chance to land, many commercial transports now delay takeoff until they get a firm OK for a time-slot to land. By eliminating this "stacking" over a crowded airport, our airlines save millions of gallons of jet fuel. Computers are a big help in keeping track of air traffic, and in figuring out minimum-fuel missions.

Before long those air traffic computers will be linked with a new microwave traffic control system that "sees" a much greater volume of space than the current ILS (instrument landing system), and sees it in more detail. The MLS (microwave landing system) has been a long time in coming. That's because it's a highly complex, nationwide system that must be bug-free before it goes into operation. Nearly all of tomorrow's commercial traffic will depend on it, and it is too crucial to the nation's business to install without exhaustive development. By the end of this century the MLS will be an international system.

Judging from progress reports, though, the MLS will be worth the wait. It will be able to identify the big commercial boomers right down to the troublesome tendencies of a given type, and will do the same for small private craft approaching the same runway. That makes it easier to guide more aircraft down safely with less delay; with all that information, we can safely isolate the planes from each other without wasting time. The fuel saving is an important side effect.

NASA Administrator James Beggs predicts that, by the turn of the century, there will be whole new populations rich enough to afford long-distance air travel. The new affluence will come, we are told, from new industrial centers in the Pacific, South America, Asia, and Africa. His reasoning goes a step further; these people will largely be flying on business, buying tickets for destinations many thousands of miles away, and that will create a big new market for supersonic transports.

We are not altogether convinced of the market, because it's risky to assume that businessmen in other cultures will follow our cultural patterns. This is especially true when electronic communication methods are improving so much; holovision will make a conference call seem like a meeting in the flesh, in the same room. (On the other hand, it's true that some Third World cultures put a high value on people being able to touch and even smell each other.) If African industry brings affluence, maybe rich Africans will do most of their flying around (or near) Africa. Asians may fly mostly within Asia; most of the business in emerging countries may be with neighboring allies; and so on. But to have 400-passenger supersonic transports (SST) capable of nonstop flight from Djakarta to Capetown, it isn't really necessary to have a big market. You only have to convince the right people that the market is waiting to be exploited—whether it is or not! When will we know about that market? Why, when we are flying the big boomers 8,000 miles nonstop. Chances are, even if NASA turns out to be wrong about the market, they will still be right about the aircraft.

Tomorrow's SST will be a very different animal from the sleek little Concorde. It will be lots bigger, and its wings will probably adjust as dramatically and efficiently as an eagle's in flight. Its engines will be much advanced over the best we have today, actually operating in different modes at various speeds. This means we can operate the engines at high efficiency for takeoff and landing, and change such features as inlet and combustion chamber geometries to keep high efficiency at Mach 3 and 60,000 foot altitude. The engine noise and sonic booms may not be all that bothersome if the aircraft is designed expressly to keep them down. And the designers will have to deal with that, if the SSTs are to serve inland terminals. It would be a rotten joke on Africans to help them get nice modern glass windows, then offer them modern SSTs that would break half of those windows.

Whether operating in Asia or America, the heavy commercial traffic in short-to-medium hops will probably find us traveling a bit slower in the interest of lower fuel consumption. The airlines will help develop still better meteorological methods to keep track of jet streams, because theose fast-moving rivers of high-altitude air can cut your fuel consumption by a third—or add to it, if you are flying upstream. The trick is finding one that's going more or less in your direction. Driving cars, we usually think of thirty miles an hour as a ruinous headwind. But those winds near ground level are slowed a lot by forests, mountains, and plain old turf. At 30,000 feet, a jet stream often wails along steadily at over 150 miles an hour.

(Footnote: While car manufacturers are beginning to pay serious attention to reducing drag coefficients, we could name some racy manufacturers who proudly announce drag coefficients of over 0.3, which is downright awful when we can get them down to 0.15. Bragging about a drag coefficient of 0.3 is like bragging about senility. They know that; but they hope you don't. Still, even with the lowest drag coefficient, the drag penalty curve begins to rise sharply when we push anything through the air at speeds higher than about sixty miles per hour.)

The commercial aircraft field is not alone in reflecting the new interest in efficiency. The business of designing and selling small private aircraft is, at this moment, in turmoil. Lots of people who used to own four-seaters like the Beech Bonanza are looking around desperately for something that is affordable. The Bonanza is a plush, fast example of yesterday's design. It is heavy, with aluminum skin and lots of rivets. It needs over 1200 feet to take off or land, burns roughly thirteen gallons of *very* expensive avgas per hour, and cruises at nearly 200 miles an hour. If you throttle back to get it under sixty-five miles an hour it falls right out of the sky. We cite the Bonanza because it's a good ship—by old standards. For over a generation we kept those standards.

Then, in the early 1970s, a friend in Oregon (John Bigelow) who designed hang gliders tipped one of the present authors off about a coming "revolution" —actually a fast evolution. Bigelow, always ahead of his time, built and flew hang gliders that almost hung in the air without stalling. He knew other people who were doing the same, and they were already casting about for power plants you could tuck under your arm. These enthusiasts felt sure they could take off from a flat pasture at thirty miles an hour, given ten or fifteen horsepower. They could hardly wait to prove it. John Moody, in Wisconsin, was among the first with proof; he installed a kart engine and a small propeller on his Icarus II hang glider in 1975 and sport flying hasn't been the same since.

These folks did not take a huffy, stuffy professional stand with all the caution that implies. They risked their backsides, and broke a few, but today everybody knows the results. These daring experimenters, hardly any of them with professional aerodynamics backgrounds, developed an entire new class of powered aircraft. We call the planes "ultralights," and they are changing the rules about future flight.

We are not trying to imply that the world had never seen an ultralight before. Most early aircraft were similar to them. Our favorite eccentric, Alberto Santos-Dumont, built his ultralight "Demoiselle" airplane before World War I. A bit later came such lightweights as the Huntington, and then the "Pou de Ciel," France's "flying flea" during the 1930's. If you have ever flown models of them you know they have a loony-tunes look; we suspect that with the real ones, while the pilot aloft was grinning, the folks down below were laughing out loud. In short, for most enthusiasts the attractions of ultralights had seemed so pale that their development had been overlooked. Some analysts say that today's ultralight developers have only reinvented the wheel. Actually there is just enough truth in that to make it sting. The rest of the truth is, they have reinvented cheap flight when nobody else seemed interested. We know a lot about engines and the stability of some configurations that we did not know before—even if we still don't know which ultralight to buy!

As with any technology, there are characteristics inherent to ultralight flying machines. On the plus side, an ultralight is cheap to buy and easy to learn. Maintenance is easy, it burns less fuel than most cars, and at this writing you do not even need a pilot's license to fly it. You can take off in a hundred yards and land in half that distance at thirty miles an hour. You really get the old "intrepid airman" feeling when you are perched on something between a lawn chair and a bicycle seat, getting bugs in your teeth at fifty miles an hour. Thousands of enthusiasts claim it's brought the fun back to flying.

On the debit side, ultralights are not supposed to be able to fly much over sixty miles an hour and they can only carry a pilot. The typical power plant is noisy as a buzz-saw. Their ranges are rarely more than 200 miles, and it's risky to fly them in bad weather. With so much wing and so little power, an ultralight is *literally* a pushover for a sudden gust of wind, and that includes the turbulence created by an old-fashioned light aircraft landing at seventy miles an hour. It's not only forbidden but foolhardy to try to land an ultralight at a terminal catering to big commercial boomers. The big jets sometimes create invisible, standing whirlwinds of turbulence that last for long minutes, which no ultralight could survive. We once heard Bill Lear speak in awe of the clear air turbulence he had just encountered while landing his Learjet, which weighs maybe a hundred times as much as an ultralight without much more wing area. With such a sturdy little bullet around him, Lear was only shaken up. Anybody in an ultralight, running into that invisible cyclone, would have hit the runway gift-wrapped in his own wings. You do not have to imagine the charges and countercharges between pilots of hot old ships and ultralights; just ask them sometime.

The argument is being settled in four ways, all in favor of the ultralights. First, ultralights now outsell other kinds of aircraft because they are cheap fun. Second, the FAA (Federal Aviation Administration) is taking a liberal view in setting rules for their design and operation. Third, some very famous, very professional folks are showing a fondness for the little critters. Take, for example, the man who first punched through Mach one in a bona fide rocket ship. When Chuck Yeager talks, people listen. Fourth and most significant, government money is boosting ultralight development. Paul MacCready's little company, Aero-Vironment, Inc., has built a prototype of a spy plane so compact, it can be packaged and parachuted into hostile territory. Given a plastic engine and a superb muffler, such a craft could fly unseen by radar and unheard by sentries.

Temporarily, the civilian ultralight movement is stagnating because FAA rules may toughen up soon, and because purchase prices have shot upward while performance has not. For one thing, even the current, relatively liberal FAA requirements set limits on ultralights including the following examples: an ultralight is required to weigh under 254 pounds empty, carry no more than five gallons of fuel, and be *incapable* of flying faster than sixty-three miles per hour. For another thing, lots of enthusiasts are bewildered at the many competing shapes. Is a highwing with forward-mounted engine better than a pusher-type, swept-wing with a little canard wing up front? Are two engines better than one?

Some manufacturers will bow out of this race very soon, while the manufacturers of future ultralights will combine successful ideas. Thanks to canard and Kasper airfoil developments, the safest ones will not stall; they will "mush," which is a slow bellyflop while moving forward—infinitely better than a sudden helpless nosedive. And if one has a structural failure in flight, the whole rig can come down safely with the parachutes already available. They will land at fifteen miles an hour and take off at twenty. They will have quieter, more fuel-efficient power plants (plastic automobile engines will pave the way for lighter aircraft engines). Along with a quieter ride and less vibration, they will have more plush, comfortable seating. They will be able to fly aerobatic maneuvers. Some of them, especially the canards with swept wings, will look ferociously fast. And the only reason they will not have ferocious speed is that, when they do, they won't fit the FAA "ultralight" category anymore. We will take up these fast lightweights, the ARVs, in a moment.

We are not trying to paint a pessimistic picture of future ultralights; far from it. We are merely pointing out that the big rush is over. Ultralights are now being touted for police patrol, aerial photography, and commuting in addition to sport flying. Now, let's put two recent developments together. First, some ultralight manufacturers are testing risky ideas by radio controlling the full-sized craft without a pilot. We know that works. Second, the Department of Agriculture is modifying a radio-controlled model with an eight-foot span to spray fruit trees in Georgia, hoping to computerize the flight patterns for perfect coverage. At last report that seemed to be workable. Now: how long before full-sized, pilotless, radio-controlled ultralights are in wide use as robots for big, precision crop-dusting operations? We will guess 1986, and we are probably being too conservative.

In passing, we cannot resist mention of the look-alike ultralights in development now. The famed Spads and Fokkers of World War I may soon be copied, approximately full-size, as kits for any of you latter-day Rickenbackers who want to build and fly them, bogus machine guns and all! Sure, they only do sixty or so, but with an imaginary Hun in your sights and your scarf trailing in the slipstream, whadda you care?

It's obvious that ultralights have borrowed technology from more powerful light aircraft, but we are betting that some of that borrowing will work both ways. For example, most of the new high-tech two and four-place craft could profit from a much lower stall speed, so they could take off and land slowly on runways only a hundred yards long. This may lead to development of hybrid, variable-geometry wings for heavier ships. You can stow a lot of Dacron cloth furled inside a fuselage or a fiberglass wing; why not furl and unfurl extra wing surface for that slow, floating glide at low speeds?

The future of "conventional" light aircraft may depend, to a large degree, on how easily they can be assembled. That's because the present *and* the future of conventional light aircraft is a long way from past conventions. Until recently, it was not conventional to build your own.

In the recent past, light aircraft were completely assembled in factories, with lots of metal welding and riveting, and a fair amount of cloth-stretching. Then a few designers like Burt Rutan invested in plastic fabrication methods, including foam-filled wings and load-carrying fiberglass shells in which the sleek plastic skin doubled as structural framework. The new methods made it fairly easy to build wondrous new efficient shapes at low cost, too. A heck of a lot of new light planes are now sold as kits to be assembled like kit cars in the owner's garage, and some of them look like interceptors from Mars. The homebuilts are considered an "experimental" category, and a lot of them fly on plain unleaded gas. Before you ask, "so what?", we point out that avgas costs almost twice as much as auto fuel. Gasoline, at least, is one thing the airplane builder can share with the car builder.

Having said that, standard practice among car enthusiasts parts company from aircraft practice in a big way. Most homebuilt cars look, um, ah—homebuilt. Tatty, ill-finished; unlovely when you look close. Most homebuilt aircraft, on the other hand, have lovely lines and nice finishes. While most are single-place designs, a goodly number are two-place and a few are four-place. It's interesting to see how near some of them come to ultralights. Take the Quickie, for example, shown in Figure 2-1.

Starting up front, it has a normal propeller and a nicely-cowled engine. So far, ho-hum; but from there back, the Quickie looks downright weird. It boasts a canard wing angling downward in a shallow inverted vee from just behind the engine. Almost hidden in the tips of those wings are the main landing gear wheels. Designer Burt Rutan quipped, "You don't have to worry about catching a wingtip. You're supposed to."

Another wing, angling upward, is back behind the cockpit bubble and the rudder fin juts far out behind on a graceful extension like a long teardrop. Yet for all its strange lines, this little ship has loads of eye appeal. It's beautifully streamlined and it is *tiny*: wingspan is under seventeen feet, shorter than many family cars. It weighs under 250 pounds empty, carries only the pilot, is made of fiberglass and foam composites, and flies with an uprated lawnmower engine producing twenty-two horses. At cruise speed it will actually take you *one hundred miles* on a

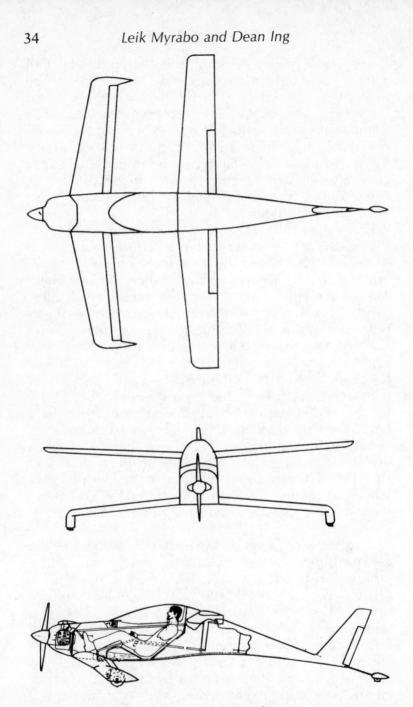

Figure 2–1. Three-view drawing of the Quickie.

gallon of fuel. Obviously an ultralight, right? Well, in truth it is. But the FAA has stuck a speed limit into its definition of the ultralight breed, and the Quickie will never get arrested for loitering. That's why the Quickie is in the ARV category; while giving you that astonishing hundred miles per gallon, it is also cruising at over 130 miles an hour!

Rutan's Varieze, Figure 2-2, is faster yet, and looks it. A canard with a pusher prop and lovely swept wings at the rear, it will cruise at 190 miles an hour. It's a two-place ship, but it only gets maybe forty miles a gallon. It would get better mileage than that if its main gear were retractable, but Varieze owners are not whining; it also gets forty admiring stares a mile. Then there's the Taylor Micro-Imp, a single-seater shown in Figure 2-3. It looks like something the Germans would have sent up against us if World War II had lasted another year. Its pusher prop is on a slender stinger behind an inverted V-tail, and with its gear retracted it looks like it should have beam weapons. Actually, using the air-cooled twenty-five horsepower engine from a Citroen 2CV, it isn't terribly fast, cruising at 110 miles an hour. Still, it gets close to a hundred miles per gallon and lands almost as slowly as an ultralight. Well, it almost *is* one. . . .

The near future of fast light ARV aircraft will owe a lot to these exquisite little ships. We will see more two- and four-place designs, advanced composites bringing weights still lower, and lighter engines with most parts (including connecting rods and casing) made of plastic. Circular shrouds around propellers, and increasingly slick low-drag shapes, will get the most from every ounce of fuel. We will probably see two-place ships getting a hundred miles per gallon, especially if they use low-drag tandem seating. But side-by-side seating is more companionable, and a delta shape with wing extensions could become very popular. We should also see a few little boomers, with spans under twenty feet, pushing Mach 1 in a few years. One of the present authors has been mak-

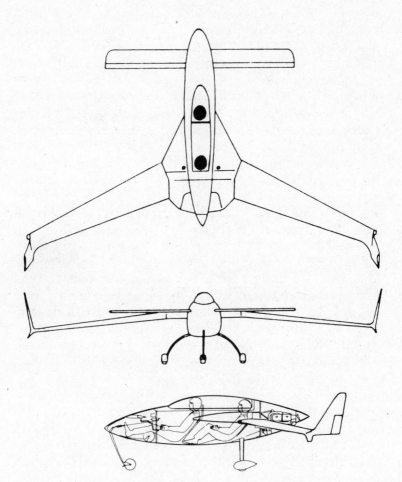

Figure 2–2. Three-view drawing of the original Vari-Eze

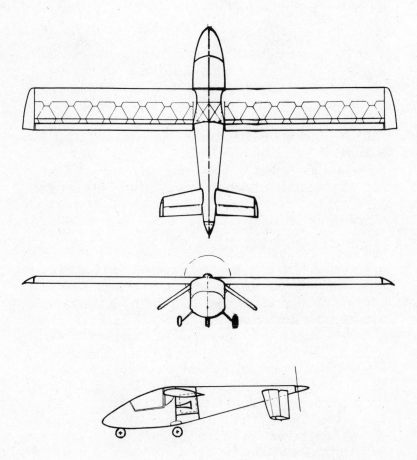

Figure 2–3. Three-view drawing of the Micro-Imp

ing calculations on a certain existing homebuilt, based on stiffer wings and an air-turborocket boost unit tucked in behind the recumbent pilot. Sure, it would be out of fuel in only a few minutes. But during those few minutes it could not be caught with tracer bullets. Somebody is sure to try something like this during the next ten years.

At Rensselaer Polytechnic Institute, they're working on a composite Kevlar sailplane, Figure 2-4. It should have a glide ratio of nearly thirty to one— double that of most sailplanes—because it weighs less than most pilots. Work is underway to apply similar innovative composite construction to ARVs.

Another idea which never became popular, but has a passable chance to, is the roadable airplane. Many years back, designer Molt Taylor certified his Aerocar, a flying automobile now being restored in the EAA Air Museum. Now, MacCready's AeroVironment people have locked onto this potential market. The real need here is for a vehicle you can fly for hundreds of miles, then drive in normal road traffic for twenty miles for business, or to avoid hangar fees. This may become more practical with tomorrow's lightweight wheels and super-adhesion tires. There is no problem in folding the flight surfaces, but they could be seriously damaged by the first yahoo that nudges them with his bumper. When you are designing "one for the road," just remember that the lighter it is, the harder it will be to control when you drive it in cross-winds with small tires. Nobody will want to share the road with a whirling propeller, so you need a driveline for your wheels. Engine development will be tough; it must idle for long periods in traffic without fouling its plugs. Individual electric motors like Bob Boucher's provide a lot of torque per pound, but they might be very expensive for this application. Instead, you may want to consider coupling your engine to a hydraulic pump, with a hydraulic motor driving each wheel.

It would be interesting to design a four-place

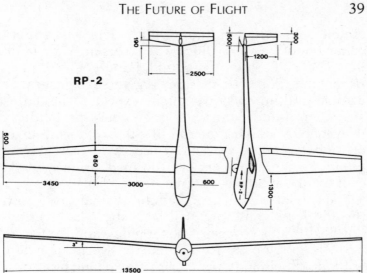

Figure 2–4. Composite sailplane design by Steve Winckler of Rensselaer Polytechnic Institute. The entire RP-2 will weigh only 172 pounds (Kevlar and carbon fiber materials). Standard aluminum and fiberglass construction could raise that figure to more than 400 pounds.

double-delta with adjustable wing extensions, a small
canard doubling *a la* Quickie as struts for your landing gear, and a hundred-pound, hundred-horse plastic engine. Some delta shapes give such insurance
against stalling that we might expect to land this
speedster at under thirty miles an hour—particularly
if we deployed extra dacron lift surface during takeoff and landing. We do not see these fast private
planes becoming cheap, or even medium-priced, except for those bought as kits.

The special record-setting aircraft will always "push
the envelope," and they will be costly. The recently-
unveiled Rutan Voyager is a stunning example (Figure
2-5). Its mission: to fly around the world, nonstop,
without refueling. It has already flown long test hops.

The more you know about aircraft, the more unbelievable the Voyager seems, until you see it in the
air. One engine pushes, one pulls. For most of the
global flight, only the pusher will be operating. It
weighs under a ton empty, but *five and a half* tons
fully fueled. No, it's not fast; its crew of two will live
for two weeks in the fuselage. Its structure is made
chiefly of Nomex paper honeycomb-faced with carbon fiber skins. It has two vertical fins, but only one
fin has a rudder. It is far and away the world's
largest composite aircraft, but when empty it weighs
less than a Volkswagen. One day, inexpensive aircraft may routinely surpass the Voyager in every
respect. Meanwhile, the record-setters will cost huge
sums, and we will not see a real market develop for
most of them.

We do envision a sort of Rolls-Royce market that
will continue turning out executive aircraft in somewhat larger numbers than they do today. These will
do the same jobs as the supercharged, twin-engined
Pipers and Cessnas of today, as well as the smallish
executive jets. They will carry six to fourteen passengers, and they will not be kits. But they will
probably be flown first as manned, perhaps two-
thirds sized, scale models. The Rutan factory special-

Figure 2–5. Rutan Voyager during fly-by at Whitman Field, Oshkosh, WI (July 1984). Designed for non-stop, around-the-world record attempt without refueling.

izes in this method of using the world for a wind tunnel, building prototypes of bigger craft-to-come and flying them first as pygmies. If we see civil aircraft taking off and landing more or less vertically like the Harrier, by deflecting jet exhausts, we will probably see it first in executive aircraft. That's because vertical takeoff requires advanced, powerful engines and deflector systems. Those systems will almost certainly be adapted first from military power plants, which are developed for pretty heavy aircraft. All bets are off if somebody builds a single-place, superlight delta with an internal hundred-horse ducted fan! The fan can be used to lift your craft a few feet up as an air cushion vehicle while you are slowly gaining forward speed. Its downwash "footprint" will not set fire to your grass, either.

So much for the very near future, using hardware already in development. It's not exactly a blueprint for that future when, as NASA's Lovelace said, you can call for fast air transportation easier than you can call a cab today. That day is likely to come only after we have gobs of cheap power available, in the form of energy beams.

In Chapter 4 we describe the scramble for more powerful engines, the limitations of chemical fuels, and ways to cheat by using air instead of, say, liquid oxygen. It's interesting to speculate on what the performance of today's interceptor aircraft *would* have been, if we had not diverted funding from research aircraft to man-carrying ballistic rockets back in the sixties. We might have hybrid air-turborocket engines boosting interceptors up to orbital speed in the atmospheric fringes by now. But they would still consume tremendous amounts of chemical fuels in the process, probably dropping empty tanks or boosters en route. The way to get around this is to feed aircraft most of their energy by beams from remote power plants. We can do that with microwave beams, which require big receiving antennas, or with laser beams, which can be focused down to relatively small receiving lenses. Obviously, when flying at high speeds we prefer to carry the smallest receiving device that's practical. The high-energy laser, then, is our energy beam of choice.

The placement and type of power plant to feed energy to a billion-watt electric laser is going to be a political question. It would probably be much cheaper to place multi-gigawatt nuclear reactors in orbit, as the Soviets have done with smaller reactors, than to erect miles-wide solar cell arrays. It would also be quite safe because it would be in high orbit. The Soviet reactor that broke up over Canada would never have posed the slightest danger had it been placed a thousand miles out to begin with.

Despite its advantages, though, we have doubts whether the orbital power reactor will gain enough adherents in this country to make massive funding popular. A politicians's first need is to see to his re-election. Political decisions on the power plant issue, we suspect, will tend to err on the side of caution—indistinguishable from what Kantrowitz labeled as "timidity." And too many voters have shut their minds against the case for reactors, anytime, anyplace. Many of those same voters take a sunnier view of solar power.

Direct conversion of sunlight to electricity *is* a reasonable alternative energy source, especially in space. It may be considerably more expensive than orbital reactors, but nobody has drummed up an orchestrated demonstration against the sun recently. Therefore, politically and economically, solar-conversion power plants seem a likely source of energy for future needs. Putting them out there will be just a big engineering project because we know how to do it (for details, see Chapter 9). Let us leave those details to their proper place and take this as an excellent bet: *sometime early in the next century, pilots will be able to request energy beams to match the flight path of their aircraft.* That is when we can expect a fully flight-integrated society.

The first airliner to use a laser for fuel might look a lot like the sketch in Figure 2-6. Hertzberg and Sun have proposed a flight demonstration using a conventional, modified cargo jet. It might use ordinary fuel to start up its turbofans, then call for a forty-two megawatt laser against its fifty-foot-diameter laser receiver. The laser energy would then be concentrated in a heat exchanger which would heat incoming air just as jet fuel would. The hot air under pressure would escape through turbines, which would power the compressor fans. A schematic of the laser-turbofan is shown in Figure 2-7. This laser would power three engines clustered atop the aircraft.

Communication between the airplane and the laser installation, in stationary orbit, must be as complete as it is with the new microwave landing system. The plane could signal that it needs only enough power to taxi, and then keep up a flow of feedback information so that the laser's aiming device will keep the power laser tracking at the same pace as the vehicle. (A low-power "pilot" laser, beamed from near the plane's tail, could provide this error-correction.)

The very first tests might be laser-powered taxiing, followed by a rendezvous between the laser and the plane in flight after it has already climbed to cruise altitude using conventional fuel. These early flight tests will answer lots of questions, such as: are our adaptive optics good enough to keep the laser centered when our plane flies through turbulent air? Is a high orbit, with its tiny built-in time delay, too high for quick pointing response to a buffeting airplane? Do we need tighter focus, or a wider receiving dish as a shield against a partial-miss by the laser?

You can think up other scenarios of interest. These tests would probably be made over calm water even though a clean miss by this particular laser, hitting the ground, might deliver only a hundred watts or so (per square inch) against the ground for a fraction of a second as it swept along. That's not a very serious

Figure 2–6. Concept for laser-powered aircraft (after Beckey & Mayer, Aerospace Corp., 1976); redrawn by artist R. Rue.

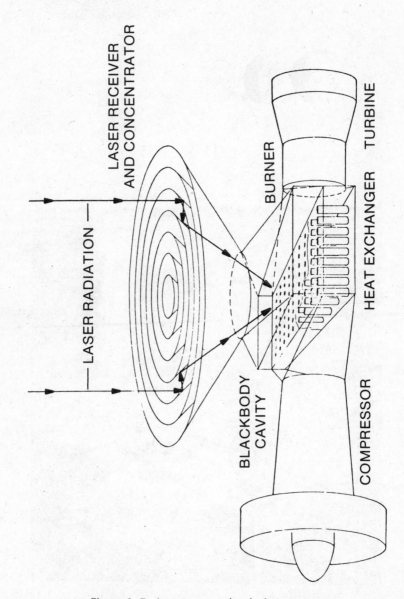

Figure 2–7. Laser-powered turbofan concept
(Hertzberg and Sun, Univ. of Washington, 1978)

fire problem, but it would not do a stargazer's eyes any good. If the laser feed were shut off for any reason, the plane could crank up its jet fuel pumps, restart in flight, and head for home. Of course it might have conventional jet engines slung under its wings for such emergencies or for routine taxi needs.

Kantrowitz and Rosa, a decade ago, worked up a patent on a laser-powered ramjet that could be fed from *below*. The patent sketches show a delta shape with its air intake and exhaust, as well as its receiving lens, on its underside. A ramjet can't produce thrust until it is boosted up to near-sonic speed, so this scheme would need some auxiliary power. We will cover several engine types in Chapters 4 and 5.

Once we have the bugs worked out of this laser-feed system, investors will be quick to invest in big space-based power plants, just as they were willing to buy stock in communication satellites. A system that can safely feed tens of megawatts, and later gigawatts, to a jumbo jet can feed lots of lesser beams to smaller consumers. All aside from fast executive transport, a fifty-mile-an-hour air taxi does not have to be airplane-shaped, nor does it need a cabbie. It needs a receiver lens, a laser-fed engine with thrust deflection for vertical and horizontal thrust, comfortable seating in a pod integrated beneath the receiver, and a comm link with an orbiting beamer. Depending on its own weight, the number of passengers, and the type of engine it uses, a laser-fed taxi might lift you from the mall pad downtown and whisk you to your backyard pad using as little as a steady fifty kilowatts. When power becomes this abundant, it will be very, very cheap. A solotaxi, only large enough to carry you alone, would cost you less than a twintaxi or a fourtaxi.

Or take a family flivver instead of a taxi. As a four-seater with safety devices, its composite shell will be filament-wound with graceful bubble viewports. The real energy-conserving type will have skirts so that, for longish trips, it can use ground effects to scud down interstate highways using no more energy than a solotaxi. At any time, however, you can request boost to the nearest bathroom or pizza joint. Your flivver's onboard computer will check out the locations nearby, give you a choice, and ask you to verify. When you do, it will then check local traffic control to make sure no one will be on collision course with you, ask for a more energetic laser from far above, and take you to that pizza as the crow flies. If you have an emergency, your computer can advise traffic control and, with any luck at all, get an okay for hot boost to the hospital.

Some of these requirements suggest a few things about the flivver's shape. If it flies four people at, say, seventy miles an hour, it should be moderately streamlined with no greater frontal area than is reasonable. It might look like a smooth ellipse from above, with its circular receiver lens spanning most of its roof. It should be flat and smooth beneath, its skirts retractable (perhaps deflatable to bumper contours). In side view its front end should slope back in unbroken contour to a relatively abrupt contour at its rear end, conforming to Kamm's minimum drag envelope. It might weigh a half-ton, empty.

But what if your flivver is designed to fly the same four people from Akron to Athens for dinner? Well, we know the trip will be hypersonic, which suggests a shallow ballistic flight for such a distance, and that means we need hundreds of megawatts for a few minutes. The roof lens must be large, and of very high quality; your windows and shell must be able to take high rates of heating. You will probably want stub wings both to stabilize and to help lift your vehicle. You will need water tanks too, because this kind of ballistic boost demands a heck of a wallop against your behind. That wallop can come from laser vaporization of water—a very sophisticated kind of "steam rocket" that we will describe in due course. This kind of flivver is really a limousine and it might weigh over a ton, with amenities like onboard air for

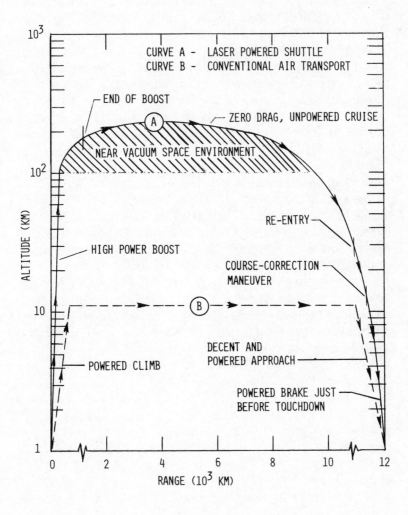

Figure 2–8. Mission profiles for laser-powered shuttle vs. conventional air transport vehicles.

breathing, and deceleration jets near the roots of your retractable stub wings.

The ways we use energy during the flight are called the "mission profile." The mission profile for our Athens trip will look very different from the same trip by today's airliner, as we can see in Figure 2-8. We go ten times as high, we coast for most of the way without power, and we make the trip in half an hour instead of half a day.

Big intercontinental transports of this later era may not look anything like those of today. For reasons we will cover later, they may look more like huge conical-topped frisbees, with many receiver lenses spaced around their upper surfaces. Figure 2-9 shows an aerospaceport with several of these craft. Passengers enter and exit from passageways below, so that their eyes will not be damaged by glinting reflection from a nearby power laser. We expect that by 2020 AD, given inexpensive beamed power, commercial flights through near-orbital space will be as common as transatlantic flights are today. This cheap power is the only technology we lack today, because we have solved virtually all of the other hardware problems.

Figure 2–9. Launch facility for laser-powered shuttles. (Artists: R. Rue and R. Carter)

Chapter 3:

PUSHING HARDWARE LIMITS

There are four major ways to haul a payload better, and that's as true for flight as it is for cars. You can haul it faster by installing a bigger and more powerful engine, but big engines are thirsty devils. You will either have to install bigger fuel tanks, or accept a shorter range. Of course the extra fuel and tankage are massive, and the engine must haul it along too, so you gain less than you thought. This is the sort of option you might use if you are not very concerned about the price of fuel over long distances.

Instead, you can install a more efficient propulsion system; an engine that makes better use of the existing fuel, or a better fuel, or both. This usually calls for more R & D (research and development), which is expensive, but in the long run it pays off by hauling a payload faster or farther. Until recently, most engineers thought we were nearing the limits of improvement in this area. Now we realize so much room for improvement exists that entire chapters (4 through 7) in this book are devoted to the new propulsion systems.

A third route to better vehicles is to spend your R & D money on making the vehicle structure itself lighter, and/or more efficient. In this case you can keep the old propulsion system and still haul payloads faster or, as with Rutan's Voyager, farther.

Finally, you can build more reliable systems: engines less likely to fail, fuels that are not as likely to deteriorate or explode, structures that haul more payloads before they are ready for the scrap heap.

The history of flight and of auto racing show that, in the long run, you get the best results with the last three approaches, and that when you step beyond old limits you are treading dangerous ground. When you develop a new vehicle, you should do it with reliability in mind. In the last part of World War II the Germans, working against time, rushed several new aircraft designs into production before they were ready. The Messerschmitt ME163 was a tiny, stunningly advanced tailless interceptor powered by a liquid-fuel Walther rocket engine; when it worked properly, the little craft knifed through Allied bomber squadrons like a razor. But often, the unstable concentrated hydrogen peroxide fuel caused the ME163 to become a ball of flame in midair, a victim not of bullets but of unreliability. The great loss here was the pilot, trained at great expense, who was not as easily replaced as the aircraft. You can imagine what these catastrophic failures did to the morale of the few remaining pilots.

Later, our own satellite-carrying Vanguard rocket suffered a similar fate: high-tech, but low reliability. Unreliability caused cancellation of our Skybolt missile and other programs—one of which author Ing will never forget because the explosion during its last test flattened him against a concrete floor. If the payload is inexpensive cargo, maybe you can use a vehicle that disintegrates once or twice every dozen missions; but the moment a human being becomes part of the payload, you have a "man-rated system" that demands very high reliability. We joke about humans being produced by unskilled labor, but we consider that product very precious, worthy of lots of extra R & D to protect life and limb. It's also true that some other payloads, including communication and research satellites, are so expensive that they are worth extra effort for high reliability.

Before we leave the topic, we must mention a fund-

amental fact of reliability engineering that explains
why new aircraft cost so much to develop. A complex
aircraft has many subsystems: landing gear, engine,
communication equipment, life-support systems,
structure, and so on. For the sake of simplicity we
will claim there are only ten subsystems (actually
there are more, but let's say there are only ten that
are critical to the mission). Through exhaustive tests
we know that each subsystem has 99% reliability.
Do we expect the whole aircraft to have 99% reliability?

We do not! If any one of those ten critical subsystems fails, the mission fails. We must multiply each
subsystem reliability figure by the next: 99% × 99%
× 99% . . . and so on,—nine multiplications in this
case. The result? A shade over 90% for the whole
system; try it on your calculator and see. The next
time you hear about the huge expense of developing
an advanced vehicle, think about how much work
goes into making each subsystem as near as possible
to 100% reliable. If we have only "two nines," as the
saying goes, we're in deep trouble. If each of those
critical subsystems can be proven reliable to three
nines (that is, 99.9% reliable), we are doing much
better.

It's not much of a jump from reliability to lighter
and more efficient structures because often a lightened structure, or one of different shape, brings higher
reliability with it. When it comes to improving a
structure, we must look at every part of it, and we
must make it as easy as possible to repair. Many
flightworthy structures today use a lot of aluminum
and, where we once used chromium-molybdenum
(chrome-moly) steels, we are using more titanium
which weighs less than steel with roughly the same
strength. We are beginning to see wider use of even
lighter structures called composites. We can depend
on seeing still more of them in the future. In fact, we
may be approaching the limits of structural lightness—
until someone comes up with unobtainium.

Unobtainium is an old engineering joke; it weighs nothing, costs nothing, has infinite strength, can be machined by a dull kitchen knife, and improves the flavor of tossed green salad. Of course it's unobtainable. No matter how much we improve a structure, it will weigh something and will have a limit to its strength, and if we exceed those limits it is going to fail. Designers must think about the unthinkable.

It's not enough to design a structure that is a world-beater so long as it suffers no damage. Designers must also consider the need for repair. It might be possible to cast a complete, thin-walled, superlight vehicle structure in one piece from, say, titanium alloy. But mechanics drop wrenches, and birds get in the way, and the chances are that those vehicles would get a few dents. When the structure is all one thin piece like an eggshell, a dent in one small area can cause the whole bloody thing to fail. Yes, it's possible to grind away the dented section and weld a new piece (if you've got one the right shape) in place—or in a pinch, to weld or glue a stiffener plate in place behind the dent. We say grind the dented section away, slowly, becaue titanium is tougher than most hacksaw blades. More troublesome yet, titanium welding is a special skill, and the best alloy for casting large thin shapes may not be one that is readily welded, and metal next to the weld might lose much of its strength. In a man-rated system, a better answer might be to discard the whole damaged structure at tremendous cost. The best answer, though, would be to design a more repairable structure in the first place.

Imagine the frustration of a penniless race car constructor who finds beautiful seamless titanium alloy tubing in a junkyard. He cannot cut it into transportable lengths without special tools, and if he can get it to the shop he will need an expert to weld it, and if he uses fasteners through it *they* must be titanium too, or stainless steel, to avoid galvanic corrosion from different metals being placed together.

Finally, if he can find affordable fasteners, how the devil will he drill all those holes through the tubing?

It does not take much imagination to swap today's weekend racer for the pilot of tomorrow's sport aircraft. We don't say it's impossible to bring high-tech to structural work in a home shop, because we have seen it done. We are pointing out that the future of flight will include future structures that will have to be repairable without the facilities of Lockheed or Boeing. To put it another way, the family flyer will not be as light as possible; it will be as light as is practical.

That is a good argument in favor of those superlight structural composites. Fiberglass is the most primitive of lightweight composites, and the cheapest. It's easily repaired, and is being used to good advantage in private aircraft today. But today's advanced composite aircraft are not molded the same way a Corvette is repaired, with spongy mats of glass fiber to soak up gobs of heavy resin. That's the easy way, but it's heavy as guilt and weak as a New Year's resolution. And a high strength-to-weight ratio is what we are after.

Glass fibers can be woven in many ways, and the correct weave must be oriented precisely to gain maximum strength. The syrupy plastic polymer that impregnates the weave before it hardens is also specially compounded, and the molds for each piece are made to exact tolerances. The lightest fiberglass pieces are made with "prepreg," cloth already impregnated with the precise amount of plastic resin needed, and the cloth is carefully placed between molds (or sometimes vacuum bagged) to be cured. That way there is no excess weight in the finished piece. If it's damaged, you can repair it at a home shop without too much trouble. The repaired piece may be a trifle heavy, but with such tricks as the fiberglass rivet technique it can be as strong as the original structure with next to no weight penalty.

The fiberglass rivet is a process developed many

years ago, and it is not patentable because the inventor made it public domain (in other words, gave it away to everybody) in *Road & Track* magazine in May of 1968. It can be argued that the process is revolutionary in a trivial way. Metal rivets cannot be safely squeezed into place through fiberglass panels without risking damage to the panels, but fiberglass rivets are, literally, composite mush. The rivets are injected as a specially processed slurry without bubbles, the consistency of toothpaste, which then shrinks very slightly while hardening. Some other techniques have been patented more recently which raise the possibility that glass rope can be used in the same way as steel cable. Why? Because the tensile strength of glass is higher than piano wire, it weighs far less, and glass rope is easy to handle when you need to flex it.

We describe these details in today's technology because they have paved the way for much more advanced composites that can be used in the same way but with greater weight savings. At present they have high price tags, but in the long run they can pay for themselves by cutting fuel consumption and structure weight, so you can stuff more payload in. Some of them are now being tested on tomorrow's flight structures. While fiberglass cloth is woven from extremely thin filaments of glass, you can get much higher strength-to-weight by weaving cloth that's processed so that only fibers of carbon are left, or even by winding the fibers around a form much as a baseball's interior is wound with cord. Boron filaments are better than carbon for some parts, but the stuff now costs over $200 per pound. For a while at least, we will not see boron fibers in wide use; but they are already used in very special structures such as the stabilizer of the Grumman F-14 and certain parts of the B-1 bomber.

Almost as strong as boron, carbon fiber has tremendous compression strength—it resists forces that try to squeeze it—and plenty of tensile strength—

resisting forces that try to pull it apart. With epoxy resin, carbon cloth is so good that it's already being used for wing spars and most of the rest of new Lear Fan aircraft structures. The famed Hawker Harrier, too, has been lightened with composite parts. Result: its range is much greater. Some experts say that by 1990, roughly half the structural weight of new aircraft will be advanced composites. We may see carbon and boron fibers, or Kevlar and glass fibers, used together where we need a part that has special strength but tolerable cost. Besides, when these composites fail they break gradually, so you may be able to spot the failure before it becomes serious. When aluminum fails, it often fails suddenly. They call it "catastrophic failure" for good reason: sudden failure of a structure while you are using it can ruin your whole day. We think there is little doubt about the future of composites. With gradual failures, more strength than the best aluminum alloys, and 20% less weight, today's advanced composite parts are previews of the structures in future flight.

Another small revolution is brewing in structures that must have very high strength-to-weight. It would be nice if we could build parts from foamed alloy steel—that is, steel parts with smooth surfaces but full of bubbles, with all the bubbles the right size. It may be practical, if we can produce those steel foams in a steel mill where there is no gravity. That's the kind of project we will be seeing when industry moves into orbit, and orbital industries can sell items that simply cannot be made on Earth. We can predict there will be revolutionary materials *from* space; we can even predict superfilaments grown in space from crystals, and metals composed of, say, steel and aluminum. Beyond that, we are grappling with Tsiolkovsky's problem. It's interesting to consider, but we are not sure exactly how it will all be done.

Finally we come to different ways to shape a structure in the interest of efficiency. We have been evolving better shapes for a long time, and there is still another revolution in progress that may prove larger than most of us think.

From the early days of flight, new shapes were tried. A long thin wing—a "high aspect ratio"—was found to be better at lifting payloads than a short fat one of the same area. Of course a wing fifty feet long must have *very* strong spars, which suggests a fairly thick airfoil. A fast, highly maneuverable fighter craft might have stubbier, thinner wings than a slow cargo-carrying craft of the same power.

Different airfoils were also tried, and even today we are learning things about the best airfoil for a given purpose. Footnote: a few years ago, a high-school physics teacher of excellent reputation learned that his best student was collecting parts for a real, live wind tunnel. The teacher was pleased until he heard that the youth actually hoped to find something new by studying oddball airfoil sections. To his credit, the teacher did not ridicule the student to his face. But he explained to one of the present authors that it was ridiculous to expect that anyone, with a home-built wind tunnel, could possibly learn things that NASA could not come up with.

Actually, an important discovery was not very likely. But it's entirely plausible, if you are working in some area of technology where NASA is not funded. NASA people often come up with ideas they cannot pursue, because all the money is earmarked for other things. Sooner or later NASA may get money for the study. But in very low-speed flight, for example, NASA has not shown any very outstanding interest. It's entirely possible that tomorrow's ten-mile-an-hour sport flyers will owe as much to home labs and college aerody-namicists as they owe to NASA. Paul MacCready's vehicles are a case in point.

MacCready, a professor at Cal Poly in San Luis Obispo, set the engineering world abuzz with his strangely-shaped, man-powered aircraft. A long-time builder of flying models, he and his team of amateur enthusiasts built structures of advanced composites and used airfoils with reverse-curves. With the pilot pedaling to drive the propeller, MacCready's *Gossamer Albatross* flew across the English Channel in 1979. Not content with this, MacCready's team then built the *Solar Challenger*, crowding solar cells onto the wing and tail so that the propeller could be powered by the sun! In 1981 the *Solar Challenger* flew a zigzag course 165 miles from France to England.

Reporters asked MacCready what use such aircraft might have. "Perhaps none," said MacCready, smiling. But if some of us are ghosting along in solar-powered flivvers twenty years from now, we will know where credit is due. The AeroVironment people, of course, are not limiting themselves to solar power.

Many of tomorrow's family flyers will owe a lot to the odd aircraft shapes designed by Burt Rutan. His small private planes are typically built from composites, and they are efficient enough to scare the exhaust pipes off of people who are still trying to sell older designs. Rutan went back to Orville and Wilbur in one respect; he likes canard shapes, with the horizontal tail in front and main wing behind. We say "main" because in the canard, the horizontal tail adds quite a bit of lift—and it can contain landing gear as well. Today, these aircraft are too heavy and too fast to be classed as ultralights. Within a few years, we can expect them to have the weight and landing speed of an ultralight, but with a cruising speed of perhaps 200 miles an hour.

The flying wing is another shape that should have a strong future. Perhaps we should say a flying wing constitutes a *family* of shapes, including lifting bodies without noticeable wings. Actually, the NASA shuttle is an aerobody with stubby wings that approach "delta"—triangular—shape. Jack Northrop designed very advanced aircraft at the end of World War II with no fuselage or separate tail. His jet-powered YB-49, in 1949, could carry sixteen tons of cargo at well over 500 miles per hour. In fact, a Northrop flying wing could carry almost as much cargo as the plane's empty weight, which many present cargo aircraft cannot match!

We mentioned earlier that politics sometimes influences design. Near the end of his life Jack Northrop stated publicly that he had been pressured by military leaders to merge his little company with a larger one. According to him, his refusal meant the cancellation of his hopes for the YB-49; a political hatchet job on a good design. But a good idea should outlive bad politicians. If Northrop's version is right, we can expect to see cargo lifted by flying wings one day.

Some of those flying wings may look something like the NASA shuttle but with thicker stub wings, especially if we continue present work in dirigibles. John McPhee wrote a wonderful book, *The Deltoid Pumpkin Seed*, about a private group that finally flew a small piloted prototype of a delta-shaped dirigible. A full-sized, cargo-carrying delta dirigible would be enormous. It could carry a hundred tons of cargo. Given certain revolutionary powerplants under study by one of the present authors (see Chapter 6) it could fly at stratospheric heights and supersonic speeds. We will be very surprised if we do not see aerobody dirigibles, with or without stubby swept-back wings, before 2000 A.D.

And *still* we have not exhausted the possibilities of new shapes. Even air scoops have become much more efficient with NASA's attention. Within the past few years, high-speed cars and aircraft have adopted the "NASA inlet," a duct without a protruding scoop. Slender fairings, called "strakes" or "fences" depending on their uses, are also being installed to guide air more efficiently over structures at high speed. Maybe we won't see such fences used both for structural support and efficiency on slower family flyers one day, but don't bet against it. Some crop-dusting aircraft have used these external fences on the tips of their wings for years.

Some revolutionary new aircraft are shaped so they will be just a bit unstable in the atmosphere.

You read it right; if we can use a computer to fly a plane, it can correct a wrong turn much faster than a human pilot, and it does not get tired. The trick is to build a shape that flies right on the feather-edge of instability, and then to guide that shape through the air using tiny control surfaces instead of big ones. The little ones do not create as much drag, so they are more efficient. But they can do much, much more.

If we put additional control surfaces on the aircraft, and operate them with great care, we can lower or raise the plane's nose (called a "pitch change") *without diving or climbing*. Or we can cause its nose to "yaw" from side to side, also without changing its flight direction. Imagine how useful that would be to an interceptor carrying a laser cannon; instead of having to keep re-aiming the cannon, the pilot could aim the entire aircraft at the target without pulling severe g-loads. But because of these added fins or tabs in the airstream, the same interceptor can bob upward or downward, or slide to one side very quickly without changing its flight attitude. This may force the pilot to take a few extra g-forces, but it can help him dodge a missile a lot more easily.

These aerodynamic tricks are called "decoupling" because normally the direction the aircraft moves is "coupled," or intimately involved, with the way it is pointing and banking. When a computer and carefully-placed small control surfaces can let the plane skid sideways without changing its attitude, or seesaw its nose up and down without changing its flight path, you have decoupled its attitude from its flight path. Sweden has such an airplane, and an Agile Combat Aircraft (ACA) is under test in Europe. Mr. Rutan must be pleased to note the canard fins on these revolutionary agile aircraft.

We have often heard that shapes will not matter as much in space because there is no atmospheric drag out there. Well—yes and no. Obviously an aerospace plane, which must operate both in the atmosphere and in space, must be able to maneuver in air. It may have adjustable wings, or it may land with a big steerable parachute. NASA has tested many versions of the Rogallo wing, which can be folded and stowed, then deployed at the right moment to carry the craft down like a payload under a delta-shaped kite. The Rogallo delta wing typically is shaped like one of the long paper darts we tossed when we thought the teacher wasn't looking.

Even if our vehicle is a pure spacecraft, not intended to deal with aerodynamic loads, its shape will depend on the maneuvers it must make. One g equals an acceleration, or velocity change, of 32.2 feet per second. Space probes like the Voyager and Galileo must take several g's while they are being boosted up to their paths, but you can be sure they do not have all their panels and instrumentation booms deployed until the heavy g-loads are done with. The Galileo's magnetometer boom is an open structure of spidery girders called an Astromast that sticks out a full hundred feet from the craft's centerline when deployed. It would buckle like toothpicks if the craft had to take several g's while the boom was extended. Yes, you *can* safely maneuver a deployed structure like Galileo, or a huge solar collector, but you must do it with very gentle pushes—tiny fractions of a g. You simply have to keep that gentle push going longer to complete a maneuver.

For two final examples of the importance of shape in space, we offer a space battle cruiser and a small space fighter. The space cruiser (Chapter 8) uses a linac (linear accelerator) for its laser weapon and that linac may be a hundred meters long! It also needs huge external radiators to get rid of excess heat. This space cruiser must be very long and will have retractable radiators as big as the masts on a clipper ship. Also, you do not want stray radiation from the linac or power plant to endanger the crew, so the crew quarters must be installed up forward beyond radiation shielding.

The little space fighter may be another matter. We will give it a pilot, and design it as a compact structure able to pull thirty g's for a few seconds without damage. We want some kind of armor against damage from enemy lasers, and an escape capsule for the pilot in case of severe battle damage. The fighter gets its power from a friendly laser (perhaps relayed from a power satellite or a highly mobile battle cruiser thousands of miles away). The laser engine works by vaporizing materials in a thrust chamber, as we will show in Chapter 4.

Here is one way to do it all. We build a long torus, an elongated doughnut, to hold the fuel. We stick the laser collector and engine at the back of it, and slide the pilot's capsule into the central hole of the torus from the front. Hydrogen is excellent fuel, but we are willing to accept a less powerful fuel if it can double as laser armor. It happens that lithium and carbon can be made into pellets or powder, and they are not too expensive. Carbon, despite its light weight, will also resist an enemy laser beam very well. Not only that, but since we are carrying our fuel as solid particles, it won't all be hopelessly lost if the enemy laser burns a hole in the tank. Incidentally, with fuel pellets, it might actually be possible to retrieve fuel that has been lost in space.

A design of this sort makes a small target, and a torus is a great structural shape for its weight. The pilot is protected by the toroidal shell full of fuel, and he can can pop his life-support capsule out if necessary like a cork from a bottle. Will the escape capsule have retractable wings for dodging back to Earth? A stowed Rogallo wing? If so, the pilot might be able to steer his way back to almost any spot on Earth—but we must remember to give him an emergency propulsion system. In future flight, we may not have to depend much on chemical rockets for that.

Chapter 4:

BEAM US UP!

This is the chapter where we wade into formula-infested waters. But we can keep the water shallow and the formulas small so they won't bite anybody. Actually, the progression from the earliest skyrockets to the latest laser propulsion system depends on the same basic principles. We can survey that progression quickly.

Until we began very recently to experiment with revolutionary propulsion systems, it was thought that the future of flight might be limited by the amount of energy we can get by burning chemicals together. For centuries, rockets were powered by gunpowder, usually a special slow-burning mixture with excess powdered charcoal. At its very best, gunpowder (a mixture of finely-powdered potassium nitrate, sulfur, and charcoal) is a low-power propellant, and the slow-burning stuff is even more inefficient.

The most common measure of a propellant's efficiency is called specific impulse, or I_{sp}. This simply means the amount of thrust impulse you can get from a chosen propellant in a rocket using using a particular exhaust nozzle. There are several formulas to express I_{sp}. We will use a simple formula here that shows what affects I_{sp} the most. For this we need to consider only two things: T_c, the temperature of hot gases in the chamber; and MW, the average molecular weight of those hot gases. Here is the relationship:

I_{sp} varies with the square root of $\dfrac{T_c}{MW}$.

Why go into it in such detail? Because THE FUTURE OF FLIGHT GREATLY DEPENDS ON IMPROVING PROPELLANT SPECIFIC IMPULSE. Notice that if you want a much higher I_{sp}, you must somehow raise the chamber temperature, T_c, or you can lower the molecular weight of the gases (MW), or both. Up to a point, you can do both by choosing chemicals that burn hotter and produce exhaust gases of low MW.

In tests, you can find the actual I_{sp} of a propellant by using instruments to see how much thrust the rocket produces, for how many seconds. You already know how much the propellant weighs, having weighed it in advance. Let's say your test rocket has two pounds of propellant, and it gives a steady fifty-five pounds of thrust for four seconds. Simply multiply the thrust in pounds, times the duration in seconds, to get total impulse, measured in pound-seconds.

In our imaginary test rocket, we get 55 × 4, or 220 pound-seconds of total impulse. Now, to find I_{sp}, we divide the *total* impulse, 220 pound-seconds, by the number of pounds of propellant we had; in this case, two pounds. We get a specific impulse of 110 for the propellant of our little rocket, which is not anything to brag about. If we did not already know, we might suspect that our propellant is gunpowder, because that's about all you can expect from old-fashioned "black powder" rockets.

By World War II, scientists were using better stuff. In general, for military munitions they still preferred solid propellants because, like a skyrocket, they can be stored easily and the whole rocket is a relatively simple gadget with few if any moving parts. The bazooka rocket, for example, used a type of smokeless powder that had nearly twice the I_{sp} of black powder. This family of propellants feels rather like plastic—in fact, it's partly made from a highly incendiary plastic called nitrocellulose. Incidentally, when used as rocket propellant, smokeless "powder" is not really powder at all, but typically a slender tube of plastic that burns furiously.

But other storable solid propellants called "composites" were developed as well. After early development at Cal Tech provided the GALCIT composites, companies like Aerojet-General and Thiokol went on to develop composite propellants for the Polaris and Minuteman missiles. Today, we see composites at their best in the boosters for the NASA shuttle. A typical composite propellant consists mostly of ammonium perchlorate and powdered aluminum, mixed with a rubbery fluid material that later cures into a firm mass. The stuff is poured, or "cast," into the rocket casing as a thick slurry, and it's often cast with a hole in the middle to provide lots of burning surface.

It is pointless to go into loving detail on these huge skyrockets because the truth is that, at best, their propellants may achieve an I_{sp} of a little over 300. (That is, each pound of propellant will provide a bit over 300 pound-seconds of impulse.) Yes, you can send small payloads into orbit with this kind of I_{sp}— the Scout rocket is proof—but you need an awfully big rocket to orbit a very small payload. And the clouds of smoky exhaust can completely obscure an entire launch complex, and those clouds are pollutants. Since the days of Robert Goddard, scientists have known a better way.

Liquid fuels can avoid many of those pollutant clouds, and—far more important—they boast higher I_{sp}s as well. The German V-2 was an early example, with huge tanks of liquid oxygen and alcohol for fuel. The fuels were pumped into a special combustion chamber where they were ignited, and the flaming exhaust shot from a flaring nozzle in the rear. The chamber temperature (T_c) was so high that it would have melted the metal chamber, if it had not been cooled. How did they cool it? By pumping the alcohol through a thin jacket surrounding the combustion chamber, before that alcohol was injected into the chamber; that's called "regenerative cooling." Though our pioneering Dr. Goddard had patented such a design long before, James Wyld of the American Rocket Society really made it popular in the late 1930's. The shuttle's main engines approach today's limits of regenerative cooling—a tour de force in heat transfer.

So the liquid propellants give higher I_{sp}, but as we might suspect from studying the formula above, they do it by very high T_c and exhaust gases of low MW. The shuttle's great engines burn perhaps the best liquid fuels of all: liquid hydrogen and liquid oxygen. This combination gives a T_c of about 3500° Kelvin, and the average MW of the exhaust gases is only about twelve (the propellants are burned fuel-rich, six pounds of oxygen for each pound of hydrogen). This is getting near the upper limit we can expect from burning chemicals.

That upper limit rises a little when you put a rocket in a vacuum, because there is no pressure outside the chamber to resist the flow of exhaust. This is true whether we use black powder or laser rockets, and a rocket designed to operate in a vacuum usually has a bigger exhaust nozzle to extract more energy from that exhaust.

The only other way to get much higher efficiency burning chemical propellants is to use liquid fluorine instead of liquid oxygen—and *that* would be a disaster! When you burn hydrogen and oxygen, you get clouds of steam as exhaust, which is not toxic when it cools. But when you burn hydrogen and fluorine, you get hydrofluoric acid, which will dissolve glass and concrete, not to mention your lungs. Some researchers have suggested adding finely powdered beryllium to liquid propellants to raise I_{sp} by a small but useful amount; but even if it was used only during high-altitude propulsion, beryllium products can be very toxic too. So the NASA shuttle's main engines make do with oxygen and hydrogen, with an I_{sp} of around 455 in space (375 at sea level). That's more than we could get a few years ago; enough to boost our first industrial experiments into orbit. But as long as we have to use up hundreds of tons of propellant for each launch, it is going to be expensive. If we could somehow find a way around the "I_{sp} barrier", we could fill the vehicle with less propellant and more payload.

Conceivably, we could float over that barrier with metastable helium. J. S. Zmuidzinas, at JPL, studied the possibility of spin-polarizing atoms so that, when some of the atoms "go normal," a great amount of heat is suddenly released. To manage this trick, you first choose a very stable element because you do not want that violent heat release until you squirt a bit of the metastable stuff into a thrust chamber. Then you learn to process and store great amounts of it. Finally you inject it into a (probably preheated) chamber and let the chamber's initial heat trigger spin-reversals in the metastable element. The result would be a tremendous exotherm, and that heat would cause expansion of the injected material.

Helium is an extremely stable gas. Scientists have verified that "spin-polarized triplet" helium, molecules with the spins of three helium atoms aligned, can be created. The jargon term for this exotic molecule is "metastable He_4." Odd as it seems, at room temperature this material would be both a crystalline solid and metallic. This means it could be stored as solid propellant.

Or could it? Apparently, like some crystalline explosives (ammonium iodide, for example) but for a different reason, metastable helium is not all *that* stable; it "goes normal" on its own within a few hours. If you had a hundred tons of it in a tank, and even a little of it decided to go normal before you were ready, your entire launch complex would be flattened by the ensuing blast.

Metastable elements, then, are a long shot at best.

He$_4$ may have an I$_{sp}$ of over 3,000, though, if we can learn to keep concentrations of it as propellant. We might even be able to use it as fuel in airbreathing boosters, raising its I$_{sp}$ an order of magnitude higher. If any of that happens, you can expect much of this whole topic to become classified. Meanwhile, we would be overjoyed if we could merely double or treble the current I$_{sp}$ figures with something more controllable—something like an energy beam.

Help, as the saying goes, is on the way. If you doubt that beamed energy can ever power an aircraft, you might check up on the pilotless helicopter which was developed by William C. Brown at Raytheon about 1964. It had a large grid slung below its structure, and the grid intercepted a powerful microwave beam. Microwaves can be power beams too, and as long as the beam was directed against that grid, the helicopter had power to fly. You could also consider MacCready's solar-powered *Challenger* as a beam-powered vehicle too, since it was powered by sunbeams. But these experimental vehicles flew with airscrews (rotors in one case, a slow-moving propeller in the other). We are interested in atmospheric future flight, but if we intend to challenge chemical rockets we need the kind of concentrated power that a laser can provide.

Our astronauts used to make good-natured jokes about *Star Trek* technology with signs like, "Beam us up, Scotty!" But Gordon Cooper was not joking when he said that a few designers are years ahead of the pack.

We already mentioned that the 1970's saw tremendous strides in the power of high-energy lasers, and that a HEL (high energy laser) beam can be sent thousands of miles without losing much energy. Well then, why can't we shoot that energy beam to the rocket, in such a way that the beam is used to heat propellants? We can; in fact, there are several ways to beam us up. First, we must clear up a few points that could cause confusion:

1. The laser transmitter is not carried by the rocket. We are talking about gigawatts—billions of watts—and that means we need a whopping big power plant to generate the electricity. At first we will probably use ground-based laser (GBL) installations. Later, we will be able to get that power from orbital solar power satellites (SPS). So a very reliable laser installation produces the HEL beam and directs it to the rocket, and the HEL beam follows the rocket as it climbs.

2. The rocket must have something to expel: a fuel mass. Within our atmosphere, we may even use air as a propellant. The HEL's job is to heat the fuel to incandescent gas and the gas then escapes from a nozzle, basically like an ordinary rocket. (Some far-out designs *look* very different, though. We will cover those in later chapters.)

3. The HEL must be aimed precisely on the "co-operative" target—the proper spot on the rocket—as long as the rocket needs that power. Pointing and tracking with great precision and reliability are absolute necessities when we feed that much power through a beam.

4. The classic mission, boosting a payload to orbit, is not the only one we are considering for high energy laser propulsion. We may want to power a vehicle as it maneuvers through the atmosphere carrying passengers, and we must consider several schemes for doing this.

When we study the design of laser rockets, maybe the simplest way to start is by separating them into two types, depending on whether the HEL is directed up the nozzle from behind, or against a mirror on the rocket's body. In the "single-port" designs the only port, or opening, is the exhaust nozzle. Propellant is pumped into a thrust chamber while the HEL is directed into the chamber through the nozzle. A basic single-port design is shown in Figure 4-1. Designers can accept a little misalignment of the beam, but you can see that a single-port laser rocket

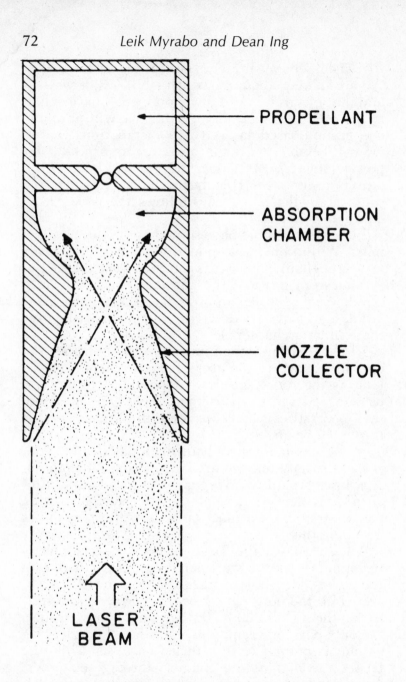

PROPELLANT

ABSORPTION
CHAMBER

NOZZLE
COLLECTOR

LASER
BEAM

Figure 4–1. Single-port engine

must keep thrusting more or less directly away from the source of the laser. If you wanted the vehicle to turn around, you would have to make other arrangements.

In the "two-port" designs the nozzle is still considered a port, but only an exhaust port; the laser does not enter there. Instead, the laser is aimed at a port somewhere on the body of the rocket, as shown in Figure 4-2. Remember that these are only the bare bones of the design; if this rocket must fly through air, we probably would mount the mirror in some way that avoids having a huge hole in the side of the rocket's body. And in airless space, the mirror could even be mounted ahead of the rocket. The basic point is that the HEL strikes a mirror that can be swiveled to receive, then reflect and focus the laser beam through a very special window. That window opens into the thrust chamber. Just as with the single-port designs, fuel is injected into the thrust chamber where it meets the tremendous, tightly-focused energy of the HEL. The HEL turns the fuel to incandescent gas which escapes through the nozzle and provides thrust.

Notice that we no longer call the chamber a "combustion" chamber? That's because we no longer need to inject great gobs of oxygen into the chamber to burn, or combust, the other fuel. Strictly speaking then, there's no combustion inside the chamber. Some researchers call it an "absorption chamber" because that's where the energy of the HEL is absorbed. It's still a thrust chamber, though, and a *very* efficient one! How efficient? Given the right propellant it can double, possibly even quadruple, the I_{sp}s of today's best chemical engines.

For over ten years it has been true that a high energy laser can vaporize any known material, so theoretically the laser rocket could use almost anything for fuel. But remember, our rough formula said that a higher I_{sp} is gained by raising T_c or lowering MW. We can raise that chamber temperature only so far before we melt the whole chamber,

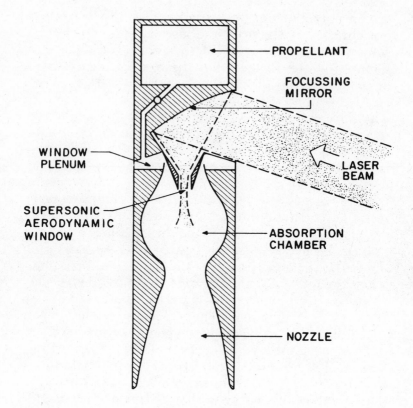

Figure 4–2. Two-port engine

so we have certain limits in that direction. How about MW? Look on any periodic table of chemical elements and you will see that some elements have atomic weights many times heavier than others. When we combine elements to make molecules, the spread of molecular weights becomes even wider. In other words, you will not get a good I_{sp} by vaporizing stuff like lead chromate; even the vaporized gases would have ridiculously high MWs. What you want for high performance is what NASA already uses for the shuttle: hydrogen.

While applauding the shuttle's oxygen/hydrogen fuels, we mentioned that the MW of its exhaust was about twelve. What is the MW of pure hydrogen, injected into a chamber and vaporized by a laser? Exactly two. Or even *one*, if the heat is enough to dissociate hydrogen into single atoms. This is more like it! Plugging in reasonable numbers, and recalling that the I_{sp} improvement varies with the *square root* of those numbers, we can see that a hydrogen-fueled laser rocket might have an I_{sp} somewhere between 1,000 and 2,000. And if we can cleverly design the thrust chamber so that the chamber itself contains extremely high temperatures without having to absorb them, it's possible that we could see an I_{sp} of 3,000.

This is a revolutionary leap in efficiency; not merely a slight rise in an old plateau, but a whole new plateau. It's a rocky plateau, however, with some unknowns. Take the question of propellant, for example. We have already established that hydrogen is great for high I_{sp}, but even when we liquify it, it is very light in weight. This means we need very large tanks to contain it, and an extra-large tank means a weight penalty. There is another kind of penalty in the sheer size of a large tank, if we have to push it through much atmosphere. Atmospheric drag becomes very important as airspeed rises. Then too, liquid hydrogen is tough to store for long periods, and it costs more than some other fuels. For these

reasons, some researchers have suggested other propellants for some missions. One of the most frequently
suggested fuels, believe it or not, is water. It might
give us an I_{sp} of "only" about 1,000, but it's cheap,
storable, nontoxic and requires smaller tankage. Still,
when you read technical papers on laser propulsion,
the fuel most often mentioned is hydrogen.

A few paragraphs back, we separated laser engines
into single-port and two-port types. Now it's time to
look at another fork in the design path: pulsed lasers
and continuous wave lasers.

A continuous wave (CW) laser is one that sends a
steady energy beam without pulsing. But a CW laser
can cause problems, and in some cases we may need
to send the beam as a series of pulses. Because we
need many repeated pulses to get enough power, we
use the term repetitively pulsed (RP).

Why would we need to pulse the beam? Because it
strikes the fuel particles with a result that boggles
your mind. Let's say the laser power is thirty megawatts. The laser is directed in a beam a yard wide
until it is reflected and focused by a mirror in a
two-port laser engine. That beam can be focused
down to an area of one square inch or less. And we
know from experiments that, in such a beam as this,
ordinary air breaks down into an electrically-conduc-
tive plasma and dust particles literally explode! This
heating effect is called a laser-supported detonation
wave—and sure enough, they have shortened the term
so there is a new meaning for LSD.

It's hard to express just how ferocious a detonation wave can be unless you have seen one smash
armor plate or shatter granite. We can use such a
shock wave, virtually a wall of superheated gas moving at supersonic velocity, to generate thrust (see
Chapter 7 for the *Orion* propulsion scheme, for
example). But we can get away with this trick only if
we keep it under perfect control. Once we trigger an
LSD wave, that supersonic wave tends to propagate
back up the beam. If we did not shut the beam off

fast, the shock wave would strike the window that admitted the beam. If the first detonation pulse did not shatter the window, a rapid series of those shocks probably would.

If we shut the beam off in time, though, the detonation wave is created, it wallops the chamber with a pulse of pressure, and the hot gases are forced out through the nozzle port. At this point we can inject another squirt of fuel, turn on the HEL again, start another detonation wave, turn off the HEL in time, and so on, in a repeated series of pulses. So an RP laser rocket is really a pulsed rocket, though we would not be able to tell by watching it if the pulses come oftener than, say, twenty per second. An ordinary light bulb in the U. S. emits pulses of light sixty times per second but that rate is so fast the light seems to be steady.

Another problem arises with continuous wave lasers beamed into a single-port chamber. Whatever fuel you use, it will be a superheated glowing gas once the laser hits it, creating a laser-supported combustion (LSC) wave—a form of plasma torch—near the focus. The gas becomes opaque, no longer transparent, to laser light when heated to such high temperatures. So, if you send a CW laser beam up the nozzle, an LSC wave moving at subsonic speed immediately blocks off the beam. This rig might keep firing, chuffing along after a fashion, but it would repeatedly blow the LSC wave out the nozzle and the fuel would be used very inefficiently. Translation: you would lose I_{sp} by the bucketload. Is there a way around this so we can use a CW design?

Yes; use a two-port engine, with the laser striking the fuel spray from the *front* end of the chamber. You must be sure you have designed the focusing mirror so that the steady CW beam gets focused just tightly enough. With the proper focus, the LSC wave velocity is exactly adjusted to the propellant flow rate. Like designing a carburetor, you must see that the correct balance is always maintained between propellant flow and the LSC wave velocity.

So far we have passed by the mirrors and windows as if they were no problem. Mirrors reflect and windows are transparent, right? Well, *mostly* right. One major problem is that even the best mirrors do not reflect quite all the energy, and the best windows do not let quite all the energy through. Instead, they absorb a small percentage of it. The mirror is not the main problem because it receives a broader, less intense beam than the window does. Also, mirror coatings are now so good that they can reflect 99.8% of the light that strikes the mirror. If we are beaming ten megawatts onto a mirror with that coating, it will absorb only a fifth of one percent of the energy.

Not much energy to absorb, you say? Maybe not much compared to what is reflected, but 0.2% of ten megawatts is still twenty kilowatts, enough energy to run a small car, and enough to heat a yard-wide mirror considerably. We need not worry too much about this, because a good mirror can handle reasonable thermal shock and moderately elevated temperature. The window, however, is another matter entirely.

Time out for a moment. We are about to use a common shorthand term, an acronym, that you saw in previous pages—only now it means something else. When we talk about rocket exhaust gas, MW means "molecular weight." But when we talk about laser energy in the millions of watts, MW means "megawatt." Once you know the term has those two possible meanings, it's no problem.

So we have a ten MW beam, reflected and focused down by a curved mirror so that, by the time it passes through the window in the front of the thrust chamber, the beam may be—oh, maybe ten square inches across. Let's say we picked the best laser wavelength and our window absorbs only 0.02% of the energy. (That is, it absorbs a *percentage* ten times less than the mirror, *per square inch*.) But the window area is roughly a *hundred* times smaller than the mirror. Every square inch of that window, then, has to take ten times as much heat from absorbed laser energy, while also taking ferocious heat from inside the chamber. This is a lot to be asking from any transparent material.

If all those finagle figures were confusing, we can put it a simpler way. The small window must deal with almost exactly the same amount of laser energy as the big mirror. That energy is very much more concentrated as it strikes the window, so the window is more likely to fail—especially when it's taking a pounding from the thrust chamber. Can we make survivable windows?

There are a few crystalline materials that show promise, with transparency (the jargon word is "transmittance") as good as we need for certain laser wavelengths. Examples? Large, specially-grown single crystals of strontium fluoride (SrF_2), zinc selenide ($ZnSe$), and a very common chemical, potassium chloride (KCl). But when we start up our laser engine, the middle of that crystal window will be heated faster than the edges. When we have a high temperature gradient building up in the window, it's likely to crack, and then all bets are off.

Can we find crystals that have almost the same transparency but much greater strength to resist the forces trying to destroy them? Oh, we know of a couple. Trouble is, we may need a regimental combat team to guard them. You may have already guessed: windows of solid diamond or sapphire.

It's not as wild as it seems. One Massachusetts firm has already grown a single sapphire crystal a foot in diameter, weighing roughly a hundred pounds. There is no basic reason why we could not create synthetic sapphires and diamonds of this size in quantity. Remember, too, that synthetic gemstone crystals could be a whole lot cheaper than they are if the prices were not kept unnecessarily high. If we find that a synthetic diamond the size of a dinner plate can let us boost a ton of payload to orbit for a dollar a pound, and can do it over and over—that diamond will be cheap at almost any price. There is also reason to hope that zero gravity will prove highly useful for growing various crystals, including diamonds.

These basic ideas—single-port and two-port engines, CW and RP lasers—have led to some far-out designs which we will cover in later chapters. But before we do, we must consider one more big factor: laser *wavelength*.

A laser is a concentrated beam of electromagnetic radiation, but not all radiation is visible. Figure 4-3 shows the range of what we call the electromagnetic spectrum. The visible spectrum of light is a fairly narrow range of wavelengths, and light beams of wavelengths shorter, or longer, than this simply cannot be seen by the naked eye. (Notice in Figure 4-3, the shorter the wavelength, the higher its frequency of waves per second.) Ultraviolet (UV) wavelengths are shorter than visible light. If you build gadgetry that produces energy waves much shorter than ultraviolet, you begin to get into the range we call X rays.

But at the other edge of the visible spectrum is red, then infrared (IR), which we call "heat waves." Even in pitch darkness, our bodies radiate enough heat—infrared wavelengths of light—to be detected by special scanners. When we rearrange logs in a fireplace, afterward we can sometimes feel dangerous heat from the poker even if it is not hot enough to be visibly red. What we are detecting then is powerful *infra*red radiation. And that's the kind of radiation we will probably want to transmit in a HEL propulsion beam, especially within the atmosphere.

Why do we care what wavelength (WL) we have, so long as the beam is powerful enough? For one thing, infrared lasers of certain wavelengths penetrate the atmosphere as well as visible blue-green

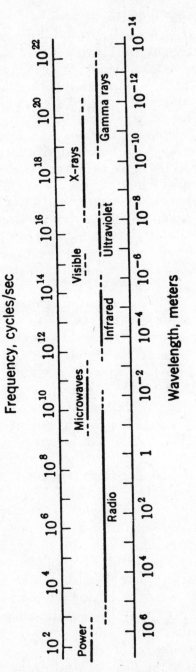

Figure 4–3. The electromagnetic spectrum. (Note that the frequency and wavelength scales are logarithmic.)

wavelengths do, and there's a possibility of severe eye damage from wavelengths shorter than 2.2 microns. For another thing, air turbulence can defocus or slightly deflect a laser beam. A very short WL visible high energy laser beam, passing through dusty air, can be scattered so much and so quickly that what reaches the target is useless for propulsion. There are ways to get around atmospheric turbulence, and one way is to choose a wavelength that isn't so vulnerable to it. The most promising wavelengths for this are in the IR range.

When we depend on a chemical laser, we have to accept the wavelengths those chemicals generate. The basic hardware of a chemical laser generally includes three items:

1. An active material—a gas—to convert "pumping" energy into laser light.

2. A pumping source—an electron beam, for example—to provide high energy to the active material.

3. Mirrors to make the beam bounce back and forth through the active material, and to collect the output.

The problem here lies in item 1. That active material emits an *exact* wavelength of laser radiation, and it may not be ideal for beaming us up. It would be nice if we could design a laser system that lets us choose whatever wavelength we want, and even to change it instantly. Presto: the free-electron laser!

The free-electron laser (FEL) fires an electron beam, but not into special chemicals. Instead, the electron beam passes within a vacuum between a set of permanent magnets or electromagnets, called the "wiggler." These magnets are of alternating polarity, and they literally shake the stream of electrons back and forth in their passage, slowing them. This causes the electrons to emit photons (light) as they slow down. We can change the energy of the electron beam and the spacing of the magnets, and this sets the frequency of the laser beam that emerges. Some scientists are openly disgusted to see so little effort spent on developing the FEL, especially since it promises to give us much higher "wallplug" efficiency than any other laser system. Its potential uses are so great, they say, that anything less than a crash program is a criminal shame.

Why haven't we seen crash programs on a national basis—spurred by NASA, for example? Well, NASA had a political hassle getting its shuttle funded, and its leaders did not want to start publicizing brand-new propulsion schemes until NASA had a working shuttle using well-proven, reliable technology. A lot of memos were written at that time, "proving" that chemical rockets were better than HEL boosters. This was a good practical move at the time, but some of those memos are still floating around quoting figures that are now sadly out of date.

It is probably true that laser propulsion won't be clearly better than chemical propellants until the laser system efficiency is around 10% or higher. It *used to be* true that solid-state ruby and neodymium glass laser systems fired less than 1% of the energy fed into them. But today we have already built IR lasers that deliver 8 to 10% of the input energy. The FEL may be able to convert 25 to 40% of its input energy into output—a tremendous improvement. Too bad so many people are still quoting the old figures.

And the efficiency figures are getting better all the time. It's high time we all agreed that the NASA shuttle is lovely, a necessary step using the best stuff we had ten years ago, but it is now time to take fresh steps.

Designers face a lot of choices in ways to beam us up; single and two-port systems, continuous wave (CW) and repetitive pulse (RP) beams, various fuels, and chemical laser or free electron laser (FEL) power beams, to list the choices we mentioned above. Today it seems the best bet for beaming a cargo to orbit will be a two-port system using an RP beam with hydrogen for fuel and an infrared chemical laser—with the chemical laser giving way to the FEL later. A few thousand words back, that last sentence might have sounded like gibberish, but we are heading for new territory. We need to speak the language.

Chapter 5:

BLASTING PAST THE SHUTTLE

The NASA shuttle is the best orbiter we could develop, a decade ago. No complaints, we needed a recoverable, orbital cargo transport that was reliable, and we needed it as soon as possible. Today we have several shuttles in operation, but there is an old saying about long-term projects: if it's operational, it's out of date. Designers of advanced aircraft like Jack Northrop, in the 1930's, must have felt the same way seeing the Douglas DC-3; we're in business, now let's develop something a whole lot better.

We do not mean to imply that NASA is ignoring revolutionary propulsion systems. For over a decade they have been studying laser-powered rockets and other advanced propulsion ideas. Now that the shuttle is in business they are studying these advances more openly. Maybe NASA scientists cannot afford to say it as frankly as they would like for political reasons, but we can: NASA should greatly expand its efforts in this direction, with less emphasis on fine-tuning of old-fashioned rocket designs that will not get much better.

What do we mean by "better"? Perhaps no improvement is more important than reducing the cost per pound of cargo. The amount of energy needed to place a pound of cargo in orbit comes to about 4.5 kilowatt hours in terms of electricity. That's a fraction of your daily electric bill. Even if our laser rocket is only 10% efficient, it could orbit a pound for *well under a dollar.* That's several hundred times cheaper than the shuttle does it. But then, the shuttle has to carry all its energy sources, and they are largely chemical rather than electrical.

We might get a clearer picture of the improvement by imagining the shuttle, which weighs 2,100 tons at liftoff though only thirty-two tons of it are payload, as it might work if boosted with a laser propulsion system. (We will have to pretend we also have a source of electrical energy to feed a laser of sufficient power to boost a shuttle. Our imaginary shuttle's empty weight is equal to its payload: thirty-two tons.)

It will still use 112 tons of hydrogen for fuel, but it will not need to carry the 633 tons of liquid oxygen propellant because the hydrogen is heated by laser. Instead of that oxygen we can carry many more tons of payload to orbit—and besides, our propellant efficiency is at least tripled, so we can plug in an I_{sp} figure of 1,460. Our launch weight, then, would be 176 tons for a single-stage-to-orbit (SSTO), laser-powered shuttle. That's about one-twelfth the weight of NASA's.

Remember that the three main engines of the NASA shuttle burn fuel at the rate of 1.69 tons *per second,* and its two huge solid-rocket boosters burn an additional ten tons per second. By the time the NASA shuttle gets up to orbit, it has only a small fraction of its prelaunch mass, and is not gulping fuel at such a great pace because it no longer needs as much thrust as it did at launch. Its mass has been pared down greatly by discarding the empty solid boosters on the way up, and discarding that enormous external tank when almost in orbit. Once in orbit, the shuttle itself masses seventy-five tons; its payload, thirty-two tons more. Even if the cost of boosting our laser-powered shuttle were the same with electrical energy as it is using chemical energy, the cost *per pound* would drop drastically because our shuttle launch weight can be so much less. This puts a gleam in the eyes of industrialists because it can put space industry on a paying basis.

Of course, we will not adapt the existing shuttle that way. Instead, we will probably build much smaller laser-powered orbital transport ships at first, carrying a ton or so of payload apiece. Why? For one thing, it is easy to ask for twenty-five GW (gigawatts) of electricity for a ten-minute shuttle boost, but not so easy to get it. Today, we would have to divert a noticeable fraction of the nation's power grid to supply that much juice for ten minutes. Grand Coulee Dam generates nearly two GW. It would not be impossible to collect the energy of a dozen Grand Coulees for that brief surge, but the initail cost of setting up the power collection grid would be high. It seems a whole lot more reasonable to choose one source—maybe one that already exists near a good launch site, like high desert near Hoover Dam—and tailor our first laser-boost payloads to what we have to work with already.

Hoover Dam could deliver about 1.6 GW to a site a hundred miles or so away. If our laser system is 30% efficient, we would have 500 MW of energy "into the engine," which could launch a vehicle weighing several tons, and half of it would be payload. This might not sound like much until we consider an automated system, tossing up two tons of payload several times a day in recoverable unmanned cargo vehicles.

As long as we are into this scenario, we ought to make it as practical as possible. The good people of Los Angeles are not going to enjoy a brownout every time we launch a couple of tons of payload, so we should time our launches to coincide with times when ordinary power demands are least. That way, we can divert Hoover Dam's output for a few minutes at a time without browning people out, or off. As we might expect, the wee small hours are the best times; but if we merely avoid launches during morning and evening peak load demands, we should be okay.

Let's remember, too, that this routine of ours is

not quite as routine as sending boxcars from a switching yard. Instead, we have a small fleet of perhaps a hundred little cargo boosters, returning by parachute or adjustable delta wings from orbit to a recovery site near the launch complex. And the high Nevada desert near Hoover Dam has lots of room for that; just ask the USAF people at nearby Nellis AFB, who use it for gunnery practice. We will have more to say about launch and recovery sites. For the moment, it's enough to say that southern Nevada looks pretty good.

At any given time, about fifty boosters will be out of service for inspection and repair. Of the remaining fifty, roughly twenty will be in some part of the loading process, about ten will be already loaded and in some phase of the launch procedure, and ten will be in orbit in some phase of maneuvering and offloading. The final ten will be in orbit awaiting a proper "time window" for return, or in the actual return and postflight process.

With this little fleet we might manage twenty launches a day, putting two tons of payload up with each launch. The daily total is forty tons a day; more than the big NASA shuttle puts up with each flight, with far less launch cost and the beginnings of an assembly-line operation. We probably have a few small crews in orbit overseeing the transfer of cargo. Some of that cargo will be orbital crew supplies— and their replacements, as crewmembers are rotated Earthside.

Even if we operated this fleet of orbiters for only 250 days a year, we would boost 10,000 tons of payload to orbit annually. We would still need big orbiters to boost a few large payloads—multiton optical telescope mirrors, for example—but our fleet of small supply craft could boost most of the supplies we need to construct and maintain our permanent orbital workshops.

Like as not, our fleet of small orbiters would be designed around the propulsion system we described at the end of Chapter 3; a two-port engine receiving an RP infrared laser of roughly 2 micron wavelength, using hydrogen for fuel. These little vehicles would be smaller than today's jet interceptors and would probably lift vertically at first, accelerating quickly and pitching over toward the east as they climbed toward orbit. But we might see other vehicles scudding across the sky on very different missions, using different propulsion systems.

Let's examine some of these other systems, starting with those that use air for fuel. This might be a good propulsion scheme for a transcontinental passenger vehicle, which might climb at a shallow angle into the fringes of space, and land halfway around the world an hour or so later. We would boost it up with a HEL and land it the same way, letting it glide for a good part of its flight. It might not need much takeoff or landing space, because we could probably lift it straight up for the first few seconds and land it the same way, helicopter-fashion, without pointing it upward. This vertical takeoff/land feature, with no need for miles-long runways, is what makes the Hawker Harrier so attractive today, and it will be more common in the future of flight. The Harrier, however, guzzles a lot of jet fuel. Our future liner might drink only air and laser energy.

We already mentioned that a HEL beam can be focused strongly enough to break air down into a conductive plasma. Just below that intensity level, we can generate LSD waves; and with a still lower intensity we can generate LSC waves. Well, we could put LSD (laser supported detonation) and LSC (laser supported combustion) wave-heating processes to work for us, letting them boost our liner and bring it down gently. But there are two general approaches to this, depending on whether we want to generate those shock waves inside a chamber, or out in the open—say, just beneath the hull to lift us upward.

If you thought we were through serving alphabet soup, we apologize; it's time to swallow IRH and

ERH. Internal radiation heating, IRH, is when the radiation is beamed into an absorption chamber as we saw in previous chapters. That is, the radiation heat is harnessed inside the engine. With *external* radiation heating, ERH, the laser is actually focused on a point (or a line) *outside* the vehicle. Figure 5-1 shows a dart-shaped passenger liner with some interesting features, and like our previous sketches, it is an IRH design.

Up until now we have described systems that use a single mirror, or set of mirrors, to bounce and focus a laser at the right spot. But some designs require more than one bounce. In these cases, we refer to the first optical element to receive the laser as our "primary optics," whether it's a lens or a mirror. The second element (or set of elements) becomes our "secondary optics." No doubt some laser propulsion systems will use tertiaries as well as secondaries, but every added bounce of laser energy means a small loss of efficiency. In Figure 5-1, our primary optics are not mirrors, but a set of rather special lenses.

Across the afterbody of the vehicle lies a specially-constructed Fresnel lens, which is really a series of thin lenses even though they may be manufactured from a single piece of material. (A normal lens would be far too heavy. The Fresnel lens was originally developed to reduce the great weight of huge lighthouse lenses.) Most Fresnel lenses are made in concentric circles, but this one is linear. It receives and focuses the HEL beam, directing it to a spot in a chamber. That chamber gulps air, and the air itself is heated inside the chamber. We can heat it with a repetitive pulse laser beam and LSD waves, or with a continuous wave laser beam and LSC waves.

If we use special valving to admit pulses of incoming air, similar to the common pulsejet engine, we can fire a repetitive pulse laser and then, if we do everything in the right sequence, we have an air-breathing laser pulsejet. Scientists Nebolsine and Pirri (among others), while at Avco Everett Research Labs,

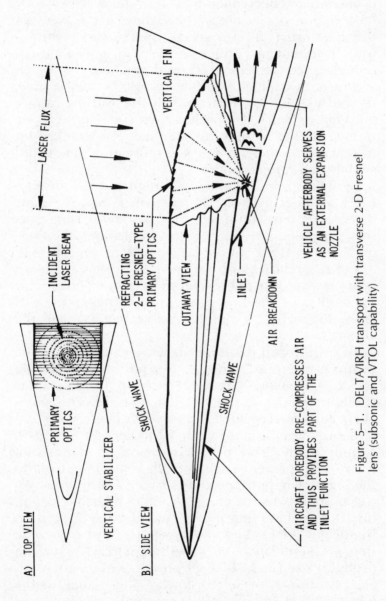

Figure 5–1. DELTA/IRH transport with transverse 2-D Fresnel lens (subsonic and VTOL capability)

experimented with RP and CW lasers using several propellants. They concluded that short pulses may be a major key to higher efficiency. A pulsejet can provide thrust at zero speed, by the way, while a ramjet cannot. A ramjet can provide more thrust, though, once the vehicle is speeding along near Mach 1 or faster. Our liner might carry both types of engine, the pulsejet for low forward velocity and the ramjet for high velocity. Or perhaps we could design our intake valving so that, as our liner gets cranked up to Mach 1 or thereabouts, the pulsejet engine could switch to a ramjet mode.

For takeoff and landing, we might want to use an ERH scheme instead, as shown in Figure 5-2. Our big Fresnel lens can direct the laser to focusing mirrors which are secondary optics (remember, the Fresnel lens is the primary as shown in Figure 5-3). These secondaries are designed to bring the laser's beam down to its tightest focus in midair, just below the hull near the tips of the stub wings, so that a laser supported detonation wave begins near the wingtips.

You will recall that an LSD wave runs back up the beam, so we must shut the laser pulse off before the shock wave works its way back up the beam far enough to damage the secondary optics. This obviously calls for repeated pulses—RP. There is a complication here because we have to keep those pulses coming many times per second, and the detonation waves may prevent enough fresh air from getting to the region where we need it between LSD pulses. We can probably overcome the problem by using a combination of laser pulse energy and pulse repetition frequency (PRF). Let's presume we have overcome that problem. If we do everything correctly, we can probably use the LSD shock waves to make the vehicle rise, hover, or settle slowly. This is one of the major advantages of such an external radiation heating (ERH) design; we can propel a vehicle without internal engines by kicking it rapidly and carefully

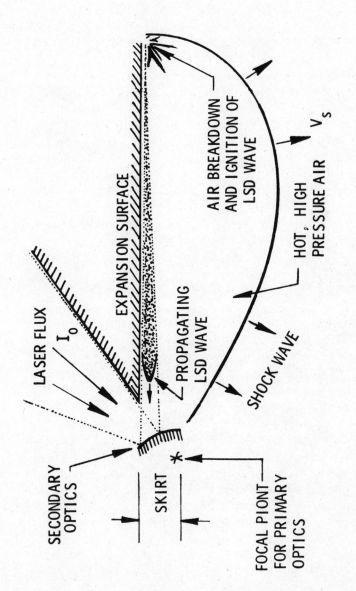

Figure 5–2. External radiation-heated (ERH) thruster concept

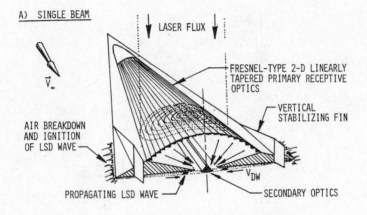

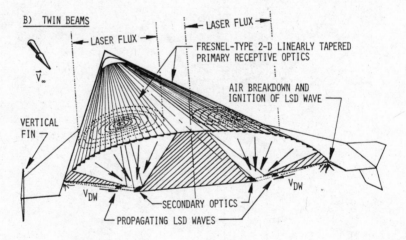

Figure 5–3. DELTA ERH/IRH transport configuration with longitudinal primary 2-D Fresnel lens (subsonic and VTOL capability)

with external shock waves. This transfers momentum to the air, driving it downward away from the vehicle.

An IRH engine will probably be noisy, but it will be a gentle whisper compared to an ERH rig. We can use an analogy here: internal radiation heating is like exploding a firecracker inside a tin can with one end cut out, while external radiation heating is like setting off the firecracker just outside its closed end. All those external shock waves, lifting a passenger liner, might not be terribly loud inside but you would not want to stand outside nearby during liftoff or landing.

Once our liner is well above the launch pad, we might divert part of the laser energy to the IRH pulsejet. This gives forward motion to the vehicle and forward motion can generate lift, which means we can phase out the ERH shock waves. As our vehicle accelerates to about Mach 1, the speed of sound, we switch over to ramjet mode. By this time our passenger liner will be starting its long shallow arc up to the fringes of space, perhaps even rising above the height of low-orbit spacecraft but at considerably less velocity.

At some point early in the flight, we shut the laser off. No problem; the liner is streaking out at hypersonic speed, and its shallow trajectory will carry it thousands of miles. Presently our vehicle will re-enter the atmosphere, and another laser will be directed onto our Fresnel lens. We may have to cope with some of the re-entry problems the shuttle faces today. Re-entry will not be as severe for our vehicle, though, because we re-enter the atmosphere at a much lower velocity than the shuttle's orbital speed of 17,000 miles an hour.

If our liner has to circle awhile, it may cruise around using its IRH pulsejet again. We can slow it down a lot by simply forcing it to "mush" ahead, nose slightly up, in a way that adds tremendous aerodynamic drag. Remember the aerodynamic decoupling of attitude and direction we described in Chapter 3? Here is a great place to use it, perhaps with small canard fins near the vehicle's nose. We can make our craft slew around while remaining horizontal, or raise or dip its nose without changing altitude. Of course there are limits to these tricks; our delta could not fly completely sideways, for example. These limited maneuvers will not be especially dangerous; even a passenger liner the size of today's Boeing 747 can take several g's, and tomorrow's transcontinental arrows will be that sturdy too. Most of these aerodynamic decoupling tricks cause drag, but they can also let us maneuver the vehicle to a perfect landing. Most likely the vehicle will undergo far less acceleration change during a flight than it could easily take, in order to keep the passengers comfortable. It's likely that the passengers will go through the entire flight without pulling more than two g's or less for a few moments, and eventually they begin a steep, flat downward glide toward the landing site.

Finally our primary Fresnel lens directs the laser to the secondary optics under the hull, which start generating ERH shock waves under the hull again. Our vehicle hovers, then settles on the landing pad with a final rumble of LSD thunder. We have carried a hundred passengers halfway around the world in less than two hours, and without burning thousands of gallons of jet fuel. That means we began with a vehicle that was not loaded down with kerosene—a safety advantage, a cost advantage, and a power-to-weight advantage rolled into one. There are also pollution advantages, but we cannot claim that our air-breathing laser engines are entirely free of pollution. When we "burn" air this way, we should expect some oxides of nitrogen to result.

By this time you may be wondering: won't we need more than a few GW of electricity to power these hypersonic transports? We might not, if and when we get system efficiencies that are high enough. But until we get system efficiencies considerably higher than 10%, yes, we'll need something like ten

GW. Where are we going to get all this power without causing brownouts in our cities?

There are two ready answers. First, commercial air travel has a way of developing whatever power sources it needs, so we can expect some very large ground-based power plants that are dedicated to feeding power lasers. But in the long run, we are going to get power from space. As we said before, orbiting nuclear plants would be cheaper, but we believe them to be politically unlikely. In any event, once we have permanent crews and orbital workshops out there, we can begin erecting vast spidery grids covered with photovoltaic cells. With this collection grid we can convert the sun's energy directly to electricity (as we did years ago with Skylab), and our big laser installations can then be moved into space. This idea is not new by any means; in fact, solar power in space is already well-developed through many years of use on satellites and space probes. Still, on the multi-GW scale it ranks as a major construction project. We cover it in Chapter 9.

We have offered scenarios for laser-powered shuttle trains to orbit, and long-range, air-breathing passenger liners. How about something a little more sporty? Actually we would expect to find small, highly maneuverable, manned hypersonic craft in the hands of the military, long before they become personal vehicles. And we should not be too surprised to hear them called "flying saucers," because some of them may be radially symmetrical.

Radial symmetry merely means that though they may have a whole family of shapes seen from the side, from the top they look circular. The more we squash them for a low side profile, the more they approach the classic frisbee shape of the flying saucer. CAUTION! We are not trying to prove that little green men in flying saucers are real, and we promise to be short-tempered with folks who claim we are proving it. But radial symmetry is one perfectly reasonable design approach and it deserves a careful look.

We start by demythologizing the design. A b-b and an artillery shell are projectiles with radial symmetry. The Garrett Corporation has built supersonic ramjets with radial symmetry for NASA, as shown in Figure 5-4. This ramjet, like an artillery shell, has a "high fineness ratio"—that is, it is considerably longer than it is wide. Now then: what if we aimed a wide-beam laser (not tightly focused) straight at the *front* of this ramjet, and designed the front spike so that it is a primary mirror that bounces the beam back to focus just inside the thin circular shroud? Figure 5-5 shows how it works. It's worth repeating that the initial wide beam is not tightly focused, so its energy is not dense enough to overheat the mirror-bright primary mirror. That energy gets *very* dense as we focus it down inside the ramjet.

The ramjet, remember, cannot produce thrust unless it is already moving around Mach 1 or more, so we take it for granted that we have already boosted it to that speed somehow. And if it has to be moving more or less straight up the beam, that HEL installation had better be a long way off—like in orbit, for example. It may seem weird to think of a laser as an old-fashioned science-fiction "tractor beam," pulling the object toward it. That's what this design *seems* to do. There is no such thing as a sucker laser, but we may see the term used for a beam that feeds a vehicle from the front.

Study Figure 5-5 for a moment. The supersonic ramjet's frontal spike creates a shock wave that just grazes the lip of that circular shroud, which is called an "annular duct." Air is rushing through the duct, and is heated by the focused laser just as it would be heated by burning jet fuel. The hot air expands as it passes out of the duct, and part of it expands to push against the curve of the ramjet's afterbody. Part of that push is felt as forward thrust, just as it is in a rocket nozzle. For this reason, that special afterbody

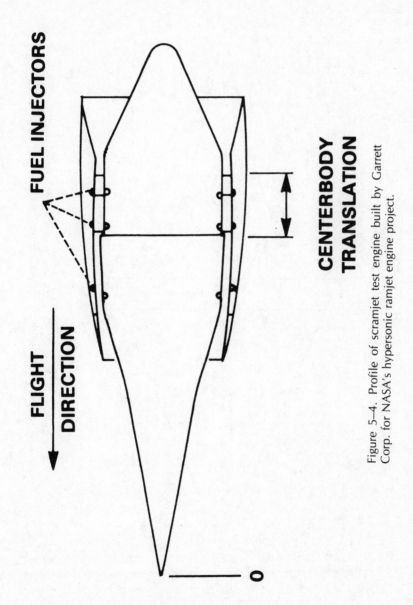

Figure 5—4. Profile of scramjet test engine built by Garrett Corp. for NASA's hypersonic ramjet engine project.

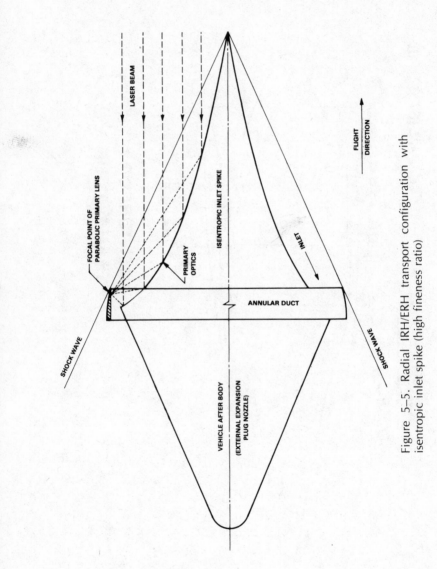

Figure 5–5. Radial IRH/ERH transport configuration with isentropic inlet spike (high fineness ratio)

is called a "plug nozzle." The ramjet is hurled forward by the thrust, climbing up the beam until it is deflected into a trajectory, or until it runs out of atmosphere.

Somebody is bound to ask about the I_{sp} of all these laser air-breathers. As long as we are getting thrust without using up any mass aboard our vehicle to get that thrust, the I_{sp} of our thruster is infinite! There is no paradox here; no matter what it's roughly proportional to, I_{sp} is calculated by how many pound-seconds of thrust we get from a pound of propellant. And if we are not using any propellant, but getting thrust anyway, our propulsion system has an infinite I_{sp}. In theory we could build an air-breather that would fly forever, or until its laser stopped.

Looking at radially-symmetrical craft, we see that it should be easy to put secondary optics, mirrors, into the annular duct. Then we could focus the laser, not inside the annular duct, but clear back at the base of the afterbody as shown in Figure 5-6. Now we can start up those LSD waves and kick the whole craft upward from a standstill. Not only that, but we could mechanically fiddle with the laser beam symmetry so that we have LSD waves whacking the bottom of the afterbody only on one side. That will make the whole vehicle move away horizontally, in whatever direction we choose. It does not rotate like a frisbee, but it looks rather like one.

It seems we have a vehicle at least as maneuverable as that hypersonic delta airliner. It can jump off the pad, land the same way, or sizzle away horizontally using its ERH thrusters. In fact, maybe it could be more maneuverable. You recall that our airliner could not fly entirely sideways? That's because its delta shape makes it unstable, probably downright unflyable, if it yaws more than fifteen or twenty degrees to one side. But our big frisbee is radially symmetrical, so it is just as stable heading north as it is heading southwest.

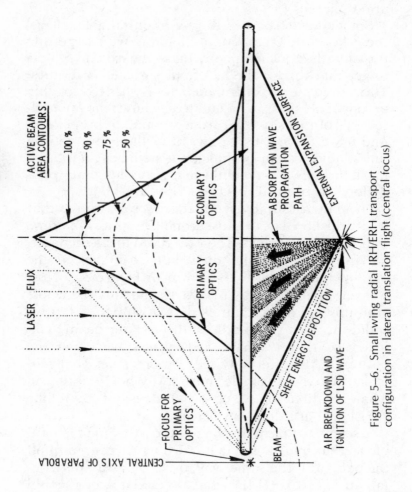

Figure 5–6. Small-wing radial IRH/ERH transport configuration in lateral translation flight (central focus)

It is not terribly efficient for horizontal travel, though, as long as that frontal spike and the afterbody give it a tall profile—i.e., a high fineness ratio. There is just too much drag on a shape like this moving horizontally. Surely we can squash this design down a little. That's what we did in Figure 5-7.

In this design we shorten the frontal spike and the afterbody too. In fact, we no longer have a spike; we have only the base of the spike left, topped by an aerodynamic fairing in the form of a low dome that forces us to distort the propulsion HEL beam into an annulus—in short, a hollow beam. With this scheme, only a low-intensity beam hits the dome and, because of the dome's squat curvature, is simply reflected away. It had *better* be, unless we want to melt the dome after a few seconds! The base of the spike below the dome, now a ring-shaped mirror, is still in place with the same curvature as before, still acting as a primary mirror that bounces laser energy to secondary mirrors at the base of the annular duct.

This design does not have much potential for aerodynamic lift from its body surfaces; after all, it has no wide surfaces that could be used like wings. We just have to count on controlling the ERH shock waves to lift and maneuver it. When those shock waves are whacking the underside of the hull, the whole craft will probably generate a sound like a huge loudspeaker. The sound will be a tone, probably at a pitch somewhere between middle C and high C depending on the frequency of shocks. (A frequency of 264 cycles per second is middle C and the frequency doubles every time the pitch rises one octave.) How many decibels? Let's just say this event could be mistaken for the blast of Gabriel, and would permanently deafen anybody nearby. Maybe we could do something about that. For example, we could reduce the laser intensity to where it sets up combustion, LSC, under the hull instead of LSD waves. This would still generate enough thrust for hovering.

If we focus only enough laser energy under the

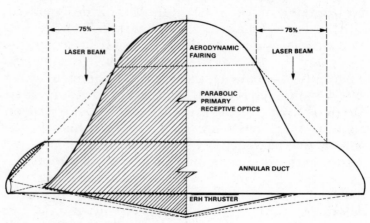

A) 75% ACTIVE AREA (ANNULAR BEAM)

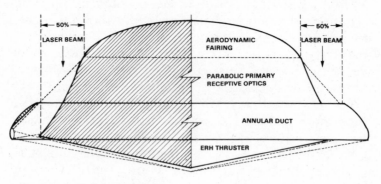

B) 50% ACTIVE AREA (ANNULAR BEAM)

Figure 5–7. Radial IRH/ERH transport configuration with rounded isentropic—spike center body inlets (lower fineness ratio)

hull to generate constant LSC waves, we have a sort of continuous plasma torch that can keep the vehicle balanced on a pressure wave of laser-supported combustion instead of detonation. That pressure need not be very high; if it were only a fraction of a pound of pressure per square inch across the entire lower hull, it should be enough to make the craft hover. Look at it this way: if our little frisbee is a scout craft carrying a crew of one, it might be fifteen feet in diameter—let's say fourteen for the underbody, since we should not count the annular duct. The area of its underbody, then, is roughly 22,000 square inches. We make a rough guess at its gross weight; say, 6,000 pounds. If we have a plasma torch exerting a one-psi pressure wave against every square inch of that underbody, we have 22,000 pounds of lift. That's more than enough to make it hover; it could boost our three-ton frisbee straight up at a rate of several g's until we run out of atmosphere.

A note for those of you who are thinking about your own first rough preliminary sketches of the future: we cannot just scale this design up indefinitely because of something called the "square-cube law." (That is, when we scale something up, as we square its area we *cube* its volume.) Example: take our little plasma-torch frisbee with its one-psi pressure limitation, and double its dimensions. If we multiply the diameter by two, its area increases by the square of two, which is four. So our underbody area is now about 88,000 square inches, and the plasma torch can lift 88,000 pounds. But the volume and mass of the ship increase by the *cube* of two, which is eight. Our scaled-up craft weighs 48,000 pounds. The one-psi force can still lift it—if we have the laser to feed it—but with only about a one-g upward acceleration. If we kept scaling it up, still limited to one-psi lift, we would find that with a frisbee of about fifty-foot diameter we would either have to lighten its weight, or it would never get off the pad with LSC wave heating. Maybe, if we intend to build big ones, we should make do with LSD waves for vertical takeoff, and get some additional help from aerodynamic lift. Let's consider a big cargo-carrying frisbee for use within the atmosphere.

Cargo craft tend to be large, but they do not have to be as maneuverable as scout ships, so they do not have to take so many g-loads. And if that is true, we do not need to keep the structure so compact. We want to spend as little laser energy as we can when transporting heavy cargo, so we really should try to gain a lot of lift from aerodynamic surfaces. We might wind up with something like Figure 5-8, carrying most of the cargo in the thick outer ring of the circular hull.

Notice that this rig does not have that annular duct anymore. It does not sacrifice so much area of its primary mirror, either. It bounces the laser down through hollow spaces in the hull to secondary optics just inside the bottom of the hull, about halfway out from the centerline. The secondaries then focus the energy near the circumference of the hull to set up LSD waves as you see in the illustration.

To guide this cargo craft, we would call for a narrower laser beam that strikes mostly, or entirely, to one side of the center of our central primary mirror as shown in Figure 5-9. Our cargo vehicle is sailing along, partly on the lift from LSD waves and partly on aerodynamic lift from its wide circular "wing." If we want it to dip downward, we just ask for the beam to be narrowed a bit and redirected aft of the centerline. That concentrates the shock waves toward the rear of the underbody, which tips the rear upward slightly. The result is that the forward lip pitches down slightly, and the craft begins to descend. We can make it rise, or roll to either side, in the same way. If we are carrying a lot of cargo we will probably want those maneuvers to be gentle.

In all these maneuvers by all our vehicles, we depend on our ability to maintain constant contact with the source of the laser to make sure that the

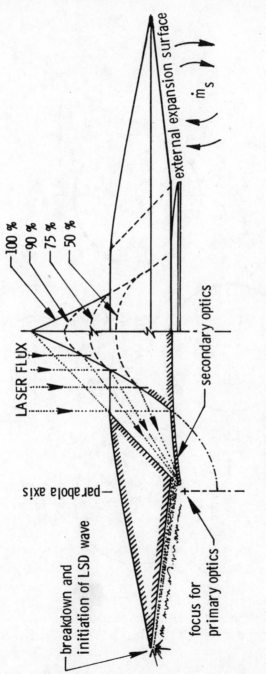

Figure 5–8. Large-wing radial/ERH transport configuration (perimeter focus)

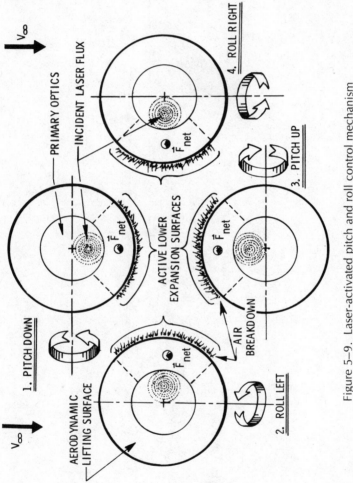

Figure 5–9. Laser-activated pitch and roll control mechanism for radial/ERH transport (perimeter focus case—top view)

HEL beam is directed exactly where we need it. And for maximum control, we might signal the source to send a smaller beam or several of them. We may also want the beam to be more energetic during part of the flight, and we may even want the wavelength of the laser to change from time to time. Remember that the free electron laser (FEL) seems to be our best bet to get all those variations. If we have the option, we will probably specify an FEL as our energy source.

If we can get exactly the beam we want, where and when we want it, we might develop a more efficient system that uses rotating chambers around the edge of our frisbee. It's called a "rotary IRH pulsejet," and one version of it is shown in Figure 5-10. In this design, the outer part of the hull *does* spin, frisbee-fashion, though it could spin on a wide bearing so that the hub section of the hull need not spin. (Imagine being a passenger in a spinning hub. The g forces would plaster you against the outer wall of the hub; definitely hazardous to your health and not much fun for whoever had to clean you off the wall with a sponge. . . .)

You will recall that the IRH scheme lets us heat our working fluid (air, in this case) inside a chamber. That chamber can be shaped for high efficiency, and there is no rule that says we can have only one chamber. So we build identical chambers all the way around the circumference of the hull, and spin them on that big bearing. As long as the spin-impulse is coming from the part that's spinning, we avoid the kind of torque reaction that would make the hub spin hard in the opposite direction. But bearings are not perfectly frictionless, and we can expect some tendency for the hub to spin anyhow. We could cure that by bleeding off some exhaust gas and using it as a stabilizing jet for the hub; or by a small auxiliary engine in the hub.

In Figure 5-10 we are already moving horizontally at supersonic speed, pushing a bow shock wave ahead

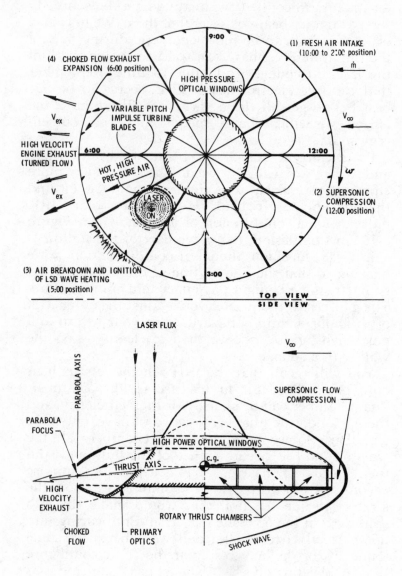

TOP VIEW
SIDE VIEW

(1) FRESH AIR INTAKE (10:00 to 2:00 position)

(2) SUPERSONIC COMPRESSION (12:00 position)

(3) AIR BREAKDOWN AND IGNITION OF LSD WAVE HEATING (5:00 position)

(4) CHOKED FLOW EXHAUST EXPANSION (6:00 position)

HIGH PRESSURE OPTICAL WINDOWS

VARIABLE PITCH IMPULSE TURBINE BLADES

HIGH VELOCITY ENGINE EXHAUST (TURNED FLOW)

HOT, HIGH PRESSURE AIR

LASER ON

V_{ex}

V_∞

ω

$\dot{m}$

9:00   6:00   12:00   3:00

LASER FLUX

PARABOLA AXIS

PARABOLA FOCUS

HIGH VELOCITY EXHAUST

CHOKED FLOW

PRIMARY OPTICS

THRUST AXIS

HIGH POWER OPTICAL WINDOWS

c.g.

ROTARY THRUST CHAMBERS

SHOCK WAVE

SUPERSONIC FLOW COMPRESSION

V_∞

Figure 5–10. Rotary IRH pulsejet configuration in supersonic lateral translation mode (sonic nozzle)

of us. Inside that bow shock wave, the air is highly compressed, just begging to be bled away somehow. Hold that thought for a moment.

This particular design has twelve chambers, each with moveable turbine blades at its exit nozzle. We set the outer part of the hull spinning so the chambers are rotating too. And then we call for a comparatively small laser beam that winks on, strikes the primary mirror for a tiny fraction of a second, and winks off again for another split-second. The laser strikes the mirror only at a spot which generates LSD waves inside only one chamber: the one nearly opposite the direction we're moving. The time sequence is critical, because that shock wave inside the chamber needs a few thousandths of a second to shoot out the exit nozzle. By the time the shock wave races out the nozzle, it is exhausting directly opposite our direction of travel. The result is highly directional thrust.

The nozzle, however, has vanes that act like turbine blades. The escaping burst of hot gas also pushes against these blades, and that force keeps the chambers spinning on the big bearing. By this time the next chamber is lined up, another wink of the laser starts an internal LSD wave which imparts thrust and spin, and so on. But that's not the whole story.

Remember that bow shock wave? The moveable turbine blades can pivot as each chamber spins toward the front of our vehicle, and can scoop a chamberful of compressed air from the bow shock wave. It keeps most of that charge of air, perhaps by closing the blades again, until that chamber has spun around to the point where it gets another wink of laser energy. Then the blades can open and function as turbine blades again. We expect higher efficiency from this system because our internal LSD shock waves are racing through denser compressed air. Since the air is more dense to start with, the chamber is exhausting more mass at each pulse. The result is more thrust per laser pulse, which equals more efficiency for the whole laser propulsion system.

Though we described this rotary IRH pulsejet in supersonic flight, it also has the potential to boost the craft from zero horizontal speed to supersonic flight very quickly. We only need a power source to start the chambers rotating at a modest rate before we start flicking the blades and winking the laser. Several versions of this basic design have been outlined in technical papers by one of the present authors.

Before we leave the rotary laser engines, we should mention rotary IRH turbojets. We would have to develop turbine blades capable of withstanding very high temperatures, maybe by forcing relatively cool air through hollow blades. That's not a new wrinkle, either. For the present, we will assume we can get as much cooling as we need. Since all turbines are rotary, we call the design in Figure 4-11 a laser-heated turbojet and take the "rotary" for granted.

Most of today's turbojets are long slender axial-flow engines, largely because their slenderness creates less drag. But some of our early turbojets were short, fat engines. They were built around a single, wide centrifugal-flow compressor, an impeller, shaped somewhat like the impeller in a vacuum cleaner. Our laser-heated turbojet uses a centrifugal compressor, which sucks air into a circular shroud at the top of our craft and compresses the air, flinging it out toward a combustion chamber near the rim of our frisbee.

Our laser also comes in through the same intake, bouncing off the spike-shaped primary mirror to generate LSC or LSD waves in the compressed air near the vehicle's rim. We could use either an RP or CW beam here. If we have the beam power, and suitably rugged structural hardware, we could generate LSD waves. In that case, as we already know, we must use an RP laser with the pulses timed perfectly. But we might be limited by any of several criteria: noise, or hardware ruggedness, or intensity of the HEL

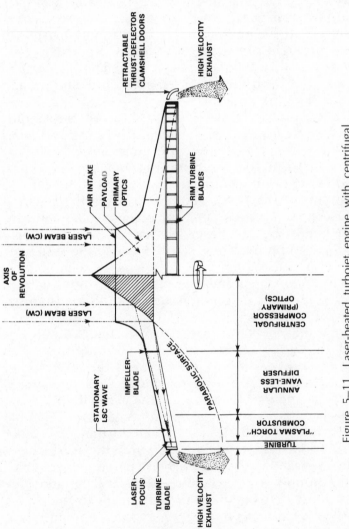

Figure 5–11. Laser-heated turbojet engine with centrifugal compressor and 'rim' turbine (subsonic VTOL configuration)

beam. In such cases we might opt for a CW laser. That means we can generate only laser supported combustion in the combustion chamber; a standing wave, in fact. A standing wave is rather like a salmon swimming as hard as it can up an almost vertical waterfall. If the mass of water is roaring downstream hard enough, the fish can't move upstream any farther. Its forward motion is matched by the onrushing impact of all those molecules of fluid, and though it's working like mad, it stands still.

The heated air rushes downstream, of course, past turbine blades that are mechanically connected to the impeller. This powers the impeller, drawing in more air. But the incoming blast of air makes the LSC wave front stand still in its effort to expand upstream. Now think about that laser that's being bounced between compressor blades to the combustion chamber. The laser obviously passes *through* that incoming pressurized air blast, so the transparent air lets energy through like a window. This feature, where the open compressor passageway admits HEL energy through a high-pressure wall of air, is called an "aerowindow."

Now that we know how it works, the bad news: it will not work very well in fast horizontal flight. The intake simply is not aligned toward the direction of flight, and our compressor might stall, causing a disastrous loss of thrust when the aerowindow effect stops. Oh, we could fiddle with a lot of adjustable parts, but it really does not seem all that promising for anything but vertical lifting within the atmosphere.

Before we pass by the turbomachinery, we should mention one use of a turbine that really might give us a boost. Let's go back for a moment to the rotary pulsejet design in Figure 5-10, and make room inside the frisbee for a small conventional turbocompressor. The little turbojet might even burn jet fuel, and its exhaust could help push or steer the craft, but its real job is to feed most of its compressed air to the main combustion chambers. We are supercharging those chambers now, and when the laser initiates an LSD pulse in a chamber that full, we really feel a kick in the backside. This afterburner effect does use up some jet fuel, but might be well worth it if we wanted really blazing performance in horizontal flight.

There are still more new propulsion schemes, but they are centered on other principles than the laser. We will save them for the next chapter. The designs we illustrated here do not exhaust all the possible variations for using an HEL to boost a payload, yet they do show how we might tailor a laser to a particular vehicle mission. It should be obvious by now that we cannot just pick an engine, then cobble up a structure and optics to fit; or pick a structure, and then squeeze an engine in to fit with whatever mirrors and lenses we have handy. We have to carefully integrate engines, optics, and airframes to find the best combination for a mission. If that mission lets us steal air from the atmosphere during nearly all of its maneuvers, we can dispense with big fuel tanks. However, if it involves lots of cargo we must count on big lifting surfaces in order to keep our laser power requirements down to reasonable levels. And if we are boosting cargoes to orbit, our first laser-boosted shuttle designs will probably be rather small, because we will not have multi-GW laser-boosts until we can dedicate whopping big power plants to the job.

So we should be able to blast past the shuttle within a few years in several respects, and yet we may not be able to orbit heavier payloads by HEL for many years to come. Pressed for a prediction, we expect NASA to build bigger, heavier launch vehicles using conventional liquid fuels during the latter years of this century. Meanwhile, laser development will progress at slow-to-moderate pace. By the time we have HELs dedicated to payload boosting, we will probably have laser propulsion efficiency up near the 20 to 30% mark. When we have a ten GW laser available, the higher efficiency should make it capable of lifting about the same payloads the NASA shuttle does today. But the cost will then be laughably low, and it can be a daily event. Upshot: expect humankind's real diaspora into space when business and industry are already out there in force, and that will happen when lasers power big shuttles.

It's a sad prediction that we will not boost big payloads with lasers in this century—but the Soviets just might. They are ahead of us in some areas of laser R & D. They are also heavily into magneto-hydrodynamics—MHD. That is another fertile field for wild new propulsion systems, and we can trek into those wilds in the next chapter.

Chapter 6:

MHD FANS AND SUPERSONIC DIRIGIBLES

Any propulsion system is basically a means for converting some kind of energy into a lusty shove. We have seen how a laser beam can do that directly, by raising the temperature of a fuel or other reaction mass and expelling it under pressure. But we could use lasers in combination with some other energy-conversion schemes, too, especially when we intend to travel through the atmosphere. The combinations could give us more thrust from a given level of laser power.

Even though air gets in our way a lot, it can be useful stuff when we know how to use it. When we give it a properly tailored electrical charge, we can transform its lightning discharges into powerful air-breathing "fans" which, in combination with vast invisible electromagnets, can provide the needed shove. Let's take the "electric fan" idea first.

We have known for many years that when a hot, conducting stream of gas passes stationary magnets, the ions (atoms with a positive or negative charge) in that gas stream can pass their charges to electrodes positioned nearby. This energy-conversion scheme deals with magnetic fields and dynamic, fast-moving hot fluids including gases, so it's called "magneto-hydrodynamics." Rather than wear their jaws out on such a mouthful, the investigators shortened it to MHD. Early MHD generators were huge, unwieldy affairs that burned rocket propellants to get enough

117

hot ionized gas, from which they extracted electrical power. Investigators worked for the same improvements we see in computers and lasers: more efficiency, smaller size.

An MHD generator is the exact electrical analogy to a mechanical turbine. In effect, an MHD generator is like a turbine coupled to an electrical generator. The great advantage of the MHD generator is that it can handle working gas temperatures that would instantly melt even the most exotic turbine blade materials.

If we could cram an MHD generator into an aircraft, how would we use it? Sure, it could run our electrical systems, but that would scarcely put a dent in the tremendous electrical supply MHD could provide. Well, if we had megawatt quantities of electricity available, we could use the electricity to power a whopping big MHD impeller fan. Today, we usually use an air-breathing gas turbine to power a high-bypass-ratio fan, such as a turbo/fanjet engine. But if we could replace the gas turbine engine with a laser-heated rocket MHD generator, we would get a much lighter, smaller, and more powerful system. We would feel all that left-over energy as added thrust. We might also use that electrical energy to power a particle-beam weapon or even to influence the air around a dirigible. If we can influence enough air in the right ways, we can use that air to provide lift or thrust for the dirigible.

We will get to the dirigibles later in this chapter. At the moment we are designing an MHD fanjet propulsion system that might improve the high-altitude performance of a hypersonic craft. The rotary IRH (internal radiation heated) pulsejet, which we designed in Chapter 4, might be a good starting point, if we combined it with an air-turborocket engine.

First, we want to inject hydrogen into the laser-heated thrust chambers to get maximum temperatures and pressures for a highly ionized rocket gas

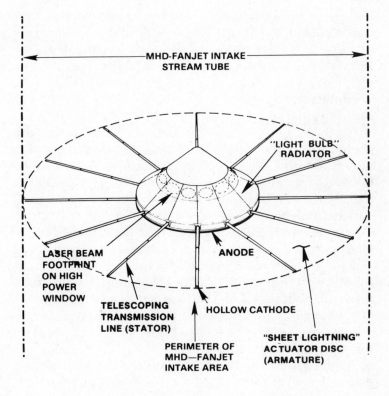

Figure 6–1. Laser-propelled MHD-fanjet configuration (air turborocket propulsion cycle)

stream. So we include a tank of liquid hydrogen in the nonrotating hub of the frisbee vehicle shown in Figure 6-1. Second, we have to modify the exhaust nozzle of each chamber so it can snap nearly shut, clamshell-fashion, as shown in Figure 6-2. Third, we install superconducting MHD generator field coils and electrodes on those nozzles. Fourth, we add a set of secondary laser optics as shown in the illustrations. Finally, we build a very flat, wide, lightweight linear electrical motor—an "accelerator"—into the craft, with telescoping electrodes serving as stators as shown in Figure 6-1.

Here's how it works: the actuator blades or paddles of this MHD fanjet are short-lived sheet lightning which also do the job of an armature. This may be tricky to envision; Figure 6-3 is an illustration showing this sheet lightning armature in the process of generating thrust.

Our remote high energy laser is still with us, bounced from primary optics out to each combustion chamber. We inject a small amount of hydrogen into the absorption chamber and start a laser-supported detonation pulse. In its passage toward the chamber nozzle, the hydrogen is transformed into an extremely high-temperature pulse of ionized gas. The MHD generator magnets induce a flow of electricity across the electrodes, and the resulting current is used to energize the big annular air-breathing fan. In this way, we impart thrust directly to our working fluid, which is air. We waste very little energy on dissociation and ionization of the air stream.

Why would we want to do this, when it requires us to carry a tank of hydrogen? Because it may give us the ability to accelerate the frisbee to a far higher altitude and velocity, with greater efficiency, than the pure air-breather—up to Mach 10 or 15, in fact— and we do not need to inject more than a tiny amount of hydrogen for each pulse. In terms of thrust per unit of fuel consumed, we might get an I_{sp} of 10,000 from the hydrogen, because 99% of the mass we

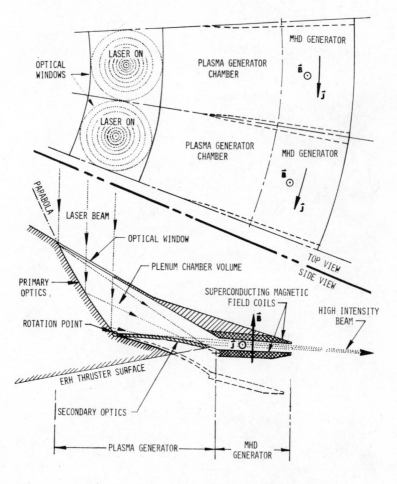

Figure 6–2. IRH plasma generator geometry for MHD-fanjet

Figure 6–3. Laser shuttle in MHD-fanjet propulsion mode.
(Artist: R. Carter)

expel for thrust is air we stole from outside. Furthermore, we are gulping all that air without having to heat it, driving our fan electrically with MHD current.

This rig might need an ERH boost on its underbody to lift off the pad, and a rotary IRH pulsejet mode for its first moments of horizontal acceleration (for this mode, the clamshell exhaust nozzles would be open). Whatever we select as a boost mode, once it gets going it should be something to see. Properly designed, it could go from trifling speeds near sea level to hypersonic cruise at 300,000 feet. That's 100 kilometers high, where there is so little air that even our furiously paddling MHD fanjet cannot gulp great amounts of it. Above that height, we would have to inject more hydrogen and operate the system as a pure laser-driven rocket. Its I_{sp} would drop to only a thousand or two, which would limit its flights in orbital regions.

Author Myrabo has worked out some modifications to his MHD fanjet propulsion system, including one that could use a continuous wave laser. Basically, the rocket chambers would "burn" hydrogen in a more or less steady state of laser-supported combustion instead of distinct pulses, and the CW laser would enter continuously through a crystal window to add enthalpy (heat content to most of us) to the gas. The big airbreathing MHD fan would still have to operate in an RP or quasi-steady mode, to minimize losses from dissociation and ionization of the airstream.

This kind of engine could give us a vehicle that climbs to orbit without dropping external tanks: a single-stage-to-orbit (SSTO) shuttle. By cleverly adjusting our chambers and on-board laser optics, we could build a single stage shuttle that uses four different propulsion schemes to take advantage of available conditions, depending on our speed and altitude. It could have an ERH thruster, integrated as shown in Figure 6-4 for a launch and landing; a rotary IRH pulsejet to boost us away horizontally; an MHD fan-

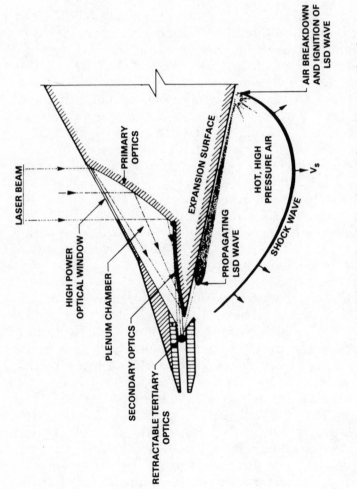

Figure 6–4. External radiation-heated thruster integrated with vehicle lower surface

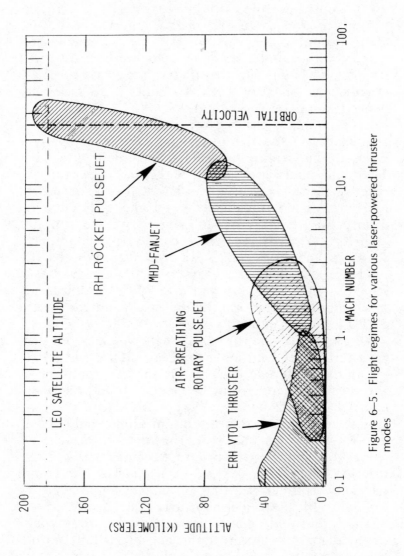

Figure 6—5. Flight regimes for various laser-powered thruster modes

jet for hypersonic flight almost to orbital heights; and an IRH rocket for maneuvering in low Earth orbit. Figure 6-5 plots the way we could use these propulsion modes for an orbital mission. All this could be automated so that it is no more complicated for the pilot than having four different gears for his dune buggy. For that matter, the rotary pulsejet is an integral part of the MHD fanjet, so the weight penalties may be very slight.

Let's evaluate the performance of three frisbee-shaped SSTO shuttles of different diameters so we can see how scaling up this design might affect it. Their diameters are sixteen and a half feet, thirty-three feet and sixty-six feet. They will each have the four propulsion modes we listed above. Each will absorb an RP laser of sufficient power to run its engines. Of course, the more combustion chambers we have, the more pulses we will need. We can fit twelve of our little chambers around the rim of the smallest shuttle; twenty-four around the middlesized craft; and forty-eight on the big one. What can these SSTO craft put in orbit?

The smallest one, at liftoff, will weigh about six tons and can deliver one man, if he and his gear don't weigh over 200 pounds. The middlesized one weighs three times as much but cannot lift much more; it can deliver two men, or 400 pounds. But the sixty-six-footer, weighing seventy tons at liftoff, could boost almost sixteen tons to orbit. That is half as much as the NASA shuttle's maximum payload, with a tiny fraction of its size! Table 6-1 summarizes the comparisons. You can see that the payload mass of the big cargo-lifting frisbee is nearly equal to the mass of the liquid hydrogen it burns. Rest assured, when payload mass begins to approach propellant mass, the air express people and your local travel agent will be clamoring for space!

We have plugged in the performance numbers as though we could depend on whatever HEL power we need, but at this point it's time to see how much

VEHICLE DIAMETER PARAMETER	5M	10M	20M
NO. OF PLASMA GENERATORS	12.	24.	48.
LASER ENERGY PER PULSEJET (MJ)	5.	5.	5.
PEAK POWER PER PULSEJET (MW)	100.-300.	100.-300.	100.-300.
PAYLOAD TO LEO (Kg)	90.	180.	15,000.
VEHICLE HEIGHT (M)	1.8	3.	5.3
INTERNAL VEHICLE VOLUME (M^3)	30.	100.	363.
VOLUME OF LH$_2$ (M^3)	26.4	78.6	303.
ERH THRUSTER AREA* (M^2)	19.6	78.5	314.
MAX. DIA. OF MHD-FAN (M)	28.	56.	80.

* ERH THRUSTER AREA IS SET EQUAL TO ENTIRE VEHICLE BASE AREA.

Table 6–1A. Shuttle Vehicle Data

power we need for these three single stage frisbees. Take a look at Tables 6-2, 6-3, 6-4, and 6-5. As we switch engine modes, we will need different amounts of HEL power. You can see that, when our big cargo-carrier is operating in space in the IRH rocket mode, it will demand somewhere between five and fifty GW of laser power. And *that*, as we mentioned earlier, implies HEL installations in orbit that are much larger than anything we have planned today.

Very well, then; our plans will just have to be expanded. We will probably see two drivers of that expansion: the economic success of our first small laser-boosted craft, and Soviet progress in larger or-bital power plants. At least we need not worry about having plenty of healthy competition. Some of the best work in HEL development has been done by the Soviets, and we do not notice them slacking off. It would be nice if we could see American space prog-ress pulled along entirely by our confidence in its future, rather than by our fear of somebody else's success. Yet what we would like, and what we really expect, are often very different.

Speaking of things that are different, how about the supersonic dirigibles we promised? Imagine a big cylinder, with a "fineness" (length-to-diameter) ratio of ten to one. If it is much under 300 feet long, it will not be a true lighter-than-air craft; but from 300 to about 3,000 feet long, we could furnish it with the classic dirigible's internal gas cells and a double-walled skin made of thin girders. Though hydrogen is still the lightest gas to fill a dirigible, it has only a 10% lifting advantage over helium. Its cost advan-tage may be much greater, yet with thin cell walls the possibility of leakage and fire is always present—so take your choice. Whichever gas we use to fill the buoyancy cells, our dirigible will not be buoyant above roughly 10,000 feet. It will not need buoyancy.

It can be independent of buoyancy because we can give it several modes of propulsion. If you predicted

| VEHICLE DIAMETER | MASS (KG) | | |
PARAMETER	5M	10M	20M
AIRFRAME & STRUCTURE	1250.	3890.	12,300.
PLASMA GENERATORS	1210.	2220.	4440.
XMHD GENERATOR MAGNETS	690.	2840.	5680.
TRANSMISSION LINES	460.	1880.	4910.
PAYLOAD	90.	180.	15,000.
VEHICLE DRY MASS	3700.	11,000.	42,300.
PROPELLANT TO LEO*	1850.	5,500.	21,200.
MASS AT LIFT-OFF	5550.	16,500.	63,500.

*ASSUMES MASS RATIO OF 1.5, FOR $\Delta V = 4$KM/SEC.

Table 6—1B. Vehicle Mass Estimate

VEHICLE DIAMETER PARAMETER	5M	10M	20M
COUPLING COEFFICIENT (d-s/J)$_L$	100.	100.	100.
MASS AT LIFT-OFF (10^3Kg)	5.55	16.5	63.5
"WING LOADING" (Kg/M^2)	283.	210.	202.
REQUIRED LASER POWER (MW)			
• HOVER (1g)	54.	162.	622.
• 3 g's ACCELERATION	162.	485.	1867.
• 10 g's ACCELERATION	539.	1620.	6220.

Table 6–2. Performance Estimate for ERH Thruster
(Sea Level, Zero Velocity)

PARAMETER \ VEHICLE DIAMETER	5M	10M	20M
MAX LASER PRF (SEC^{-1})	168.	192.	240.
COUPLING COEFFICIENT (d-s/J)$_L$	20.	20.	20.
MAX REVOLUTIONS/SECOND	14.	8.	5.
VEHICLE MASS (10^3kg)	5.5	16.5	63.5
MAX ABSORBED LASER POWER (MW)	670.	770.	960.
MAX THRUST (10^5 NEWTONS)	1.37	1.56	1.95
MAX THRUST/WEIGHT RATIO	2.54	0.96	0.31

Table 6–3. Performance Estimate for Airbreathing Rotary Pulsejet(Sea Level Altitude)

VEHICLE DIAMETER PARAMETER	5M	10M	20M
VEHICLE MASS (10^3 kg)	5.55	16.5	63.5
ELECTRICAL COUPLING COEFFICIENT $(d-s/J)_e$	95.	95.	95.
LASER COUPLING COEFFICIENT $(d-s/J)_L$	47.5	47.5	47.5
CENTER-BODY DRAG (GW)	0.124	0.496	1.98
ACTUATOR VELOCITY (M/S)	330.	330.	330.
PROPULSIVE EFFICIENCY (%)	81.	81.	81.
REQUIRED LASER POWER (GW)			
• 1g ACCELERATION	0.239	0.836	3.29
• 3 g's ACCELERATION	0.467	1.52	5.91
• 10 g's ACCELERATION	1.27	3.90	15.1

Table 6–4. Performance Estimate for MHD-Fanjet
(31.1 km, 300 m/s)

VEHICLE DIAMETER PARAMETER	5M	10M	20M
VEHICLE MASS (10^3 kg)	~5.55	~16.5	~63.5
LASER COUPLING COEFFICIENT $(d-s/J)_L$	12.5	12.5	12.5
REQUIRED LASER POWER (GW)			
● 1g ACCELERATION	0.435	1.29	4.98
● 3 g's ACCELERATION	1.31	3.88	14.9
● 10 g's ACCELERATION	4.35	12.9	49.8

Table 6—5. Performance Estimate for IRH Rocket Pulsejet
(>70km, >4 km/s)

pulsejets again, you are right; both the external and radiation and internal radiation (ERH and IRH) type should work handily. A less predictable guess might be aerodynamic lift, especially using vortex generators; but that, too, may be in the offing. And if you guessed propulsion from a huge electromagnetic field, our hats are off. This last option seems very unlikely until you study it a bit. Let us cover all our options, starting from the top.

First we take a smallish version, Figure 6-6. It needs at last one special end cap called a "power head" (both ends could be adapted this way) with the optics to receive and focus a laser. Inside the power head is an articulated "beam catcher" mirror that directs the laser to one chosen area of the curved primary optics. The laser's job is to generate ERH pulses outside the hull. For simplicity's sake we will give it one power head. The HEL beam emerges from one port of the power head, runs the length of the underside of the vehicle a few centimeters from its surface, and is focused to start a LSD blast wave near the *other* end of the vehicle. The detonation wave is allowed to run back up through the beam for almost the entire length of the cylinder, as shown in Figure 6-7. The beam pulse is then shut off to protect the optics. The detonation wave slaps the underside of our cylinder and propels it upward for a brief pulse, and as the expanding gas moves away it is replaced by fresh cool air. Another laser pulse starts this ERH cycle all over again.

We can get lateral (horizontal) movement, force the vehicle downward, and so on by shifting the optics to cause blast waves on other parts of the surface, as shown in Figure 6-8. In a scheme like this, we must maintain very close control over the LSD waves. If we don't, we will have some unexpected pitch or yaw maneuvers by the vehicle. We will also have to develop very tough surface plates for the vehicle skin—perhaps tied to structural stringers—because the LSD waves will slap the skin with some-

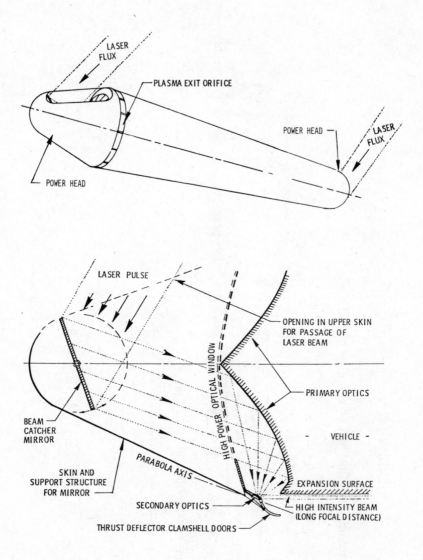

Figure 6–6. Engine/optical/airframe configuration for cylindrical laser-powered shuttlecraft

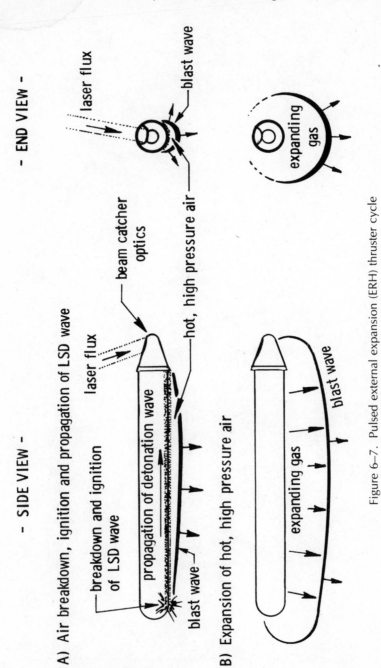

Figure 6—7. Pulsed external expansion (ERH) thruster cycle

- SIDE VIEW -

A) Air breakdown, ignition and propagation of LSD wave

breakdown and ignition
of LSD wave

laser flux

beam catcher
optics

propagation of detonation wave

hot, high pressure air

blast wave

B) Expansion of hot, high pressure air

expanding gas

blast wave

- END VIEW -

laser flux

blast wave

hot, high pressure air

expanding
gas

A) LATERAL MOTION (controlled by proper projection of beam upon primary concentrating optics by "beam catcher" mirror).   - END VIEW -

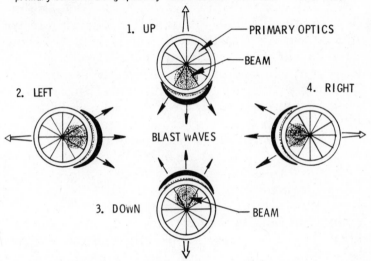

B) PITCH AND YAW MANEUVERABILITY (controlled as above, except with laser pulses of shorter duration)   - SIDE VIEW -

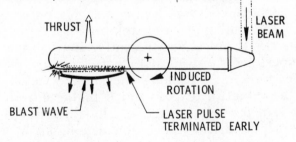

Figure 6–8. Flight maneuverability and control for cylindrical shuttlecraft by ERH thrusters

thing like 100 atmospheres (1500 psi) of sudden pressure.

We can install an IRH system also; a rotary pulsejet system that works very much the same way as those we met earlier. (After all, this is still a vehicle with "radial symmetry"—it's just a very long one.) If those variable-pitch blades are adjusted properly, we can induce the whole cylinder to roll. Figure 6-9 shows how we do that, combining the IRH pulsejet with the beam catcher mirror. You may remember that, by using a tank of liquid hydrogen and a few other tricks, we turned an IRH air-breather into a hydrogen-fueled, laser-boosted rocket for orbital missions. We could employ the same trick here and operate our power head(s) either as air-breathers with hydrogen-injection, or—if we can afford to carry big hydrogen tanks for orbital missions—as pure IRH rockets.

We can also get aerodynamic lift, even from a cylindrical vehicle. Santos-Dumont and his colleagues knew they could push their primitive dirigibles higher by forging ahead at a nose-high attitude, and we can do the same. But because we can use the exhaust of our pulsejet, we can use another trick they lacked. This is called "vortex-augmented lift."

Some of today's ultralight aircraft use vortex-generating airfoils first developed, not long ago, by Kasper. The trapped vortex above a "Kasperwing" can lower the stall speed and sink rate of a glider to half the normal values. Very recently, Swedish wind-tunnel experiments proved that a vortex can be maintained by blowing air along the span of a wing, toward the wingtip, to gain much higher lift than the wing can provide otherwise. We can apply this trick to our cylindrical vehicle too, as long as we are satisfied with fairly low speeds. When we start approaching sonic speed we run into trouble with the compressibility of air, which disturbs the vortex.

We generate our vortex by directing exhaust gases from the power head to spiral along the length of the cylinder. These gases excite surrounding air to move

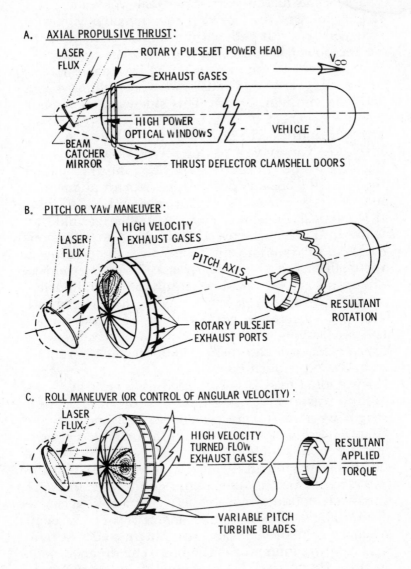

A. AXIAL PROPULSIVE THRUST:

LASER FLUX

ROTARY PULSEJET POWER HEAD

EXHAUST GASES

V_∞

HIGH POWER OPTICAL WINDOWS

VEHICLE

BEAM CATCHER MIRROR

THRUST DEFLECTOR CLAMSHELL DOORS

B. PITCH OR YAW MANEUVER:

HIGH VELOCITY EXHAUST GASES

LASER FLUX

PITCH AXIS

RESULTANT ROTATION

ROTARY PULSEJET EXHAUST PORTS

C. ROLL MANEUVER (OR CONTROL OF ANGULAR VELOCITY):

LASER FLUX

HIGH VELOCITY TURNED FLOW EXHAUST GASES

RESULTANT APPLIED TORQUE

VARIABLE PITCH TURBINE BLADES

Figure 6–9. IRH pulsejet mode of cylindrical shuttlecraft

in the same direction. Because the vortex effect is
strongest near the nozzles, the invisible vortex is
somewhat cone-shaped, with its largest diameter nearest the power head, its tip trailing away beyond the
opposite end of the cylinder. The cylinder is acting
like a very fat wing, and the whole thing moves
sideways through the air. This sideways movement,
when we expect a long cylinder to move like an
arrow, is hard to visualize; but that's how it works.

By now you may be asking, "Why do we need it?"
Because we need cheap propulsion, and the smaller
the HEL, the cheaper our mission. Vortex-augmented
lift lets us use a relatively low-power HEL to force
IRH exhaust gases to set up a swirl, like a small hot
whirlwind. The whirlwind influences an enormous
mass of surrounding air to follow suit, creating a
vortex like a tornado which creates lift on our vehicle.
The result is a faster rate of climb for our cylindrical
craft, using a given laser energy to the power head.
This is a scheme we might employ when the vehicle
is first climbing up from the pad. As our craft speeds
up near Mach 1, the vortex would become too inefficient to do us much good.

For a lot of missions—say, fast passenger travel—we
tend to waste energy in the interest of speed. But for
cargo, we tend to pinch pennies and cheapen the
ride. If we stowed our cargo in a dirigible cylinder
and accepted slow subsonic flight, we could give it a
pretty cheap ride all the way to its service ceiling.

We might use another gimmick, if we could spin
the whole cylinder like a roller. This would generate
a kind of lift known as the Magnus effect. Baseball
pitchers spin the ball and use Magnus-effect lift to
generate the infamous curve ball. The dreaded hook
or slice of a golf ball is a curve produced by the same
phenomenon. A spinning hull would definitely not
work with passengers, unless their compartment were
isolated from the spin. It seems likely, though, that
Magnus-effect spin could generate lift at speeds far
higher than we could manage with the nonspinning

hull. Upshot: if we spin the hull, we might manage Mach 1 speeds and cheap transportation too, as long as we stayed within the atmosphere.

But what if we want to boost our dirigible at hypersonic speeds? We cannot manage that in dense air unless we squander energy. The solution is to climb out to the fringes of space and find some way to boost us along without using air. Would you believe we might warp the Earth's geomagnetic field for the purpose?

We do not suggest perturbing the entire global magnetic field, but we might manage *local* perturbations, for ten miles or so around our vehicle. After all, we have climbed many miles above the Earth to the ionosphere now, and in previous chapters we designed ultralight MHD generators to create tremendous electrical power. If we build a really big dirigible—say, 3000 feet long—we can construct it so that the structure includes electromagnetic thrusters. (This might seem like a mind-boggling vehicle until we recall that it's only three times the length of the Graf *Zeppelin*, which was built fifty years ago.)

When we start tossing out terms like "geomagnetic repulsors" and "electromagnetic thrusters," we run a credibility risk. The science fiction fan rubs his hands in glee because he has seen these jawbreakers mentioned, if not explained, before. Some readers will want to throw this book across the room because they smell a hoax. But the engineering physics student sighs and digs in his heels because, like as not, he has often considered how he could make use of huge natural forces. Two of those forces are the vast charges that create lightning bolts, and Earth's magnetic field. Author Myrabo has worked out some of the early preliminary designs making use of these forces. Like most preliminary designs, these are speculative; but they look very promising. They do not depend on any new fundamental laws, although we are still a long way from off-the-shelf hardware. What hardware? We saw it in previous pages.

Let's furnish our big dirigible's power head with MHD hardware: superconducting electromagnets, insulating walls, and electrodes at the exhaust nozzles. When we apply magnetic fields through the laser-heated hydrogen exhaust, we can draw electrical power from the MHD generator's electrodes. With such a big vehicle, we can easily install linear accelerators (linac) and feed them some of the power from our laser-MHD power heads. We can also make the vehicle's structural longerons double as superconductors, as shown in Figure 6-10. For travel within the atmosphere, we eject a beam of protons or positrons from one end of the cylinder and a beam of electrons from the other, which should create oppositely-charged clouds of ionized air for a distance of a mile or so behind the vehicle. When we have pumped up these clouds to the point where they begin a natural glow-discharge in the volume between them, we use our MHD generators to deliver a great wallop (between a million and a billion amps) of current into this glow-discharge volume. The glow-discharge volume is full of air—a tremendous amount of it with a total mass at least equal to our vehicle's mass. This air and the vehicle repel each other, giving us an electromagnetic thruster. We have shown the process in Figure 6-11.

There are several variations on this theme, using charged volumes of air to repel our vehicle. By the way: this is not the kind of propulsion system to use on a spy ship. In its progress across the sky, it will probably leave a series of lightning discharges behind it as the oppositely-charged clouds neutralize their charges. You can't sneak overhead trailing lightning bolts.

Another kind of repulsor is rooted in experiments that date back over twenty years, to the work of Way and his colleagues. Way built a ten-foot model submarine and propelled it with a single long electromagnet as shown in Figure 6-12. The constant electromagnetic field surrounded the model and reached

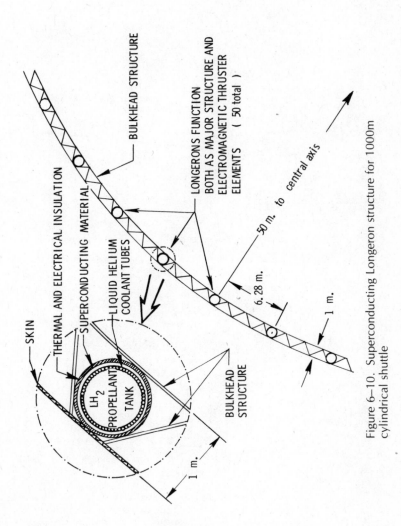

BULKHEAD STRUCTURE

LONGERONS FUNCTION
BOTH AS MAJOR STRUCTURE AND
ELECTROMAGNETIC THRUSTER
ELEMENTS   (50 total)

THERMAL AND ELECTRICAL INSULATION

SUPERCONDUCTING MATERIAL

LIQUID HELIUM
COOLANT TUBES

SKIN

LH₂
PROPELLANT
TANK

BULKHEAD
STRUCTURE

50 m. to central axis

6. 28 m.

1 m.

1 m.

Figure 6–10. Superconducting Longeron structure for 1000m
cylindrical shuttle

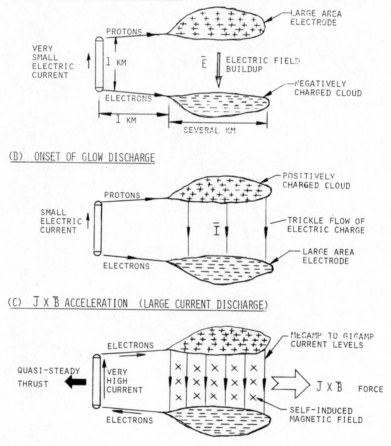

Figure 6–11. Stratospheric "glow discharge" propulsion concept (20 to 100 km altitude)

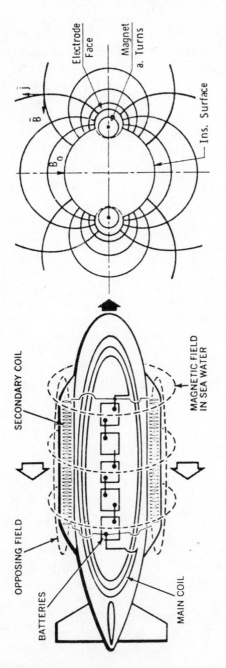

Figure 6–12. Magnetic field and current flow configuration for Way's electromagnetic submarine. Electric current flowing perpendicular to magnetic field produces "Lorentz force" that pushes sea water backwards (like armature of electric motor).

far out into the water. Electrodes on the model's surface fed a current into the nearby (conductive) sea water, and water in the core of the magnetic field was ejected to the rear. This water jet propelled the model. Way studied scaled-up versions in which huge cargo subs could be propelled this way. One major problem, of course, would be the attraction of magnetic materials from the ocean floor.

We could put Way's ideas to use in atmospheric flight by using structural longerons as electrodes. We use our dirigible's power head to generate LSD pulses in the air around the huge cylinder, and the blast wave (as usual) is a conductive plasma of hot gases. We send a heavy jolt of current from one long surface electrode to the next, through that conductive blast wave. Because the LSD blast wave is a moving pulse, it influences a great volume of surrounding air to move with it. The pulse was generated so that it moves rearward, and as all that air is repelled backward, our vehicle moves forward. But like the other electromagnetic thruster schemes we have shown, this one needs at least a modest amount of air. For dirigibles in orbit, we might have to use something more subtle.

We promised a geomagnetic repulsor, and space (our ionosphere) is the place to use it. Yes, we must carry our tank of hydrogen—but using this scheme it might give us an I_{sp} of 100,000. We use hydrogen with HEL power at the power heads to produce whopping amounts of electric power. You'll recall we discussed the Magnus-effect lift; well, the geomagnetic repulsor is just the electrical analogy of the Magnus effect. In our scheme, instead of an aerodynamic vortex created by a spinning cylinder, we have a cylindrical magnetic field. We produce this field by conducting high current, from one end of the huge cylinder to the other, through the superconducting structural stringers. And instead of an external atmosphere, we have Earth's geomagnetic field.

In operation, our vehicle's cylindrical electromag-

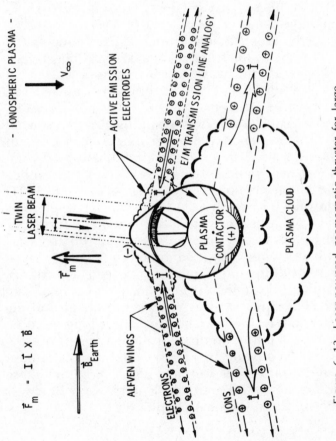

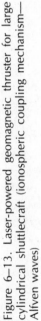

Figure 6–13. Laser-powered geomagnetic thruster for large cylindrical shuttlecraft (ionospheric coupling mechanism—Alfven waves)

netic vortex field interacts with the local part of Earth's linear magnetic field. This creates the Lorentz force which propels our spacecraft. The free electric charge, ejected from the end point electrodes of our vehicle, is conducted away by the sparse plasma of the ionosphere—mostly along local external magnetic field lines. This is shown in Figure 6-13 as Alfven waves.

So maybe those fictional mile-long hovering spaceships are not so far from reality. We can boost various shapes all the way to orbit using a variety of propulsion systems. The one thing they all have in common is the HEL energy source—an endless extension cord from God's own wallplug, so to speak. If you want the pencil-and-paper exercise, you might try cobbling up a stub-winged design using adjustable power heads and surface electrodes. Given multi-GW laser power, you could wind up with an SSTO shuttle that hovers on LSD blast waves, accelerates to the fringes of space with electromagnetic thrusters, then uses geomagnetic repulsors to climb to orbit. Why give it wings? So it can maneuver on its return without needing much more laser feed. Of course, you could call for the HEL again for your final moments of landing, so your craft could hover and descend VTOL-fashion without a miles-long landing strip. At this point, you can probably dream up several versions of your own for special missions. About the only big missions we have not covered are those taking us beyond Earth orbit—and we will cover some of those in the next chapter.

Chapter 7:

STARSHIP DRIVES

Until recently many scientists, even some of the young ones, tended to snicker at the idea of manned flight beyond the Earth-moon system. If we cannot boost vehicles at thousands of miles per second (and we can't, burning old-fashioned chemical propellants with three-digit I_{sp}s), we might as well forget deep-space voyages—especially those beyond our own solar system. Actually, that is a very reasonable view if we are limited to I_{sp}s of three, or four, or five digits. Where starships are concerned, a four-digit I_{sp} is about as much help as a one-digit IQ. The distance to the nearest neighboring star system, Alpha Centauri, is literally astronomical. It's so far away that we can only get a vague impression of the distance by comparing it with distances we travel today. In case you have not seen such comparisons lately, let's do a minute's refresher.

With air travel today, we can get an idea, an internal feeling, for the great size of our Earth. It's 24,000 miles in circumference; a good, understandable measure of long distances. The moon is ten times that far away, almost a quarter of a million miles from us. That's so far that it takes a light beam about 1.3 seconds to make the trip—the longest round-trip to date for human beings. The sun is about 93 million miles from us, so its light takes roughly 8.3 minutes to reach us. And its near neighbor Alpha Centauri? Light takes 4.3 *years* to span that vast interstellar gulf. Interstellar distances are commonly measured by light years—the distance light travels in one year. (The parsec is an even larger unit, a distance of 3.26 light years.)

If we built a model to scale those distances up, we might pick some central spot like Peoria, Illinois, and put a tiny jewel on the ground there. That's our Earth. An inch away from it we put a smaller stone to represent the moon. Now measure off about thirty-two feet and place a bright disk there to represent our sun. Okay: ready to pace off the distance to our model Alpha Centauri? Better make a few sandwiches and check your canteen; your destination is San Diego, or maybe Kamloops in British Columbia, because you have a walk of over 1600 miles ahead of you. That, at least, is a comparison we can handle; we do not get as clear a picture of the scale if we just say Alpha Centauri is over a hundred million times as far away as the moon, or two-and-a-half billion times around the world. And this is our next-door neighbor system; other star systems in the neighborhood include Barnard's Star (six light years away) and big, bright Sirius (over eight light years away). These figures begin to give a rough idea why, when we want to say something's bigger than big—maybe bigger than we can comfortably imagine—we say it is astronomical. No wonder so many scientists were pessimistic about space travel.

Pessimists admitted that we might send one-way probes to nearby planets; but provisioning a crew for a round-trip of several years, they said, required a payload that was simply out of the question. About that time, we began to send those probes. It's comforting to realize that at the beginning of the 1980s the human race had already landed spacecraft on three other bodies in the solar system (the moon, Venus, and Mars), and had made flybys of two more (Jupiter and Saturn). Maybe, said the pessimists; but the distances are piddling (astronomically speaking) and the payloads are tiny.

And then we started seeing designs like the Orion project of Taylor and Dyson, Bussard's deepspace ramjets, and antimatter engine schemes like Robert Forward's. These folks are designing engines with I_{sp}s that go from the thousands up to infinity. Not by stealing our atmospheric air, but *in deep space*, mind you! It's beginning to look like a new ballgame.

One of the simplest means to get high impulse has been known since the 1950s, though the whole scheme was never really put together with all its elements. We will see why in a moment; it was called the Orion project.

In an early atmospheric A-bomb test, scientists had placed graphite-covered steel spheres below the tower and later found the spheres little the worse for wear, with only a bit of the graphite missing. Bomb designer Ted Taylor realized that the graphite could, in principle, have been spread over a stout pusher-plate, fastened to a payload, and aimed so the bomb would have given it one almighty push. In fact, you could erect a structure the size of a small building, attach a pusherplate below it with enormous shock absorbers, and fire the whole shebang a goodly distance by detonating a single A-bomb fifty yards below the plate. A moment later, you could eject another A-bomb like a soft-drink can from a dispenser, detonate it below the pusherplate, and so on until your whole building was in orbit.

Taylor and Freeman Dyson both got cracking on this scheme, which was funded by the Air Force even though it sounded brutally simple and bizarre at the same time. The designers realized that this was a peaceful way to dispose of lots of our A-bombs, and they calculated that we could put a thousand tons of payload on the moon in a single mission. Or we could set out for Mars with a crew of a hundred, not worrying about minimum-energy trajectories.

It all sounded wonderful and weird, but there were lots of doubts whether those repeated detonations could send up a payload under reasonable control.

So the Orion team built and fired bullet-shaped scale models with flat bottoms, injecting hunks of high explosive into the air below the pusherplate and detonating them. We are told the injection mechanism was actually based on a soft-drink can dispenser! At least one yard-long model climbed until its store of explosives was exhausted, then returned by parachute while movie cameras whirred below. Werner von Braun evidently thought the scheme harebrained until he saw a film of the thing climbing into the sky on its pusherplate, boosted by a string of high-explosive pulses. After that, von Braun was a convert to Orion.

Of course a skyscraper-sized rig propelled by atom bombs would be a health hazard if we fired it from the Earth's surface. But Orion could be assembled in high orbit, and then boosted away for a round-trip to Neptune carrying a labful of people, a planetary landing craft, food for everybody and a bowling alley if they wanted one. They would start out with a basementful of A-bombs and return without them. But Orion depended entirely on exploding nuclear bombs, and the test ban treaty in 1963 forbade nukes in space. Orion went into cold storage. It is there today, metaphorically covered with the frost of neglect.

It may be impossible for most of us to appreciate the disappointment felt by Taylor and Dyson when Orion hit the deepfreeze. They had a proven design for a tour of the solar system over twenty years ago, but it was—still is—politically unpopular. The Orion story has been chronicled in captivating detail by John McPhee in *The Curve Of Binding Energy*.

Orion would have been improved in many respects, had they kept the project alive. The design of the bombs, for one thing, called for as much directional energy-release as possible. A low-yield explosion could actually be more efficient than one of higher total yield, if more of its energy could be converted into thrust against the pusherplate. But then, that had been Ted Taylor's business. That pusherplate, or baseplate, still would not make very efficient use of the total energy detonated below. Its I_{sp} would be many thousands, but in conversion from mass to energy it would boast a fraction of 1% efficiency. What about other, more efficient schemes?

Bob Bussard's deep-space ramjet vehicle would be much more efficient, but would have to start out from a parking orbit for a different reason. We know that even in the deepest black voids of known space, a few atoms—mostly hydrogen—cruise around in a galactic Brownian movement, aimlessly waiting for some useful employment. Bussard decided to employ them. He would rig a huge funnel-like scoop in front of his vehicle, boost it up to *many* miles a second, and then process all that hydrogen by actually scooping it into a collector. We have seen some ways to use hydrogen for fuel, including laser heating from an HEL sent far into space to mirrors on the vehicle. Bussard suggested that the scooped hydrogen could be used as fuel for a fusion engine.

The ramscoop itself, by the way, would be an enormous gossamer structure—far larger than the vehicle. Seen through a telescope, it would probably look like a funnel, miles in diameter, with a tiny blob (the vehicle hull) at its apex and a glare of exhaust issuing from behind the blob. In the interests of lowering mass, the ramscoop structure would be so flimsy that we would have to keep the accelerations very, very low. But even a thousandth of a g, applied steadily for a few months, would give us enough velocity to tour beyond our solar system. Using an on-board reactor, our ramscoop craft would be independent of laser energy piped from home, but it's strictly a vehicle for gradual velocity changes in covering astronomical distances. We would have to furl and stow the ramscoop if we wanted to apply heavier g loads using some auxiliary boost propulsion system. Even if we used the gravitational force of our target body (such as another star) to swing the vehicle around for a return trip, we would either have to make a very wide, time-consuming swing or furl the ramscoop for the maneuver.

These restrictions may disappear if we can design a force field somehow to perform the scoop duties. In such a case, our interstellar ramscooper could accelerate at a full g or more, right up to relativistic speeds (meaning a sizeable fraction of light-speed). The exhaust nozzle of a rocket spewing plasma exhaust could be a rickety-looking structure using magnetic fields to create a huge efficient nozzle. Such magnetic nozzles have already been designed on paper.

Whitmore and Jackson added a canny idea in case we have to use a ramscoop of solid material: fire tiny pellets of frozen heavy-hydrogen out ahead of it, before it begins to accelerate! The deuterium pellets would have to be accelerated to tremendous speed, in line with the vehicle's intended path. Then the ramjet would simply accelerate, gulping pellets as it went, and could use a modest-sized scoop for the purpose. You could think of this as a kind of in-flight refueling system. If we used this scheme for an interstellar run, the "pellet runway" might be a tenth of a light year long, the vehicle accelerating at one-fifth of a g for a year. At the end of that time it would be going one-fifth light-speed. It would have also gulped nearly fifty times its own mass in fuel pellets.

Bussard's interstellar ramjet may be a long way in the future, but its I_{sp} could be infinite as long as it scooped up its fuel en route and had an energy source to heat the fuel. We just have to bear in mind that it's not a vehicle for sudden maneuvers if it has to make them with an enormous scoop of solid material poking out in front. If we can stow it readily, or if we can energize a force-field scoop as easily as flicking a switch, we might manage those maneuvers. We could not count on the ramjet for power, of course, when its scoop is stowed away. Or could we? Why not store up a little interstellar hydrogen en route, then use it for abrupt maneuvers while our scoop was furled? Maybe we could. We can probably find better solutions than that; but somebody has to think of them first.

And then there's antimatter, long thought to be the province of science fiction. Antimatter consists of particles spinning in opposite directions from those of "normal" matter. An antielectron (called a positron) has the same mass as a normal electron; an antiproton the same mass as a normal proton. We could create atoms of antihydrogen; indeed, somewhere in the universe there may be entire galaxies of antimatter. But our universe seems to be composed of normal matter, and if any antiparticles are created, they disintegrate the instant they collide with any normal matter. Not only do they cease to exist, but both the normal particles and the antiparticles completely annihilate each other, with a total conversion of their masses to raw energy. "Cute," say the skeptics. "So if you had some, what would you keep it in?" Good question.

Well, we now have some answers *and* some antimatter. At the CERN facility in Switzerland, they have managed to store high-speed antiprotons for eighty-five hours. CERN's scientists generated the high-speed particles with a powerful proton beam, then injected and stored their antiprotons in a magnetic storage ring. How do we make antimatter? With fiendishly complex equipment, resulting in some simple energetic particles.

If we fire a proton beam against a tungsten target, the staggering kinetic energy of those fast-moving protons causes them to be converted into a spray of other particles. Some of those particles will be antiprotons. These particles are moving at relativistic speeds. In this country, our Fermilab scientists intend to fire proton beams of eighty giga-electron-volts (GeV) against tungsten, collecting the high-speed antiprotons with a special magnetic field and aiming them into a particle decelerator. Those particles are not all moving at the same speed, but they are all moving right along. We *must* slow them down before we can store them for propellants.

Two deceleration methods have been proven. CERN adds or subtracts energy in the antimatter madly whirling in its containment ring, smoothing out speed fluctuations in the particles and gradually slowing them all down to "cool" them. Fermilab does it in much less time, injecting a beam of electrons with the antiprotons. The electrons are moving at uniform speed and by energy exchange with the antiparticles, they bring them to a fairly uniform speed too. This speed can be reduced very quickly—in fractions of a second.

Once we have a slow-moving stream of antiprotons we could inject a beam of positrons (antielectrons) with them. And just as the combination of an electron and a proton make an atom of hydrogen, combining antiparticles could create antihydrogen. Antihydrogen atoms would be electrically neutral then, but we would need to slow them down still more. They would still be a hot gas until we cooled the antihydrogen atoms to the point where we could liquify them. Though there are several ways we might succeed in this, we still have problems here. It may be that the problem of storing liquid antihydrogen will turn out to be greater than that of building a big doughnut-shaped magnetic storage tank for the gaseous stuff.

The trouble with all the American plans is that we have been twiddling our accelerators while the Europeans built better research labs. The proton/antiproton collider ring at CERN is a mile and a half in diameter, a gigantic gadget. In the U.S. at this writing, our bureaucrats are still having hissyfits over where to build our huge new collider facility. It's going to be a biggie, remember; the physicist's counterpart to the Palomar telescope. The Japanese want to get in on ours, and so will the Canadians if we can make it worth their while. Key presidential scientist George Keyworth recently made a speech to leaders of the

project-on-paper, and made no secret of his impa-
tience. In so many words, he suggested that the project leaders get their buns in gear. That collider facility
will be the free world's Number One (or will it be
ichi ban?) center for antimatter research, and time's
a-wasting.

We might not need many pounds of gaseous antimatter to tour the solar system. Scientist/author Bob
Forward points out that we could keep antihydrogen
as tiny particles and inject them with equally small
amounts of normal hydrogen in a pulsed-rocket mode.
Since the total conversion of one pound of matter to
energy would equal the energy of some twenty billion pounds of TNT, we're talking I_{sp}s in the trillion range. Anyone for spaceflight?

Studies at JPL and elsewhere show that we probably could use the annihilation of matter to get anywhere we liked (assuming we had the time, our speed
being limited by the speed of light). Dipprey concluded that the best way to use antimatter is to use
it very sparingly to heat a greater amount of normal
fuel. According to Dipprey, if we keep our final velocity below about 30% light-speed (!), regardless of the
mission, we can get by with a mass of antimatter
that is well under 1% of the total spacecraft mass. Another conclusion by several sources is that for any
mission, unless we want to go faster than 50% light-
speed, our total fuel mass need not be over four
times the payload mass. This will probably be a
no-sweat item unless the antimatter storage "tank"
is beefier than we would like.

If we used the high-energy plasma resulting from
annihilated matter to heat larger amounts of hydrogen fuel as Dipprey suggested, according to Cassenti
we could get over 40% efficiency. Here we are talking about 40% of utter and total conversion of matter into energy; I_{sp}s in the hundreds of billions.
Forward gave one mission example: a one-ton payload could be accelerated to 0.2 c (that is, 20% light-
speed) with a two-stage antimatter rocket toward

Alpha Centauri. The first stage would use four tons of normal hydrogen fuel and twenty pounds of antihydrogen to get us up to 0.1 c. The second stage would use twenty tons of hydrogen fuel and 400 pounds of antihydrogen to accelerate us up to 0.2 c in less than a year. (Several months? Right; it takes awhile to accelerate us to over 37,000 miles per second.)

The ship's second stage would then coast the rest of the way for 21.5 years at relativistic speed before using the rest of its fuel. Much lighter now, the vehicle would burn its last four tons of normal fuel with eighty pounds of antihydrogen to bring it to rest in the gravitational grasp of far Centaurus. Its tanks now empty, the vehicle would weigh one ton and would begin processing data to be beamed back to Earth. The whole trip would take twenty-five years. We would begin to receive data from Alpha Centauri 4.3 years later. Would we learn of habitable planets to lure human colonists soon afterward? There is one way we might make sure. . . .

If we are going to produce antimatter in useful quantities, we will need vast quantities of energy to start producing it with. There is no denying that even a few grams of antimatter, stored in one place on Earth, would have local folks picketing the storage facility in short order. Either of those reasons would be enough to make us plan our antimatter factory as a space-based industry. There, our solar energy is limited only by the size of the collector we build. We produce and store our antihydrogen in orbit, perhaps lunar orbit or at an L5 location, and we take the antimatter fuel onto our starship in space where the hazards will not be passed on to everybody else.

It is quite possible to build atmospheric vehicles using an antimatter drive. After all, a tenth of a gram of the stuff could power a family flivver to orbit and back. But no machine is perfect, and even that tiny smidgin of antimatter would devastate the countryside if anything went wrong. When antimatter drives first become practical, we can expect treaties banning its use for propulsion within Earth's atmosphere. There are other potential uses for it on Earth; for example, as an ultimate compact source of energy to power an MHD electric plant. The exhaust product is a high-temperature plasma, which we met before in Chapter 6. MHD power does not have to be used to propel vehicles; it could also take care of those demand surges on a nation's electrical power grid. Will the treaties ban this use, too? We will risk a guess: yes. We will have other sources of energy from space by that time, and they do not involve the potential destruction of even a milligram of antimatter gone astray. So far as we know, antimatter drives are the ultimate in propulsion efficiency. They may have to wait, however, for those orbital factories.

As a footnote of interest, Jon Post reminds us that *if* we ever find so much as a single antimatter molecule of heavier stuff that we did not make—anti-uranium, for an extreme example—it would prove the existence of an antistar in which antihydrogen was cooked into heavier nuclei. This in turn would prove the existence of an antigalaxy. We could communicate with its citizens from a mutually safe distance, but handshakes between us would be a mite hazardous to our health.

The light sail, with some very cute twists including separable stages, is a propulsion system we may use while we are waiting to build those antimatter factories. The World Space Foundation, an amateur group with very professional members, has been developing a prototype solar sail for several years. With the help of JPL (under a technical assistance agreement), they are working out the details of guiding gossamer kitelike probes here and there, pushed by photon pressure—the impact of light from the sun.

The first three problems are sail construction; stowage in a small package that can unfurl properly in orbit; and controlling its attitude—the way the sail faces. Now if this were a government program, these guys would still be hassling over what to call the project. But they are amateurs, doing it for love. They had already built and unfurled a half-scale test version of their solar sail in Pasadena by August of 1981. It looked very much like a diamond-shaped kite with aluminized Mylar panels, but it was nearly fifty feet on a side. Their full-scale solar sail prototype has been complete for some time now. They are still working on attitude control vanes at the corners of the hundred-foot sail, and trying to figure out what to do with the static charge that will build up as ions strike the sail. But if they ever get the go-ahead to plop their gargantuan kite into the shuttle (it will be a small package when stowed, of course), they will be ready.

We were tickled to learn that a French group has something a little more sporting in mind: they would like to sponsor a race, with competitors steering their solar sails to the moon! Naturally, the racers would be remotely steered. The pressure of "solar wind" is almost infinitesimally slight, so the payload could not be anything more than communication gear and sensors. Sounds like fun, though. . . .

Over twenty years ago, Forward suggested unfurling an absolute mind-boggler of a sail in space, many miles wide. He did not intend it to be at the mercy of "solar wind," light pressure from the sun. He intended to beam light against it with a laser. The sail, of course—like its amateur-built predecessor—would have to be many times lighter than canvas.

Before we hang a label of "unobtainium" on such a structure, we should reflect that Drexler has designed some, based on a thin aluminum film (much thinner than foil) sail. If the sail is made to rotate slowly with ballast weights at the end of its arms, a six-mile-wide sail might weigh only about an ounce for every thousand square yards. Of course, a circular sail six miles wide would have some eighty-four million square yards of area, weighing roughly 5,000 pounds. That is a very manageable little package when carefully packed. We could tote it up to orbit today and set it rotating while our shuttle crew watched. Light pressure from the sun would very, very slowly accelerate it away from the sun. Naturally, we have a light source more energetic than that in mind.

A laser beam, *not* focused to a pencil-beam but sent from light years of distance if necessary, could gently accelerate the sail and anything it was attached to. This parachute-like device would be only a one-way probe unless we specify something to decelerate it with. Forward did suggest an electrically-charged spacecraft which could turn in an interstellar magnetic field, even if it could not slow down. Then Norem, in 1969, put those concepts together (whereupon Forward charged himself with a lack of imagination, a whimsy he can easily afford).

Norem would launch his sailcraft with a laser toward the vicinity of a target star—not directly toward that target. When it was up to cruise speed the light sail would unreel *very* long wires to increase the ship's capacitance, then electrically charge the ship, sail and all, with on-board equipment. If the sail were moving correctly through the magnetic field between stars, the sail would begin to circle around carrying the payload with it. With this long pass, the sail and ship would circle behind the target star, then head back toward us again and could be decelerated by the laser we aim from home. If we decelerated it properly, we could make the probe go into orbit around the target star. The advantage, of course, is that our probe could then stay in orbit to accumulate and transmit all the data we need, instead of making one fast flyby as the Voyager probes did near Saturn a few years ago.

There might be a problem in the added time required for the roundabout approach of Norem. There is some doubt, too, whether the interstellar magnetic field is strong enough to provoke the turn we need. Forward, as usual, has another card to play: a two-stage light sail.

The light sail is built so that it can separate into an inner circle and an outer ring. The outer ring is roughly ten times the mass of the smaller circle and can be considered the first stage because we intend to discard it in flight. Note that this mission is one-way, so everything must work automatically. We separate the outer ring when the vehicle is approaching Alpha Centauri, then pivot the inner circular sail so that it faces the big ring sail. A still more powerful laser, turned on years before so its arrival is properly timed, hits the sails. The ring sail is flexed so that, while it's being pushed harder, it reflects almost all that light onto the efficient front face of the small sail. This starts decelerating the small sail. The big ring sail is soon far ahead, reflecting energy from our laser which keeps slowing the second stage sail.

This deceleration involves so much energy reflected onto the circular sail that it might actually get hot enough to melt the sail material. We must design around that problem, maybe by lengthening the time and lessening the laser power a bit. But since virtually *all* the power hitting the big ring sail is then reflected back on the second stage which is one-tenth its mass, the little one slows down many times more quickly than the big one speeds up. Our mission ends with the first stage ring sail continuing on and the second stage sail going into orbit in the Centauri system. Other missions using these basic techniques seem limited only by our cleverness in modifying light sails. Would you believe three-stage light sails? With such a rig we could make a round-trip, detaching a still-smaller center portion of the sail again and making the stages accelerate away from each other as before. Of course, this suggests a crew, which suggests one bodacious big light sail craft to start with.

If we send a power laser to another star system, the lens will be a whopper. Forward assumes a Fresnel lens over 600 miles in diameter. O'Meara has designed one like a spiderweb that is half empty space and half gossamer Kapton plastic, and its weight is a little daunting: nearly 200,000 tons. That is no more massive than an oil tanker, but it's big, all right. It is so big it can focus its light down to a "spot" only sixty miles wide at the distance of Alpha Centauri. That spot would contain our two-stage interstellar sailcraft, assuming we keep the laser aimed correctly. Forward's two-stage probe would have a ring sail sixty miles wide and a circular inner sail twenty miles wide. The laser would need nearly six *terawatts* (TW), six trillion watts, to accelerate it away from our solar system. It would need a tremendous uprating, from six to twenty-one TW, for the second-stage deceleration beam. Well, we will simply have to build some big collectors close to home. We might build them in orbit around Venus for that matter, which is nearer the sun and has a handy gravitational field to anchor our laser hardware.

Part of our trouble in boosting starships, or even one-way starprobes, is that the bloody things are so massive. Until we can breed people with normal intelligence and one-pound mass, we may be stuck with certain minimum weights for manned missions. But with our passion for miniaturizing things, surely we can steal some ideas for gossamer unmanned probes. Physicists have been cudgeling their brains on this one for years, and Bob Forward has designed one he calls the Starwisp.

The Starwisp owes some of its design to a conversation between Forward and Freeman Dyson. Seems that Dyson already had stuffed into his files some notes on a sail propelled by microwaves. Such a sail can be made of a mesh of wires, and the holes in the mesh can be very much wider than the diameter of the wire. As it happens, Forward had been working out ideas for wire mesh probes using microchips at the wire junctions. Result: a design for a mesh sail only a thousand yards in diameter, weighing half an ounce, carrying a hundred billion microchips! That may sound pretty far-fetched, but it might be buildable.

To send Starwisp to probe the Centauri system, we need a solar-power facility to generate ten GW of microwaves. Then we build a really huge transmitter dish, actually a set of wire mesh rings separated by empty space, which works like a Fresnel lens. This dish beams its microwave energy against our mesh sail, which is made of aluminum wire of one-micron thickness. At each juncture of wire in the sail is a microchip that performs several jobs. The microchips control electrical flow through the mesh and can keep the sail oriented correctly. They are incredibly thin (half a micron thick) but five microns square, wide enough to act as sensors for light waves from infrared through ultraviolet. More about that in a moment; right now, we are accelerating our kilometer-wide sail with microwaves, boosting it toward a neighboring star.

The entire area of the wire mesh sail is feeling the push of that microwave beam, and the sail weighs next to nothing because the wire and the microchips are so thin. A ten-gigawatt beam will accelerate that sail at 115 g's—such a tremendous constant shove (actually not quite constant, diminishing a little with distance) that the sail reaches 0.2 c, one-fifth light-speed, in a few days. Then we can turn off the beam awhile. Our Starwisp will keep going until, twenty-one years later, it makes a flyby of Alpha Centauri.

Our microwave lens sends its power at light-speed, of course, so its beam can still "catch" our probe. As the probe begins to approach its target star, we bathe the probe again with the beam from home. The microchips, using the wire mesh as microwave antennas, collect the microwave energy. Some of those microchips are also acting as detectors, "looking" at the new star system, and then sending back what they see by modulating a return microwave beam. At a given moment, a single microchip may only report that it saw a certain amount of light in the visible spectrum—but when you collect the reports of few billion microchips, you can assemble all those spots of light and darkness into a picture of high resolution.

Our probe might send back a new picture every three minutes as it flew past the Alpha Centauri system. We could not send highly-detailed pictures much faster because, from that distance, the signal-to-noise ratio at our home receiver limits our rate of data reception. If we did not care about such high resolution, we could send pictures faster. But Starwisp will be passing through the system for hours. Plenty of time to send a hundred good pictures back.

You want to slow Starwisp down during its flyby so it could gather and report lots more data? So do we. Who is to say we could not design a two-or-three-stage probe—a Stagewisp? Some of the building blocks are already in our notes, thanks to the mental leapfrogging of Norem, Forward, Dyson, and others. Just remember that a more massive probe requires more power or less acceleration. On the other hand, we accelerated Starwisp up to interstellar cruising speed in just a few days, which is pretty inconsequential if it will coast for twenty-one years. Hmm. We *could* triple its mass without adding much time to the mission, by adding—oh, never mind. Your imagination can take it from here.

By now you probably have enough rough-cut design data to work out some starships of your own. You can start with a given propulsion system and see what missions it can be bullied into making. Or you can start with a given mission and see which propulsion system seems best for it. Always bear in mind that humans do not function well when pulling more than one or two g's for long periods. If you intend to boost your starship at a hundred g's for a quick trip, give it silicon chips for brains.

Also, unless you know something the professionals don't, you will be limited to velocities below light-speed. That means years-long trips between stars and, if you want human crews, you must design life-support systems to keep them happy—or asleep. Whatever we use for power, it seems likely that our first starships will *not* make a single jump from Nevada to the stars. If it's Orion, it pollutes. If it's a light sail, you cannot unfurl it in the air. If it's antimatter, nobody wants that much potential bang inside the atmosphere. And then there are the facilities you must have, and so on. When you study what's involved in assembling, fueling, testing, or launching these deep-space craft, you tend to conclude that we should do it in space. Our atmosphere is not an ideal environment for a starship.

Chapter 8:

FLYING MILITARY MISSIONS

We mentioned in Chapter 1 that space enthusiasts, both professionals and amateurs, are still debating the wisdom of "weaponizing" space. Meanwhile, the Soviet Union and the U.S. have demonstrated weapons that can intercept and destroy targets at orbital heights. These early space weapons do their damage by kinetic-energy kill; that is, by hitting the target with a small hunk of material at miles-per-second velocity. It's almost certain that several nations will soon have more advanced weapons flying inside and outside our atmosphere. We ought to have some idea how these military craft might be designed.

The U.S. has developed an Airborne Laser Lab (ALL) which, after some teething troubles, has proven that an airplane can shoot down a missile in flight with a HEL beam. That means we have laser installations light enough and powerful enough to install in a Boeing jet transport, and pointing/tracking devices that can point a hurtling missile for a kill using radiant energy. In aiming for a radiant-energy kill, you do not have to worry much about "leading" a cruise missile target because the beam is traveling hundreds of thousands of times faster than the target. Before long, we may adapt ALL techniques against low-flying cruise missiles.

The cruise missile is a troublesome little gadget because it flies so low and it isn't very big. We need highly developed IR sensors to spot and track several cruise missiles at the same time. Tomorrow's cruise missiles may use stealth technology and, in any case, it's hard to pick up their radar signatures when they are hedge-hopping. Flying at stratospheric heights, our ALL may have to identify and track cruise missiles from their hot exhausts, ignoring factory smokestacks and friendly low-flying aircraft which also have hot IR signatures. Future cruise missiles may be equipped with countermeasures—perhaps a very intense flare trailing on a wire-thin tube which emits a stronger signature than the engine exhaust. The ALL's detectors must then decide where the target really is, and then hit it.

A third-generation ALL might draw its own propulsion power and the energy for its HEL cannon from a ground-based laser installation, or even from one in space. We would just feed the beam to optics on the ALL and let the aircraft sort out what it needs for propulsion and shooting. But the more deadly it proves against cruise missiles, the more likely it is to draw an enemy HEL beam. This brings up a scheme suggested some years ago in a highly unclassified article (all right, then: in a science fiction paperback!) by one of the present authors.

If you are flying in the atmosphere and you're worried about taking a hit from an enemy space-based laser, you might give your vehicle a fairly thick carbon skin with sensors spread over it. It might take a second for the laser to hurt you through your carbon carapace (longer still, if it were spinning) and before that time elapses, your craft can be jittering in a pattern the enemy can't know in advance. Sure, the enemy space-based laser may track you, but it's hundreds, if not thousands, of miles away. It takes a few milliseconds for the enemy to sense that you dodged, to readjust his HEL beam, and for his next beam to reach you. It's unlikely that the beam would do more than scar your upper skin while your ship is virtually "trembling" at, say, five-g jitters, jerking several feet sideways and not in a predictable pattern.

And if you don't hold still long enough for the HEL to seriously damage you in a given spot, you can get away with minor damage. You might use aerodynamic decoupling (explained in Chapter 2) to generate those jitters, or you might use lateral jets. Why not jitter at twenty g's? We're thinking of the pilot, who will wish he had stayed home. If your aircraft isn't carrying live payload, you might jitter it quite a bit harder.

For a laser-dodger of this kind, you probably want to have your energy source on-board instead of feeding your own craft with remote laser energy. Maybe you could readjust your remote laser with perfect communication, and maybe you couldn't depend on it while jittering. No military commander wants to fight with iffy hardware. The best solution for long missions might be the laser feed, with auxiliary on-board power for the jitter mode.

Well, if that is a plausible way to dodge a space-based laser, why can't cruise missiles do it to escape the nearby ALL? Because the ALL is cruising over home territory, only twenty miles or so away from its approaching targets, and can readjust its aim in less time. We are talking about milliseconds for the readjustment, remember. Frankly, we know there must be figures on the exact times needed to adjust and fire another HEL beam. But if we knew what they were, the information would surely be classified. The point to remember is that the cruise missile is a relatively slow aircraft, and it carries neither the armor nor the power to escape a well-aimed HEL beam. The cruise missile is far from home, limited to on-board energy. Our carbon-armored craft would probably roam friendly skies; it could have an infinite I_{sp} for unlimited cruise—and it just might be there as a hunter/killer of cruise missiles.

Whether we employ jittering carbon-armored craft or not, we expect beam weapons to be contenders for air and space superiority. They may strongly affect the balance of world power—which explains why many countries are developing them. Any operational mobile platform (an interceptor, for example) that directs beam weapons must be designed from square one with the weapon's limitations in mind. If structural vibrations can get the optics out of alignment, those vibrations must be isolated. A beam weapon needs gobs of energy too; and if we decide not to depend on remote feed during a fight, our first beam-firing interceptors will have HEL beams of only modest energy. So *if* our laser energy is carried onboard, somewhere between a hundred KW and one MW is the best we can expect from these weapons for the next fifteen years or so. A big lumbering craft with the lifting capacity of a 747 might be able to fly a weapon with one to ten MW. It might even be uprated with carbon armor, just as the Harrier was uprated with advanced composites.

There's another problem with lasers on a light-weight platform: the laser and its power supply are themselves sources of vibration. Even if you solve that one, it's well known that laser energy is impeded by atmospheric effects. Heated by the laser, air can cause "thermal blooming" that defocuses the beam. Air can also deflect and scatter a beam. These effects are less severe for certain wavelengths, and it is also possible to adapt the transmitter optics to account for some of the trouble. Still, if we send a powerful laser at a long slant through the atmosphere, we can expect some problems. We would like to avoid them as much as possible. We're cobbling up a military system here, and military systems are expensive because they absolutely, positively *must* work when you need them. Later of course, we can adapt reliable military stuff to commerce, just as we have always done in the past. Meanwhile, a system that cannot be proven reliable is likely to be axed from the military budget. From a reliability standpoint, the problems of flying beam-weapon platforms begin to look overwhelming until we take a second hard look at remote power sources.

One way to minimize the problem is to screw the laser installation down firmly to the Earth, but on carefully-chosen high ground: a GBL installation on a high mountaintop. At a 10,000 foot altitude, air pressure is only two-thirds that at sea level so it creates less trouble for an energy beam. Because we are still on Earth's surface we have the advantages of easy access and repair, vibration isolation, and "hardening" under concrete or solid rock. By the end of this century we might have mountaintop GBLs of fifty to a hundred MW power. A mountaintop is a big hunk of real estate—enough for us to install three or four GBLs.

We tend to think of 10,000 foot mountains as rare, but Colorado alone has about forty of them. If we chose a network of sites carefully (we might lease a few in places like New Zealand, the Dominican Republic and Turkey), we could beam HEL power to relay satellites overhead and from there to any spot on Earth or above it. Some of those mountaintop locations are near known geothermal areas, which could power the turbines that generate those megawatts the lasers need.

Very well, then; we now have a dozen mountaintops spaced around the globe with, say, three 100-MW lasers on each. They are high enough to deal reliably with atmospheric effects, but how do we fight with them? If we keep a string of relay satellites in orbit waiting for targets, those satellites will be awfully easy for an enemy to find and target. Then when big trouble brews, those satellites might be among the first casualties. They might be able to defend themselves with great verve—they *can*, after all, dispense hundred-megawatt punishment—but they would be much more effective if they were highly maneuverable.

Few ships are more maneuverable than a single stage to orbit (SSTO) shuttlecraft of the sort we described in Chapter 4. Aerospace companies have studied several versions that would scramble for space when the red alert sounded. Like today's interceptors of the Air Defense Command, they would be maintained and serviced on Earth, always ready to go on the bounce at a moment's notice. They might not need human crews, however. We intend to bounce them to orbit and use them as fighting mirrors.

The "monocle" approach has been proposed by Lockheed. It involves a circular or elliptical platform, with a mirrorlike underside. The mirror consists of adaptive optics (flexible panels) in a phased array. The monocle's job is to receive and redirect a HEL beam, focusing the beam at chosen targets. The structure above the mirror contains hardware for pointing and tracking. The basic design assumes that the monocle is already in space, either in orbit or roughly at orbital height.

If we want to integrate the monocle into an SSTO shuttle using a laser boost, we will either have to wait for gigawatt GBLs or use a dozen mountaintop lasers beaming simultaneously. We have already described the kind of laser power it takes to boost even a one-man interceptor to orbit, and we don't expect to have that much power available from a single laser during this century. Our first SSTO monocles, then, may need several laser inlet ports and its underside must be kept mirror-bright. Our propulsion system might be the rotary IRH pulsejet described in Chapter 4, and/or the MHD fanjet covered in Chapter 6. The entire Monocle Shuttle would have a fat delta or radial (disk) shape, and it would not be over twenty feet long. We could build larger ones when we have more powerful lasers, in the next century.

Let's assume that we don't want to wait for lasers powerful enough to toss a monocle mirror up to fighting altitude. What else could we use during the next few years? As it happens, we have been decommissioning old missiles for a long time, which might serve as boosters for monocle mirrors. We need boosters that can be fired on a moment's notice. Our Minuteman and Poseidon missiles are solid-fuel ballistic birds designed for instant readiness, and the

Poseidons are stationed on submarines. Instead of destroying the Poseidons as Tridents become available, we might adapt the Poseidon to carry a monocle mirror instead of several warheads. On command, the Poseidon would lift its mirror to orbital height. The mirror would have to be stowed during boost phase and would deploy itself, perhaps unfolding its segments like a flower, as it gained orbital height. It would be available as a fighting mirror for several minutes before it fell back into the atmosphere. By that time, another Poseidon would be boosting its relatively cheap fighting mirror into place.

This scheme would be fairly cheap because it would use reliable boosters that we have already paid for. It would find its best employment against a salvo of enemy ballistic missiles, where one monocle mirror might zap dozens of warheads in its brief trajectory into space.

Several other designs have been proposed, including Lockheed's "binocle" and BDM's "perinocle." The binocle would use two telescopes linked together with an optical train of several smaller mirrors; one large dish to receive the feed laser, and another to transmit the final beam against a target. This scheme has some advantages; it permits us to isolate vibrations, track the feed laser beam, and point the final output beam more easily. On the other hand, we would have to cope with a lot of heat generated within the system when the entire power beam is focused down onto the series of very small mirrors between the two large ones. We repeat: the binocle is not two separate optical trains, but two sets of beam expanders linked end-to-end.

The perinocle design uses only two large mirrors, rather like a periscope with a rotary joint in the middle. It would not have so much waste heat to dispose of, because it completely eliminates the need for the small mirrors. But like the binocle, it might also be complicated. Since this is a military system, and since we already have some nifty future designs hanging around from Chapter 4, we think it might be most useful to combine a monocle fighting mirror with a radially symmetrical shuttle. This could be a marriage made in—well, if not in heaven, at least in orbit.

Let's assume we have already crammed some first-generation monocles into Poseidon payloads and it is now the turn of the century. We have the military big beamers in development, so it is time we developed a military SSTO shuttle to use them. That SSTO craft might look something like Figure 8-1. It's a bit over fifteen feet in diameter, with radial jet exhausts ranged around its circumference, and the flexible mirror covering its underside has about twenty layers of thin film coatings for very high reflectivity. It will take (and redirect for fighting) a fifty MW laser, but even if it reflects 99.9% of that energy it still absorbs fifty KW of it. This is roughly one-fourth of a watt per square centimeter surface area, not much different from the heat deposited by the sun in Earth orbit. That means we do not need to install a cooling system across the inner surface of that mirror's underside. The whole craft might weigh in at 2800 pounds. It is not very big. You could mock this thing up full-scale, with plywood and cardboard in your garage.

On its upper surface it will be more or less cone-shaped. If we can get a lot of aerodynamic lift from this frisbee on a long slanting acceleration to orbit, we might get by with less laser power during the boost to orbit. With aerodynamic help we might boost it up with a dozen lasers each beaming a hundred MW to the craft. If we don't get much aerodynamic help, and if the system efficiency is low, each of those dozen lasers might have to beam 300 MW each. We may very well fly this rig as an RPV (remotely piloted vehicle) to save weight.

On the other hand, an onboard pilot might not be much of a weight penalty. This is a true SSTO shuttle, capable of popping up into orbit and back down

Figure 8–1. SSTO Monocle Shuttle configuration for space-superiority fighter (Artist: R. Rue)

again within a few minutes, so we might not have to furnish the pilot with much more than an acceleration couch, a ham sandwich, and a hefty bottle of breathing oxygen. While on-station in space, this scout craft could use the adaptive optics on its mirror-bright underside to receive, adapt, and focus a beam against any military target within sight, even if that target is thousands of miles away.

Later, when we get more powerful lasers or more of them to gang for boost power, we could build a much larger version of this craft for a different purpose. We played with larger versions in Chapter 5 and found that we would have to make the structures of large craft very light. Author Myrabo has crunched some numbers to get a sixty-six footer which can haul about sixteen tons of cargo, half the payload of the NASA shuttle, to orbit. Bear in mind that with laser boost, we could do it every hour on the hour—but we might need ten gigawatts to lift it.

When we start talking about cargo, some of you may wonder if we are going from military to commercial missions. We're not; at least, not right away. Military outposts in space need resupply on schedule, and a radially-symmetrical SSTO (otherwise known as a sixty-foot frisbee) could do the job. A few years later, we should not be surprised to see all that military hardware and procedure used by commerical carriers. If it weren't for military transportation systems developed during World War II, we would have needed many more years to develop the globe-girdling commercial air transportation network we have today.

We have sketched out several future military flight systems, largely using designs borrowed from earlier chapters. We waited until now to rough out a real space cruiser, because it's a bit of a departure from all those frisbees.

For one thing, we think a real battle cruiser will probably have to cruise the deeps of space with only occasional support, in true dreadnaught tradition. It will be on-station, call it picket duty if you like, for long months. It will require a crew of at least a couple of dozen. And if it has to operate on its own, it will have to carry its own power. Well into the next century we may have antimatter engines, and then all that onboard power will be a cinch. But like it or not, until then we will have to use more well-developed technology. As with their deep ocean submersible counterparts, our first space cruisers will probably ply the void with nuclear power plants.

Many years ago, we developed solid-core nuclear reactors for the rocket engines of the NERVA project. We learned a lot from it—including the fact that solid-core reactors would almost certainly not serve us for the cruiser. For weapon energy, we have to put sudden, extreme power demands on our cruiser's engines. The heat buildup in solid-core elements would cause tremendous stresses inside the reactor. It might fail the first time we made a heavy demand on it. Sorry.

A particle bed reactor is another matter, though. It could accept those sudden peak demands, assuming we have some means for radiating waste heat away from the reactor after it's shut down. That is a mighty big assumption, because we will need hu*mong*ous radiators. There are lots of radiators that could handle the waste heat of a few gigawatt-rated reactors, but most radiator designs would mass more than the rest of the entire cruiser. That, to understate the case, is no small mass. Figure 8-2 shows a three-view of our space cruiser.

This critter is *big*. Notice the old NASA shuttle, docked under the chin of our cruiser in side view? We have a craft 500 feet long, with radiator return manifolds like enormous legs. Each return manifold extends about 300 feet from the cruiser's centerline. It has to, because smaller radiators would let the ship fry in its own waste heat.

These radiators are very special gadgets, originally proposed by Mattick and Hertzberg. They are called liquid droplet radiators, designed to dispose of prodi-

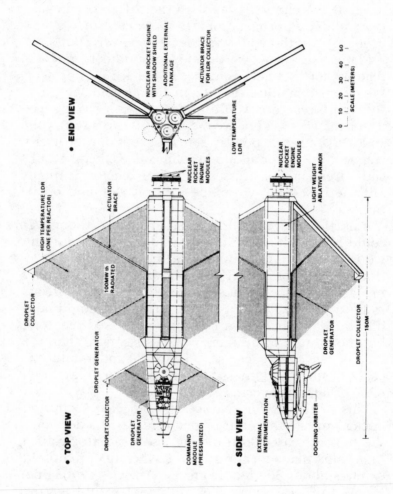

Figure 8–2. Manned space battle cruiser: Post-2000 Era

gious amounts of waste heat in moments. Here's how it works: each particle bed reactor sends its waste heat to a fluid-filled heat exchanger. That hot fluid, which may be a lightweight metal or an oil that is stable at high temperature, is then pumped to an array of nozzles lying along the fuselage of the cruiser. This array, like a very elongated (linear) showerhead, sprays the hot fluid into space. But not very far into space, because every one of those spray nozzles is aimed at a collector scoop on the end of that long, extended radiator return manifold.

The smaller a droplet, the more surface area it has per unit mass; and we are spraying billions of tiny droplets per second. As the droplets fly through the vacuum of space, they radiate their heat away. But we are not through yet. The droplets continue through space for a moment, then we catch them with the collector scoop and pump them back into the system, recycling for the next thermal load. Here is where we may have to get cute with the fluid. If we mix exceedingly tiny particles of iron or magnetic iron oxide into the oil, every droplet can be dragged along by a magnetic field. We embed magnetic coils in the collector out at the tip of that extension, and simply let a moving magnetic field sweep all those billions of droplets into a scavenger collector pump. The pump returns the cooled fluid back to the reactor heat exchanger, and we are ready to reuse it.

Notice the end-view in Figure 8-2; we have three separate engines, and for reliability each engine has its own reactor. These are multimode engines; we can use them all for propulsion, or for electrical energy to power onboard weapons, or some of each simultaneously. Each reactor is rated at about 2.5 GW; and the engines need propellant, and weapons require coolant. Much of the rearmost two-thirds of our cruiser's hull will be filled with tanks of liquid hydrogen. In between the tankage we install: the big guns.

For weaponry, the space cruiser may carry a massive free-electron laser, a neutral particle beam weapon, perhaps a microwave weapon, and an electromagnetic cannon. There is no doubt that you can accelerate lumps of material to meteorite velocity using a mass driver. In space, it could spit anything from steel pellets to compressed garbage without releasing much of a weapon signature. The projectiles would be slow in comparison to an energy beam, but they would be hard to see coming, and at several miles per second, a little dab would do you. If we installed an electromagnetic cannon fifty yards long in our cruiser and accelerated its projectiles at 50,000 g's, each projectile would emerge at about 4.3 miles per second. If a projectile the size of a golf ball hit a piece of enemy hardware at that speed, the kinetic energy of the collision could do terrific damage.

The free-electron laser is a whopper, as you can see in the cutaway, Figure 8-3. Its linac runs most of the length of the hull and the wiggler magnet is near the midpoint of the hull. As an alternative accelerator, we could use a storage ring which would also be located at the hull midpoint. We can call for whatever wavelengths we want against a given target, and the HEL beam is fired from final optics that retract into a turret near the forward end of the cruiser.

The neutral particle beam is another matter. It pours out radiation like clinkers from a tin horn, and we want to avoid firing it past the crew up front. So we fire the particle beam generally rearwards, and shoehorn its accelerator and optics into the hull near the FEL goodies.

We have a pretty potent cruiser here, self-sufficient and capable of long missions. We need enough crew to stand watches around the clock—at least two dozen people. Except for inspection and repair, the entire crew will probably live and work in the command module, which is the forward fifty-yard segment of the cruiser. We know that long space missions without gravity tend to rob our bodies of calcium, and several long missions may cause irreversible weakening of our bones. Well, how would *you* like to volun-

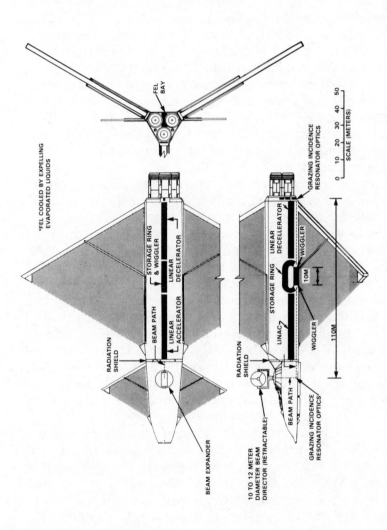

Figure 8–3. FEL system integration: accelerator alternatives

teer for a career that's guaranteed to cripple you? Or, looking at it from another angle, why spend huge sums to train our best people, knowing they will be good for only one or two missions?

This is depressing; it's wasteful and tragic and, with something the size of a space cruiser, it is unnecessary. The solution is in Figure 8-4: a one-g centrifuge for our crew quarters. Crew members will probably be *ordered* to stay there for a certain portion of every twenty-four hours when not on alert. The centrifuge is over sixty feet in diameter, and at its outer wall you feel Earth-normal force—a synthetic gravity.

Near the front of the command module, up ahead of the crew quarters, is the bridge, where the crew stands duty watch. The cutaway shows how we integrate the bridge, the centrifuge, and the FEL turret. The bridge windows give us a fair idea of the scale. It might get a little cramped for two dozen people after a few months, but submariners have it worse. And no one can complain about the view! The entire command module is fitted with radiation barriers, but the fighting bridge is especially well-armored. This is necessary protection both from enemy weapons and from stray radiation coming from our own onboard weapons. When the klaxon calls for battle stations, the entire crew will probably strap down in the armored bridge section.

One day we may have the power to boost cruisers of this size up from Earth and return them intact, but it will not happen in the next fifty years. Our prototype cruiser must be built in segments, probably here on Earth, then boosted to orbit piecemeal for final assembly. The big brute was not intended to fly in the atmosphere; it's a pure spacecraft. Even during major overhaul it will hang in a parking orbit.

We have become used to pure spacecraft looking like an orgy of granddaddy longlegs with pingpong balls, without any need for aerodynamic shape. Yet

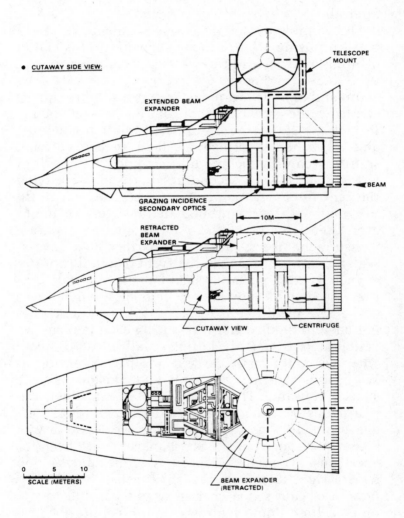

Figure 8–4. FEL system integration: telescope.

we must boost this monster up through the air for initial assembly, even if we do it in pieces. Don't be surprised, then, if it ends up looking pretty slick after all.

The command module is one segment we might boost up using a lot of today's hardware. Instead of orbiting a NASA shuttle, we might consider the option shown in Figure 8-5. Yes, the fifty-yard-long command module is a monster, but it's light. And we can leave the crew centrifuge out for the time being. In fact, we can bring up all the radiation shielding and other heavy furnishings later in conventional shuttles leaving the module stripped for its first voyage. We have a second good reason for leaving the centrifuge out momentarily, because we can fill the void with extra propellant tankage. We might even use elements of those tanks later as separate pressure chambers, just as submarines have several sealable compartments in the event of a hull rupture.

There is one infuriating detail about external tanks that you may already know: the biggest single piece of the NASA shuttle, its leviathan external tank, does not have to be thrown away during each launch! We deliberately discard it, letting it fall into the ocean, when we could easily carry it into permanent orbit. We have heard the arguments and consider it little short of criminal. There is still a lot of extra fuel, and many tons of structure, and potentially a lot of storage room, in that expensive tank we throw away. "No-deposit, no-return," is a bankrupt idea even for beer cans. When your deposit is in megabucks, you have a right to ask why it isn't stashed in orbit for later use. Our space cruiser would be able to use nine of those liquid hydrogen tanks for interior propellant storage, and perhaps others as exterior strapons. What other uses would the empty tanks have? Too many to list here.

Some of our cruiser hull structure might be largely constructed in orbit but, as we see in Figure 8-5, we could boost the entire command module in one shot.

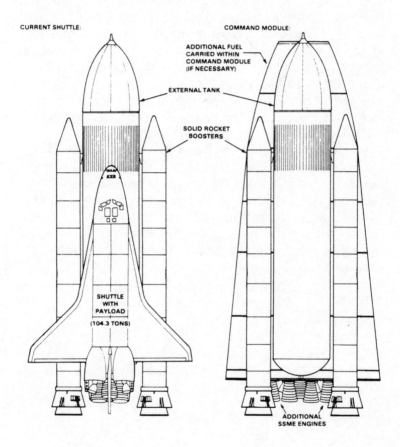

Figure 8–5. Command module launch configuration

Our next step would be to clear out the empty bay and install the crew centrifuge, radiation shields, and other interior furnishings. During the entire final orbital assembly process, the assembly crew can spend their off-duty hours in a one-g environment.

Did we hear someone say we need a pilot module like the shuttle's to boost this hunk into orbit? Right; and we have one. The command bridge is already installed in the cruiser's forward segment, and there's plenty of room for several mission specialists. Just don't forget to kiss this vehicle goodbye; it isn't coming back. It will soon be the smart end of a very large space-superiority cruiser, fitted out for long-duration missions in near-Earth space.

We could bore everybody to tears with discussions of trade-offs, and the "small" retractable liquid droplet radiators up front for environment control, and refitting our cruiser for antimatter engines and the Alpha Centauri trip; but we have to stop somewhere. Even if our military space cruisers never fire a shot in anger, some of them will make dandy vehicles for cargo and exploration.

Chapter 9:

THE ORBITING BONANZA

This is sometimes overstated, but history *does* tend to repeat a lot of broad patterns. Often, the repeated parts are those that worked like clockwork in the past, even if coincidence played a part the first time. We know now that the solar system offers riches to dwarf any treasure found in mankind's history. How are these discoveries likely to affect future flight?

For help with the answer we take another quick look backward, though it means we must shift our focus behind transportation for the moment, to the events that drive its progress. To keep from losing sight of our main topic in the first part of this chapter, we will say "TAKE NOTE" when those events suggest special designs in the future of the flight.

The California gold rush offers some insights for future bonanzas. There would have been no rush without voyages of discovery, and big ships that followed with settlers and their supplies. TAKE NOTE. Immigrant John Sutter had title to the huge area in central California where gold was discovered, but he would have needed an army to keep people out if enough of them wanted it. Sutter knew his history too, and tried to suppress the news about the big find at his millrace. San Francisco, at that time, had about 1,000 citizens. It also had a good harbor. When the rush began, treasure-seekers came from all over the world by every means of available transport. TAKE NOTE.

There were no transcontinental highways then, and the trip was dangerous, but if you gave a hoot you didn't belong out there anyhow. Ten years later, a few men had grown rich selling their gold but the hidden bonanza was in commercial supply. You could see it in the growth of San Francisco, which became *the* West's center of commerce during that short time. Shipowners got rich hauling passengers and freight to the frontier; farmers and storekeepers and teamsters fought frontier perils, and reinvested buckets of money. And in 1861 the big windfall began with the incorporation of the Central Pacific Railroad Company.

Everybody knows about the success of the transcontinental railroad, and the stunning wealth it brought to industrialists. TAKE NOTE. Now there were genuine cities to supply out West. The engineering of railroads was fairly well understood, and soon huge advanced vehicles were on the drawing boards. The juggernaut intermountain express locomotives eventually became early equivalents of uprated NASA shuttles, thrilling brutes designed to haul the thousands of tons of cargo and passengers headed for those new centers of commerce. Studebaker set up a manufacturing facility out where the action was, and became famous with improved wagon chassis, catering to transportation needs we might call feeder lines today. TAKE NOTE. Horse breeders made their piles (there's a pun in there someplace). A man like Levi Strauss with a better idea for clothing on the new frontier could become legendary with his Levi's. Much of the real bonanza, then, came in transportation and services.

Some of this was repeated in the Klondike. You can find other parallels, including South Africa and the Australian opal mining regions. We will see some of them again when we begin to mine the valuables circling our sun. It's going to bring some fast evolution in the future of flight.

Just for fun, before examining the riches beyond

Earth, let's toss out a few scenarios of the future, based on the gold rush. Story 1: A tailor with an eye for materials development improves the fit and toughness of space suits. A century later, most space suits are called by his name no matter who makes them. Story 2: Commercial space travelers, sick of sudden accelerations and vibrations during boost and deceleration, start getting choosy about the spacecraft they are willing to ride. One firm designs much better vibration-isolation fittings, and sets up shop in orbit to refit any ships that can pay. Pretty soon, if a commercial spacecraft *doesn't* have this firm's logo on its airlock, travelers are likely to wait for one that does. Generations later, that firm is building entire fleets of spacecraft for private citizens. Story 3: A prospector, down on his luck, wins title to a worked-out asteroid in a poker game. It's a big asteroid, but all it has left now is a lot of mass. Then nearby asteroids are found that are worth billions, and our prospector finds his new property is valuable as a spa because it has enough gravity to be a favored hangout for other miners. Let's add a kicker appropriate to the new setting: the orbit of the spa gradually carries it away from the popular region and it's so massive the owner cannot afford to change its orbit. He sells it cheap—and then a new bonanza is discovered in the region the big asteroid is slowly approaching. Story 4 is one we'll have to guard against: A few freighter barons, through fraud, get legal claim to moonlets near Saturn. Their goon squads browbeat settlers, and they force out competition, until legislation and outright brush wars with settler groups finally bring them under a sort of control. In time their names show up on the labels of universities, natural features, and hotels famous throughout the solar system.

Of course, science fiction writers have been mining history books and processing plots like these for many years. Today, some of those writers include renowned scientists and engineers like Arthur Clarke and Robert Heinlein who, like Kantrowitz, see that the only things separating us from a future of abundance are two avoidable failures: nerve and imagination. These world-class futurists are doing their level best to tell us that the big bonanza is out there now, and has been out there since our planet was new, orbiting the sun and awaiting those who can couple nerve and imagination.

We did not need to go beyond Earth until its human population grew beyond four billion or so. It is headed for six billion now, and humanists across the globe are predicting disaster within the next few generations, in books like *The Limits To Growth*. A few high-tech humanists see our clear alternative, which we choose to call the orbiting bonanza.

Mining the resources of the solar system is not yet taken seriously by enough people; we are only beginning to understand the staggering, unbelievable wealth out there. To begin with, there is enough energy out there to feed cheap kilowatts to every citizen on Earth, including those of Bangladesh. (Footnote: Sutter's gold was discovered while a crew was building a millrace to tap the cheap energy of the American River. Watch for a future parallel.) Skylab proved that even a small solar power satellite (SPS) can be a prime producer of energy, feeding sixteen KW to the lab from its array of solar cells. With the right hardware, Skylab could have beamed some of that power down Earthside just to demonstrate that it works. Peter Glaser, in his pioneering studies, suggested that we make them larger—*vastly* larger—and place them 22,300 miles out. This is the geosynchronous Earth orbit (GEO), where our media satellites are today. The spidery structure of the SPS can be unbelievably gossamer because it does not have to deal with gravitational loads, merely orienting its great glittering flat expanse of solar cells toward sunlight, twenty-four hours a day. The solar array can directly generate electricity which will be fed to the transmitter module, then beamed down to a simple receiving antenna on Earth. Such a receiving antenna would be much easier for an emerging country to build than massive hydroelectric dam projects.

An SPS about three miles wide by seven miles long can generate roughly five billion watts, equal to several of today's nuclear power plants. It will not gobble up fossil resources and it will not pollute our earthly nest either. There's enough room in GEO for literally thousands of them, and they could spell the difference between life and death for Third World countries where most of the local biomass has already been burnt for energy. We suggest (in fact, we expect) collaborations with needy countries for cheap SPS electricity.

The SPS is one of the most obvious solutions to crushing problems in most parts of the world today. Typically, some political figures wave it aside saying it's a solution we cannot put into use for twenty years or so—*but they don't find any other long-term solution.* Notice the pattern? If the solution cannot be soon enough to boost them back into office in the next election, they are likely to ignore its long-term value. It takes a special kind of politician to focus on solutions that can be fully appreciated only after he has retired. Huge engineering projects, like mass-transit networks (TAKE NOTE) and space assets, tend to be solutions of that sort.

Right about now, somebody with a calculator is figuring out how many tons a three-by-seven mile solar cell array would mass, and is wondering if we *really* expect to boost all that stuff up from Earth. No, we fully intend to get it from the moon and, a bit later, from asteroids. The materials will be a whole lot cheaper that way and we know bloody well they are out there. We have talked to the men who collected lunar regolith (moondirt), and we have handled the stuff, and they have proved that surface mining on the moon is a cinch. You can separate some magnetic ores just by magnetizing a garden rake and pulling it across the surface.

Lunar regolith is about 40% oxygen, combined with other elements. Next time we are next door (on the moon), we really ought to set up a little automated processing plant. It would run on solar power and would start filling tanks with oxygen for storage. Life-sustaining oxygen, in enormous quantity: surely a treasure on our airless moon. Nor would we toss the other materials aside.

Silicon is there, lots of it, along with plenty of iron and aluminum. There is enough titanium and magnesium and phosphorus to repay us. We can see the structural uses of the metals, but phosphorus? Right; we need it (and some other stuff) if we intend to raise crops in processed moondirt. And silicon? This is the main element we need to make trillions of solar cells. There are other important elements in lunar regolith, but we can see that the moon has the raw materials we need to account for nearly all of the mass of an SPS. Or of ten *thousand* of them, if we need them. We can separate the materials on the moon, boost them up from its weak gravity, and take them to Earth orbit much more cheaply than we could boost them from Earth itself. TAKE NOTE.

The lack of atmosphere on the moon is another advantage, because we do not have to fight air drag during boost. It even allows us to use one orbital boost system that'd be impractical on Earth: the mass driver. We could lay the mass driver flat on the lunar surface like a miles-long drag strip, or on a very shallow ramp, and boost materials to lunar orbital velocity before they rise very far. The next step would be orbital transfer from the moon to GEO, which requires comparatively low energy.

The mass driver is not considered a candidate for practical payload launches from Earth because we do not have launch sites high enough and it would be impractical to build them. A payload boosted from Earth to orbital velocity from a 10,000 foot high mountain might be incinerated by air friction before it got beyond most of our atmosphere. A few schemes have been suggested in which a mass driver payload from Earth would carry its own particle beam projector and literally punch a partial vacuum hole for itself through the air. It might be possible. One thing certain: it would create quite a racket, following its own thunderbolt to orbit.

One more thing about lunar mass drivers. We noted in Chapter 8 that our battle cruiser's magnetic cannon—which is a mass driver adapted as a weapon—has to accelerate its small payloads at thousands of g's. We can lower the acceleration a great deal by making a lunar launch track many miles long, but that gets expensive. It's also more expensive when you accelerate more bulky or more massive payloads. Chances are, early lunar mass drivers would not be designed to boost humans up from the moon. With life-support systems and whatnot, people are just too bulky and tender to be part of those payloads on a short fast track.

Things might be different a century from now, when the moon has its own physics institute and industrial centers. With travelers constantly leaving the lunar surface, we might find it practical to build mass drivers energetic enough to carry human cargo, and long enough to do it without acceleration loads that mash folks flat. TAKE NOTE. The moon is almost certain to be prime real estate for some of our first off-Earth population centers, and commerce there will support a lot of big projects. Sure, lunar processing will produce vital materials for low-energy shipment around the solar system; but the development of our moon will go far beyond the mining ventures. San Francisco's Golden Gate Bridge was not built for hauling gold dust; the commerce across it is more important than gold.

Quite possibly other crucial elements, lacking from the lunar samples we have collected, lie in wait on the moon for prospectors. That could include water in the form of ice, but at this writing we cannot be sure the moon, by itself, has all the materials we need. We will need hydrogen, nitrogen, and carbon in great quantities, which the moon seems to lack. Must we ship these elements from Earth at great expense? We probably could, but it now seems certain that we will not have to. The Asteroid Belt, a region of tiny planetoids circling the sun between the orbits of Mars and Jupiter, is all but certain to have the missing materials.

We have gathered enough information about asteroids to know that there are tens of thousands of them, perhaps millions more too small to study from Earth. We can learn a little about their composition when a sizeable asteroid passes between us and a known source of light, such as a star, because we can spot some materials from their spectrographic signatures. We are sure that many big asteroids are of the carbonaceous class. That means they are rich in organic stuff, the hydrogen and nitrogen and carbon we do not yet find on the moon. Another class of asteroid is the metallic class, chiefly nickel and iron. Scientists are wary about saying, "Most meteorites that strike the Earth are asteroids," in blunt terms. That's the overwhelming opinion, though. If it is true, then the asteroid belt will furnish us with water, high-strength steels, carbon, nitrogen, and so on—by the billions of tons. Astronomers doubt that all those asteroids were ever a planet, but there is no doubt whatever that altogether, they would make a sizeable planet for mining.

For our purposes, though, they are even better than a single planet, because they are in so many small chunks. During their formation, they may have cooled quickly enough (thanks to their small size) to concentrate some elements in veins or pockets that we can mine easily. We are just not yet sure how easy it will be. We know that this vast whirligig of materials beyond Mars deserves its own missions of discovery during the next few years. TAKE NOTE. We repeat that there is no real doubt that the needed materials are there; it's only a question of finding

enough nerve and imagination to find the best ways
of bringing them back.

Ceres is the largest known asteroid, a ball of rock
and organic stuff about 600 miles across. Ceres is big
enough to have useful gravity, yet small enough that
you could escape from it with no sweat. However, it
is a long way off. We would use lots of energy to get
there and back with a mining expedition if we wanted
to do it in a few weeks or months. It would take
much less energy if we were sending megatons of
processed materials back to lunar orbit by automated
slow freighter, spending years for the trip. TAKE
NOTE.

At this writing, the *L5 News* publishes a running
technical debate on the merits of the moon vs. asteroids as our most likely source of stuff for early space
construction projects. Now we find a welcome complication; Eleanor Helin (rhymes with "colleen") of
JPL is discovering asteroids near the Earth. With
support from The Planetary Society and other scientists, Helin has plots of several asteroids that whiz
near the Earth every so often in elliptical orbits. One
or more of these little renegades may be ripe for a
rendezvous with a mining expedition before the turn
of the century. These bodies are "little" in comparison to Ceres, by the way. Each one probably has
more mass than Mount Everest, and may have more
necessary materials than we can use for years to
come.

The great debate, moon vs. asteroids, will not be
properly settled until we have lots more information on those near-Earth asteroids. We see no other
mining candidates as likely for the year 2000 or
thenabouts. That is not to say there are no other
possible candidates. How about a comet, a ball of
dirty ice with a reflective vapor tail, that we could
mine for water? A few thousand tons of ice nudged
to lunar orbit would be a wonderful source of water
and of hydrogen for fuel. Comets are often newly
discovered, looping in on long elliptical paths from

a light year away, and we simply cannot know whether we will find one coming in on a near-Earth pass at matchable velocity a few years from now.

(Another pesky footnote: we still don't know, but it is likely that several wild-and-wooly events in our past were the results of asteroids or comets that did not pass us by. Forget the Sunset Crater in Arizona; what about the hot debate over the extinction of most dinosaurs about sixty-four million years ago? If it was caused by an asteroid impact, at least we can be pretty sure some asteroids are treasure troves of rare metals like osmium and iridium because such stuff is relatively plentiful in strata that lay exposed on Earth's surface at that time. And the Tunguska Event of 1908 in Siberia? A small comet might have been the culprit, melting away into steam in its furious miles-per-second passage into our atmosphere. Whatever the heck it was, it blew entire forests over with the blast of a Mount St. Helens without leaving a detectable crater. TAKE SPECIAL NOTE.

Now let us assume a strong likelihood that we will be mining the moon and asteroids, and maybe cometary nuclei, within thirty years. Is that the sum total of the orbiting bonanza? For the short term, maybe yes. But by then we will be able to cruise out to the other planets for mining ventures. We will probably put people on Mars, but Mars has a hefty gravity nearly equal to Earth's. All else being equal, we are more likely to keep favoring small bodies that do not make us pay heavy boost penalties in escaping their gravities. Since the Voyager probes, we have discovered valuables to be mined from the moons of Saturn. Would you believe natural gas?

Saturn's biggest moon, Titan, is bigger than ours— 3,000 miles in diameter. It has more gravity than we would like, but it has an atmosphere too. Titan's "air" is a hellish rust-colored smog, more dense than our own air and utterly fatal to breathe, but it includes nitrogen, methane, ethane and other organic stuff we need. Though we could use the ethane,

methane, acetylene and other stuff as we use natural
gas, we could separate its hydrogen and carbon for
other purposes, without ever landing on Titan. We
could send ramscoop ships down in orbital passes
and scoop up countless tons of that smog, compress
it in tanks, and send it back liquified or frozen to
lunar orbit. TAKE NOTE.

Saturn has smaller moons, and literally countless
hunks of hardpan forming its rings. If we need that
stuff, we can get it. Unlike the asteroids, it's all in the
same locale and we can use Saturn's gravity as a
pivot to swing us into position for stealing whatever
we want. That doesn't mean our theft is cheap in
terms of energy; Saturn is way, *way* out there past
Jupiter and sunlight is a hundred times fainter there
than, say, on the moon. We may use solar panels
there, but at that distance from the sun they will not
have the electrical output we like. Power beams from
Earth orbit can fill the need if necessary, with huge
phased-array transmitters.

Solar panels near Jupiter will not generate the
juice we need either, but this giant planet is nearer
the sun than Saturn. And while we will not want to
land on Jupiter, we can steal his daughters blind!
Some of Jupiter's moons are nearly as large as Titan,
with more gravity than our moon; but they just
might be worth a landing. Why? Well, Europa is a
frigid miss, covered with ice. We could use it and she
would never miss a few billion tons of it. The same
with Ganymede and Callisto. Io must be a problem to
old Jupiter; she's a fiery one, with almost constant
volcanic eruptions that spatter her with pancake
makeup (sulfur). Voyager photos show that some of
those eruptions send sulfur and its oxide at least 200
miles high. Since sulfur dioxide is a gas containing
lots of oxygen, this is one place where we could
scoop up oxygen without landing. We could hang
around with a scoopship and make a pass at Io to
steal pure sulfur, but the maneuver could be in-
sanely dangerous. You would never know when the

stuff you were scooping might become denser than you bargained for, and the plume might send up some stones too. Io is definitely not a lady; she can throw rocks at you.

So much for metaphors with the names of Jupiter's daughters, which astronomers borrowed from mythology. The scientific spacecraft Galileo should give us much better information when it nearly grazes Io in the summer of 1988. Io's atmosphere is not thick enough to muster a good sneeze, but it might be worth mining. Jupiter's other moons may have different attractions for us. We will just have to get off our buns and find out.

It is clear that the known resources in our solar system can be mined and processed to give us cheap solar energy, and materials for colonies beyond the Earth. What the moon lacks, we can provide from other sources. But we have not mentioned food yet, and we cannot afford to boost a million TV dinners a week up from Earth. What about growing crops out there?

Some plants can be grown without gravity, as the Soviets proved in Soyuz experiments with cabbages and wheat. The lunar soil lacks water and nitrogen, but we can supply both from asteroid sources. We have already grown plants in soil brought back from the moon, but we had to add nitrates and water. Some crops (pineapples are one famous case in point) need special trace elements, but if necessary we could ship a few tons of those materials from Earth. We need not worry about potato bugs and tomato worms unless we are idiots enough to carry them from Earth. The same goes for mosquitoes, biting flies, and lots of other small beasties we must deal with here.

Growing crops beyond Earth is really just a special case of greenhouse farming, which has become better understood and more useful during the past few years. A lot of Americans, Europeans, Japanese and Middle-East Islamics already eat a lot of greenhouse food even though many of them don't know it.

When you can control nearly all the variables on your farm, you get heavier yields and premium-price crops. It's a fair prediction that today's controlled, virtually closed-cycle agribiz will lead directly to greenhouse farming—chickens and all—beyond the Earth. TAKE NOTE. General Electric may seem an unlikely source of expert help, but they have been developing closed-cycle farming of this type for years. Go ahead, ask them; just don't expect them to share all their high-tech secrets because they can turn them into cash.

It would be too optimistic to say that GE, or anybody else, could set up greenhouse farming on the moon and be sure of instant success. Some plants may get too enthusiastic in the low gravity, which could lower their yield of edible stuff. Maybe we can genetically tailor our cash crops to lunar conditions; agriculture labs in state universities have enough experience in this field to have a start on the problem. And maybe some crops will just have to be grown in special greenhouses in orbit around the moon. The greenhouses will rotate for artificial Earth-normal gravity and the atmosphere might be so rich in carbon dioxide the greenhouse workers will have to wear masks and carry their own breathing mixtures.

The first successful greenhouse in lunar orbit, or in Earth orbit for that matter, will show that we can do the same anywhere else in the solar system, given the energy. It will probably be solar energy during the next century, out to (at a guess) the Asteroid Belt. We may not necessarily have to carry vast solar arrays out that far, however. We can convert sunlight to laser power near Earth and beam it to our mining colonies much more efficiently than the sun does it. Can we grow cash crops in asteroidal dirt? High time we started finding out. We would bet even money that someone has crushed meteorites into dirt for rough-order experiments along this line.

We could go on with details of the great shining L5 colonies near Earth where many of our grandkids may want to migrate, of patrol craft, and so on. Perhaps we do not need to; we have already taken note of a dozen future needs for special flight missions. Those needs will drive the designs, and they will call for pilots and crews who will be picked for virtues that match the mission. Your ideal fighter pilot isn't your ideal supertanker captain. We took note of missions that will require both kinds.

Our first big ship for a voyage of discovery was mandated by President John Kennedy, and it was flying before some of our readers were born. Ten years ago you could buy rocket-powered models of our Saturn monster with its Apollo module perched on top like a dinghy. Nowadays you can fly models of our first supply ship, the NASA shuttle. No guesswork there! The guesswork begins when we try to foresee the sequence that actually begins the rush.

Most likely our next major operational craft will be a space station in LEO, while we develop bigger shuttles already on the drawing boards. (In the trade we call them Heavy Lift Launch Vehicles, or HLLV.) We will still be using old-fashioned chemical propellants and cursing their inefficiency. These big express brutes will lift, section by prefab section, the ships we assemble to put our first settlers on the moon.

Those ships, too, will probably use chemical propellants (or possibly closed-cycle nuclear electric [ion] drives), because we will not yet have the big SPS arrays to beam gigawatts of propulsion power to our moonships. Our first moonships will probably leave a small multipurpose "lifeboat" module in lunar orbit and land the great majority of their mass on the moon's surface. (Footnote on power: for political reasons we may try to avoid putting nuclear power plants there. A solar array deployed over an area a hundred yards wide by two hundred long, three acres or so, will provide a steady megawatt when Earth's shadow is not hiding the sun. We will store power for the dark times. It is possible that our first SPS will be placed at a libration point, beaming constant laser power to receiving antennas on the moon.)

The settlers, who probably will not think of themselves that way, will use a lot of moondirt and a little plastic to form hard, thick reflective shells over their inflatable domes. By deflating the domes slightly they could reduce thermal conductivity to the shells. This book is not the right place to detail all the tricks they could use; the point is that the domes will house people who set up the mining and processing equipment. Early products will include iron girders, aluminum sheet and wire, and an endless quantity of doped silicon cells for more solar arrays. Before long they will have solar panels spread out on the lunar surface so wide you can see them from Earth with an amateur's telescope. That means they will have hundred-megawatt power available. There will be enough slag from the processing to form armor plate against solar flare radiation, and you can bet on a military side to that.

Military craft of this period may include the first of the cruisers we have described, assembled in orbit and maintained at irksome expense; and at least one could be refitted for the Mars landing. Properly scheduled and fueled, this leviathan might go on to prospect for the goodies in Jupiter's vicinity. The crew, remember, can luxuriate in one-g artificial gravity. Every member of that crew, like the volunteers with Lewis and Clark, might sell the story to the media later. (Ironic footnote: Meriwether Lewis demanded that his men keep journals, then bitterly resented their attempts to publish them. He was publishing his *own* journals, you see. Captains can be like that. . . .)

By this time we should have laser-boost developed enough to build the earthly fleet of little automated SSTO craft with small payloads, described in Chapter 5. Those payloads will then be repacked in orbit and used to supply our moonminers with stuff they cannot yet produce, like food and hydrogen. Meanwhile, we build a mass-driver with locally-produced wire and girders on the moon. We kick sheet aluminum and solar cells up to lunar orbit with the mass driver. Then we use a hundred MW laser from our moon power station, which gently boosts an endless train of smallish payloads toward a precise high Earth orbit. We may need the multipurpose "lifeboat" crew to oversee some of this. They will need very special little vehicles, the equivalent of rocket-powered scrambler bikes, to secure errant payloads. There will be hair-raising stories about their emergencies, and women may prove better at this particular duty than men. It's also possible that we will use tele-operation, remotely-piloted machines to do the most dangerous parts of this work. Who wants to be first to repeat the John Henry legend on this job?

The rush to orbit will not start yet; not until our orbital crews have built several—maybe several dozen—big SPS units near Earth, using hardware coaxed from raw materials on the lunar surface. Only then will power be cheap enough to tempt industrialists into building affordable, commercial SSTOs boosted by energy beams. And those energy beams can be sent from orbit with SPSs providing the power. Even if the French chose to build only one size, the Japanese and Americans would build something different. Soon after that, we would see commercial SSTOs carrying hundreds of travelers to orbiting labs and medical facilities with each launch. We would also see smaller craft, eventually some intended to carry a few VIPs, like executive jets or limousines today. These vehicles will create the feeder lines into near space, and they will feed the rush into space.

These varied SSTO craft, many of them using engines we have already described, will be different from the heavy cargo carriers that move payloads from orbit to orbit. Orbital transfer vehicles (OTV) need not carry weight penalties of aerodynamic wings, heat shields, and so on because they are pure space freighters and tugs. Energy will still cost money, and the competition will carve away what the OTVs don't need.

Translunar freighters will look as lumpy and unflyable as local OTV ships. By strapping on more external tanks, an OTV might do double-duty for lunar trips. The long half-elliptical curve of this trip, from Earth orbit to lunar orbit, will take five days at the most—less, if we are willing to squander more energy.

We have suggested that later ships of discovery, out to Mars and beyond, may look like the military cruisers they were before refitting. But they might also look like bundles of tanks and girders with a rotating crew wheel, if we choose. The scoop modules for atmospheric mining, and the sailplane-winged probes for flight in other-world atmospheres, will be strapped on to girders beefed up to take external loads during acceleration. Since payload mass will be at a premium during these voyages of discovery, it might make sense to carry probes convertible to several missions. You might try roughing out a design for a recoverable probe powered by laser from the mothership, with provision for wings and mass-collection scoop as appropriate. Will the probes be remotely piloted or manned? You decide, but don't send the kid out in a crate without life-support. A pilot makes the probe more massive, so you will need a good reason for that decision.

Commercial mining in the Asteroid Belt has its hazards, including unwelcome traffic. We are thinking of tiny asteroidal lumps, moving at speeds different enough from yours that they could zap your ship. You may want to hide your ship in cavities of larger asteroids—and that means you might even want to design it in modules so you can hide tanks in one cavity, crew quarters in another. In any case, you will probably carry radiators, and massive armor against that gravel traffic. One thing sure: you will not need wings out there. Asteroids don't have atmospheres.

We will probably bring processed materials back from the Belt by slow freight. A specially-valuable cargo—say, a few thousand tons of rare metals for lunar research labs—might be worth a faster orbit, and passengers will prefer to return in a few months rather than years. So design your Belt freighters with room for a few paying passengers. If you are carrying no live cargo, you can bundle the cargo up and use a detachable tug to inject it into a trajectory that sends it back toward lunar orbit. The tug with its engines will weigh a fraction of that payload, and one tug can fire off a hundred cargoes a year.

What will Belt tugs and freighters use for energy? They are so far from the sun that a nearby SPS may not be as practical as closed-cycle, solid-core nuclear reactors. Frankly, we expect to see nuclear power in the Belt; it's to mankind's advantage, and the Belt is a long way off. HEL beams from Earth orbit may be good power sources too. Just remember that the HEL mirrors must be huge to maintain useful focus diameters across half of the solar system. The receiving optics may be bigger than the tug, and we must not forget the danger from local gravel traffic. Perhaps you will want to design an armored collapsible receiving mirror. If you do, make sure your tolerances are very close; your mirror must open out just exactly right every time.

The reaction mass for Belt freighters can be hydrogen, because the carbonaceous asteroids can furnish it. On the other hand, they can furnish lots of other stuff that is not worth shipping back. It may seem wasteful to use oxygen as a reaction mass, but oxygen is plentiful on the moon, probably not worth the transshipment from the Belt. Oxygen does not have the I_{sp} of hydrogen either, but so what? It may be cheaper if the supply is plentiful out there.

Ramscoop ships for mining Titan's atmosphere should have adjustable wings, compressor pumps, radiators so the gases can be frozen, and whopping big engines. On a given pass the miner might cruise low, deploy the scoop, inhale a charge of gas, then swing his wings out and boost up beyond the smog. Then he will wait until his radiators have disposed of waste heat, retract his wings, and make another pass. We might design radiators *into* the wings, while we're at it. The ramscoop need not be wider than (at a guess) the ship itself, and should be retractable. Titan's smog is thicker than our sea-level air, so you will need power to cruise through it. The scoop will generate a lot of drag. What if your scoop stuck open during a low-level pass? Maybe you would have to jettison it. A designer's life is not a simple one—but compared to a ramscoop miner, he has it easy.

Obvious danger lurks in all these ventures, and we are sure to see lifeboat modules on some ships. You can have a field day designing them, distress beacons and all. The search and rescue ships, and their crews, will have to be rigged for speed and ready for dumb blunders in panic situations.

Previous writers—Clarke among them—have suggested protection of mother Earth against future collisions with comets and asteroids. We might refit Belt tugs for this, using their big engines to match speed with anything that looks threatening. On the other hand, it might work the other way around with early comet interceptors being refitted as Belt tugs. The tug would not have to break up the interloper, just nudge it off to a harmless path. But let's imagine an asteroid on collision path with Earth, with too much mass for the tug to handle directly. Maybe this would be a situation where Ted Taylor's Orion system would be welcomed by everybody. The tug might place special propulsion nukes against the asteroid, maybe with directional pusher-plates if there is enough time to attach them, then detonate the bombs to change the asteroid's course a bit. This is an iffy scenario, but better than another Tunguska Event over London or Chicago.

We mentioned orbiting greenhouses because they are vehicles, in a way, and because they will need medium-sized OTV supply craft. The first ones will probably be perfected in lunar orbit, processing moondirt with asteroidal water and nitrogen. It would probably take years for an economical trip, but we could ferry a mile-long orbital greenhouse to the orbit of Mars or the Belt for settlers there. The gravity of Mars is almost that of Earth, so it would not pay to boost Mars dirt up to orbit. If the soil of Mars can be made to yield crops, then our Mars greenhouses should be built on the planet itself. Yes, we could ferry the greenhouse to the Belt more cheaply if we left the dirt out until we got there. But so far, we do not know whether asteroid dirt will grow our vittles. In lunar orbit, a greenhouse gets all the sunlight it needs. In Mars orbit, it might get adequte sunlight without external reflector mirrors. Near the Belt, it will need huge external reflectors or power for interior lights. Supply ships will carry trace elements and organic materials to the greenhouse, and will haul away a roughly equal mass of food. This resupply is necessary because the organics and trace elements are constantly depleted. They become part of the food which gets harvested and taken away by the next supply ship.

So it looks like the orbiting bonanza will create a lot of different missions, and that means several very different designs. We will see wings over Mars and Titan and any other atmosphere we poke around in. We will see ships refitted, especially old military ships, for long missions. And when the energy gets cheap enough, we will see a lot of ships used for missions they were never designed for. That could get to be a problem. But we never said bonanzas did not create problems; we just said that this one can solve most of our present problems.

Chapter 10:

THE PANIC BUTTON

The history of flight has had its little panics and its big disasters since the myth of Icarus, and it would be wrong-headed to pretend that we could altogether escape them in the foreseeable future. We do expect fewer unpleasant surprises, because now we can model so many experiments with computers, and we can test some new hardware by remote control. We will not become infallible, though. In Chapter 1 we suggested that citizens might casually call for megawatts like demigods calling fire from heaven; when we control this much energy, we must be ready for trouble. So far in this book we have concentrated on ways to make things go right, but if we want reliable systems we must study how things go wrong. One major part of reliability engineering is developing unlikely scenarios that require the panic button. In a way, their charter includes science fiction.

(Footnote: some useful fiction has been published involving this kind of scenario. What if a lovely stowaway adds enough mass to assure that keeping her aboard will, with utter certainty, cause a crucial spaceflight to fail? Tom Godwin wrote the answer a generation ago. Might it be possible to transfer passengers to a rescue ship in a vacuum, *lacking pressure suits or life-support equipment*, without killing them? Arthur Clarke worked out the details of that one. What tricks would help a mechanic trouble-shoot and repair the malf that crippled an orbiting spacecraft? Ing addressed the problem in 1955. The literature is full of other examples.)

In surveying systems we have described, we soon run across some likely problems. We ought to make the problems and bailout procedures as realistic as we can, up to a point. Beyond that point, avoiding unnecessary gore on one hand and boredom on the other, we can study some scenarios with what one reliability engineer called "the lighter side of panic."

Beginning with realism, let's take the fleet of small cargo craft we outlined in Chapter 5, carrying a ton or so of supplies to orbit. If we have not yet built the SPS or reactor to feed an orbiting laser, we could kick those little cargo deltas up to orbit using ground-based lasers. In that case, we might use a single-port engine in which the laser is beamed straight up the exhaust nozzle into the thrust chamber.

We may need to seed the hydrogen fuel with tiny, precisely metered amounts of other chemicals to get enough thrust—and you will recall that the laser must penetrate the exhaust stream. The scenario: landing near the launch complex in Nevada, one small automated shuttle ground-loops as the tip skid of one stub wing hits a hapless pronghorn. (The USAF has often had to deal with herds of deer on its runways.) Damage seems to be minor. The filter of the seed chemical pump is damaged by sudden g forces, yet not enough to fail during routine postflight checks. Naturally, the filter mesh does not begin to fail until the next flight, when the little SSTO is under full boost up from southern Nevada.

The only new factor is a few particles of filter mesh, and extra-large seed particles, fed into the thrust chamber after a minute or so, when the delta is hypersonic. Unfortunately, that is enough to make the exhaust partly opaque to the HEL beam, which can no longer "see" into the nozzle very well. The result: a disastrous loss of thrust. We have a system malf, a malfunction affecting the whole mission, and telemetry tells us this is one cargo that is not going to make it.

In this case we might not lose the whole show. We stop the laser feed and, as soon as the ship's trajectory brings it back within the atmosphere, we divert the hydrogen fuel to small hypersonic ramjets deployed in the stub wings. (This is another good reason to use hydrogen.) Those ramjets, firing within the upper atmosphere, provide enough thrust to get the delta within glide distance of an abort site. We will have two abort sites; one near Holbrook, Arizona and the other near Las Cruces, New Mexico. We guide the little delta down but, with its heavy payload, its sink rate is that of a flat rock. We save our payload of chemicals slated for the lunar factories, but the delta's skin is buckled and its structure has taken a terrible beating. This little ship will not fly again.

However, it could have been much worse if the delta had augered down in Flagstaff. Bailout procedures saved some lives and a vital payload as well. And those little hypersonic ramjets, normally carried at a slight weight penalty, paid for themselves while powering the delta to an abort site.

A few years later, still waiting for orbital laser feed, we send up a small manned experimental frisbee fed from a GBL. Its engines use electric current from onboard rotary MHD generators. The anodes conducting this electricity are very special alloys, but we know that they do corrode and wear away. That is why the crew chief must inspect those MHD fanjet anodes carefully after every flight, just as crew chiefs used to crawl up warm tailpipes to inspect for worn turbine blades.

However, this crew chief has recently replaced all the anodes, and they always seem to wear at about the same rate, so after the previous test flight he only checked a couple of anodes. The gauge said they were fine. If he had checked them *all*, he would have suspected they were from a substandard batch, be-

cause three of the others have already begun eroding
away like spark plug tips, much too quickly for safety.

The pilot goes through warmup without trouble,
calls for full HEL boost, gets it, and soon is booming
across the California desert in rotary IRH pulsejet
mode. Then, calling out each step in the bored, good-
ol'-boy cadence favored by test pilots, he flicks the
protect cover from the MHD boost switch and ener-
gizes the MHD fanjet mode. So far, so good; in
moments, the little frisbee is rocketing upward in a
steep spiral. The spiral is not an ideal path from an
energy standpoint, but this is an experimental flight
using its own dedicated ground-based laser station.
The frisbee must not move so far downrange that it
is out of line-of-sight from its dedicated GBL.

No fear of that on this flight, as the frisbee climbs
out above 60,000 feet and two more of the anodes
begin to erode away. The three worst ones are irregu-
larly spaced around the ship's circumference and,
one by one, they just quit conducting current. Ordi-
narily the pilot could switch back to laser-fed IRH
pulsejet mode, but now he is too high for that to be
useful and some of the anodes are still working. The
current is still propelling the great electric fan, but
the magnetic pulses are no longer evenly spaced
around the frisbee. This sets up a surging vibration
that begins to shake the entire ship, pilot and all.

The pilot manages to kill the MHD boost, which
instantly stops the killing vibration. He still has laser feed, but no big hydrogen tanks for laser rocket
operation and at that altitude, the IRH pulsejet will
not keep him aloft. He elects to ride it down, back to
thicker air, but finds that the vibration has loosened
some of the moveable IRH exhaust vanes. It gets
worse as he descends to dense air. He radios the bad
news below, confirming what Ground Control knows
from telemetry, and they tell him to get out while he
can. The laser feed is stopped. The pilot ejects, riding
up in a pod on a half-second pulse of solid rocket
thrust, and deploys his personal chute safely. He can

only watch from above as his experimental frisbee slices downward at a steep angle, wiping out a dozen cars in the base parking lot.

Including the crew chief's uninsured Thunderbird and the base commander's customized Mercedes. For the experimental program, this day has been a setback. For the crew chief it has been a disaster.

Years later, we complete our orbital laser installations and begin furnishing laser power to commercial aerospace planes. Only a few private firms own executive IRH pulsers so far, and at first only a few feed lasers are available in orbits 2,000 or 3,000 miles out. An oil baron with his own ten-place executive pulser wants to fly home from Oklahoma City to Alpine, Texas, but must wait for an orbital feed laser to come within range. Commercial traffic has priority, though; Mr. Baron fumes and frets, knowing he can cover the 500 miles to Alpine in fifteen minutes if only he can get confirmation of a feed laser.

Finally he gets one, lifts off, and streaks toward the southwest. He is warned to stay above 30,000 feet because of weather conditions. But Baron has some new oil wells near Odessa, and the radar shows no clouds nearby; using manual override he drops down to 10,000 feet just to ogle his holdings. This is a grave error, because "weather" can mean many things to a laser installation. Baron is passing through a region that was filled by a dust storm a few hours ago, and trillions of fine dust particles still hang in the dense air below 20,000 feet.

The laser controller warns him again, but by now it is too late and getting later every second. Baron realizes he is losing power, and calls for more. He does not realize that the small, intense beam to his pulser is trying to punch through miles of dust particles, much of the beam "shining" away, scattered by dust. The more power he gets, the sooner those dust particles trigger air breakdown, completely blocking the beam from him. By this time, Baron would dearly love to lift up above the danger level, but cannot get enough power and he is now barreling along at tumbleweed level.

West Texas ranchers later report a line of fire sweeping across the sky and a ripping sound, the result of laser-supported detonation of dust particles, just before Mr. Baron's pulser cuts a ditch half a mile long in the baked earth near the Pecos River. After this, the FAA puts tighter restrictions on private pulsers.

Some years after Mr. Baron's fatal mistake, we might see hypersonic craft in common use around the world. Not all countries have federal agencies as responsible as ours, and in some regions the flight regulations might be as readily ignored as driving regulations are ignored today in some countries we decline to list. One of the present authors, in more cavalier days, took part in outlaw racing events that involved power restricted only by the limits of ingenuity, and a mix of automotive designs ranging from inane to brilliant. One pit manager, studying a race from the safety of a tree, aptly described this type of event as ". . . a paroxysm of dumb." We may see such outlaw events in future flight.

Imagine an outlaw drag race, in the year 2035, by young speedfreaks in a mythical Middle-East country. Prizes are offered for minimum elapsed time and top speed over a straight-line course that stretches 20,000 cubits between start and finish lines. A dozen teams build special vehicles, which must fly low to trip the timing devices. Some of these teams can buy the very latest equipment; others must beg, borrow, and steal theirs.

As the traditional "Christmas tree" staging lights begin to flash at the start line, we see a startling variety of vehicles lined up across desert sand. The favorites lie supine, dressed in g suits of the latest type with primary lenses across the tops of their delta hulls. One young man has bribed a Libyan laser controller to feed him ten per cent more than the maximum permitted power. Least likely to succeed is the lunatic who sits in a homemade pod ahead of an ancient, stolen Soviet solid rocket booster which lies horizontal on a detachable wheeled undercarriage. He cannot afford laser-powered engines. He has tied tourniquets above his knees and elbows, and a big one around his waist, because he cannot afford a g-suit. He cannot afford a false start, either, but he hits the ignition button an instant early.

The booster man is off, illegally and hopelessly; you do not shut off the spark in those old solid boosters. Everyone else is off an instant later, some of them hurtling up the tremendous, opaque smokescreen boiling out behind the old booster. The booster sheds its undercarriage at Mach 1, which flips and disintegrates, picking off two of the onrushing competitors.

The bribe man is safely to one side, overtaking the booster with his superior ERH thrustors which are deafening every camel within ten leagues. Three similar ships are falling behind because a bribe can also be used to crank down the wick on an opponent's feed laser. But one slick customer has stolen a tank of metastable helium to feed his rocket engine and, already pulling seven g's, firewalls his throttle to beat the ERH ship ahead.

Seeing himself passed, the briber uses that illegal extra power to fire a charged particle-beam. His ship now forges ahead into the partial vacuum created by the particle beam, and at this point both leaders lapse from insanity to unconsciousness, thanks to excessive g-forces. Their autopilots were programed not to follow ground contour but to maintain a straight course, and this they do.

We need not worry about who won. Our main concern is with the two leaders who regain consciousness in low Earth orbits, since both of these hotshots exceeded the 17,000 mile-per-hour velocity required to reach orbit. We stress the comic side of this event because the other side is too gory to detail here. Sooner or later, every country that contains vehicles with such power will learn to enforce reasonable restrictions in the public interest.

Some of those restrictions will probably include automated flight paths that put private aerospace flights in the fully-automatic category. Complete automation may be our best choice because, in the interest of everyone's safety, computers can respond more reliably and more quickly to new information than any human could. In this respect we may have to trade away some freedom of trivial choice when we choose to use great amounts of energy.

Our next scenario shows how this energy might become a social problem—call it "light pollution" if you will. A mail cargo craft, fully automated, is nearing its destination near Des Moines. The entire trip from Denver has been very cheap because, after a few minutes of laser boost, the cargo plane continued for most of the way without power, coasting through a vacuum in a ballistic arc. It needs another laser feed only for landing and braking. Now the ship is easing back down through the atmosphere, bumbling along with wings extended at subsonic speeds. Because Traffic Control has the mail slated for a simple, straight-in approach, a controller decides to switch the landing feed laser to another craft with an urgent request. He instantly provides an alternate beam for the mail ship.

This alternate beam comes not from another power station in low orbit, but from one located in geosynchronous orbit, 22,000 miles out. This is so far away that light, including HEL beams, needs an eighth of a second to cover the distance. A closed cycle, round-trip response takes twice that time—a fourth of a second. The controller knows that the mail ship is coming in "on rails," and decides its path and speed are perfectly predictable. An eighth of a second's delay in feedback from the mail ship, he thinks, should not be a problem for the laser tracker.

But Des Moines lies in the tornado belt, and vast whirling eddies of air are cavorting in the mail ship's path. Eddies form, break up and re-form, often without creating a clear trace on instruments. While slowing to land near Des Moines the mail ship flies through one of these invisible whirlwinds and, for only a second or two, is buffeted back and forth. During that brief moment, the feed laser is slow to react (because it is so far away) as the ship jerks back and forth in the buffeting wind. The beam strays from the receiver lens; the mail ship instantly feeds back the error, but that instant uses up an eighth of a second and *another* eighth-second elapses before the corrected beam can reach its target. With a jittering target and tiny delays in the laser tracker, the feed laser may partly miss its target for a full second or so.

The mail gets through, regaining its full laser feed and landing on schedule. But a thousand citizens in Des Moines had glanced up at the drone of the mail ship, and fifty of them were watching at the moment when the aircraft jerked aside. When the beam strayed from the center of the receiver lens, some of this "beam stray" struck other parts of the ship's skin. Some of it struck the ground, and people on the ground. Believe it or not, this beam probably would not create third-degree skin burns if it passed by at an airliner's pace, but it could certainly produce serious eye damage. Even the laser's reflection from the side of the ship might cause permanent corneal damage to anyone looking at it.

For some, the damage would be slight. But for a half-dozen people, the mail plane was the last thing they would see until after surgery. One second they watched the ship's slow descent, its feed laser appearing as a lance of light visible from dust reflections. The next second, a tremendous flash, and then blindness. This scenario would probably end in eye operations paid for by the power company's insurance. No doubt, new restrictions would prevent power companies from offering laser feed to aircraft from such great distances. We suspect that complaints about light pollution will be one that plagues orbital laser power companies for many years.

In all honesty, our mail ship scenario is pretty unlikely in a couple of particulars. First and foremost, an air terminal designated for laser boost will have *rigidly* controlled, and enforced, flight corridors. Those corridors would avoid heavily populated areas. In fact, when landing, most craft would drop almost vertically into the port of destination. Second, traffic controllers will know better than to feed a distressed vehicle—for example, one at a low altitude over a cityful of people—from a laser transmitter 22,000 miles up. Even from very low orbits, the laser feed to vehicles in the atmosphere involves milliseconds of delay. We can probably match receiver hardware and transmitter feed power to safely accommodate closed-loop delays of fifty milliseconds or so (we're guessing at that number), but this means the laser feed must be from low orbit. How low? We can't give an exact answer, but we can say this: respected military people are *not* planning on zapping nuclear missiles from geosynchronous orbit. If we had to decide today on one exact orbit for laser feed to vehicles on Earth, we would see a lot of panic buttons pushed.

The lowest orbits involve special problems. Below 200 miles, atmospheric drag takes its toll and without frequent little added boosts, a laser installation (or any other satellite) would be slowed enough to fall into the atmosphere within a year. We do not need to create scenarios for this; our media have gloried in them when early Soviet and American low-orbit satellites disintegrated during re-entry.

Even in a thousand-mile orbit—safe from orbital decay for many years—a feed laser would pass over a given point on Earth's surface so fast that it could not keep a target in its *effective* field of view for more than a few minutes. If the target is moving at hypersonic speed in the same general direction as the laser transmitter, the laser in thousand-mile orbit can feed it for an extra minute or so. After that, the job of feeding power must either be passed off to another laser installation (or relay mirror) following in a similar orbit, or someone must push the panic button.

The higher its orbit, the more slowly a laser installation would pass a point on Earth's surface. As Arthur Clarke told us many years ago, at orbital velocity 22,300 miles up, the installation no longer passes a point on Earth's surface, but stays above it forever in geosynchronous orbit. (This is why geosynchronous orbit is sometimes called "Clarkeian orbit.") But this, as we have seen, involves feedback delays too long to safely feed a moving target.

Incidentally, an object in GEO will not stay *precisely* above a given point on Earth's surface unless the orbit stays directly above Earth's equator. In an inclined orbit, the orbiting object will seem to move back and forth a bit in a north-south figure-8 pattern. That pattern is very predictable and we can still use a laser feed in GEO to stationary objects on the ground.

As if we didn't already have enough problems, the power of the feed laser decays a bit in passing through miles of atmosphere. When feeding a beam straight down from any orbit, the vertical beam path through the air is shortest and loses the least energy. As the laser tracks a target at an increasing angle from vertical, it loses more and more energy. At an angle of 60° from vertical, the laser's "slant range" through atmosphere is doubled, and its power is seriously reduced. This angle is roughly the limit of its effective field of view where beam-feed is concerned.

So: a higher orbit allows an orbital laser to feed a target longer, but it increases the lag in control information. Surely we can find a decent compromise.

The best compromise for laser transmitter or relay feed to vehicles is probably an orbital height of a few thousand miles. For example: 1800 miles up, a laser looking 60° ahead of vertical can begin to feed a target with increasing efficiency for about ten minutes as the laser transmitter continues its orbit and the angle to its target grows nearer to vertical. For another ten minutes then, after the laser installation passes the vertical, the angle grows greater again, eventually to more than 60°. The total time for effective field of view: twenty minutes. A lot of taxi rides and executive pulser ships may need power beams for at least that long, so the 1800 mile orbit is probably as low as we should go for feeding vehicles.

In an orbit 2840 miles out, the laser's overhead pass is slower, and it could effectively feed a target for twice as long: forty minutes. The total two-way control delay for a corrected beam from that orbit grows to over sixty milliseconds at the 60° slant range—more than a twentieth of a second. This is pushing our luck if we need fast beam correction, so perhaps the 2800-mile orbit is as high as we should go for vehicle feed.

In a future where we call for laser feed for casual short trips in perfect weather, we might prefer the lower orbit. (For all-weather operation, we *must* develop microwave power beams, even if the antennae are many times larger than we would like. And because microwave WLs are orders of magnitude longer than laser WLs, the microwave transmitter or relay station must be in very low orbit.) The shortness of a low-orbit control delay gives us a safety margin, and our trips across the city in a laser-boosted taxi may take less than five minutes—especially if some of them shoot us across in a ballistic arc. This would be a much faster, more exhilarating way to go than by slow, steady hovercraft. It might also mean our panic button should be attached to a parachute. Perhaps we should check out a panic situation in a solotaxi, brought on by the "shower curtain effect."

This effect was named for a phenomenon many of us have experienced with common shower curtains. If you are in the shower, very near a semitransparent curtain, you can see only vague shapes and light through the curtain. But if you are standing twenty feet away looking at someone else who is in the shower, you can see quite well through the curtain; the bather's secrets are on full display.

We find a very similar effect when we study a laser beamed through a disturbance such as air turbulence. If the disturbance is near the receiver lens and far from the transmitter, the laser gets through with little interference. But if the disturbance is near the transmitter, your beam sees a lot of interference. There are adaptive optics that can minimize the shower curtain effect, but without the expensive optics you might keep your finger on that button.

Our scenario: you are taking your fresh rumcake to the county fair at the civic center and, late as usual, you call a solotaxi. The weather is generally fair, with lots of puffy low cumulus clouds. Your taxi arrives with an orbital laser feed beam, dropping down through a sunny opening between widely-spaced clouds, making more noise than your neighbors would like. The solotaxi is designed to boost one passenger at low acceleration, no more severe than you feel at the start of a fast elevator ride, so you feel secure in placing your prize rumcake on your lap.

Your destination is a commercial landing pad near the civic center. Your laser beam is fed from a mountaintop GBL somewhere in the sun belt, to a low-orbit relay mirror, which bounces it down to you. Your onboard computer must call for an orbital laser feed to boost you into a shallow ballistic arc for a few miles. After coasting weightless for a minute or so your solotaxi receiver will be fed again, briefly, for braking energy to let you down gently. The computer must make these arrangements for both laser feeds at the launch and destination sites before boosting you. Part of the computer's job is to consider the weather at both locations.

You program your destination; the solotaxi computer decides you need a fractional g boost for twenty seconds and, for gentle braking at the end of your trajectory, a bit more power for a similar timespan. The computer gets a firm commitment for both the boost laser and the braking laser, and winks a green light at you. Your launch window has arrived; up you go.

You go up through a temperature inversion layer, missing those cumulus clouds. The boost leg of your trip comes off without a hitch. But during the zero-g part of your trajectory, while you are coasting without power, a sudden storm is developing far away over that mountaintop GBL installation. The atmosphere *looks* clear above the GBL site, but clear-air turbulence levels begin to set ten-year records.

But near the civic center, hurtling nearer to that commercial landing pad, you bloody well notice that something is missing because this cut-rate power station outfit on the mountaintop has not kept its adaptive optics properly maintained and it is severely overstressed. The GBL beam spears up through the atmospheric disturbance, gets defocused, and only a small portion of that power beam is bounced off the orbital relay mirror. That pathetic remnant of a beam arrives at your solotaxi receiver in sorry shape to slow a sofa pillow, much less a solotaxi.

You are descending at several hundred feet per second, so fast that the landing pad tracker barely has time to adjust and upgrade its power beam. However, you have made solotaxi trips before and none of them looked like kamikaze runs but this one definitely does, and the panic button is there, and you push it.

The parachute attached to your solotaxi is popped upward just before the GBL beam, uprated to emergency power, manages to vaporize a channel through an offending cloud. The uprated beam comes through, sears a hole through your parachute, and strikes your solotaxi receiver lens full-strength. The solotaxi takes two separate jolts of heavy deceleration, one from the parachute and the other from emergency laser braking thrust, and you land as gently as dandelion fluff. Landing pad attendants rush toward you because you are not getting out.

You are not getting out because your legs are rubbery with relief, but also because you no longer hold a prize rumcake on your knees. What you have is a sticky mass a yard wide and an inch thick spread across your lap and the floor, the result of sudden emergency braking at fifteen g's. An attendant says something about the shower curtain effect, which reminds you that you need a bath before you see your lawyer.

A thorough treatment of all the possible problems in the future flight will fill volumes, and those volumes will be carefully studied by agencies like NASA and FAA. Perhaps we should make brief mention of a few more potential problems, leaving the full scenarios for others to flesh out.

The "dusty mirrors" problem might plague the development of ERH thrusters (Chapter 5). The secondary optics that focus beams under a vehicle's hull must be as free from dust as we can manage, and electrostatic cleaners will probably be installed for this purpose. But a malf of the cleaner on one secondary mirror might cause that mirror to absorb a sizeable fraction of the beam. This would create two problems. Instantly, the ERH detonation wave under that portion of the hull would be degraded, and the upward thrust would no longer be evenly applied. The craft might bank away crazily. Within a second or so, the dusty mirror would be overheated by absorbed energy and its coating might be ruined, possibly shattering it, which would suddenly worsen the asymmetrical thrust.

The "cracked or shattered mirror" problem could bring catastrophe in a two-port laser rocket (Chapter 4). A big sapphire window might have an undetected flaw, or it could be installed with uneven pressure on its circumference. Or perhaps its cooling system malfunctions; any of these problems could result in extreme stresses within the crystal window. If that window cracks, the concentrated energy beam will be partly deflected by the crack and thrust will be degraded. Heat will quickly build up in the window unless the laser feed is stopped, and if the thrust chamber is still working at all, chamber pressure might blow the window out entirely. The effect might be that of a grenade exploding at the front of the thrust chamber.

The "pilot beam failure" problem is a real systemic malf. We have shown what can happen when a feed laser strays from its target receiver, for whatever reason. The feedback control system from vehicle to feed laser will probably include at least three redundant, low-power "pilot" laser beams. A pilot beam constantly informs the HEL transmitter about the correctness of its aim and beam strength. The shapes of some vehicles, and their receiver lenses, may require a short fin-like extension which carries the pilot laser transmitter. But no matter where it is placed, if that little transmitter ever gets out of alignment it could misdirect the HEL beam. The beam stray might be slight, or it might be catastrophic both for the vehicle and for people below.

The "damaged radiator" problem could put a military space cruiser out of action. We studied the huge retractable radiator coolant collectors in Chapter 8, and saw how liquid droplet radiators must recycle their coolant fluid. If a tiny meteorite or an enemy particle beam drives a hole through one of those spray heads along the fuselage, we might lose a lot of fluid into space. It is possible that, when the fluid freezes, some or all of it might actually be recovered by a crewman in a small emergency vehicle. If that coolant includes metal liquid or powder, it should be detectable with radar. These radiators will surely be designed so that a damaged portion can be blocked off instantly to minimize the loss of coolant. In a radiator malf of medium seriousness, the commander might limit the use of weapons, or propulsion, or some of both.

The "vehicle mix" problem is the last one we will sketch out here. We encounter it today, and it may be more severe in the future. Pilots of ultralight aircraft are often denied access to runways because those runways are in demand by much larger, faster planes. The pilot of an ultralight is at the very bottom of the pecking order. The speeds and wing loadings of these different classes of aircraft make them a danger to each other. In the future we may find the skies filled with a mix of craft even more incompatible. Light aircraft may soon be capable of 40,000 foot altitudes or more, and they might not fare well in the wake of supersonic dirigible. The most likely solution will be more restricted flight corridors and more specialized landing facilities for these different vehicle classes.

We tried to show in this chapter that we expect more panics than disasters in future flight. That seems likely because designers will have better tools, including computer simulation, to study the problems before they occur. Old aircrew jokes aside, panic buttons *are* hooked up to emergency systems that can save your mission—or at least your skin. Flight is safer now than it used to be, and it will almost certainly be still safer tomorrow.

Chapter 11:

PROBLEMS, REMEDIES, AND FUTURE PROMISE

The ideas we have collected in these pages, even if most of them become fact, will be only a few threads woven into the crazy-quilt tapestry of our future. We avoid the metaphor of the jigsaw puzzle because, when put together right, the puzzle makes a charming picture—and this is probably too much to ask of human affairs. In general, only the past seems to have charm. The present has problems; the future holds threats and promises. When we are living in it we will have to admit that our future, like the past and present, is a hodgepodge of elements; a crazy-quilt of old and new ideas, some charming, some troublesome. We described some of the new ideas, and in some cases we will need remedies when they do not mesh easily.

New ideas are often like that. They can be especially troublesome when they involve, not just means to exert power, but power itself; vast energies. At the core of this book is the search for ways to tap and control vast energies. That search is as old as religion, and it will continue in science as well, with or without books like this one. Some major issues on energy use will be decided in part by the public. We think the decisions should be based on understanding, not doctrine. If we have helped a bit toward that understanding, we are content.

Our study of the possibilities offered by future flight shows that it can immeasurably improve the human condition. The best possibility, now being seriously pursued by the Soviet Union and modestly pursued in the West, is that both industry and colonization will spread beyond Earth, returning goods and energy without ecological damage to our home planet. Perhaps the worst possibility is that through timidity or lack of vision, we will sit back and watch while others develop a major driver of this improvement, propulsion technology. If that happens the United States will be a quaint economic backwater, stagnating in a pool of past glories, within the next fifty years. We need only a few moments to review worrisome evidence.

Americans have already relinquished leadership in some areas that are crucial to us, though we are becoming an economic challenger again. Specifics? Our mass transit common carriers, the railroads, are woefully far behind the times. The British travel 120 miles an hour between commuter stops, using trains as cheaply as we use crosstown buses. Some commute with their bicycles stowed for quick removal in baggage cars. The French TGV (very high speed) trains seem capable of moving masses of commuters at 300 miles an hour. In a gesture of friendship, one Japanese industrialist has donated millions of dollars to promote the excellent Japanese high-speed rail technology in the United States. We are still mucking about with the underfunded studies on magnetic levitation trains, when we ought to be riding in them.

Clearly, these other countries needed cheap, efficient mass transit even more than we do. Their mass transit bottlenecks forced them to excellence, and they met the challenge. Much the same has happened in the automotive world.

Japanese and German cars met American needs better than Detroit did for many years, and sales figures prove that we now know it. Few of us know, however, that some of the most striking recent improvements in American cars were developed in

Germany by Porsche under contracts specifying secrecy. To its credit, our domestic auto industry is now fighting back with engineering as well as tariffs. It is crucial to our future that we meet the design challenges head to head; for if we hide behind tariffs, our products will fail to meet future challenges. If we find it necessary to import more and more technology because our own stuff has become inferior, we will soon be up to our necks in economic backwater.

But all of this is (very recent) history, and we still lead in several technological areas. We should continue doing what we do best, especially when that path leads us toward the orbiting bonanza. Our lead in computers is, in some respects, a commanding one. We lead in some areas of aerospace technology, though the plans for a permanent American space station are still in trouble at every step from hostile budget-cutters. At this writing, our media seem unaware that the Soviets *already* have a functioning space station—perhaps because our Soviet friends have learned some vital lessons about us and our media.

In the past, the Soviets trumpeted their technical advances over the West, pleased to see the coverage they received in our free media. They were less than pleased to see us overtake and pass them. Examples: the race to land men on the moon, and the development of returnable spacecraft. They now deny there was ever a race to the moon. The lie is understandable and fairly transparent. They would have a tougher time denying their struggle to overtake us in spacecraft design. The Australians recently photographed a subscale Soviet delta shuttle after its re-entry, which indicates a shape of Soviet shuttles to come. It looks like a chick from an egg our NASA shuttle might have laid.

With Salyut 7, however, the Soviets are going about the business of uprating their existing permanent space station without so much press agentry. This time, evidently, they prefer to avoid the kind of Western media coverage that might alert us. Alert us to what? To their head start toward the orbiting bonanza. They are on their way to the treasures out there, and by starting early they intend to avoid the rush. Their stated long-range plans are for cosmograds, perhaps in L5 locations; their unstated near-term plans probably include a manned mission to Mars and/or a permanent facility on the moon. They have grown experimental food crops in orbit; their experience with human crews beyond Earth amounts to a commanding lead; and they have the best of reasons for keeping that lead: future economic world leadership.

Economic leadership can be measured many ways, but one of the better ways is to see how much energy a nation uses. Americans, with a mountainous variety of plug-in devices, a nationwide electrical power grid, and comparatively cheap fuel, use more energy than most of the rest of the entire world. Our per capita energy use, compared to many Third World countries, seems absurd to some and obscene to others. But our standard of living depends on our ability to buy energy more cheaply. In part, this is true because improved transport of people and goods leads to improved lifestyles. And as we have shown in these pages, improved transport often requires control of more energy.

If our talk of megawatts has appeared a bit grandiose, you might add up your family's recent use of house current. Chances are, within a couple of months the total is around 1,000 kilowatt-hours. That equals a megawatt for an hour. Today, many American families use five or ten megawatt-hours of house current per year, plus a similar amount (often much more) of energy in fossil fuels. A hundred years ago we used a very small fraction of that energy. A hundred years from now we may each use megawatt-hours per day instead of kilowatt-hours. Citizens of developing countries may then use more energy than we do today.

They can do it only with someone's help, and the energy provider will have tremendous economic clout. This is easily equated with standards of living. We can help others improve theirs without imperiling ours.

Across the globe, energy use and standard of living are so tightly related that if you know one, you can closely predict the other. This is not so much a deliberate process as a natural outcome; your industry, your food production, and your transportation networks all consume fat shares of energy which you pay for even if that payment is indirect. Americans produce more, eat more, and travel more than most, and these items are crucial to our standard of living. Obviously, we waste a lot of energy, and that's bad. But we would be suicidally short-sighted to stop searching for better sources of it.

Today we have wallplugs that tap into a nationwide power grid. Tomorrow, if we lead in propulsion technology, we will be able to tap into orbital "plugs." Even if we do not lead, we still might be able to tap those orbital energy sources—but we would pay someone else for them. If you harbor any doubt about the danger in that, consider the trouble we have inherited through "plugging into" (and depending on) foreign oil. We will be wise to develop our own energy sources for our future transport needs, and that is directly linked to future propulsion needs.

Some of the schemes for much-needed further advances in laser propulsion are described in this book. Today, the factor that limits our advance seems to be in uprating laser beams to much higher power levels. We can fire intense beams, but they are beams of very small diameter with relatively low total (time-average) power. These beams are more suitable for weapons than for long-duration propulsion systems. The power requirements for antiballistic missile beam weapons are roughly equal to the power levels we would need to drive engines for moving a payload to a higher orbit (a basis for many interesting scenarios).

But a boost from ground to orbit takes five or ten times these power levels. Weapon technology is also concerned with scaling up the beam power, however. Designers will borrow all of this military technology that they can, for peaceful purposes. Like it or not, the human race developed steel first for swords, then adapted it to plowshares. The governments now developing laser weapons will soon adapt them to laser engines, and orbital transfer missions are likely candidates for first commercial use.

In key experiments with present laser engines, we find few if any real barriers to the scaling-up toward big, high-thrust propulsion units. We even have the proven ability to make hundred-pound sapphires for laser engine windows. We can borrow from earlier propulsion developments to handle such stuff as liquid hydrogen, and to dispose of waste heat using state-of-the-art conductors and radiators.

For airbreathing electrostatic engines, the thruster technology is largely unknown territory. So little research has been done on microwave thruster concepts that we cannot yet pinpoint the design bottlenecks, if any. We already have the necessary multi-megawatt microwave power beams, though, and kiloamp electron accelerators as well. The most we can say now is that we already have some of the hardware for force field propulsion systems, but that we are still a long way from flying supersonic dirigibles in this fashion. We need not stay far from it if the concepts prove interesting enough to students of physics.

Metastable helium drives are a long shot. But we must remember that, not so many years back, some experts grew nervous at the very thought of filling a rocket's tanks with something as dangerous as liquid hydrogen. It is still a tricky process. We perform that trick regularly with success. Designers may yet perform a trickier operation with metastable helium.

The antimatter drive may not be such a long shot, eventually. For one thing, the stuff is so clearly an "ultimate fuel" that we may see considerable pressure to pursue research on it in orbital laboratories. We would need only a little of it to power a starship. Even if its containment vessels were many times heavier than the fuel itself, it *far* outstrips anything else we currently see for propulsion through the deep interstellar gulfs.

Both of these exotic fuels have a very important advantage over beamed energy: they do not require support from a remote power source. With either of them in our bag of propulsion tricks, we would see a rush to the orbiting bonanza as soon as the purchase prices became bearable. A big interplanetary vessel, carrying prodigious amounts of onboard power, could provide all the room and the spin-inducted artificial gravity needed for a large research staff. Such a vessel could carry its own small patrol craft and might use electrical fields to propel them, using the miles-long cruiser itself as reaction mass as shown in Figure 11-1. In some ways, life on such a vessel might be much the same as on a permanent L5 colony. Within the next century, several nations will probably develop propulsion systems that make such huge vessels practical.

Whatever means we use to obtain cheap propulsion, the concentration of tremendous energy contains a built-in, basic threat that we touched lightly in Chapter 10. We may illustrate the problem best by describing the propulsion systems available to an adult American in various eras. An ordinary citizen in Lincoln's day, sufficiently drunk or deranged, could ride a half-ton stallion onto your porch at thirty miles an hour. During prohibition, he could drive his one-ton flivver into your parlor at sixty per. Today, impacting at a 120 miles an hour in his two-ton sedan, he could go all the way through your house and into your neighbor's. Kinetic energy is equal to one-half mass times velocity squared, so each of these small disasters involved eight times as much impact

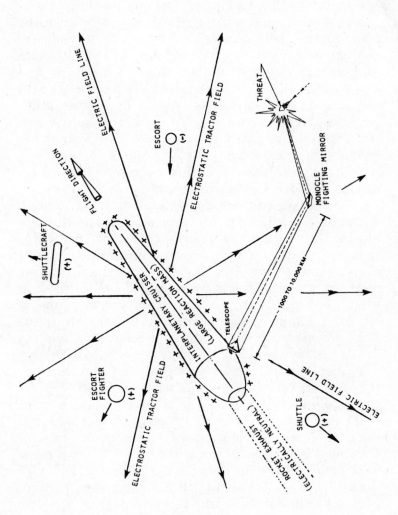

Figure 11–1. Large interplanetary vehicle provides inherent reaction mass and "electrostatic tractor field" for propulsion of escort shuttlecraft

energy as the one before it. These are rare events, but they are not rare enough.

And fifty years from now? At the present rate of increase we would expect an ordinary citizen to be able, for whatever reason, to lay waste to your entire neighborhood by plowing through it at 240 miles an hour in a four-ton vehicle. This is a bit much, and it only assumes a steady rise in the numbers. With revolutionary advances, we might find those numbers growing larger, faster. We will eventually reach the point where abuse of vast energies becomes too easy, without external control.

At first glance the situation begins to look like a dilemma. Without more available energy for everyday living, we become an also-ran nation. With it, we could live in fear of wholesale death through almost anyone's casual miscalculation. We *could* live that way—but we do not have to. Instead we can opt for reasonable controls, and strict enforcement, *varying with the potential forces we request*. With caution to match our advances, we can escape the dilemma. A few rough approximations of the controls are in order here, because we must avoid painting ourselves into a tightly regimented corner.

To begin with, we have had some controls since the first speeding ticket was written. Flight regulations followed; to obtain a license today, a pilot must pass examinations proving the competence to fly over other people's heads. These exams require far more competence than a driver's license does, with good reason. Furthermore, a license to fly a cub does not permit you to fly a faster, larger twin-engined craft. In short, the more impact energy you might exert, the more competence you must prove. We think this principle can work well in the future. We may not need more controls for the levels of force we control now; to repeat an important point, we must balance the controls so that we have both reasonable freedom of choice and reasonable protection against abuse.

Some folks complain that the graded license principle is not democratic. Rather than argue the point we merely assert that all pilots were not created equal. Until flight becomes entirely automated, relatively few pilots will be granted the privilege of flying over our heads in executive IRH pulsers.

Complete automation is, of course, the great leveler. No human reflexes can approach computer-directed, electromechanical responses. The time may come when manual control of *any* vehicle becomes so thoroughly unnecessary that some will label manual operation as macho. In any case, some of today's cars and aircraft are already performance-limited more by the human in the system than by any other factor. If we want higher performance in the future, and if we know that performance is degraded by our "help," it seems likely that high-performance classes of future aircraft will eventually be guided by computers. No doubt, a few of us grizzled recidivists will prefer to fly our own craft just for the fun of it. And we should be allowed to, so long as we do it in classes of aircraft, and flight corridors, suited to our competence. Existing flight regulations in the United States already keep the vehicle mix separated so well that flying is safer than driving.

Our best guess, then, is that we can meld the new hot ships into our society without too much regimentation. In the near term, we will do it with graded licensing and frequent re-examination. In the long term, we can do it with fully automated flight controls so that everyone can enjoy a trip that surpasses human ability to control. For recreational flight, we can still enjoy manual control in aircraft, and corridors, suitable for it.

We claimed at the outset that the future of flight can remove the limits to growth, and we believe that the evidence is compelling. There is a powerful synergism between cheap megawatts for propulsion and cheap kilowatts for gracious living in yet-undeveloped nations. When the poorest nation on the globe boasts a living standard equal to the richest nations today, perhaps human societies can mature without war or crushing coercion. Thanks to this energy connection, the future of humankind is entwined with the future of flight.

BIBLIOGRAPHY

For the convenience of the users, the bibliography has been sorted into eight major categories and their subdivisions. All entries are listed in chronological order.

The compilers hope that this gathering of the information will be of use in generating revolutionary new vehicles for The Future of Flight.

INTRODUCTION

The bibliography is divided into subsections as follows:

1. SPACE COLONIZATION AND INDUSTRIALIZATION
    1.1 Colonization of Free Space
    1.2 Lunar Colonization
    1.3 Planetary Colonization
2. SATELLITE SOLAR POWER STATIONS (Microwave Power Beaming)
3. STANDARD PROPULSION TEXTBOOKS
4. BEAMED ENERGY SYSTEMS (REMOTE POWER SOURCE)
    4.1 Beamed-Energy Propulsion Concepts
    4.1.1 Laser Rocket Propulsion
    4.1.2 Laser Airbreathing Propulsion
    4.1.3 Microwave Rocket Propulsion
    4.1.4 Microwave Airbreathing Propulsion
    4.2 High-Power Lasers and Laser Power Stations
    4.3 Laser/Gas Interactions
    4.4 Laser/Surface Interactions
    4.5 High Power Laser Propagation
    4.6 Precision Pointing and Tracking Systems
    5.7 High-Power Laser Windows and Large Optics
    4.8 Useful Reference Materials
5. SELF-SUFFICIENT PROPULSION SYSTEMS (local power source)
    5.1 High Altitude Airscooping Propulsion
    5.2 Magnetohydrodynamic ship Propulsion
    5.3 Propulsion by Energy Exchange with Magnetic and Electric Fields
    5.4 Hybrid Nuclear-Electric Propulsion
    5.5 Fission Rocket
    5.6 Fusion Rocket
    5.7 Orion Pulsed Propulsion System
    5.8 Bussard Interstellar Ramjet
    5.9 Antimatter Propulsion
    5.10 Light Sails
    5.11 Miscellaneous
6. Warbirds of the 21st Century
7. Ultralight and ARV Aircraft
8. Advanced Composite Materials

1. GENERAL DISCUSSIONS OF SPACE COLONIZATION AND INDUSTRI-ALIZATION

1.1 Colonization of Free-Space

Tsiolkovsky, K.E., "Investigation of World Spaces by Reactive Vehicles", *Vestnik Vozdukhoplavaniya (Herald of Astronautics)*, Vol. 9, 1912, pp. 7–8.

Bernal, J.D., *The World, the Flesh, and the Devil*, 1929, 1968.

Dyson, F.J., "Search for Artificial Stellar Sources of Infrared Radiation", *Science*, 3 June 1960, pp. 1667–1668.

"Space Station Studies", special section in *Astronautics & Aerospace Engineering*, Vol. 1, No. 7, Aug. 1963, pp. 38–56.

Hilton, B., "Hotels in Space," in *Commercial Utilization of Space*, Advances in the Astronautical Sciences, Vol. 23, American Astronautical Society Publications Office, Tarzana, 1968, pp. 251–58.

Ehricke, K.A., "Space Tourism", in *Commercial Utilization of Space*, Advances in the Astronautical Sciences, Vol. 23, American Astronautical Society Publications Office, Tarzana, 1968, pp. 259–291.

Boretz, J.E., "Large Space Station Power Systems", *J. Spacecraft*, Vol. 6, No. 8, 1969, pp. 929–936.

Clarke, A.C., "Island in the Sky", in *The Promise of Space*, The Walter Reade Organization, Inc., New York, 1970, pp. 148–57.

Donlan, C.J. and Johnson, R.W., "Activity Planning for the Space Station", *IEEE Transactions on Aerospace and Electronic Systems, AES-6*, Vol. 4, 1970, pp. 551–555.

Aldiss, B., "City in the Sky", *The Illustrated London News*, 16 May 1970.

Adelman, A. and Kemp, K.J., "Space Station Information Management", *IEEE Transactions on Aerospace and Electronic Systems, AES-6*, Vol. 6, 1970, pp. 746–763.

Day, L.E. and Noblitt, B.G., "Logistics Transportation for Space Station Support", *IEEE Transaction on Aerospace and Electronic Systems, AES-6*, Vol. 4, 1970, pp. 565–574.

Ehricke, K.A., "Planning Space Stations for Long-Range Utilization of Space for Earthians", Rockwell International Report SD71-562, 1971.

Dyson, F.J., et al., "Astroengineering Activity: The Possibility of ETI in Present Astrophysical Phenomena", in *Communication With Extraterrestrial Intelligence*, Carl Sagan, ed., MIT Press, Cambridge, 1973, pp. 188–229.

"Out of this World", *Fortune*, Vol. 89, No. 6, June 1974, p. 120.

"Colonies in Space", *Time*, 3 June 1974.

"Notes and Comments", *The New Yorker*, Vol. 50, No. 17, 17 June 1974, p. 23.

O'Neill, G.K., interview, "Colonization of Space", by Richard Reiss, *Mercury*, July/Aug. 1974, pp. 4–10, 23.

O'Neill, G.K., "A Lagrangian Community?", *Nature*, Vol. 250, 23 Aug. 1974, p. 636.

O'Neill, G.K., "The Colonization of Space", *Physics Today*, Vol. 27, No. 9, Sept. 1974, pp. 32–40.

Chedd, G., "Colonization at Lagrangia", *New Scientist*, 24 Oct. 1974, pp. 247–249.

Davies, P.C.W., "Arrival of the Age of Rama", *Nature*, Vol. 252, 13 Dec. 1974.

Taylor, T., "Strategies for the Future", *Saturday Review/World*, Vol. 2, No. 7, 14 Dec. 1974, pp. 56–59.

Berry, A., "Flying City-States", in *The Next Ten Thousand Years*, The New American Library, New York, 1975, pp. 128–141.

Berry, A., "Building the Giant Sphere", in *The Next Ten Thousand Years*, The New American Library, New York, 1975, pp. 142–155.

Nicolson, I.K.M., "Aspects of Some Problems Concerned with the Construction of Dyson Spheres", in *The Next Ten Thousand Years*, by Adrian Berry, New American Library, New York, 1975, pp. 173–181.

Asimov, I., statement in *Future Space Programs 1975, A Compilation of Papers etc.*, 1975, p. 1.

Ruzic, N.P., "Possible Future National Space Programs", in *Future Space Programs 1975, A Compilation of Papers, etc.*, 1975, pp. 805–865.

Coon, C.S., "Living Together in Space", in *Future Space Programs 1975, A Compilation of Papers etc.*, 1975, pp. 46–58.

Friesen, L.J., "Future United States Space Programs", in *Future Space Programs 1975, A Compilation of Papers etc.*, 1975, pp. 338–403.

O'Neill, G.K., in *Future Space Programs 1975, Hearings etc.*, 1975, pp. 111–188.

Robinson, G., *Living in Outer Space*, Public Affairs Press, Washington, 1975.

Agosto, W.N., "Far Out: The Case for Extraterrestrial Colonization", *Harper's Weekly*, Vol. 64, 21 Feb. 1975, p. 7.

Bainum, P.M. and Evans, K.S., "Three-Dimensional Motion and Stability of Two Rotating Cable-Connected Bodies", *J. Spacecraft*, Vol. 12, No. 4, April 1975, pp. 242–250.

Dempewolff, R., "Cities in the Sky", *Popular Mechanics*, Vol, 143, No. 5, May 1975, pp. 94–97, 205.

The Proceedings of the May 1975 Princeton/AIAA/NASA Conference on "Space Manufacturing Facilities (Space Colonies)", available from American Institute of Aeronautics and Astronautics, N.Y., 1975.

Sagan, C., interview, "Lots of Space Mysteries Still Left to Explore", *U.S. News & World Report*, Vol. 78, No. 20, 19 May 1975, pp. 69–74.

"Colonizing Space", *Time*, 26 May 1975.

Asimov, I., "Colonizing the Heavens", *Saturday Review*, Vol. 2, No. 20, 28 June 1975, pp. 12–17.

O'Neill, G.K., "Space Colonization and Energy Supply to the Earth", testimony before the Subcommittee on Space Science and Technology, Committee on Science and Technology, U.S. House of Representatives, 23 July 1975.

Parker, P.J., "Lagrange Point Space Colonies", *Spaceflight*, Vol. 7, July 1975, 269–273.

"Space Suburbia", *Science Digest*, Aug. 1975, pp. 10–11.

Cravens, G., "The Garden of Feasibility", *Harper's Magazine*, Aug. 1975, pp. 66–76.

Salisbury, D.F., "Cities in Space, Once Science Fiction, Are Plausible Now—But Very Costly", *The Christian Science Monitor*, Vol. 67, No. 189, 22 Aug. 1975, pp. 1, 11.

Paine, T., "Humanity Unlimited", *Newsweek*, 25 Aug. 1975, p. 11.

O'Neill, G.K., "The High Frontier", *Co-Evolution Quarterly*, Fall 1975.

O'Neill, G.K., "Space Colonization and Energy Supply to the Earth", *Co-Evolution Quarterly*, Fall 1975.

O'Neill, G.K., interview, "Is the Surface of a Planet Really the Right Place for an Expanding Technological Civilization?", *Co-Evolution Quarterly*, Fall 1975.

O'Neill, G.K., "The Colonization of Space", *Science Year*, Field Enterprises, Inc., Chicago, Sept. 1975.

O'Neill, G.K., et al., "Colonies in Space", *Physics Today*, Vol. 28, No. 9, Sept. 1975, pp. 13–15, 74.

Salkeld, R., "Space Colonization Now?", *Astronautics & Aeronautics*, Vol. 13, Sept. 1975 , pp. 30–34.

"Lagrangia: Pioneering in Space", *Science News*, 21 Sept. 1975, p. 183.

O'Neill, G.K., et al., "Detente in Space", *Harper's Magazine*, Vol. 251, Oct. 1975, p. 12.

"Space Colonies by 1990: A Solution to Global Crises?", *The Futurist*, Vol. 9, No. 5, Oct. 1975, pp. 273–274.

"A City in Space", *NASA Report to Educators*, Vol. 3, No. 3, Oct. 1975, pp. 6–8.

Friedman, P., "Colonies in Space", *New Engineer*, Vol. 4, No. 10, Nov. 1975, pp. 36–39.

O'Neill, G.K., "Space Communities: The Next Frontier", *Aerospace*, Vol. 13, No. 4, Dec. 1975, p. 1.

Harr, K.G., Jr., "Will We Become Colonists?", *Aeorspace*, Vol. 13, No. 4., Dec. 1975, p. 1.

O'Neill, G.K., "Space Colonies and Energy Supply to the Earth", *Science*, Vol. 190, 5 Dec. 1975, pp. 943–947.

Burgess, E., "Colonies in Space", *Astronomy*, Vol. 4, No. 1, Jan. 1976, pp. 18–25.

Michaud, M.A.G., "Two Tracks to New Worlds", *Spaceflight*, Vol. 8, Jan. 1976, pp. 2–6.

Gatland, K.W., "Cities in the Sky", *Spaceflight*, Vol. 8, Jan. 1976, pp. 7–9.

Macomber, F., "Cities in the Sky Capture Center Stage During 1975", *The San Diego Union*, A-11, 4 Jan. 1976.

Chernow, R., "A Physicist Finds that Colonies in Space May Turn Out to be Nice Places to Live", *Smithsonian*, Vol. 6, No. 11, Feb. 1976, pp. 62–69.

"Interest in Space Colonies Rises", *The Futurist*, Vol. 10, No. 1, Feb. 1976, pp. 32–33.

O'Neill, G.K., "Space Colonies: The High Frontier", *The Futurist*, Vol. 10, No. 1, Feb. 1976, pp. 25–33.

"Asimov Supports Space Colonization", *The Futurist*, Vol. 10, No. 1, Feb. 1976, p. 30.

"Space Settlement a Cinch—If We Want to Do It", *National Space Institute Newsletter*, Vol. 1, No. 3, March 1976, pp. 4–5.

Asimov, I., "The Nightfall Effect", *The Magazine of Fantasy & Science Fiction*, Vol. 50, No. 3, March 1976, pp. 144–154.

L-5 News, Newsletter of the L-5 Society, 1620 N. Park Ave., Tucson, Arizona 85719, various issues.

Heppenheimer. T.A. and Hopkins, M., "Initial Space Colonization: Concepts and R&D Aims", *Astronautics & Aeronautics*, March 1976, pp. 58–72.

Agosto, W.N., "Space Production of Solar Power Stations", *IEEE Spectrum*, May 1976.

O'Neill, G.K., *The High Frontier: Human Colonies in Space*, William Morrow & Co., N.Y., 1977.

Michaud, M.A.G. "Expanding the Human Biosphere", *JBIS*, Vol. 30, No. 3, March 1977, pp. 83–95.

Michaud, M.A.G., "Manned Interstellar Flight and the Colonization of Other Systems", *JBIS*, Vol. 30, No. 6, June 1977, pp. 203–212.

Puttkamer, J., "The Next 25 Years: Industrialization of Space: Rationale for Planning", *JBIS*, Vol. 30, No. 7, July 1977, po. 257–264.

Freitag, R., "NASA Philosophy Concerning Space Stations as Operations Centers for Construction and Maintenance of Large Orbiting Energy Systems", *JBIS*, Vol. 30, No. 7, July 1977, pp. 265–271.

"Space Colonization", special issue of *JBIS*, Vol. 30, No. 8, Aug. 1977.

Michaud, M.A.G., "The Consequences of Colonization", *JBIS*, Vol. 30, No. 9, Sept. 1977, pp. 323–331.

1.2 Lunar Colonization

Clarke, A.C., "Electromagnetic Launching as a Major Contribution to Space Flight", *JBIS*, Vol. 9, No. 6, Nov. 1950, pp. 261–267.

Buna, T., "Thermal Aspects of Long-Term Propellant Storage on the Moon", *J. Spacecraft*, Vol. 1, No. 5, Sept.–Oct. 1964, pp. 484–491.

Halacy, D.S., Jr., *Colonization of the Moon*, D. Van Nostrand Company, Inc., 1969.

Henry G.E., *Tomorrow's Moon*, 1969.

Clarke, A.C., "The Uses of the Moon", and "The Lunar Colony", in *The Promise of Space*, The Walter Reade Organization, Inc., New York, 1970, pp. 221–238.

Zwicky, F., "Systems for Extracting Elements and Chemical Compounds from Lunar Materials Needing Manned Operations on the Moon", in *Applied Sciences Research and Utilization of Lunar Resources*, F.J. Malina, ed. 1970.

Sharpe, M.R., in Encyclopedia Britannica's *Yearbook of Science and the Future*, 1972, p. 13.

Ehricke, K.A., "Lunar Industries: Their value for the Human Environment on Earth", *Acta Astronautica*, Vol. 1, May–June 1974, pp. 585–622.

Armstrong, N.A., "Out of this World", *Saturday Review/World*, Vol. 1, No. 25, 24 Aug. 1974, pp. 32–34, 118.

Parkinson, R.C., "Take-Off Point for a Lunar Colony", *Spaceflight*, Vol. 16, No. 9, Sept. 1974, pp. 322–327.

Berry, A., "The Beckoning Moon", and "The Lunarians", in *The Next Ten Thousand Years*, New American Library, New York, 1975, pp. 39–60.

Dossey, J.R. and Trotti, G.L., "Counterpoint: A Lunar Colony", *Spaceflight*, Vol. 7, July 1975, pp. 259–267.

"Why Not a Moon Colony?", *The Futurist*, Vol. 10, No. 1, Feb. 1976, p. 28.

1.3 Planetary Colonization

Sagan, C., "The Planet Venus", *Science*, Vol. 133, 24 March 1961.

Huang, S.S., "The Sizes of Habitable Planets", in *Interstellar Communication*, A.G.W. Cameron, ed., 1963.

Morowitz, H. and Sagan, C., "Life in the Clouds of Venus?", *Nature*, Vol. 215, 16 Sept. 1967.

Clarke, A.C., "The Commerce of the Heavens" and "Tomorrow's Worlds", in *The Promise of Space*, The Walter Reade Organization, Inc., New York, 1970. pp. 281–302.

Libby, W.F. and Seckbach, J., "Vegetative Life on Venus? Or Investigations with Algae Which Grow Under Pure Carbon Dioxide in Hot Acid Media at Elevated Pressures", *Space Life Sciences*, Vol. 2, 1970, pp. 121–143.

Baker, F.A., Seckbach J. and Shugarman, P.M., "Algae Thrive Under Pure Carbon Dioxide", *Nature*, Vol. 227, 15 Aug. 1970.

Berry, A., "After the Rain", *Daily Telegraph Magazine*, 30 April 1971, p. 340.

von Hoemer, S., "Population Explosion and Interstellar Expansion", in *Einheit und Vielheit*, Scheibe & Sussman, eds., Gottingen: Vandenhoeck & Ruprecht, 1972.

Dyson, F.J., "The World, the Flesh, and the Devil", in *Communication With Extraterrestrial Intelligence*, Carl Sagan, ed., MIT Press, Cambridge, 1973, pp. 371–389.

Sagan, C., "The Venus Detective Story" and "Venus is Hell", in *The Cosmic Connection*, Dell Publishing Company, Inc., New York, 1973, pp. 81–94.

Sagan, C., "The Moons of Barsoom", in *The Cosmic Connection*, Dell Publishing Company, Inc., New York, 1973, pp. 101–114.

Sagan, C., "Terraforming the Planets", in *The Cosmic Connection*, Dell Publishing Company, Inc., New York, 1973, pp. 148–154.

Sagan, C., "Astroengineering", in *The Cosmic Connection*, Dell Publishing Company Inc., New York, 1973, pp. 229–232.

Berry, A., "Search for Habitable Worlds", in *The Next Ten Thousand Years*, New American Library, New York, 1975, pp. 106–116.

Berry, A., "Venus, the Hell-World" and "Making it Rain in Hell", in *The Next Thousand Years*, New American Library, New York, 1975, pp. 61–78.

Murray, B.C., "A Future Elsewhere?", Chapter 4, in *Navigating the Future*, Harper & Row Publishers, Inc., New York, 1975.

Dole, S., *Habitable Planets for Man*.

2.   SATELLITE SOLAR POWER STATIONS (Microwave Power-beaming)

Stewart, W.L., et al., "Brayton Cycle Technology", presented at the Space Power Systems Advanced Technology Conference, NASA Lewis Research Center, Cleveland, Ohio, 23–24 Aug. 1966, NASA SP-131, pp. 95–145.

Lubarsky, B. and Shure, L.I., "Applications of Power Systems to Specific Missions", presented at the Space Power Systems Advanced Technology Conference, NASA Lewis Research Center, Cleveland, Ohio, 23–24 Aug. 1966, NASA AS-131.

Glaser, P.E., "The Future of Power From the Sun", Proceedings *IECES*, IEEE Publication 68C21-Energy, 1968, pp. 93–103.

Glaser, P.E., "Power from the Sun: Its Future", *Science*, Vol. 162, pp. 857–861, 1968.

Robinson, W.J., "The Feasibility of Wireless Power Transmission from an Orbiting Astronomical Station", NASA Technical Memorandum 53806, May 1969.

Ostrander, N.C., "Longitudinal Station Keeping of Nearly Geostationary Satellites", RAND Corporation Report No. RM-6166RR, Santa Monica, CA, Nov. 1969.

Boretz, J.E., "Large Space Station Power Systems", *J. Spacecraft*, Vol. 6, No. 8, 1969, pp. 929–936.

Goubau, G., "Microwave Power Transmission From an Orbiting Solar Power Station", *J. Microwave Power*, Vol. 5, No. 4, Dec. 1970, pp. 223–231.

Brown, W.C., "A Microwave Beam Power Transfer and Guidance System for Use in an Orbital Astronomy Support Facility", NASA Contract No. HAS-8-25374, Final Report, 10 Dec. 1970.

Glaser, P.E., "Power Without Pollution", *Journal of Microwave Power*, Vol. 5, No. 4, Dec. 1970.

Glaser, P.E., "Power from Space—Technology Transfer for Human Survival", AAS Science and Technology Series, Vol. 26, *Technology Utilization Ideas for the 70's and Beyond*, edited by F.W. Forbes and P. Dergarabedian, pp. 263–280, AAS Publications, Tarzana, CA, 1971.

Miller, T.J. et al., "Design and Preliminary Testing of a Brayton Space Radiator Concept", *Proceedings IECEC*, 1971.

Brown, W.C., "Transmission of Energy by Microwave Beam", *Proceedings 1971 Intersociety Energy Conversion Engineering Conference*, Boston, MA., Aug. 1971, pp. 5–13.

Glaser, P.E., "A New View of Solar Energy", Paper No. 719002, *Proceedings 1971 Intersociety Energy Conversion Engineering Conference*, Boston, MA, Aug. 1971.

Brown, W.C. and Maynard, O.E., *Microwave Power Transmission in the Satellite Solar Power Station System*, Raytheon Technical Report, 27 Jan. 1972.

Williams, J. and Kirby K., "Exploratory Investigation of an Electric Power Plant Utilizing a Gaseous Core Reactor with MHD Conversion", presented at the Nuclear Power for Tomorrow Conference sponsored by the American Nuclear Society, 24 Aug. 1972.

"Sensitivity of Attitude Control Propellant Requirements to SSPS Deviation Angle Limits", Grumman Aerospace Corporation Report No. ASP-611-M-1004, Aug. 1972.

"SSPS Microwave Transmission Model and Assumptions", Engineering Memorandum, File B11-P, Raytheon Company, Wayland, MA., 28 Aug. 1972.

Mockovciak, J., "A Systems Engineering Overview of the Satellite Power Station", *Proceedings for the 7th IECEC*, Paper No. 73911, Sept. 1972, pp. 712–719.

Woodcock, G.R., "On the Economics of Space Utilization", 23rd Congress of the IAF, Oct. 1972.

Wolf, M., "Photovoltaic Conversion of Laser Energy", *Proceedings of Laser-Energy Conversion Symposium*, NASA Ames Research Center, Moffett Field, Ca., 18–19 Jan. 1973, NASA TM-X-62269, pp. 6–18.

Raytheon Company, "Applications of Microwave Power Transmission to the Satellite Solar Power Station", Presented at the NASA Lewis Research Center, Cleveland, Ohio, 14 Feb. 1973.

Patha, J.T. and Woodcock, G.R., "Feasibility of Large Scale Orbital Solar Thermal Power Generation", Eighth Intersociety Energy Conversion Engineering Conference, 1973.

Brown, W.C., "Satellite Power Stations: A New Source of Energy?", *IEEE Spectrum*, Vol. 10, pp. 38–47, 1973.

Glaser, P.E., "The Satellite Solar Power Station", *Proceedings of the IEEE International Microwave Symposium*, June 1973, pp. 186–188.

Brown, W.C., "Adapting Microwave Techniques to Help Solve Future Energy Problems", *Proceedings of the IEEE International Microwave Symposium*, June 1973, pp. 189–191.

McCarthy, J.F., Jr., et al., "Satellite Solar Power Station", Student Project Report, Dept. of Aeronautics and Astronautics, M.I.T., Cambridge, MA, July 1973.

Glaser, P.E., "Solar Power Via Satellite", *Astronautics and Aeronautics*, Aug. 1973, pp. 60–63.

Gordon, G.D., "Assessment of On-Orbit Servicing of Synchronous Orbit Spacecraft", Comstat Laboratories, Final Report NASA Contract NAS 8-30285, Dec. 1973.

Brown, W.C., "Adapting Microwave Techniques to Help Solve Future Energy Problems", *IEEE Transactions on Microwave Theory and Techniques,* Dec. 1973, pp. 755–763.

Glaser, P.E., "Method and Apparatus for Converting Solar Radiation to Electrical Power", United States Patent 3,781,647, 23 Dec. 1973.

Patha, J.T. and Woodcock, G.R., "Feasibility of Large-Scale Orbital Solar/ Thermal Power Generation", *J. Spacecraft and Rockets,* Vol. 11, 1974, pp. 409–417.

Brown, W.C., "The Technology and Application of Free-Space Power Transmission by Microwave Beam", *Proc. IEEE,* Vol. 62, No. 1, Jan. 1974, pp. 11–25.

Pritchard, E.I. and Mead, O.J., "Business Risk and Value of Operations in Space (BRAVO)—Analysis of Solar Cell Power Satellite System", Aerospace Corporation, El Segundo, CA, 18 Jan. 1974.

Glaser, P.E., Maynard, O.E., Mackovciak, J. and Ralph, E.L., "Feasibility Study of a Satellite Solar Power Station", NASA CR-2357, NTIS N74-17784, Feb. 1974.

Ehricke, K.A., "The Power Relay Satellite: A Means of Global Energy Transmission Through Space", Rockwell International, Report E74-3-1, March 1974.

Woodcock, G.R. and Gregory, D.L., "Derivation of a Total Satellite Energy System", AIAA Paper 75-640, April 1975 (submitted to *Journal of Energy*).

Kline, R. and Nathan, C.A., "Overcoming Two Significant Hurdles to Space Power Generation: Transportation and Assembly", AIAA Paper No. 75-641, AIAA/AAS Solar Energy for Earth Conference, Los Angeles, CA, April 1975.

Williams, J.R., "Geosynchronous Satellite Solar Power", Chapter Eight, *Solar Energy for Earth,* Killian, Dugger and Grey, editors, an AIAA Assessment sponsored by the AIAA Technical Committee on Electric Power Systems, American Institute of Aeronautics and Astronautics, New York, 21 April 1975, pp. 59–71.

Woodcock, G.R. and Gregory, D.L., "Orbital Solar Energy Technology Advances", Tenth Intersociety Energy Conversion Engineering Conference, 1975.

"Sonnenenergie-Satelliten", AEG-Telefunken, Summary Report, Contract No. RVII-V67/74-PZ-BB74, May 1975.

Williams, J.R., "Geosynchronous Satellite Solar Power", *Astronautics & Aeronautics,* Nov. 1975, pp. 46–52.

"Solar Power From Satellites", Hearings before the Subcommittee on Aerospace Technology and National Needs of the Committee on Aeronautical and Space Sciences, United States Senate, 94th Congress, Second Session January 19 and 21, 1976, U.S. Government Printing Office, Washington, D.C., 1976.

"Space-Based Solar Power Conversion and Delivery Systems Study", Interim Summary Report, ECON, Inc., Princeton, N.J., Report No. 76-145-1B, 31 March 1976.

ECON, Inc., "Space-Based Solar Power Conversion and Delivery Systems," NASA Marshall Space Flight Center, Contract NAS 8–31308, Final Report, April 1976.

Agosto, W.N., "Space Production of Solar Power Stations", *IEEE Spectrum*, May 1976.

Committee on the Peaceful Uses of Outer Space, "Solar Power Stations in Space", Background paper prepared by the Secretariat, United Nations, General Assembly, A/AC.105/CXIX) CRP.1, 1 June 1976.

"Systems Concepts for STS-Derived Heavy Lift Launch Vehicle Study", Boeing Aerospace Co., NASA JSC Final Report NAS4-14710, June 1976.

"Space Station Systems Analysis", Grumman Aeorspace Corp., NASA MSFC Contract No. NAS8-31993, Program Review, 17 June 1976.

"Space-Based Solar Power Conversion and Delivery Systems Study", Grumman Aerospace Corp., NASA MSFC Contract No. NAS8-31308, Second Interim Report, Vol. II, Engineering Analysis of Orbital Systems, 30, June 1976.

"Space-Based Solar Power, Conversion and Delivery Systems Study", ECON, Inc., NASA MSFC Contract No. NAS8-31308, Second Interim Report, Vol. III, 30 June 1976.

"Space-Based Solar Power Conversion and Delivery Systems Study, Second Interim Report, Vol. III, Economic Analysis of Space-Based Solar Power Systems", ECON, Inc., Princeton, N.J., Report No. 76–145–2, 30 June 1976.

"Initial Technical, Environmental and Economic Evaluation of Space Solar Power Concepts", NASA JSC–11568, Aug. 1976.

"Systems Definition-Space Based Power Conversion Systems", Boeing Aerospace Co., NASA MSFC Contract No. NAS8-31628, Fourth Performance Review Briefing, 11 Aug. 1976.

O'Neill, G.K., "Engineering a Space Manufacturing Center", *Astronautics & Aeronautics*, Vol. 14, No. 10. 1976, pp. 20–28.

Drummond, J.E. and Drummond, R.N., "Derivation of a Low Cost Satellite Power System", *11th IECEC Proceedings*, Vol. 1, AICHE, Sept. 1976, pp. 64–71.

Woodcock, G.R. and Davis, E.E., "Transportation Options for Solar Power Satellites", *11th IECEC Proceedings*, Vol II, AICHE, Sept. 1976, pp. 1400–1407.

"Satellite Power System Concept Definition", Rockwell International Mid-Study Executive Summary, Sept. 1976, NASA MSFC Contract No. NAS8-32161.

Glaser, P.E., "Evolution of the Satellite Solar Power Station (SSPS) Concept", *J. Spacecraft*, Vol. 13, No. 9, Sept. 1976, pp. 573–576.

"Application of Station-Kept Array Concepts to Satellite Solar Power Station Design", The Aerospace Corp., NASA MSFC Contract No. NAS8-31842, Third Performance Review, 30 Sept. 1976.

Kline, R.L., "The Role of Space Stations in the Assembly and Maintenance of Large Space Structures", Int. Space Hall of Fame, Dedication Conference, Alamogordo, N.M., Oct. 1976.

Gehrig, J.J., "Geostationary Orbit-Technology and Law", Paper No. IAF-ISL-76-30, 27th Int. Astronautical Congress, Anaheim, CA, 10-16 Oct. 1976.

Glaser, P.E., "Solar Power From Satellites", *Physics Today*, Feb. 1977, pp. 30–38.

Glaser, P.E., "Perspectives on Satellite Solar Power", *J. Energy*, Vol. 1, No. 2, March-April 1977, pp. 75–84.

Gregory, D.L., "Alternative Approaches to Space-Based Power Generation", *J. Energy* Vol. 1, No. 2, March-April 1977, pp. 85–92.

Hazelrigg, G.A., Jr., "Economic Viability of Pursuing a Space Power System Concept", *J. Energy*, Vol. 1, No. 2, March-April 1977, pp. 93–99.

Glaser, P.E., "Satellite Solar Power—An Option for Power Generation on Earth", presented at the World Electrotechnical Congress, Moscow, UUSR, 21–25 June 1977.

Woodcock, G.R., "Solar Satellites—Space Key to Our Power Future", *Astronautics & Aeronautics*, Vol. 15, No. 7/8, July/Aug. 1977, pp. 30–43.

Grumman Aerospace Company studies: "The Development of Space Fabrication Techniques" for NASA/MSFC and "Orbital Assembly Demonstration Study" for NASA/JSC.

NASA, "Space Station Systems Analysis," (studies being performed under contract for Johnson Space Flight Center, Houston, Texas by McDonnell Douglas; and for Marshall Space Flight Center, Huntsville, Alabama by Grumman Aerospace Corporation).

Boeing Aerospace Company, "Space-Based Power Conversion and Power Relay Systems", Contract No. NAS8-31628.

"Performance Evaluation and Parametric Sizing of the Baseline SSPS", Grumman Aerospace Corporation Report No. ASP-611-M-1010.

Snyder, N.W., editor, *Energy Conversion for Space Power—v.3*, forty-five selected reprints, available from AIAA Publications Dept., N.Y., 1977.

Brown, W.C., "Transmission of Power From Space to Earth", AIAA/EEI/IEEE Sponsored Conference on New Options in Energy Technology, San Francisco, CA, 2–4 Aug. 1977.

3. STANDARD PROPULSION TEXTBOOKS

Shapiro, A.H., *The Dynamics and Thermodynamics of Compressible Fluid Flow*, Vol. 1, 1st ed., Ronald Press Co., New York, 1953.

Hesse, W.J. and Mumford, N.V.S., Jr., *Jet Propulsion for Aerospace Applications*, 2nd ed., Pitman Publ. Corp., New York, 1964.

Hill, P.G. and Peterson, C.R., *Mechanics and Thermodynamics of Propulsion*, 3rd ed., Addison-Wesley Publ. Co., Reading, MA, 1965.

Jahn, R.G., *Physics of Electric Propulsion*, 1st ed., McGraw-Hill Book Co., New York, 1968.

Shepherd, D.G., *Aerospace Propulsion*, 1st ed., American Elsevier Publ. Co., Inc., New York, 1972.

4. BEAMED-ENERGY SYSTEMS (REMOTE POWER SOURCE)

4.1 Beamed-Energy Propulsion Concepts
4.1.1 Laser Rocket Propulsion

Marx, G., "Interstellar Vehicle Propelled by Terrestrial Laser Beam", *Nature*, Vol. 211, 2 July 1966, pp. 22–23.

Redding, J. L., "Intersteller Vehicle Propelled by Terrestrial Laser Beam", *Nature*, 11 Feb. 1967, pp. 588–589.

Forward, R. L., "Ground Based Lasers for Propulsion in Space", Hughes Research Laboratories internal paper, Malibu, CA, 19 May 1967.

McLafferty, G. H., "Laser Energy Absorption in the Exhaust Nozzle of a Laser-Powered Rocket", United Aricraft Research Laboratories Report UAR-G256, 15 Jan. 1969.

Norem, P.C., "Interstellar Travel, A Round Trip Propulsion System with Relativistic Velocity Capabilities", American Astronautical Society Paper No. 69-388, June 1969.

Kantrowitz, A., "The Relevance of Space", *Astronautics & Aeronautics*, Vol. 9, No. 3, March 1971, pp. 34–35.

Klass, P. J., "Laser Propelled ABM Studies", *Aviation Week*, 17 April 1972.

Minovitch, M. A., "The Laser Rocket—A Rocket Engine Design Concept for Achieving a High Exhaust Thrust with High I_{sp}", Jet Propulsion Laboratory, TM 393-92, 18 Feb. 1972.

Arno, R. D., MacKay, J. S. and Nishioka, K., "Applications Analysis of High Energy Lasers", NASA Technical memorandum, NASA TM X-62, 142, March 1972.

Rom, F. E. and Putre, H. A., "Laser Propulsion", NASA Technical Memorandum, NASA TM-X-2510, April 1972.

Kantrowitz, A., "Propulsion to Orbit by Ground-Based Lasers", *Astronautics & Aeronautics*, Vol. 10, No. 5, May 1972, pp. 74–76.

"Advanced Propulsion Concepts—Project Outgrowth", Tech. Report AFRPL-TR-72-31, Mead, F.B., Jr., Editor, Air Force Rocket Propulsion Laboratory, United States Air Force, Edwards, CA, June 1972.

Pirri, A. N. and Weiss, R. F., "Laser Propulsion", AIAA Paper No. 72-719, Boston, MA., 26-28 June 1972.

Minovitch, M.A., "Reactorless Nuclear Propulsion—The Laser Rocket", AIAA Paper No. 72-1092, New Orleans, Lousiana, 1972.

Nakamura, Y. et. al., "Interim Progress Report on Propulsion Concepts for Advanced Systems", NASA No. 113-31-08-00, Sept. 1972, (JPL internal document).

Kizner, W., "Optimization of a Thrust Program for an Orbiting Laser Rocket Using One Ground Based Laser Generator—Maximum Eccentricity With Minimum Fuel and Time", Phaser Telepropulsion, Inc., Technical Report No. 101-1, Sept. 1972.

Harstad, K. G., "Review of Laser-Solid Interaction and Its Possibilities for Space Propulsion", Technical Memorandum 33-578, Jet Propulsion Laboratory, Pasadena, CA, Nov. 1972.

Moeckel, W. E., "Propulsion by Impinging Laser Beams", *J. Spacecraft and Rockets*, Vol. 9, Dec. 1972, pp. 942–944.

"Laser-Energy Conversion Symposium", NASA Technical memorandum X-62, 269, Proceedings of the First NASA Conference on Laser Energy Conversion, Billman, K. W., editor, Ames Research Center, Moffett Field, CA, Jan. 1973.

Garbuny, M., "Laser Engine Operating by Resonance Absorption" at Laser-Energy Conversion Symposium, NASA-Ames, 18-19 Jan. 1973, NASA TM X-62, 269.

Buonadonna, V. R., Knight, C. J. and Hertzberg, A., "The Laser Heated Wind Tunnel—A New Approach to Hypersonic Laboratory Simulation", AIAA Paper 73-211, Washington, D.C., 1973.

Bloomer, J. H., "The Alpha Centauri Probe", *Proc.. 17th Int. Astronautical Congress* (Propulsion and Re-Entry), Madrid, 1966; Gordon and Breach, Inc., New York, 1967, pp. 225–232.

Chapman, P. K., "Laser Propulsion to Relativistic Velocities for Interstellar Flight," *Proc. 24th I.A.F. Congress*, Baku, U.S.S.R., 7–13 Oct. 1973.

Buonadonna, V. R., Knight, C. J. and Hertzberg, A., "The Laser-Heated Hypersonic Wind Tunnel", *AIAA Journal*, Vol. 11, No. 11, Nov. 1973, pp. 1457–1458.

Baty, R. S., "Space Propulsion—Let's Do it Better Electrically", *Air University Review*, Nov.–Dec. 1973, pp. 10–25.

Cohen, W., "New Horizons in Chemical Propulsion", *Astronautics and Aeronautics*, Vol. 11, No. 12, Dec. 1973, pp. 46–51.

Poole, J. W. and Thorpe, M. L., "Seeded Gas Thrusters and Related System Components", Report No. NASA-CR-2364, Contract NAS3-17192, Humphreys Corp., Concord, N.H., Jan. 1974.

Pirri, A. N., Monsler, M. J. and Nebolsine, P. E., "Propulsion by Absorption of Laser Radiation", *AIAA Journal*, Vol. 12, No. 9, Sept. 1974, pp. 1254–1261.

Proceedings, Second NASA Conference on Laser Energy Conversion, NASA SP-395, Billman, K. W., editor, NASA Ames Research Center, Moffett Field, CA, Jan. 1975.

Byer, R. L., "Initial Experiments with a Laser Driven Stirling Engine", at Second Symposium on Laser Energy Conversion, NASA-Ames, CA, Jan. 1975.

Caledonia, G. E., Wu, P. K. S. and Pirri, A. N. "Radiant Energy Absorption Studies for Laser Propulsion", Physical Sciences Inc., PSI TR-20, NASA Cr-134809, Andover, MA, March 1975.

"Frontiers in Propulsion Research: Laser, Matter-Antimatter, Excited Helium, Energy Exchange and Thermonuclear Fusion", NASA Technical Memorandum 33-722, Papailiou, D. D., editor, 15 March 1975.

Forward, R. L., "Advanced Propulsion Concepts Study: Comparative Study of Solar Electric Propulsion and Laser Electric Propulsion", Under JPL Contract No. 954085, Subcontract under NASA contract NAS7-100, Task Order No. RD-156, Hughes Research Laboratories, Malibu, CA, June 1975.

Moeckel, W. E., "Optimum Exhaust Velocity for Laser-Driven Rockets", *J. Spacecraft*, Vol. 12, No. 11, Nov. 1975, pp. 700–701.

Minovitch, M. A., "Performance Analysis of a Laser Propelled Interorbital Transfer Vehicle", Final Report, Contract NAS 3-18536, NASA CR-134966, Feb. 1976.

Caledonia, G. E., Root, R. G., Wu, P. K., Kemp, N. H. and Pirri, A. N., "Plasma Studies for Laser-Heated Rocket Thruster", PSI TR-47, Physical Sciences Inc., Andover, MA, 1976.

Barchukov, A. I., Bunkin, F. V., Konov, V. I. and Prokhorov, A. M., "Laser Air-Jet Engine", *JETP Lett.*, Vol. 23, No. 5, 5 March 1976, pp. 213–214.

Wu, P. K. S. and Pirri, A. N., "Stability of Laser Heated Flows", *AIAA Journal*, Vol. 14, No. 3, March 1976, pp. 390–392.

Garbuny, M. and Pechersky, M. J., "Laser Engines Operating by Resonance Absorption", *Applied Optics*, Vol. 15, No. 5, May 1976, pp. 141–1157.

Kemp, N. H., Root, R. G., Wu, P. K. S., Caledonia, G. E. and Pirri, A. N., "Laser-Heated Rocket Studies", NASA CR-135127, May 1976.

Pirri, A. N., Simons, G. A. and Nebolsine, P. E.Pulsed, "The Fluid Mechanics of Laser Propulsion", ARPA Order No. 3176, PSI TR-60, Physical Sciences Inc., Woburn, MA, July 1976.

Bunkin, F. V. and Prokhorov, A. M., "Use of a Laser Energy Source in Producing a Reactive Thrust", *Sov. Phys. USP.*, Vol. 19, No. 7, July 1976, pp.561–573.

Larson, V. R., "Future Propulsion Options for Performance Growth", AIAA Paper No. 76–708, AIAA/SAE 12th Propulsion conference, Palo Alto, CA, July 26–29, 1976.

Huberman, M. et al., "Investigation of Beamed Energy Concepts For Propulsion: Systems Studies—Volume I", AFRPL-TR-76-66, TRW Defense and Space Systems Group, Redondo Beach, CA, Oct. 1976.

Huberman, M. et al., "Investigation of Beamed Energy Concepts For Propulsion: Laser/Propellant Coupling Analysis—Volume II", AFRPL-TR-76-66, TRW Defense and Space Systems Group, Redondo Beach, CA, Oct. 1976.

Huberman, M., et al., "Investigation of Beamed Energy Concepts for Propulsion: (Classified)—Volume III", AFRPL-TR-76-66, TRW Defense and Space Systems Group, Redondo Beach, CA, Oct. 1976.

Lo, R. E., "Propulsion by Laser Energy Transmission", IAF-76-165, 27th International Astronautical Federation Congress, Anaheim, CA, 10-16 Oct. 1976.

Selph, C. and Horning, W., "Laser Propulsion", IAF-76-166, 27th International Astronautical Federation Congress, Anaheim, CA, 10–16 Oct. 1976.

Shoji, J. M. and Larson, V. R., "Performance and Heat Transfer Characteristics of the Laser-Heated Rocket—A Future Space Transportation System", AIAA Paper No. 76-1044, AIAA International Electric Propulsion Conference, Key Biscayne, FL., Nov. 1976.

Wu, P. K., "Similarity Solution of the Boundary-Layer Equations of Laser Heated Flows", *AIAA Journal*, Vol. 14, No. 11, Nov. 1976, pp. 1659–1661.

Wu, P. K., "Real Gas Effect in a Laser Heated Thruster", *AIAA Journal*, Vol. 14, No. 12, Dec. 1976, pp. 1766–1768.

Kantrowitz, A. R. and Rosa, R. J., "Ram Jet Powered by a Laser Beam", U.S. Pat. No. 3,818,700.

Caledonia, G. E., "Conversion of Laser Energy to Gas Kinetic Energy", *J. Energy*, Vol. 1, No. 2, March–April 1977, pp. 121–124.

Wu, P. K., "Convective Heat Flux in a Laser Heated Thruster", PSI TR-80, Physical Sciences Inc., Andover, MA, April 1977.

Simons, G. A. and Pirri, A. N., "The Fluid Mechanics of Pulsed Laser Propulsion", AIAA Paper No. 77-699, AIAA 10th Fluid and Plasma Dynamic Conference, Albuquerque, N. Mex., June 1977.

Kemp, N. H. and Root, R. G., "Nozzle Flow of Laser-Heated, Radiating Hydrogen with Applications to a Laser-Heated Rocket", AIAA Paper No. 77-695, AIAA 10th Fluid and Plasma Dynamics Conference, Albuquerque, N. Mex., June 1977.

Weyl, G. M. and Shui, V. H., "On Water-Vapor Plumes, Condensation, and Their Effect on Laser Propagation in the Laser Propelled Rocket", AIAA Paper No. 77-696, AIAA 10th Fluid and Plasma Dynamics Conference, Albuquerque, N. Mex., June 1977.

Legner, H. H. and Douglas-Hamilton, D. H., "CW Laser Propulsion", AIAA Paper No. 77-657, AIAA 10th Fluid and Plasma Dynamics Conference, Albuquerque, N. Mex., June 1977.

Whitmire, D. P. and Jackson, IV, A. A., "Laser Powered Interstellar Ramjet", *JBIS*, Vol. 30, No. 6, June 1977, pp. 223–226.

Chapman, P. K., "Optimal Trajectories for Laser-Powered Launch Vehicles", AAS/AIAA Astrodynamics Specialist Conference, Jackson Lake Lodge, Grand Teton National Park, Wyoming, 7–9 Sept. 1977.

Molmud, P., "Laser Assisted Propulsion-Coupling Mechanisms", R&D Status Report 6, Contract FO4611-76-C-0003.

Shoji J. M., "Laser Heated Rocket Thruster", Contract No. NAS3-19728, (Final Report To Be Published).

Sellen, J. M., Jr., "Laser Receiver System Study", R&D Status Report 6, Contract FO4611-76-C-0003.

"Laser Rocket Systems Analysis Study," Lockheed Missiles and Space Co., LMSC-D564671, October 1977.

Dyson, F. J. and Perkins, F. W. Jr., "JASON Laser Propulsion Study, Summer 1977", Stanford Research Institute, Menlo Park, CA, Technical Report JSR-77-12, December 1977.

Felber, F. S., "Laser Acceleration of Reactor-Fuel Pellets," General Atomic Project 2101, EPRI Contract RP-323-2, December 1977.

Nebolsine, P. E., Pirri, A. N., Goela, J. S., and Simons, G. A., "Pulsed Laser Propulsion," Proceedings of 1978 JANAF Conference, Incline Village, Nevada, 14 February 1978; See also Report No. PSI-TR-108 submitted under DARPA Order No. 3176, Physical Sciences, Inc., Andover MA, February 1978.

Nebolsine, P. E., Pirri, A. N., Geola, J. S., Simons, G. A. and Rosen, D. I., "Pulsed Laser Propulsion," Physical Sciences, Inc., TR-142; presented at the AIAA Conference on Fluid Dynamics of High-Power Lasers, October 1978.

Douglas-Hamilton, D. H., Kantrowitz, A. R. and Reilly, D. A., "Laser Assisted Propulsion Research, *Radiation Energy Conversion in Space*, Progress in Astronautics and Aeronautics, Vol. 61, pp. 264–270, 1978.

Ageev, V. P., Barchukov, A. I., Bunkin, F. V., Konov. V. I., Korobeinikov, V. P., Putryatin, B. V. and Hudyakov, V. M. (1978) "Experimental and Theoretical Modeling of Laser Propulsion", Paper 78-221, presented at the XXIX-th Congress of the International Astronautical Federation, Dubrovnik, 1978; *Acta Astronautica* (1980), *Vol. 7*, pp. 79–90.

Weiss, R. F., Pirri, A. N. and Kemp, N. H., "Laser Propulsion," *Astronautics and Aeronautics*, Vol. 17, No. 3, March 1979, pp. 50–58.

Jones, W. S., Forsyth, J. B. and Skratt, J. P., "Laser Rocket System Analysis," Lockheed Missiles and Space Co., NASA CR159521, 15 March 1979.

Chapman, P. K., "Laser Propulsion from the Moon," Arthur D. Little, Inc., *Space Manufacturing III, Proceeding of the 4th Princeton/AIAA Conference*, Princeton, NJ, 14–17 May 1979.

Fowler, M. C. Newman, L. A. and Smith, D. C., "Beamed Energy Coupling Studies".—Final Report AFRPL-TR-79-51, January 1980.

Kemp, N. H. and Lewis, P. F., "Laser-Heated Thruster—Interim Report," NASA CR-161665, Physical Sciences, Inc., Andover, MA, February 1980.

Jones, L. W., "Laser Propulsion—1980," AIAA Paper No. 80-1264, AAIAA/SAE/ASME 16th Joint Propulsion Conference, Hartford, Connecticut, 30 June—2 July 1980.

Kemp, N. H. and Krech, R. H., "Laser-Heated Thruster," Physical Sciences, Inc., NASA CR-161666, Andover, MA, September 1980.

Rather, J. D. G., Borgo, P. A. and Myrabo, L. N., "Laser Propulsion Support Program," BDM/W-80-652-TR, prepared for NASA Marshall SFC, 1 November 1980.

Ageov, V. P., et al., "Some Characterisics of the Laser Multi-Pulse Explosive Type Jet Thruster," Lebedev Physical Institute, Moscow, USSR, IAF Paper No. 80-F-272, XXXI Congress of the International Astronautical Federation.

Andrews, D. and Grim, D., "Advanced Propulsion System Concepts for Orbital Transfer", The Boeing Company, Mid-term Briefing to NASA/MSFC, February 1981.

4.1.2.   Laser Airbreathing Propulsion.

Bekey, I. and Mayer, H., "1980–2000: Raising our Sights for Advanced Space Systems", *Astronautics and Aeronautics*, July/Aug. 1976, pp. 34–63.

Myrabo, L. N., "MHD Propulsion by Absorption of Laser Radiation", *J. Spacecraft & Rockets*, Vol. 13, No. 8, Aug. 1976, pp. 466–472.

Weber, R., "Laser Powered Propulsion for Aircraft," Memorandum to NASA Headquarters, Research Div., dated June 11, 1976.

Hertzberg, A., Sun, K. C. and Jones, W. S., "A Laser-Powered Flight Transportation System," AIAA preprint 78-1484, AIAA Aircraft Systems and Technology Conference," See also *Gas Flow and Chemical Lasers*, J. F. Wendt, Ed., McGraw Hill, 1978.

Myrabo, L. N., "Solar-Powered Global Air Transportation", presented at the AIAA/DGLR 13th International Electric Propulsion Conference, San Diego, CA, 25-27 April 1978.

Jones, W. S., "Laser-Powered Aircraft and Rocket Systems with Laser Energy Relay Units," *Radiation Energy Conversion in Space*, Progress in Astronautics and Aeronautics, Vol. 61, 1978, p. 264–270.

Myrabo, L. N., "Laser Boosted Advanced LTAV as a Heavy Lift Launch Vehicle," AIAA Paper No. 79-1403, presented at the 4th Princeton/AIAA Conference on Space Manufacturing, Princeton, New Jersey, 14–17 May 1979.

Myrabo, L. N., "High Altitude Surveillance Drone Powered by Beamed Energy," Report No. WJSA-80-176, W. J. Schafer Associates, Inc., Wakefield, MA, 28 July 1980.

Myrabo, L. N., "A Concept for Light-Powered Flight", Paper No. 82-1214, AIAA/SAE/ASME 18th Joint Propulsion Conference, Cleveland, Ohio, 21–23 June 1982.

Myrabo, L. N. and M. Martinez-Sanchez, M., and Heimerdinger, D. "Laser-Driven MHD-Fanjet" Paper No. 83-1345, AIAA/SAE/ASME 19th Joint Propulsion Conference, Seattle, Washington, 27–29 June 1983.

Maxwell, C. D., and Myrabo, L. N., "Laser-Driven Repetitively-Pulsed MHD Generators: A Conceptual Study", *Orbit Raising and Maneuvering Propulsion: Research Status and Needs*, Progress in Astronautics and Aeronautics, Volume 89, Ed. by L.H. Caveny, publ. by AIAA, New York, 1984.

Myrabo, L. N., "Advanced Beamed-Energy and Field Propulsion Concepts," BDM/W-83-225-TR, prepared for the California Institute of Technology and Jet Propulsion Laboratory (Pasadena, Calif.) under contract No. NAS7-100, Task Order RE-156, 31 May 1983.

4.1.3. Microwave Rocket Propulsion

Willinski, M.I., "Beamed Electromagnetic Power as a Propulsion Energy Source", *American Rocket Society Journal*, Vol. 29, Aug. 1958, pp. 601–603.

Luedde, J.C., "Conversion of RF Energy to Propulsion Power", unpublished, 13 June 1960.

Slocum, R.W., Jr. and Zapola, A.G., "Microwave Rocket Propulsion", *American Rocket Society Journal*, Vol. 31, 1961, p. 657.

Willinksi, M.I., "Microwave Powered Ferry Vehicles", *Space Flight*, Vol. 8, No. 6, June 1966, pp. 217–225.

Bonneville, J.M., "Propulsion Assisted by Microwave Power", *The Journal of Microwave Power*, Vol. 3, No. 4, December 1968, pp. 187–193.

Moriarty, J.J. and Brown, W.C., "Toroidal Microwave Discharge Heating of Gas", Vol. 3, No. 4, December 1968, pp. 180–193.

Chapman, R., Filbus, J., Morin, T., Snellenberger, R., Asmussen, J., Hawley, M.C. and Kerber, R., "Microwave Plasma Generation of Hydrogen Atoms for Rocket Propulsion", Paper No. AIAA 81–0675, AIAA/JSASS/DGLR 15th International Electric Propulsion Conference, Las Vegas, Nevada, 21–23 April 1981; see also, *Journal of Spacecraft and Rockets*, Vol. 19, No. 6, Nov.–Dec. 1982.

Hawley, M., Morin, T., Chapman, R., Filbus, J., Asmussen, J., and Kerber, R., "Measurements of Energy Distribution and Thrust for Microwave Plasma Coupling of Electrical Energy to Hydrogen for Propulsion", Paper No. AIAA 82–1950, presented at the AIAA/JSASS/DGLR 16th International Electric Propulsion Conference, New Orleans, LA, 17–19 November 1982.

Hawley, M.C. and Morin, T.J., "Theory of Modeling of Collision Processes in H-atom Generation for Propulsion", MSU/NASA Workshop of Advanced Propulsion Concepts Using Time Varying Electromagnetic Fields, 23–25 February 1982, E. Lansing, MI.

Micci, M.M., "Prospects for Microwave Heated Propulsion", Paper No. AIAA 84–1390, AIAA/SAE/ASME Joint Propulsion Conference, Cincinnati, Ohio, 11–13 June 1984.

4.1.4. Airbreathing Microwave Propulsion

Brown, W.C., "The Microwave Powered Helicopter", *The Journal of Microwave Power*, Vol. 1, No. 1, 1966.

Brown, W.C., "The Microwave-Powered Helicopter System", Report No. MTO-103, Raytheon Co., 23 January 1967.

Brown, W.C., "The Case for the Microwave Powered Helicopter as a Communications Platform at 5000-10,000 Foot Altitude", Microwave and Tube Division, Raytheon Co., 19 November *1964*.

Brown, W.C., "Experimental System for Automatically Positioning a Microwave-Supported Platform", Technical Report No. RADC-TR-68-273.

Brown, W.C., "Experimental Airborne Microwave-Supported Platform", Technical Report No. RADC-TR-65-188.

Brown, W.C., Mims, J.R. and Heenan, N.I., "An Experimental Microwave-Powered Helicopter", *1965 IEEE International Convention Record*, Vol. 13, Pt. 5, pp. 225–235.

Okress, E.C., "Microwave-Powered Aerospace Vehicles", *Wave Power Engineering*, Academic Press, Inc., New York, Vol. II, 1968, pp. 268–285.

Myrabo, L.N., "High Altitude Surveillance Drone Powered by Beamed Energy", Report No. WJSA-80-176, W.J. Schafer Associates, Inc., Wakefield, Mass., 28 July 1980.

Sinko, J.W., "High Altitude Powered Platform Cost and Feasibility Study", SRI Project 5655-502, prepared for NASA Headquarters under Contract NASW-2962, 12 October, 1977.

Myrabo, L.N., "Advanced Beamed-Energy and Field Propulsion Concepts," BDM/W-83-225-TR, prepared for the California Institute of Technology and Jet Propulsion Laboratory (Pasadena, Calif.) under contract No. NAS7-100, Task Order RE-156, 31 May 1983.

4.2.   High-Power Lasers and Laser Power Stations

Pike, C.A., *Lasers and Masers*, Howard W. Sams & Co., Inc., The Bobbs-Merrill Co., Inc., 1968.

Smith, R.C., "Lasers—Present Achievements and Applications", *Adv. of Science*, Vol. 26, 1970, pp. 346–354.

Lubin, M.J., "Laser-Produced Plasmas for Power Generation and Space Propulsion", *Astronautics and Aeronautics*, Vol. 8, No. 11, Nov. 1970, pp. 42–48.

Gerry, E. J., "Gas Dynamic Lasers", *IEEE Spectrum*, Vol. 7, No. 11, Nov. 1970, pp. 51–56.

Ulsamer, E.E., "Laser—A Weapon Whose Time is Near", *Air Force*, Dec. 1970, pp. 28–34.

Emmett, J. L., "Frontiers of Laser Development", *Physics Today*, Vol. 24, March 1971, pp. 24–31.

Lengyel, B.A., *Lasers*, John Wiley & Sons, Inc., 1971.

Ahlstrom, H.G., Christiansen, W.H. and Hertzberg, A., "Laser Power Transmission", *The Trend in Engineering*, Vol. 23, No. 4, Oct. 1971, pp. 20–29.

Ulsamer, E.E., "Status Report on Laser Weapons", *Air Force*, Jan. 1972, p. 63.

Hansen, C.F. and Lee, G., "Laser Power Stations in Orbit", *Astronautics and Aeronautics*, Vol. 10, No. 7, July 1972, pp. 46–51.

Klass, P.J., "Special Report: Laser Thermal Weapons", *Aviation Week and Space Technology*, Vol. 97, Part I—Research Nears Application Level, pp. 12–15, Aug. 14; and Part II—Power Boost Key to Feasibility, pp. 32–40, 21 Aug. 1972.

Eleccion, M., "The Family of Lasers: A Survey", *IEEE Spectrum*, Vol. 9, 1972, pp. 26–40.

Hertzberg, A., Christiansen, W.H., et al, "Photon Generators and Engines for Laser Power Transmission", *AIAA Journal*, Vol. 10, No. 4, April 1972, pp. 394–400.

De Maria, A.J., "Review of CW High Power Co_2 Lasers", *Proceedings of the IEEE*, June 1973.

Klass, P.J., "Major Hurdles for Laser Weapons Cited", *Aviation Week and Space Technology*, Vol. 99, 9 July 1973, pp. 38–42.

Christiansen, W.H. and Hertzberg, A., "Gasdynamic Lasers and Photon Machines", *Proceedings of the IEEE*, Vol. 61, No. 8, Aug. 1973, pp. 1060–1072.

Lacina, W.B. and McAllister, G.L., "High Energy Scaling Generalization for CO Electric Discharge Lasers", Northrop Research and Technology Center, Hawthorne, CA, 1974.

Reilly, J.P., "High-Power Electric Discharge Lasers (EDLs)", *Astronautics and Aeronautics*, March 1975, pp. 52–63.

Kantrowitz, A., "High-Power Lasers", *Astronautics and Aeronautics*, March 1975, pp. 50–51.

Warren, W. R., Jr., "Chemical Lasers", *Astronautics and Aeronautics*, April 1975, pp. 36–49.

Russell, D.A., "Gasdynamic Lasers", *Astronautics and Aeronautics*, June 1975, pp. 48–55.

Klass, P.J., "Progress Made on High-Energy Laser", *Aviation Week and Space Technology*, 7 March 1977, pp. 16–17.

Fenstermacher, C., editor, *High Energy Short Pulse Lasers*, AIAA Selected Reprint Series, Vol. XIX, Special Publications Department, Department D, American Institute of Aeronautics and Astronautics, Inc., New York, N.Y. 1977.

Myrabo, L. N., "Power-Beaming Technology for Laser Propulsion", *Orbit Raising and Maneuvering Propulsion: Research Status and Needs*, Progress in Astronautics and Aeronautics, Volume 89, Ed. by L.H. Caveny, publ. by AIAA, New York, 1984.

4.3   Laser/Gas Interactions

Ramsden, S. A. and Davis, W.E.R., "Radiation Scattered From the Plasma Produced by a Focused Ruby Laser Beam", *Physical Rev. Letters*, Vol. 13, No. 7, Aug. 1964, p. 227.

Tozer, B.A., "Theory of the Ionization of Gases by Laser Beams", *Phys. Rev.*, Vol. 137, No. 6A, 15 March 1965, pp. 1665–1667.

Raizer, Y.P., "Heating of a Gas by a Powerful Light Pulse", *Soviet Physics JETP*, Vol. 21, 1965, p. 1009.

Phelps, A.V., "Theory of Ionization During Laser Breakdown", in *Physics of Quantum Electronics*, Ed. Kelley, Lax, Tannenwald, McGraw-Hill, 1966.

Gregg, D.W. and Thomas, S.J., "Kinetic Energies of Ions Produced by Laser Giant Pulses", *Journal of Applied Physics*, Vol. 37, No. 12, Nov. 1966, pp. 4313–4316.

Wilson, K.H. and Grief, R., "Radiation Transport in Atomic Plasmas", *J.Q.S.R.T.*, Vol. 8, 1968, p. 1061.

Raizer, Y.P., "Possibility of Igniting a Traveling Laser Spark at Beam Intensities Much Below the Breakdown Threshold", *Soviet Physics JETP Letters*, Vol. 7, 1968, p. 55.

Monsler, M.J., "An Acoustic Instability Driven by Absorption of Radiation in Gases", Ph.D. thesis, M.I.T., Dept. of Aeronautics and Astronautics, Cambridge , MA, 1969.

Bunkin, F.V., Konov, V.I., Prokhorov, A.M. and Fedorov, V.B., *JETP Lett.*, Vol. 9, 1969, p. 371.

Raizer, Y.P., "The Feasibility of an Optical Plasmatron and Its Power Requirements", *Soviet Physics JETP Letters*, Vol. 11, 1970, p. 120.

Steinhauer, L.C. and Ahlstrom, H.G., "Laser Heating of a Stationary Plasma", Report 70-4, Univ. of Washington, Dept. of Aeronautics and Astronautics, Seattle, Washington, Sept. 1970.

Raizer, Y.P., "Subsonic Propagation of a Light Spark and Threshold Conditions for the Maintenance of a Plasma by Radiation", *Soviet Physics JETP*, Vol. 31, No. 6, Dec. 1970.

Molmud, P., "Laser Heating of Air Via Aerosols", TRW, Redondo Beach, CA, 11 Oct. 1971.

Vincenti, W.G. and Traugott, S.C., "The Coupling of Radiative Transfer and Gas Motion", *Annual Review of Fluid Mechanics*, Vol. 3, 1971. pp. 89–117.

Generalov, N.A., Zimakov, V.P., Kozlov, G.I., Masyukov, V.A., and Raizer, Y.P., "Experimental Investigation of a Continuous Optical Discharge," *Soviet Physics JETP*, Vol. 34, April 1972, p. 763.

Montgolfier, P., "Laser-Induced Gas Breakdown: Electron Cascade", *J. Phys. D: App. Phys.*, Vol. 5, 1972, pp. 1438–1447.

Triplett, J.R. and Boni, A.A., "The Interaction of Suspended Atmospheric Particles with Laser Radiation", SSS-R-71-1167, Systems, Science and Software, La Jolla, CA, June 1972.

Rob, B.S. and Turcotte, D.L., "Laser-Produced Spherical Shock Waves", AIAA Paper No. 72-720, AIAA 5th Fluid and Plasma Dynamics Conference, Boston, MA, June 1972.

Daugherty, J.D., Pugh, E.R., Douglas-Hamilton, D.H., "A Stable, Scalable, High Pressure Gas Discharge as Applied to the CO_2 Laser", 24th Annual Gaseous Electronics Conf., APS, Oct. 1971, Gainesville, FL; see also *Physics Today*, Vol. 25, No. 1, 1972, p. 18.

Klosterman, E.L., Byron, S.R. and Newton, J.F., "Laser Supported Combustion Wave Study", Mathematical Sciences Northwest, Inc., Report 73-101-3, 1973.

Smith, D.C., et al., "Investigation of Gas Breakdown with 10.6 μm Wavelength Radiation", AFWL-TR-72-182, Air Force Weapons Laboratory, Feb. 1973.

Schlier, R.E., Pirri, A.N. and Reilly, D.J., "Air Breakdown Studies", AFWL-TR-72-74, Air Force Weapons Laboratory, Feb. 1973.

Lencioni, D.E., et al., "The Effect of Dust on 10.6 μm Laser Induced Air Breakdown", LTP-20, MIT Lincoln Laboratory, Lexington, MA, April 1973.

Hall, R.B., Maher, W.E. and Wei, P.S.P., "An Investigation of Laser-Supported Detonation Waves", AFWL-TR-73-28, Air Force Weapons Lab., N. Mex., June 1973.

Stegman, R.L., Schriempf, J.T. and Hettche, L.R., "Experimental Studies of Laser-Supported Absorption Waves with 5-ms Pulses of 10.6 μm Radiation", *Journal of Applied Physics*, Vol. 44, No. 8, Aug. 1973, pp. 3675–3681.

Raizer, Y.P., *Laser-Induced Discharge Phenomena*, Plenum Press, New York, 1974 (in preparation).

Klosterman, E.L. and Byron, S.R., "Experimental Study of Subsonic Laser Absorption Waves", Mathematical Sciences Northwest, Rept. MSNW-73-101-4, Seattle, Wash., Dec. 1973; or Air Force Weapons Laboratory Rept. AFWL-TR-73-28, Kirkland AFB, Albuquerque, N. Mex., 1974.

Stallcop, J.R. and Billman, K.W., "Analytical Formula for the Inverse Bremsstrahlung Absorption Coefficient," *Plasma Physics*, Vol. 16, 1974, pp. 1187–1189.

Boni, A.A. and Su, F.Y., "Subsonic Propagation of Laser Supported Waves", AIAA Paper 74-567.

Klosterman, E.L. and Byron, S.R., "Measurements of Subsonic Laser Absorption Wave Propagation Characteristics at 10.6 μm", *J. Appl. Phys.*, Vol. 45, 1974, p. 4751.

Jackson, J.P. and Nielsen, P.E., "Role of Radiative Transport in the Propagation of Laser Supported Combustion Waves", *AIAA Journal*, Vol. 12, No. 11, Nov. 1974, p. 1498.

Walters, C.T., Barnes, R.H. and Beverly, R.E., III, "An Investigation of Mechanisms of Initiation of Laser-Supported Absorption (LSA) Waves", Final Report for DAAHO1-73-C-0776, Battelle Columbus Laboratories, Columbus, Ohio, Sept. 1975.

Thomas, P.D. and Musal. H.M., "Laser Absorption Wave Formation", *AIAA Journal*, Vol. 13, Oct. 1975, pp. 1279–1286.

Lencioni, D.E., "Real Air Breakdown", presented at HELREG Propagation Subpanel Meeting, MITRE Corp., Bedford, MA, Nov. 1975.

Su, F.Y. and Boni, A.A., "Non-Linear Model of Laser-Supported Deflagration Waves", *The Physics of Fluids*, Vol. 19, No. 7, July 1976, p. 960.

4.4   Laser/Surface Interactions

Gregg, D.W. and Thomas, S.J., "Momentum Transfer Produced by Focused Laser Giant Pulses", *J. Appl. Phys.*, Vol. 37, No. 7, June 1966, pp. 2787–2789.

Basov, N.G., Gribkov, V.A., Krokhin, O.N. and Sklizkov, G.V., "High Temperature Effects of Intense Laser Emission Focused on a Solid Target", *Soviet Physics JETP*, Vol. 27, No. 4, Oct. 1968, p. 575.

Anisimov, S.I., Imas, Ya.A., Romanov, G.S. and Khodyko, Yu. V., *Effects of High-Power Radiation on Metals*, Nauka, M., 1970.

DeMichelis, C., "Laser Interaction with Solids—A Bibliographical Review", *IEEE Journal of Quantum Electronics*, Vol. QE-6, No. 10, Oct. 1970, p. 630.

Ready, J.F., *Effects of High Power Laser Radiation*, Academic Press, New York, 1971.

Locke, E.V., Hoag, E.D. and Hella, R.A., "Deep Penetration Welding with High Power CO_2 Lasers", *IEEE Journal of Quantum Electronics*, Vol. QE-8, No. 2, Feb. 1972, pp. 132–136.

Pirri, A.N., Schlier, R. and Northam, D., "Momentum Transfer and Plasma Formation Above a Surface with a High Power CO_2 Laser", Avco Everett Research Laboratory Report, AMP-350, Everett, MA, June 1972.

Pirri, A.N., Schlier, .R., and Northam, D., "Momentum Transfer and Plasma Formation Above a Surface With a High-Power CO_2 Laser", *Applied Physics Letters*, Vol. 21, No. 3, Aug. 1972, pp. 79–81.

Barchukov, A.I., Bunkin , F.V., Konov, V.I. and Prokhorov, A.M., "Low-Threshold Breakdown for Air Near a Target by CO_2 Radiation, and the Associated Large Recoil Momentum", *JETP Letters*, Vol. 17, No. 8, 20 April 1973, p. 294.

Lowder, J.E., Lencioni, D.E., Hilton, T.W. and Hull, R.J., "High-Energy Pulsed CO_2 Laser-Target Interaction in Air", *J. Appl. Phys.*, Vol. 44, No. 6, June 1973, pp. 2759–2762.

Thomas, P.D. and Musal, H.M., "A Theoretical Study of Laser-Target Interaction", Lockheed Palo Alto Research Laboratory, Palo Alto, CA, Rept. LMSC-D 352890, Aug. 1973.

Pirri, A.N., "Theory for Momentum Transfer to a Surface With a High-Power Laser", *The Physics of Fluids*, Vol. 16, No. 9, Sept. 1973, pp. 1435–1440.

Hettche, L.R., Schriempf, J.T. and Stegman, R.L., "Impulse Reaction Resulting from the In-Air Irradiation of Aluminum by a Pulsed CO_2 Laser", *J. Appl. Phys.*, Vol. 44, No. 9, Sept. 1973, p. 4079.

Thomas, P.D., Musal, H.M. and Chou, Y.S., "Laser Beam Interaction—Part II", Lockheed Palo Alto Research Lab., LSMC-D403747, 1974.

Boni, A.A., Cohen, H.D., Meskan, D.A. and Su, F.Y., "Laser Interaction Studies", System, Science and Software, Rept. 74-2344, La Jolla, CA, Aug. 1974.

Reilly, D.A. and Rostler, P.S., "Pre-Breakdown Laser Target Vaporization and Enhanced Thermal Coupling, Final Technical Report", Avco Everett Research Laboratory Report for Contract N00014-73-C-0457, Aug. 1974.

Pirri, A.N., "Anyltic Solutions for Initiation of Plasma Absorption above Laser-Irradiated Surfaces", Physical Sciences Inc., Andover, MA, Rept. PSI TR-15, Oct. 1974.

Stamm. M.R. and Nielsen, P.E., "Sensitivity of Laser Absorption Wave Formation to Nonequilibrium and Transport Phenomena," *AIAA Journal*, Vol. 13, No. 2, Feb. 1975, pp. 205–208.

Klosterman, E.L., "Experimental Investigation of Subsonic Laser Absorption Wave Initiation from Metal Targets at 5 and 10.6 μm", Mathematical Sciences Northwest Rept., MSNW-75-123-2, Seattle, Wash., March 1975.

Jackson, J.P. and Jumper, E.J., "Mechanisms of Enhanced Coupling by a Pulsed Laser", Laser Division Digest, AFWL-TR-75-229, Air Force Weapons Laboratory, Oct. 1975, p. 172.

Thomas, P.D., "Laser Absorption Wave Formation", *AIAA Journal*, Vol. 13, No. 10, Oct. 1975, pp. 1279–1286.

Pirri, A.N., "Analytic Solutions for Laser-Supported Combustion Wave Ignition Above Surfaces", *AIAA Journal*, Vol. 15, No. 1, Jan. 1976, pp. 83–91.

Marcus, S., Lowder, J.E., and Mooney, D.L., "Large-Spot Thermal Coupling of CO_2 Laser Radiation to Metallic Surfaces", *Journal of Applied Physics*, Vol. 47, No. 7, July 1976, p. 2966.

Hall, R.B., Wei, P. S.P. and Maher, W.E., "Laser Beam Target Interaction—Vol. II, Laser Effects at 10.6 μm", AFWL-TR-75-342, Vol. II, Air Force Weapons Laboratory Report, N.M., July 1976.

Boni, A.A., Su, F.Y., Thomas, P.D. and Musal, H.M., "Theoretical Study of Laser-Target Interactions", Mid-Term Technical Report, SAI 76-722-LJ, Science Applications, Inc., La Jolla, CA, Aug. 1976.

McKay, J.A., Stegman, R.L. and Schriempf, J.T., "Thermal Effects of Pulsed Laser Irradiation", *2nd DoD High Energy Laser Conference Proceedings*, Col. Springs, CO, Nov. 1976.

Pirri, A.N., Kemp., N.H., Root, R.G. and Wu, P.K.S., "Theoretical Laser Effects Studies", Final Report, PSI TR-89, Physical Sciences Inc., Andover, MA, Feb. 1977.

Boni, A.A., Su, F.Y., Thomas, P.D. and Musal, H.M., "Theoretical Study of Laser-Target Interactions", Final Technical Report, SAI 77-567 LJ, Science Applications Inc., La Jolla, CA, May 1977.

Pirri, A.N., Root, R.G. and Wu, P.K.S., "Plasma Energy Transfer to Metal Surfaces Irradiated by Pulsed Lasers", AIAA Paper No. 77-658, AIAA 10th Fluid and Plasmadynamics Conference, Albuquerque, N. Mex., 27–28 June 1977.

4.5   High Power Laser Propagation

McCoy, J.H., "Atmospheric Absorption of Carbon Dioxide Laser Radiation near Ten Microns", Technical Report 2476-2 (Ohio State University), prepared for AFAL, AFSC, 10 Sept. 1968.

Hayes, J.N., Ulrich, P.B. and Aitken, A.H., "Effects of the Atmosphere on The Propagation of 10.6-μm Laser Beams", *Applied Optics*, Vol. 11, No. 2, Feb. 1972, pp. 257-260.

Sutton, G.W., "Propagation Limitations Due to Atmospheric Turbulence", AMP 353, Avco Everett Research Laboratory, Everett, MA, May 1972.

McClatchey, R.A. and Selby, J.E.A., "Atmospheric Attenuation of HF and DF Laser Radiation", Report No. AFCRL-72-0312 (for AFSC, USAF, Environmental Research Papers No. 400), 23 May 1972.

Ulrich, P.B. and Wallace, J., "Propagation Characteristics of Collimated, Pulsed Laser Beams Through an Absorbing Atmosphere", *Journal of the Optical Society of America*, Vol. 63, No. 1, Jan. 1973, pp. 8–11.

McClatchey, R.A., Benedict, W.S., et al., "AFCRL Atmospheric Absorption Line Parameters Compilation", Report No. AFCRL-TR-73-0096 (for AFSC, USAF, Environmental Research Papers No. 434), 26 Jan. 1973.

Aitken, A.H., Hayes, J.N. and Ulrich, P.B., "Thermal Blooming of Pulsed Focused Gaussian Laser Beams", *Applied Optics*, Vol. 12, No. 2, Feb. 1973, pp. 193–197.

Vetter, A.A., "Phased Arrays of Lasers for Power Transmission", *Proceedings of the Technical Program, Electro-optical Systems Design Conference*, New York, 18–20 Sept. 1973, pp. 283–293.

McClatchey, R.A. and Selby, J.E.A., "Atmospheric Attenuation of Laser Radiation from 0.76 to 31.24 um", Report No. AFCRL-TR-74-0003 (for AFSC, USAF, Environmental Research Papers No. 434), 3 Jan. 1974.

Busar, R.G. and Rohde, R.S., "Transient Thermal Blooming of Long Laser Pulses", *Applied Optics*, Vol. 14, No. 1, Jan. 1975, pp. 50–55.

Teare, J.D., "Aerosol Propagation Effects", PSI TR-33, Contract No. N00014-75-C-0526, Physical Sciences Inc., Woburn, MA, 15 Aug. 1975.

Buser, R.G., Rohde, R.S., Berger, P.J., Gebhardt, F.G. and Smith, D.C., "Transient Thermal Blooming of Single and Multiple Short Laser Pulses", *Applied Optics*, Vol. 14, No. 11, Nov. 1975, pp. 2740–2745.

Wallace, J. and Lilly, J.Q., "Thermal Blooming of Repetitively Pulsed Laser Beams", *Journal of the Optical Society of America*, Vol. 64, No. 12, Dec. 1974, pp. 1651–1654.

Lencioni, D.E. and Herrman, J., "Comparison of CW and Repetitively-Pulsed Laser Beams", Lincoln Laboratory, Lexington, MA, 1976.

Gebhardt, F.G., "High Power Laser Propagation", *Applied Optics*, Vol. 15, No. 6, June 1976, pp. 1479–1493.

Hayes, J.H., "Propagation of High Power Laser Beams Through the Atmosphere: An Overview", *1976 AGARD Conference Proceedings*, No. 183—Optical Propagation in the Atmosphere, 1976, pp. 29–1 through 29–15.

Reilly, J.P., et al., "Multiple Pulse Propagation in Fog, Rain, and Dust at 10.6 μm", Avco Everett Research Laboratory, Contract N00173-76-C-0059, Everett, MA, July 1976.

Gebhardt, F. G., Phillips, E.A., Hancock, J.H. and Whitney, K.G., "Report on Nonlinear Propagation and Atmospheric Aerosol Investigation", SAI-164-416-03, Contract No. N00014-75-C-0530, Science Applications, Inc., Arlington, VA, 1 Oct. 1976.

Cordray, D.M., "MPLAW: A Multipulse-Scaling-Law Code Using Data-Base Interpolation", NRL Report 8055, Naval Research Laboratory, Optical Radiation Branch, Optical Sciences Division, Washington, D.C., 6 Oct. 1976.

Ruquist, R.D. and Phillips, E.A., "Meteorological Effects on High Energy Laser Propagation", AIAA Paper No. 77-655, AIAA 10th Fluid & Plasmadynamics Conference, Albuquerque, N. Mex., 27–29 June 1977.

Reilly, J., Singh, P. and Weyl, G., "Multiple Pulse Laser Propagation Through Atmospheric Dusts at 10.6 Microns", AIAA Paper No. 77-697, AIAA 10th Fluid & Plasmadynamics Conference, Albuquerque, N. Mex., June 1977.

4.6   Precision Pointing and Tracking Systems

Fosth, D.C., "A Survey of Precision-Pointing Systems", NASA SP-233, 1970, pp. 73–81.

"Parametric Analysis of Microwave and Laser Systems for Communication and Tracking", Operational Environment and System Implementation, Vol. IV, NASA CR-1689, Feb. 1971.

Higgins, R.A., "Alignment Control of a High Energy Laser System", UCRL-74050, Lawrence Livermore Laboratory, Livermore, CA, July 1972.

4.7   High-Power Laser Windows and Large Optics

"Optical Telescope Technology", NASA SP-233, 1970. Workshop Proceedings, Marshall Space Flight Center, Huntsville, AL, 29 April 1969.

Schmidt, F.J., "Electroforming of Large Mirrors", NASA SP-233, 1970, pp. 165–171.

Schroeder, J.F., "Materials Considerations for Large Spaceborne Astronomical Telescopes", NASA SP-233, 1970, pp. 141–148.

Sahagian, C.S. and Pitha, C.A., "Compendium on High Power Infrared Laser Window Materials", AFCRL Report 72-0170, 9 March 1972.

Giordmaine, J.A., "Optics at Bell Laboratories—Lasers in Science", *Appl. Optics*, Vol. 11, 1972, pp. 2435–2449.

"Large Space Telescope, Phase A", TM X-64726, NASA, 1972.

Parke, S., "Through a Glass Lightly", *Electronics and Power*, Vol. 18, Nov. 1973, pp. 401–403.

Glass, A.J. and Guenther, A. H., "Laser Induced Damage of Optical Elements—A Status Report", *Appl. Optics*, Vol. 12, 1973, pp. 637–649.

Boling, N.L., Crisp, M.D. and Dube, G., "Laser Induced Surface Damage", *Appl. Optics*, Vol. 12, 1973, pp. 650–660.

Jacobs, S.F., Norton, M.A. and Berthold, J.W., "Lasers—Studies of Dimensional Stability Over Long Periods of Time", *Optical Sciences Center Newsletter* (Univ. Arizona, Tucson), Vol. 7, Dec. 1973, pp. 68–72.

Fradin, D.W., "Laser-Induced Damage in Solids", *Laser Focus*, Vol. 10, Feb. 1974, pp. 39–45.

O'Keefe, J.D. and Johnson, R.L., "Optical Response of High-Power Laser Windows-Ultrashort Pulse Regime", *Appl. Optics*, Vol. 13, 1974, pp. 1141–1146.

Andrews, C.R. and Strecker, C.L., in *Proc. 4th Annual Conference on Infrared Laser Window Materials*, Air Force Materials Laboratory, Wright-Patterson Air Force Base, Ohio 45433.

4.8   Useful Reference Materials

Gilmore, F.R., "Equilibrium Composition and Thermodynamic Properties of Air to 24,000 K", RM-1543, The Rand Corp., Santa Monica, CA, 1955.

Cobine, J.D., *Gaseous Conductors*, Dover Publications, New York, 1958.

Molmud, P., "The Electrical Conductivity of Weakly Ionized Gases", STL (TRW), Redondo Beach, CA, Sept. 1962.

Yos, J.M., "Transport Properties of Nitrogen, Hydrogen, Oxygen and Air to 30,000 K", Avco-Everett Research Corporation, Technical Memorandum, RAD-TM-63-7, Everett, MA, March 1963.

Zel'dovich, Y.B. and Raizer, Y.P., *Physics of Shock Waves and High-Temperature Hydrodynamic Phenomena*, Academic Press, New York, 1966.

Patch, R.W., "Thermodynamics Properties and Theoretical Rocket Performance of Hydrogen to 100,000 K and 1.013 10^8 N/m²", NASA SP-3069, 1971.

Ready, J.F., *Effects of High Power Laser Radiation*, Academic Press, New York, 1971.

5. SELF-SUFFICIENT PROPULSION SYSTEMS (LOCAL POWER SOURCE)

5.1 High Altitude Airscooping Propulsion

Demetriades, S.T. and Kretschmer, C.B., "The Use of Planetary Atmospheres for Propulsion", Paper No. 57-46, Fourth Annual Meeting of the American Astronautical Society, 31 Jan. 1958; Also AFOSR TN 58-229, ASTIA No. AD 154.132, April 1958.

Demetriades, S.T. and Kretschmer, C.B., "A Preliminary Investigation of an Atomic-Oxygen Power Plant", AFOSR TN 58-325, ASTIA Document No. AD 154.229, 4 March 1958; Also summarized in *J. Aero/Space Sci.*, Vol. 25, 1958, p. 653.

Berner, F. and Camac, M., "Air Scooping Vehicle", Avco-Everett Research Lab., Everett, MA, Research Rept. 76, Air Force Ballistic Missile Div. TR 59-17, Aug. 1959.

Demetriades, S.T., "A Novel System for Space Flight Using a Propulsive Fluid Accumulator", *Journal of British Interplanetary Soc.*, Vol. 17, Oct. 1959, pp. 114-119; See also Northrop Corp./Norair Division, Document NB-59-161, CA, Dec. 1958 (ASTIA AD-226-086).

Demetriades, S.T., "Orbital Propulsion System for Space Maneuvering (PROFAC)", *Astronautical Science Review*, Vol. 1, Oct.-Dec. 1959, pp. 17-18, 26.

Corliss, W.R., *Propulsion Systems for Space Flight*, 1st ed., McGraw-Hill, N.Y. 1960, pp. 147-152.

French, E.P., "Operation of an Electric Ramjet in a Planetary Atmosphere", AAS Preprint, Aug. 1960, pp. 60-90.

Demetriades, S.T. and Young, C.F., "Orbital Refueling Satelloid", SAE/AFOSR Research Paper 230H, Standard Research Corp., Arcadia, CA, Oct. 1960.

Camac, M. and Berner, F., "An Orbital Air Scooping Vehicle", *Astronautics*, Vol. 6, Aug. 1961, pp. 28-29, 70-71.

Reichel, R.H., Smith, T.L. and Hanford, D.R., "Potentialities of Air-Scooping Electrical Space Propulsion Systems", *American Rocket Soc.*, Preprint No. 2391-62, March 1962; and in *Electric Propulsion Development*, Vol. 9 of Progress in Astronautics and Aeronautics, Academic Press, New York, 1963, pp. 711-743.

Dolgich, A., "Soviet Studies on Low-Thrust Orbital Propellant-Scooping Systems", *Foreign Science Bulletin*, Vol. 5, No. 7, July 1969, pp. 1-9. (Available CFSTI: N69-39104).

Glassmeyer, J.M., AFRPL "Ideagram", A-SCOR, Air Force Rocket Propulsion Lab, Edwards AFB, CA, 3 May 1970.

Cann, G.L., "Advanced Electric Thruster (A Space Electric Ramjet)", Air Force Rocket Propulsion Lab., Wright-Patterson AFB, Ohio, Technical Report AFRPL-TR-73-12, April 1973.

Cann, G.L., "A Space Electric Ramjet," AIAA Paper 75-377, New Orleans, LA, 1975.

Reichel, R.H., "Airscooping Nuclear-Electric Propulsion Concept for Advanced Orbital Space Transportation Missions", IAF-76-161, 27th International Astronautical Federation Congress, Anaheim, CA, 10–16 Oct. 1976.

5.2   Magnetohydrodynamic Ship Propulsion

Way, S., "Examination of Bipolar Electric and Magnetic Fields for Submarine Propulsion", preliminary Memorandum Communication to U.S. Navy Bureau of Ships, 15 Oct. 1958.

Rice, W.A., U.S. Patent 2997013, 12 Aug. 1961.

Friauf, J.B., "Electromagnetic Ship Propulsion", *A.S.N.E. Journal*, Feb. 1961, pp. 139–142.

Phillips, O.M., "The Prospects for Magneto-hydrodynamic Ship Propulsion", *Journal of Ship Research*, March 1962, pp. 43–51.

Doragh, R.A., "Magnetohydrodynamic Ship Propulsion Using Superconducting Magnets", *Transactions of the Society of Naval Architects and Marine Engineers*, Vol. 71, 1963, pp. 370–386.

Way. S., "Propulsion of Submarines by Lorentz Forces in The Surrounding Sea", ASME paper 64-WA/ENER-7, Winter Meeting, New York City, 29 Nov. 1964.

Way, S. and Devlin, C., "Construction and Testing of a Model Electromagnetically Propelled Submarine", *Proc. Eng. Aspects of Magnetohydrodynamics*, Stanford Univ., CA, 1967.

Way, S. and Devlin, C., "Prospects for the Electromagnetic Submarine", AIAA Paper No. 67-432, AIAA 3rd Propulsion Joint Specialist Conference, Washington, D.C., 17-21 July 1967.

Way, S., "Electromagnetic Propulsion for Cargo Submarines", *Journal of Hydronautics*, Vol. 2, No. 2, April 1968, pp. 49–57.

Way, S. "Research Submarines with Minimal Ocean Disturbance", SAE Paper No. 690028, presented at SAE Conference on 13-17 Jan. 1969.

Anderson, G.F. and Wu. Y., "Drag Reduction by Use of MHD Boundary-Layer Control", *J. Hydronautics*, Vol. 5, No. 4, Oct. 1971, pp. 150–152.

5.3   Propulsion by Energy Exchange with Magnetic and Electric Fields

Cook, J.C., "Electrostatic Lift for Space Vehicles", in *Ballistic Missile and Space Technology*, Vol. II, Academic Press, New York, 1960.

Petschek, H.E., "Magnetic Field Annihilation", Proceedings of the AAS-NASA Symposium on the Physics of Solar Flares, NASA SP-50, Goddard Space Flight Center, Greenbelt, MD, 28–30 Oct. 1963, pp. 425–439.

Forward, R.L., "Zero Thrust Velocity Vector Control for Interstellar Probes", HRL Research Report No. 294, Hughes Research Laboratories, Malibu, CA, Dec. 1963.

Forward, R.L., "Zero Thrust Velocity Vector Control for Interstellar Probes: Lorentz Force Navigation and Circling", AIAA Journal, Vol. 2, No. 5, 1964, pp. 885–889.

Forward, R.L., "Zero Thrust Velocity Vector Control for Interstellar Probes", AIAA Bull., Vol. 1, Jan. 1964, p. 20; Also AIAA Preprint No. 64–53.

Engelberger, J.F., "Space Propulsion by Magnetic Field Interaction", J. Spacecraft, Vol. 1, No. 3, May-June 1964, pp. 347–349.

Gross, R.A., "On Alfven Wave Propulsion", Advanced Propulsion Concepts. Proceedings of the 4th Symposium, Palo Alto, CA, 26–28 April 1965, pp. 65–69.

Drell, S.D., Foley, H.M. and Ruderman, M.A., "Drag and Propulsion of Large Satellites in the Atmosphere: An Alfven Propulsion Engine in Space", Journal of Geophysical Research, Vol. 70, No. 13, 1 July 1965, pp. 3131–3145.

Sterkin, C.K. (Compiler), "Interactions of Spacecraft and Other Moving Bodies with Natural Plasmas", Literature Search No. 541, Jet Propulsion Laboratory, Pasadena, CA, Dec. 1965.

Moore, R.D., "The Geomagnetic Thrustor—A High Performance 'Alfven Wave' Propulsion System Utilizing Plasma Contacts", AIAA Paper No. 66–257, AIAA Fifth Electric Propulsion Conference, San Diego, CA, 7–9 March 1966.

"Magnetic Field Annihilation of Plasmas for Advanced Plasma Engine Design", TRW No. 14649-6001-RO-00, AFOSR-TR-71-0328, Contract No. F44620-70-C0035, TRW Systems Group, Redondo Beach, CA, 31 March 1971.

Alfven, H., "Spacecraft Propulsion: New Methods", Science, Vol. 176, 1972, p. 4031.

Banks, P.M. and Williamson, P.R., "Draft of Report on a Study of Ionospheric Currents Generated Through Shuttle-tethered Subsatellite $\vec{V} \times \vec{B}$ EMF", Dept. of Applied Physics & Information Science, University of California at San Diego, La Jolla, CA, 1975.

Papailiou, D.D., "A Proposed Concept for the Extraction of Energy Stored in Magnetic or Electric Fields in Space", AIAA Paper No. 76-707, AIAA/SAE 12th Propulsion Conference, Palo Alto, CA, 26–29 July 1976.

5.4 Hybrid Nuclear-Electric Propulsion

Stuhlinger, E., Berlin. 5th International Astronautical Congress, Springer, Vienna, 1954, p. 100.

Stuhlinger, E., "Design and Performance Data of Space Ships with Ionic Propulsion Systems", 8th IAF Congress, Barcelona, Oct. 1957, p. 403.

Rosa, R.J., "An Electromagnetic Rocket System of High Specific Thrust", Avco Research Report 103, Avco-Everett Research Laboratory, Everett, MA, April 1958.

Ackeret, J., "A System of Rocket Propulsion Using Rockets and Gas Turbines", *International Astronautical Congress, 9th. Proceedings*, Vol. 1, 1959, pp. 277–281.

Corliss, W., *Propulsion Systems for Space Flight*, McGraw Hill, 1960, pp. 182–183.

Goldsmith, M., "Augmentation of Nuclear Rocket Specific Impulse Through Mechanical-Electrical Means", *ARS Journal*, Aug. 1959, pp. 600–601.

Berry, E.R., "Effect of Electrical Augmentation on Nuclear Rocket Flight Performance", *ARS Journal*, Jan. 1961, pp. 92–93.

Resler, E.L., Jr. and Rott, N., "Rocket Propulsion with Nuclear Power", *ARS Journal*, Nov. 1960, pp. 1099–1100.

Rosa, R.J., "Propulsion System Using a Cavity Reactor and Magnetohydrodynamic Generator", *ARS Journal*, July 1961, pp. 884–885.

Rosa, R.J., "The Application of Magnetohydrodynamic Generators in Nuclear Rocket Propulsion", AERL Research Report 111, AFBSD-TR-61-58, Contract No. AF 04(647)-278, Avco-Everett Research Laboratory, Everett, MA. Aug. 1961.

Rosa, R.J., "Magnetohydrodynamic Generators and Nuclear Propulsion," *ARS Journal*, Aug. 1962, pp. 1221–1230.

Rosciszewski, J., "Rocket Motor with Electric Acceleration in the Throat", *J. Spacecraft*, Vol. 2, No. 2, March-April 1965, pp. 278–280.

Bussard, R.W., "The Role of Nuclear Energy in Space Flight", in *Nuclear Thermal and Electric Rocket Propulsion*, R.A. Willaume, A. Jaumotte and R.W. Bussard (editors), AGARD/NATO 1st and 2nd Lecture Series with Université Libre de Bruxelles, Nov. 1962-Sept., Oct. 1964, Gordon and Breach, New York, 1967.

Rosa, R.J., *Magnetohydrodynamic Energy Conversion*, 1st ed., McGraw-Hill, N.Y., 1968, pp. 189–193.

Stuhlinger, E., Hale, D.P., Daley, C.C. and Katz, L., "The Versatility of Electrically Powered Spacecraft for Planetary Missions", AIAA Paper 69-253, Williamsburg, VA, 1969.

Shepherd, D.G., *Aerospace Propulsion*, American Elsevier Publ. Co., 1972, pp. 258–259.

"General Electric Final Report—Nuclear Electric Propulsion Mission Engineering Study", Document No. 73 SD4219, March 1973.

Byers, D.C. and Rawlin, V.K., "Electron Bombardment Propulsion System Characteristics for Large Space Systems", AIAA Paper No. 76-1039, AIAA 12th International Electric Propulsion Conference, Key Biscayne, FL, 15–17 Nov. 1976.

Pawlick, E.V. and Phillips, W.M., "A Nuclear Electric Propulsion Vehicle for Planetary Exploration", AIAA Paper No. 76-1041, AIAA International Electric Propulsion Conference, Key Biscayne, FL, 14–17 Nov. 1976.

Atkins, K. and Terwilliger, C., "Ion Drive: A Step Toward 'Star Trek' ", AIAA Paper No. 76-1069, AIAA International 12th Electric Propulsion Conference, Key Biscayne, FL, 15–17 Nov. 1976.

5.5   Fission Rocket

Kerrebrock, J. and Meghreblian, R., "An Analysis of Vortex Tubes for Combined Gas-Phase Fission-Heating and Separation of the Fissionable Material", Rept. CF 57-11-3, Rev. 1, Oak Ridge National Lab., 1958.

Bussard, R.W. and DeLauer, R.D., *Nuclear Rocket Propulsion*, McGraw-Hill, New York, 1958.

Rosenzweig, M.L., Lewellen, W.S. and Kerrebrock, J.L., "The Feasibility of Turbulent Vortex Containment in the Gaseous Fission Rocket", ARS Paper No. 1516A-60, Dec. 1960.

Sänger, E., "Nuclear Rockets for Space Flight", *Advances in Astronautical Propulsion*, Corrado Casci (editor), Pergamon Press, New York, 1962, pp. 147–164; *Astronautical Sciences Review*, July–Sept. 1961.

Kerrebrock, J.L. and Meghreblian, R.V., "Vortex Containment for the Gaseous-Fission Rocket", Rep. No. TR 34-205, Jet Propulsion Lab., Calif. Institute of Tech., Pasadena, CA, Sept. 1961; Also *Journal of Aerospace Sciences*, Vol. 26, 1961, pp. 710 ff.

Rom, F.E. and Ragsdale, R.G., "Advanced Concepts of Nuclear Rocket Propulsion", *Nuclear Rocket Propulsion*, NASA SP-20, Dec. 1962, pp. 3–15.

Ragsdale, R.G., "Outlook for Gas-Core Nuclear Rockets," *Astronautical Aerospace Engineering*, Vol. 1, Aug. 1963, pp. 88–91.

Bussard, R.W. and DeLauer, R.D., *Fundamentals of Nuclear Flight*, 1st. ed., McGraw-Hill Book Co., New York, 1965.

Cooper, R.S., "Advanced Nuclear Propulsion Concepts", AIAA Paper No. 65–531, 1965.

McLafferty, G.H., "Survey of Advanced Concepts in Nuclear Propulsion", *Journal of Spacecraft and Rockets*, Vol. 5, No. 10, Oct. 1968, pp. 1121–1128.

Moeckel, W.E., "Propulsion Systems for Manned Exploration of the Solar System", *Astronautics and Aeronautics*, Aug. 1969, pp. 66–77.

McLafferty, G.H., "Gas-Core Nuclear Rocket Engine Technology Status", AIAA Paper No. 70–708, AIAA 6th Propulsion Joint Specialist Conference, San Diego, CA, 15–19 June 1970.

Gabriel, D.S., et al., "Nuclear Rocket Engine Program Status—1970", AIAA Paper No. 70-711, AIAA 6th Propulsion Joint Specialist Conference, San Diego, CA, 15–19 June 1970.

Ragsdale, R.G., "To Mars in 30 Days by Gas-core Nuclear Rocket", *Astronautics and Aeronautics*, Vol. 10, No. 1, 1972, pp. 65–71.

Hyland, R.E., "A Mini-Cavity Reactor for Low-Thrust High-Specific Impulse Propulsion", *J. Spacecraft and Rockets*, Vol. 9, No. 8, 1972, pp. 601–606.

Thom, K.H., "Review of Fission Engine Concepts", *J. Spacecraft and Rockets*, Vol. 9, No. 9, 1972, pp. 633–639.

Moeckel, W.E., "Comparison of Advanced Propulsion Concepts for Deep Space Exploration", *J. Spacecraft*, Vol. 9, No. 12, Dec. 1972, pp. 863–868.

5.6   Fusion Rocket

Sänger, E., "Stationäre Kernverbrennung in Raketen", *Astronautica Acta*, Vol., 1, 1955, pp. 63–88; (Translation) NASA TM-1405, Washington, D.C., 1957.

Clauser, M.U., "The Feasibility of Thermonuclear Propulsion", Conference on Extremely High Temperatures, Air Force Cambridge Research Center, 18–19 March 1958.

Clauser, M.U., "Application of Thermonuclear Reactions to Rocket Propulsion", in *Space Technology*, H.S. Seifert (editor), John Wiley and Sons Inc., New York, Chapt. 18, Sect. 10, 1959.

Masten, S.H., "Fusion for Space Propulsion", *Institute of Radio Engineers-Transactions on Military Electronics*, Vol. Mil-3, No. 2, April 1959.

Roth, J.R., "A Preliminary Study of Thermonuclear Rocket Propulsion", American Rocket Society Preprint 944–59, presented at the ARS 14th Annual Meeting, Washington, D.C., 16–20 Nov. 1959; *J. British Interplanetary Society*, Vol. 18, 1961–1962, pp. 99–108.

Sänger, E., "Atomraketen für Raumfahrt", ("Atomic Rockets for Space Travel"), *Astronautica Acta*, Vol. 6, 1960, pp. 3–15; (Translation) "Nuclear Rockets for Space Flight", *Astronautical Sciences Review*, July–Sept. 1961, pp. 9–15.

Luce, J.S., "Controlled Fusion Propulsion", in *Advanced Propulsion Concepts*, Vol. 1, Gordon and Breach, New York, 1963; Proceedings of 3rd Symposium on Advanced Propulsion Concepts, Cincinnati, Ohio, Oct. 1962, pp. 343–380.

Englert, G.W., et al., "Towards Thermonuclear Rocket Propulsion", *New Scientist*, Vol. 16, No. 307, 4 Oct. 1962, pp. 16–18.

Linlor, W.I. and Glauser, M.U., "Fusion Plasma Propulsion System", in *Advanced Propulsion Concepts*, Vol. 1, Gordon and Breach, New York, 1963; Proceedings of 3rd Symposium on Advanced Propulsion Concepts, Cincinnati, Ohio, Oct. 1962, pp. 381–407.

Cooper, R.F. and Verga, R.L., "Controlled Thermonuclear Reactions for Space Propulsion", ASDTDR-63-696, Air Force Sys. Comm., Wright-Patterson AFB, Ohio, Aeronautical Systems Div., Sept. 1963.

Hilton, J.L., "Plasma and Engineering Parameters for a Fusion Powered Rocket", *IEEE Trans. on Nuclear Sci.*, Vol. NS-10, No. 1, Jan. 1963, pp. 153–164.

Spencer, D.F., "Fusion Propulsion System Requirements for an Interstellar Probe", Technical Report No. 32-397, Jet Propulsion Laboratory, Pasadena, CA, 15 May 1963.

Hilton, J.L., Luce, J.S. and Thompson, A.S., "Hypothetical Fusion Propulsion Rocket Vehicle", *J. Spacecraft*, Vol. 1, No. 3, May–June 1964, pp. 276–282.

Sänger, E., "Pure Fusion Rockets", in *Space Flight*, McGraw-Hill Book Co., New York, 1965, pp. 241–255.

Samaras, D.G., "Thermodynamic Considerations of Thermonuclear Space Propulsion", *Proc. 16th Int. Astronautical Congress: Propulsion and Re-entry*, (Athens, 1965), Gordon and Breach, N.Y., 1966, pp. 305–322.

Cooper, R.S., "Prospects for Advanced High-Thrust Nuclear Propulsion", *Astronautics and Aeronautics*, Jan. 1966, pp. 54–59.

Spencer, D.F., "Fusion Propulsion for Interstellar Missions", in *Annals of the New York Academy of Sciences*, Vol. 140, Art. 1, Planetology and Space Mission Planning, 16 Dec. 1966, pp. 407–418.

Fowler, T.K., "Fusion Research in Open-ended Systems", *Nuclear Fusion*, Vol. 9, 1969.

Powell, T.C., "Fusion Power for Interstellar Flight", Ph.D. Thesis, Kentucky University, Lexington, KY, 1970, 186 pages, available through NTIS (N71-38275 STAR abstracts).

Matloff, G.L. and Chiu, H.H., "Some Aspects of Thermonuclear Propulsion", *Journal of the Astronautical Sciences*, Vol. 18, No. 1, July–Aug. 1970, pp. 57–62.

Roth, J.R., et al., "Technological Problems Anticipated in the Application of Fusion Reactors to Space Propulsion and Power Generation", NASA TMX-2106, Oct. 1970.

Fisbach, L.H., "Performance Potential of Gas-Core and Fusion Rockets: A Mission Applications Survey", NASA TMX-67940, 1971.

Dooling, D., Jr., "Controlled Thermonuclear Fusion for Space Propulsion", *Spaceflight*, Vol. 14, No. 1, Jan. 1972, pp. 26–27.

Roth, T.R., et al., "Fusion Power for Space Propulsion", *New Scientist*, 20 Apr. 1972, pp. 125–127.

Reinmann, J.J., "Fusion Rocket Concepts", paper presented at 6th Symposium on Advanced Propulsion Concepts, Niagara Falls, New York, 4–6 May 1971; NASA Technical Memorandum TM X-67826.

"Advanced Propulsion Concepts—Project Outgrowth", Tech. Report AFRPL-TR-72-31, Mead, F.B., Jr., editor. Air Force Rocket Propulsion Laboratory, Edwards AFB, CA, June 1972.

Fisbach, L.H. and Willis, E.A., Jr., "Performance Potential of Gas-Core and Fusion Rockets: A Mission Applications Survey", *J. Spacecraft*, Vol. 9, No. 8, Aug. 1972, pp. 569–570.

Powell, C., Hahn, O. J. and McNally, J.R., Jr., "Energy Balance in Fusion Rockets", *Astronautica Acta*, Vol. 18, No. 1, Feb. 1973, pp. 59-69.

Papailiou, D.D., Editor, "Frontiers in Propulsion Research: Laser, Matter-Antimatter, Excited Helium, Energy Exchange and Thermonuclear Fusion", NASA Technical Memorandum 33-722, Jet Propulsion Laboratory, Pasadena, CA, 15 March 1975.

5.7   Orion Pulsed Propulsion System

Everett, C.J. and Ulan, S.M., "On a Method of Propulsion of Projectiles by Means of External Nuclear Explosions", LASL Report LAMS-1955. Los Alamos Scientific Laboratory, Los Alamos, N. Mex., Aug. 1955.

"Nuclear Pulsed Propulsion Project (Project Orion)", Technical Summary Report (4 volumes), RTD-TDR-63-3006, General Dynamics Corp., General Atomic Div., 1963–1964.

Sänger, E., "Periodic Pure Fusion Rockets", in *Space Flight*, McGraw-Hill Book Co., New York, 1965, pp. 215–219.

Nance, J.C., "Nuclear Pulse Propulsion", *IEEE Trans. on Nuclear Science*, Vol. NS-12, No. 1, Feb. 1965, pp. 177–182; General Atomic Report GA-5572, Oct. 1964.

Hadley, J.W., Stubbs, T.F., Janmen, M.A. and Simons, L.A., "The Helios Pulsed Nuclear Propulsion Concept (OUO)", Report UCRL-14238, Lawrence Radiation Lab., Livermore, CA, June 1965.

Dyson, F.J., "Death of a Project", *Science*, Vol. 149, 9 July 1965, pp. 141–144.

Dyson, F.J., "Interstellar Transport", *Physics Today*, Oct. 1968, pp. 41–45.

Lubin, M.J., "Laser Produced Plasmas for Power Generation and Space Propulsion", *Astronautics and Aeronautics*, Vol. 8, No. 11, Nov. 1970, pp. 42–48.

Cottler, T.P., "Rotating Cable Pusher for Pulsed-Propulsion Space Vehicle", LA-4668-MS, Los Alamos Scientific Laboratory, Los Alamos, NM, Apr. 1971.

Balcomb, J.D., et al., "Nuclear Pulsed Propulsion Study", LASL Report LA-4694-MS, Los Alamos Scientific Laboratory, Los Alamos, N.M., May 1971.

Boyer, K. and Balcomb, J.D., "System Studies of Fusion Powered Pulsed Propulsion Systems", AIAA Paper No. 71-636, AIAA/SAE 7th Propulsion Joint Specialist Conference, Salt Lake City, UT, 14–18 June 1971.

Winterberg, F., "Rocket Propulsion by Thermonuclear Microbombs Ignited with Relativistic Electron Beams", *Raumfahrtforschung*, Vol. 15, No. 5, Sept.–Oct. 1971, pp. 208–217.

Hyde, R., Wood, L. and Nuckolls, J., "Prospects for Rocket Propulsion Laser-Induced Fusion Microexplosions", AIAA Paper No. 72-1063, AIAA/SAE 8th Joint Propulsion Specialist Conference, New Orleans, LA, 29 Nov.–1 Dec. 1972.

Reynolds, T.W., "Effective Specific Impulse of External Nuclear Pulse Propulsion Systems", *Journal of Spacecraft and Rockets*, Vol. 10, No. 10, Oct. 1973, pp. 629–630; NASA TN D-6984, Sept. 1972.

Winterberg, F., "Rocket Propulsion by Staged Thermonuclear Microexplosions", *JBIS*, Vol. 30, No. 9, Sept. 1977, pp. 333–340.

5.8   Bussard Interstellar Ramjet

Karlovitz, B. and Lewis, B., "Space Propulsion by Interstellar Gas", in *Proc. 9th Int. Astronautical Congress*, Amsterdam, 1958, Vienna, Springer-Verlag, 1959, pp. 307–311.

Bussard, R.W., "Galactic Matter and Interstellar Flight", *Astronautica Acta*, Vol. 6, No. 4, 1960, pp. 179–194.

Kraus, A.A., "Proposed Method of Accelerating Space Vehicles to Relativistic Velocities", *Bull. Am. Phys. Society*, Series II, Vol. 6, No. 6, 1961, p. 516.

Öpik, E.J., "Is Interstellar Travel Possible?", *Irish Astronomical Journal*, Vol. 6, Dec. 1964, pp. 299–302.

Sänger, E., "The Photon Ramjet", in *Space Flight*, McGraw-Hill Book Co., New York, 1965, pp. 261–264.

Froning, Jr., H.D., "Some Preliminary Propulsion System Considerations and Requirements for Interstellar Space Flights", *Proc. 18th Int. Astronautical Congress*, Vol. 3 (Propulsion and Re-Entry), meeting in Belgrade, Yugoslavia, 1967, Pergamon Press, New York, 1968; Douglas Aircraft Company Technical Paper No. 4752.

Mallove, E.F., "Fusion Ramjet Propulsion for Interstellar Flight—A Critical Review", submitted for subject 16.561 (nuclear rockets), Massachusetts Institute of Technology, Cambridge, MA, 15 Jan. 1969.

Fishback, J.F., "Relativistic Interstellar Spaceflight", *Astronautica Acta*, Vol. 15, No. 1, 1969, pp. 25–35.

Friedman, D., "Comments on Bussard Concept Quoted by Poul Anderson in correspondence to Robert L. Forward", 31 Dec. 1971.

Martin, A.R., "Structural Limitations on Interstellar Spaceflight", *Astronautica Acta*, Vol. 16, 1971, pp. 353–357.

Martin, A.R., "Some Limitations of the Interstellar Ramjet", *Spaceflight*, Vol. 14, No. 1, Jan. 1972, pp. 21–25.

Martin, A.R., "Magnetic Intake Limitations on Interstellar Ramjets", *Astronautica Acta*, Vol. 18, No. 1, Feb. 1973, pp. 1–10.

Grant, T.J., "Interstellar Ramjet", correspondence in *Spaceflight*, Vol. 15, No. 4, April 1973, p. 157.

Cox, J.E., "An Intragalactic Magnetohydrodynamic Ramjet Using Externalized Force Fields", senior project at California State Polytechnic University, Pomona, CA, 5 June 1973.

Fennelly, A.J. and Matloff, G.L., "A Magnetic Interstellar Spacecraft", unpublished paper abstracted in *Bulletin American Physical Soc. II*, Vol. 19, March 1974, p. 279.

Matloff, G.L. and Fennelly, A.J., "Vacuum-Ultraviolet Laser and Interstellar Spaceflight", Paper presented at 1974 Spring Meeting of the Optical Society of America, 22 April 1974.

Matloff, G.L., "A Superconducting Ion Scoop and Its Application to Interstellar Flight", *JBIS*, Vol. 27, No. 9, Sept. 1974, pp. 663–673.

Bond, A., "An Analysis of the Potential Performance of the Ram Augmented Interstellar Rocket", *JBIS*, Vol. 27, No. 9, Sept, 1974, pp. 674–685.

Whitmire, D.P., "Relativistic Spaceflight and the Catalytic Nuclear Ramjet", *Astronautica Acta*, Vol. 2, 1975, pp. 497–509.

Roberts, W.B., "The Relativistic Dynamics of a Sub-Light Speed Interstellar Ramjet Probe", AAS Paper No. 75-020, July 1975.

Matloff, G.L. and Fennelly, A.J., "Interstellar Applications of Several Electrostatic/ Electromagnetic Ion Collection Techniques", *JBIS*, Vol. 30, No. 6, June 1977, pp. 213–222.

5.9   Antimatter Propulsion

Agnew, L.E., et al., "Antiproton Interactions in Hydrogen and Carbon below 200 MeV," *Phys. Rev.*, Vol. *118*, pp. 1371–1391, 1 June 1960.

Potapkin, V.S., "Use of Annihilation for Setting in Motion of Photon Rockets," NASA TT F-8969, 12 October 1964, translation from Russian (N64-33377).

Forward, R.L., "Interstellar Flight Systems," AIAA Paper No. 80-0823, AIAA International Meeting and Technical Display, Baltimore, MD, 6–8 May 1970.

Morgan, D.L. and Hughes, V.W., "Atomic Processes Induced in Matter-Antimatter Annihilation," *Physical Review D*, Vol. 2, pp. 1389–1399, 1970.

Hora, H., "Estimates for the Efficient Production of Anti-Hydrogen by Lasers of Very High Intensities," *Opto-Electronics*, Vol. 5, pp. 491–501, 1973.

Morgan, D.L., "Investigation of Matter-Antimatter Interactions for Possible Applications," NASA CR-14136, Jet Propulsion Laboratory, Pasadena, CA, 1974.

Steigman, G., "On the Feasibility of a Matter-Antimatter Reactor Propulsion System", Yale University Observatory, New Haven, CT, 1974.

Dipprey, D.F., "Matter-Antimatter Annihilation as an Energy Source in Propulsion," Appendix in "Frontiers in Propulsion Research," JPL TM-33-722, D.D. Papailion, editor, Jet Propulsion Laboratory, Pasadena, CA, 1975.

Morgan, D.L., "Coupling of Annihilation Energy to a High Momentum Exhaust in a Matter-Antimatter Annihilation Rocket," JPL Contract JS-651111, 1976.

Morgan, D.L., "Rocket Thrust from Antimatter Annihilation," JPL Contractor Report CC-571769, 1975.

Forward, R.L., "Antimatter Revealed," *Omni*, November 1979.

Jackson, A.A., "Some Considerations of the Antimatter and Fusion Ram augmented Interstellar Rocket," *Journal of the British Interplanetary Society*, Vol. 33, pp. 117–120, 1980.

Cassenti, B.N., "A Comparison of Interstellar Propulsion Methods," *Journal of the British Interplanetary Society*, Vol. 35, pp. 116–124, 1982.

Massier, P.F., "The Need for Expanded Exploration of Matter-Antimatter Annihilation for Propulsion Applications," *Journal of the British Interplanetary Society*, Vol. 35, pp. 387 ff., September 1982.

Forward, R.L., "Antimatter Propulsion," J. British Interplanetary Soc., Vol. 35, pp. 391–395, September 1982.

Cassenti, B.N., "Design Considerations for Relativistic Antimatter Rockets," *J. British Interplanetary Soc.*, Vol. 35, pp. 395–404, September 1982.

Morgan, D. L., "Concept for the Design of an Antimatter Annihilation Rocket," *J. British Interplanetary Soc.*, Vol. 35, pp. 405–412, September, 1982.

Zito, R.R., "The Cryogenic Confinement of Antiprotons for Space Propulsion Systems," *J. British Interplanetary Soc.*, Vol. 35, pp. 414–421, September 1982.

Chapline, G., "Antimatter Breeders?" *J. British Interplanetary Soc.*, Vol. 35, pp. 423–424, September 1982.

Cassenti, B.N., "Optimization of Relativistic Antimatter Rockets," AIAA Paper No. 83-1343, 19th Joint Propulsion Conference, Seattle, WA, 1983.

Forward, R.L., "Alternate Propulsion Energy Sources", AFRPL TR-83-067, Air Force Rocket Propulsion Laboratory, Edwards AFB, CA, December 1983.

Cassenti, B.N., "Antimatter Propulsion for OTV Application," Paper No. 84-1485, AIAA/SAE/ASME 20th Joint Propulsion Conference, Cincinnati, Ohio, 11–13 June 1984.

Forward, R.L., "Antiproton Annihilation Propulsion," Paper No. 84-1482, AIAA/SAE/ASME 20th Joint Propulsion Conference, Cincinnati, Ohio, 11–13 June 1984.

5.10 Light Sails

Tsander, K., *From a Scientific Heritage*, NASA TTF-541, 1967 (quoting a 1924 report by the author).

Tsiolkovskiy, K.E., *Extenstion of Man Into Outer Space*, 1921. (cf. also, K.E. Tsiolkovskiy, *Symposium on Jet Propulsion*, No. 2, United Scientific and Technical Presses (NTI), 1936 [in Russian]).

Wiley, C., (pseudonym: R. Sanders), "Clipper Ships of Space," *Astounding Science Fiction*, pp. 135 ff., May 1951.

Garwin, R.L., "Solar Sailing—A Practical Method of Propulsion With the Solar System," *Jet Propulsion*, Vol. 28, pp. 188–190, March 1958.

Tsu, T.C., "Interplanetary Travel by Solar Sail," *ARS Journal*, Vol. *29*, pp. 442–447, June 1959.

Forward, R.L., "Pluto—The Gateway to the Stars," *Missiles and Rockets*, Vol. 10, pp. 26–28, 2 April 1962; reprinted as "Pluto: Last Stop Before the Stars," *Science Digest*, Vol. 52, pp. 70–75, August 1962.

Marx, G., "Interstellar Vehicle Propelled by Terrestrial Laser Beam," *Nature*, Vol. 211, No. 5044, pp. 22–23, 2 July 1966.

Redding, J.L., "Interstellar Vehicle Propelled by Terrestrial Laser Beam," *Nature*, Vol. 213, No. 5076, pp. 588–489, 11 February 1967.

Norem, P.C., "Interstellar Travel, A Round Trip Propulsion System with Relativistic Velocity Capabilities," Amer. Astronautical Soc. Paper No. 69-388, June 1969.

Rather, J.D.G., Zeiders, G.W. and Vogelsang, R.K., "Laser Driven Light Sails—An Examination of the Possibilities for Interstellar Probes and Other Missions," W.J. Schafer Assoc. Report WJSA-76-26, Redondo Beach, Calif., JPL Contract EF-644778, NASA CR-157326, December 1976.

Forward, R.L., "A Program for Interstellar Exploration," *Journal of the British Interplanetary Society*, Vol. 29, pp. 611–632, 1976.

Friedman, L., et al., "Solar Sailing—The Concept Made Realistic," AIAA Paper 78-82, AIAA 16th Aerospace Sciences Meeting, Huntsville, Alabama, 16–18 January 1978.

Friedman, L.D., "Solar Sail Development Program," Final Report, Vol. 1, JPL Report 720–9, 30 January 1978, Jet Propulsion Laboratory, Pasadena, California.

Drexler, K.E., "Design of a High Performance Solar Sail System," MS Thesis, Dept. of Aeronautics and Astronautics, MIT, Cambridge, MA, May 1979.

Drexler, K.E., "High Performance Solar Sails and Related Reflecting Devices," AIAA Paper 79-1418, Fourth Princeton/AIAA Conference on Space Manufacturing Facilities, Princeton, NJ, 14–17 May 1979.

Forward, R.L., "Interstellar Flight Systems," AIAA paper 80-0823, AIAA Int. Meeting, Baltimore, MD., 6–8 May 1980.

Forward, R.L., "Light-levitated Geostationary Cylindrical Orbits," *Journal of the Astronautical Sciences*, Vol. XXIX, No. 1, pp. 73–80, January–March 1981.

Forward, R.L., "Roundtrip Interstellar Travel Using Laser-Pushed Lightsails," *Journal of Spacecraft and Rockets*, Vol. 21, No. 2, pp. 187–195, March/April 1984.

Forward, R.L., "Starwisp," Research Report No. 555, Hughes Research Laboratories, Malibu, CA, June 1983; accepted for publication in *Journal of Spacecraft and Rockets*, 1984.

Forward, R.L., "Alternate Propulsion Energy Sources," AFRPL TR-83-067, Air Force Rocket Propulsion Laboratory, Edwards AFB, CA, December 1983.

5.11   Miscellaneous

Ehricke, K.A., "Solar-Powered Space Ship", American Rocket Society Paper No. 310–36, June 1956.

Corliss, W.R., *Propulsion Systems for Space Flight*, 1st. ed., Maple Press Co., York, PA, 1960.

Forward, R.L., "Guidelines to Anti-Gravity", *American Journal of Physics*, Vol. 31, 1963, pp. 166–170.

Berner, F., "MHD Turborocket Engine for Recoverable Launch Vehicles", AERL Research Report 206, BSD-TR-64-183, Contract No. AF 04(694)-414, Avco-Everett Research Laboratory, Everett, MA, March 1965.

Forward, R.L., "Far Out Physics", *Analog Science Fiction/Science Fact*, Aug. 1965, pp. 148–166.

Wild, J.M., "Nuclear Propulsion for Aircraft", *Astronautics and Aeronautics*, March 1968, pp. 24–30.

Escher, W.J.D., "Composite (Rocket/Airbreathing) Engines; Key to the Advanced (Staged) Space Transport Vehicle", Presented at the University of Tennessee, Space Institute, 18–22 Aug. 1969.

Godfrey, C.S., "Uses of Explosive Driven Gases", *Technology Review*, Vol. 72, No. 3, Jan. 1970, pp. 40–47.

Latyshev, V., "YANTAR, a Flying Accelerator", NASA TT-F-13676, Nat. Aeron. Space Admin., Washington, D.C., 1971.

Forward, R.L., "General Relativity for the Experimentalist", *Proceedings of the IRE*, Vol. 49, No. 5, May 1971.

Mead, Jr., F.B., editor, "Advanced Propulsion Concepts—Project Outgrowth", Technical Report AFRPL-TR-72-31, Air Force Rocket Propulsion Laboratory, Air Force Systems Command, Edwards AFB, CA, June 1972.

Mallove, E.F. and Forward, R.L., "Bibliography of Interstellar Travel and Communication—1972", Research Report 460, Hughes Research Laboratories, Malibu, CA, Nov. 1972.

Back, L.H. and Varsi, G., "Detonation Propulsion for High Pressure Environments", *AIAA Journal*, Vol. 12, No. 8, Aug. 1974, pp. 1123–1130; Also AIAA Paper No. 73–1237, AIAA/SAE 9th Propulsion Conference, Las Vegas, NV, Nov. 1973.

Papailiou, D.D., editor, "Frontiers in Propulsion Research: Laser, Matter-Antimatter, Excited Helium, Energy Exchange and Thermonuclear Fusion", NASA Technical Memorandum 33-722, Jet Propulsion Laboratory, Pasadena, CA, 15 March 1975.

Forward, R.L., "A National Space Program for Interstellar Exploration", Research Report 492, Hughes Research Laboratories, Malibu, CA, July 1975.

Kim, K., Back, L.H. and Varsi, G., "Measurement of Detonation Propulsion in Helium and Performance Calculations," *AIAA Journal*, Vol. 14, No. 3, March 1976, pp. 310–312.

6.0 WARBIRDS OF THE 21ST CENTURY

Ing. D., "Vehicles for Future Wars", Destinies Magazine, Vol. 1, No. 4, Aug.–Sept. 1971, pp. 237–277.

Myrabo, L.N., "The Monocle Shuttle", 1983 JANNAF Propulsion Meeting, Monterey, CA, 14–17 February 1983.

7.0 ULTRALIGHT AND ARV AIRCRAFT

Burke, J.D., "The Gossamer Condor and Albatross: A Case Study in Aircraft Design", Report No. AV-R-80/540, AIAA Professional Study Series, Aero Vironment, Inc., Pasadena CA, 16 June 1980.

Davisson, B., *The World of Sport Aviation*, Hearst Books, New York, 1982.

Markowski, M.A., *Ultralight Aircraft*, Ultralight Publications, Inc., Hummelstown, PA, Oct. 1983.

Markowski, M.A., *ARV: The Encyclopedia of Aircraft Recreational Vehicles*, Ultralight Publications, Inc., Hummelstown, PA, 1984.

Boucher, R.J., "History of Solar Flight", Paper No. 84-1429, AIAA/SAE/ASME 20th Joint Propulsion Conference, Cincinnati, OH, 11–13 June 1984.

8. ADVANCED COMPOSITE MATERIALS

Fiber Composite Materials, Proceed. of a Seminar of the American Society of Metals (held 17–18 October 1964), publ. by the American Society for Metals, Metals Park, OH, 1965.

Holliday, L., Ed., *Composite Materials*, Elsevier Publ. Co., NY, 1966.

Holister, G.S. and Thomas, C., *Fibre Reinforced Materials*, Elsevier Publ. Co., NY, 1966.

Advanced Fibrous Reinforced Composites, Proceed. of the 10th National Symposium and Exhibit (held in San Diego, CA, 9–11 Nov. 1966), publ. by the Society of Aerospace Materials and Process Engineers, North Hollywood, CA, 1966.

Advanced Composite Hardware: Major Status Report, Conf. Proceed., sponsored by Air Force Materials Laboratory and coordinated by the Southwest Research Institute, Air Force Materials Laboratory, Advanced Composites Division, Wright-Patterson, AFB, OH, Sept. 1966.

Broutman, L.J. and Krock, R.H. Eds., *Modern Composite Materials*, Addison-Wesley Publ. Co., Reading, MA, 1967.

Tsai, S.W., Halpin, J.C. and Pagano, N.J., *Composite Materials Workshop*, Progress in Materials Science Series, Vol. 1, Technomic Publ. Co., Stamford, CT, 1968.

Ashton, J.E., Halpin, J.C. and Petit, P.H., *Primer on Composite Materials: Analysis*, Technomic Publ. Co., Stamford, CT, 1969.

Davis, L.W., *Metal and Ceramic Matrix Composites*, Cahners Publ. Co., NY, 1970.

Wendt, F.W., Liebowitz, H. and Perrone, N., Eds. *Mechanics of Composite Materials*, Proceed. of the 5th Symposium on Naval Mechanics (held in Philadelphia, PA, 8–10 May 1967), Pergamon Press, NY, 1970.

Corten, H.T., Ed., *Composite Materials: Testing and Design*, Proceedings of the Second Conference, sponsored by the ASTM (held in Anaheim, CA, 20–22 April 1971), publ. by the American Society for Testing and Materials, Philadelphia, PA, 1972.

Whitney, J.M., Ed., *Analysis of the Test Methods for High Modulus Fibers and Composites*, Proceed. publ. by American Society for Testing and Materials, Philadelphia, PA, 1973.

Composites—Standards, Testing and Design, National Physical Laboratory, 8–9 April 1974, Conference Proceedings, publ. by IPC Science and Technology Press, Surrey, England, 1974.

Jones, R.M., *Mechanics of Composite Materials*, McGraw-Hill Book Co., 1975.

Vinson, J.R. and Chou, T., *Composite Materials and Their Use in Structures*, Applied Science Publishers, London, England, 1975.

Holister, G.S., *Developments in Composite Materials—1*, Applied Science Publ. Ltd., London, England, 1977.

Renton, W.J., Ed., *Hybrid and Select Metal Matrix Composites:* A State-of-the-Art Review, publ. by American Institute of Aeronautics and Astronautics, NY, 1977.

Lenoe, E.M., Oplinger, D.W. and Burke, J.J., Eds., *Fibrous Composites in Structural Design*, Proceedings of the 4th Conf. on Fibrous Composites in Structural Design (held in San Diego, CA, 14–17 Nov. 1978), Plenum Press, NY, 1980.

Noton, B., et al., Eds., *ICMM/2*, Proc. of the 1978 International Conf. on Composite Materials, Publ. by the Metallurgical Society of AIME, Warrendale, PA, 1978.

Piatti, G., *Advances in Composite Materials*, Applied Science Publ. Co., London, England, 1978.

Tewary, V.K., *Mechanics of Fibre Composites*, John Wiley and Sons, NY, 1978.

Tsai, S.W., Ed., *Composite Materials: Testing and Design*, Proceedings of the Fifth Conference (sponsored by the American Society for Testing and Materials, New Orleans, LA, 20–22 March 1978), publ. by The American Society for Testing and Materials, Philadelphia, PA, 1978.

Christensen, R.M., *Mechanics of Composite Materials*, John Wiley and Sons, New York, 1979.

Agarwal, B.D. and Brontman, L.J., *Analysis and Performance of Fiber Composites*, John Wiley and Sons, NY, 1980.

Bunsell, A.R., et al., Eds. *Advances in Composite Materials*, Proc. of the Third International Conf. on Composite Materials (held in Paris, 26–29 Aug. 1980), Vols. 1 and 2, Pergamon Press, NY, 1980.

Piggott, M.R., *Load-Bearing Fibre Composites*, Pergamon Press, NY, 1980.

Tsai, S.W. and Hahn, H.T., *Introduction to Composite Materials*, Technomic Publ. Co., Westport, CT, 1980.

Hayashi, T., Kawata, K. and Umekawa, S., Eds., *Progress in Science and Engineering of Composites*, Vols. 1 and 2, Proceedings of the Fourth International Conference on Composite Materials (25–28 Oct. 1982, Tokyo, Japan), Publ. by the Japan Society for Composite Materials, Tokyo, Japan, 1982.

Design and Use of Kevlar Aramid Fiber in Composite Structures, Technical Symposium V, sponsored by the DuPont Co., Industrial Fibers Division (held in Reno, Nevada, April 1984), document available from E.I. duPont de Nemours & Company, Wilmington, Delaware, 19898.

Lambie, J., *Composite Construction for Homebuilt Aircraft*, Aviation Publishers, Hummelstown, PA, 1984.

Schwartz, M.M., *Composite Materials Handbook*, McGraw-Hill Book Co., 1984.

INDEX

279

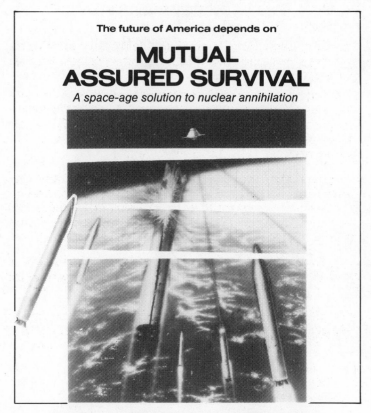